ROACH MAN

by

Charles D. Lewis

Dorrance Publishing Co
585 Alpha Drive
Pittsburgh, PA 15238
Visit our website at *www.dorrancebookstore.com*

ISBN: 978-1-6853-7239-2
eISBN: 978-1-6853-7778-6

ROACH MAN

by

Charles D. Lewis

CONTENTS

Contents

CHAPTER ONE
THE FUNERAL

I am not a teacher, but some of life's circumstances put us in a bad situation. Sneaking out of your own home at 1:30 a.m. is not a good thing. On this mission, I was the look out. There was a total of four young men and one young girl who were scared to death. Classes just ended; yes, classes. You see, I was stealing from the local gangbangers. My basement was the site of GED classes for some of those who wanted to get out, and I had literally promised them the world if they followed my instructions. But for now, I just had to get them to the alley without getting caught. For me, this was easy. But it did not remove the anxiety of those knowing the penalty of being caught getting an education.

I went to my garbage can and yelled, "5-0!" from the alley, seeing that this was the universal signal that the police were coming. It gave enough time for the five of them to get moving into whatever gangbangers do at night.

Once back in my home safe, I checked on my children before getting ready for my shift at the foundry, where I was an iron pourer. Sleep didn't come easy that night. I had plenty of worries, starting with the fact that I just gave away half of my gas money for the week to a couple of the kids, so they could eat. You know, bring home food for their siblings or whoever was home? Don't get it twisted because they are gang members and have to stand on the corner and sell drugs. That doesn't mean that they have money or know how to manage it.

J Roc hit my mind first. Just a neighborhood kid that got caught up. Now he is facing time in jail on a possession charge with no money for a lawyer. I had my ways of handling these things. After I got off work tomorrow, I had a meeting with a couple of cops who might be able to help, but they wanted him to testify in court. That was a death sentence for any gang member. I was not going to lose him like that. I had a trade school in Tennessee with his name on it. Well, truth be told, he didn't have much going for him but his looks. He was fair skinned with some good hair. Other than that, he just had a desire to get out. The thing was, when he talked about getting out, it was his eyes begging and his heart that said he was for real.

I could talk forever about these kids, but the truth remained without help they didn't stand a chance.

Let me stop before I get too far ahead of myself. I'm an ex-soldier who came back to the city I love, and it is fucking heartbreaking. I've already lost my marriage to crack. I had one son with her, and I am his guardian. He is eight years old. I am also the guardian of five other children, all mine; even the stepson is mine. Yes, their mother left me with six children. I had a total of five on my own. The oldest, who was also eight years old, is also my stepson, but you can't tell him that. Their mother was not a crackhead; quite the opposite. Very intelligent and ambitious. Maybe I was a little slow for her in that department. Plus she didn't understand that I was not in a relationship with her mother. Their scheme to get me into marriage didn't work. I saw how she treated and spoke to her husband, and that shit was not in the cards for me, but my children, I love them with every fiber of my existence. It's summertime, so they don't have school tomorrow. I have to get up at least one hour early, so that I can write out homework assignments. There is no running outside when you get up; no, you have homework and book reports due. I tried not to make this a habit. Climbing into bed and not even getting a shower was routine for me. Just another night that your principles outweighed everything. If you know what has to be done, why not just do it and get it over with? That is pretty rich coming from me. I must tell you that I am the world's greatest procrastinator, but once I start something, I finish it.

WHAT THE FUCK IS THAT NOISE?

It's 4:30 a.m. That's the alarm clock.

Rolling over and getting up was not my problem. My routine was set before my eyes opened, walking to my dresser to get my stash of weed and roll me a joint. Grab my coffee, go to the enclosed back porch, open some windows, light my joint, and then start making math problems and spelling words and give each a book for their reports. My biggest problem was trying to keep up with my oldest son Terrell. I was running out of shit to give him because his IQ was higher than mine. This might have come from his mother or his biological father, who I found out later in life was a pretty good man. I had to figure out something soon. I was stressing for no reason, because shortly after that, he figured out he was the smartest of us two. So one day he just started doing the homework assignments for the other kids.

OH yeah, speaking of kids. I had some other ones at my house. No different from any other family in the early eighties and nineties. I had children that belonged to my siblings, three of my sisters and a few others who came and went, depending on how stable their parents were at the time. Casualties of the crack wars that were fought on our streets of Chicago. Yes, that is where I live and try to survive. Englewood to be exact. This is the place that produces some of the best and the worst of everything. Not 100 yards from my home lived Mr. Philpott, a world class artist who has artwork in the Smithsonian. But right on the same block and around the corner lived the family of the man who is the reason they call this place Moe Town. I don't mean music; I mean murder, drugs, guns…you name it. This was one of the most dangerous places in the world. But somehow, this is where the fuck I was with my children, trying to make an escape with all of the kids intact. My ex put it in my head about the kids' education, so I was paying tuition even for the preschoolers.

By the time I finished my joint and coffee. It was off to the shower and trying to remember all the shit that had to be done today, like getting my cousin's wife or one of the neighbors to do the girls' hair. Don't laugh. They told me that my French braids were tight, but I can't part hair straight to save my life.

And it was Tuesday; cleaning day. I hate housework, so I pay a couple of the neighbors to take care of that. I usually leave them a couple of joints and some beer money. Plus, while the kids were out at the library, they had use of my apartment and pool table.

On my way out the door, I heard my niece Nichole calling my name. She was a fragile child, and there was no way possible I could know what she had been through. All I knew was that it was my job to make sure she was safe now. Again, I can't speculate, but I know she has been to some seedy places with her mother. I stop to see what she wants, and she tells me that I might have to stop letting her mom and uncle come to the house because they were stealing from the house. Sometimes meat and sometimes other little shit that fit in their pockets, like all my fucking jewelry. I hugged her and sent her back to bed and told her that I would look into it. I knew she wasn't lying, but I don't think I had the mental capacity to deal with it at the time. Where I was headed, there was no room for error. I had to be precise, pouring hot metal that was over 3,000 degrees all day long.

I had to clear my head and fast, and I'm only allowed one joint before my shower. From here on, it was going to have to be mental. That would not be a problem; I was born for labor work. Yes, I said it: I was born for this shit. I was physically the strongest person at the plant. Using common sense, I made it look easy, but most of the old timers thought I was going to burn out soon, because I took every overtime shift that I could get. There was not enough time in the day to tell them what my obligations were, and why they would probably didn't give a shit.

Walking into the locker room to put on my work uniform, the jokes started as soon as I stepped in: "Oh shit, here comes the money man!" Which was a reference to the fact that I worked a lot of overtime. Or just the fact that I made a little money on the side, loan sharking. If you don't know what that is, I loan money to people who want to smoke crack during the week and have no money, so I was their money until Friday. I charged 50 cents on the dollar. Not only that, I would introduce them to my cousin, who would bring it by the job.

As I was getting undressed, I could always feel eyes on me. I am not your average guy. I'm only 5 feet, 8 inches tall, but I wear a size 50 jacket; 52 for comfort, weighing around 235 pounds. I know, how is that possible without being fat? Well, I'm big on hitting the weights and jogging. Something like a freak to look at naked, especially when you are well endowed or blessed, but most of the time it was a curse. A big dick and a large ego ain't nothing but trouble.

I let the old dudes talk shit and did what I normally do, and that's strutting through the locker room like a young peacock. I wasn't what you would call cute or anything like that. Let's put it this way: I have never had a woman meet me, look me in the face, and say, "You are cute. I want to fuck you." What I have had happen was a woman got to know me as a gentleman and looked at me from the back and said, "Can I just hug you?"

Well, you know where that went, looking up at me or looking at a pillow with her ass in the air. I didn't have to say a fucking word; the package spoke for itself. But I couldn't help myself by telling Mr. Nathan Carter (he was the union steward I didn't like) that if I catch his wife on Friday with his paycheck again, I was going to fuck her for free and accept his paycheck as a tip. Then I turned to him and shook eight-and-a-half inches of fat, limp dick in his face.

Mr. Carter sat on the bench and looked up at me, and all he saw was a gap tooth smile, a six-pack, a 50-inch chest, and 18-inch guns plus a dick that was two inches longer than his at its hardest, and this mofo was still soft. As a man, I didn't have to brag, but this dude was a special type of asshole. He didn't protect his union brothers, plus I was not a fan of his mulatto looks and slick demeanor. Don't get me wrong. He worked his way up, just as I was doing now. But this 6-foot, 3-inch walking magazine cover was a fucking snake in the grass.

As I walked over to the uniform rack, the whole locker room went up in laughter, which meant I could not take one minute longer for lunch or break because Mr. Carter would be there on my ass today. He didn't know that I was on my way out the door, and I wanted to drag his disloyal ass with me. I wasn't worried about it. I just hadn't found the right worker who would give up the goods for a few dollars, but I was still searching.

The workday was going smoothly as a mother fucker. By lunch, I had poured about 200,000 pounds of iron off the big pot and was now waiting for the temperature to get back up to finish pouring. I was proud of the fact that I worked hard for my money. It made me feel a little manlier, and Lord knows I didn't need any extra shit boosting my ego. Sitting there having lunch gave me a chance to talk shit with most of the fellas in the break room and play a few numbers and get into the lottery pool. Talking shit came easy to me, but when you work in a large vat of straight testosterone, you better be on your game because in one day at work you can go from seeing a grown man laugh, cry, or die. It was dangerous work that carried every human attribute.

After pouring the last of the iron and reloading the furnace for the next shift, on my way out the door stood Mr. Carter, the fake union man taking requests for overtime work, but for some reason, I couldn't get in this week. I didn't trip. I knew that I had a little over $1,200 coming from the work crew. The hard part was catching up with those slick mother fuckers. Middle aged men have more tricks than I knew what to do with. So I paid a so-called tough guy at work to collect the money, and he wanted every dime because he got 15 percent. This motherfucker looked like something straight out of a movie. His eyes were dead, and his skin looked like it needed maybe 10 less scars. I didn't worry about trusting him because he wasn't that bright. Sometimes when we made a little extra, I always gave him a $100 bill. This kept him blinded and off balance. But I knew he was ambitious, so I still had to keep an eye out.

Another bad decision came as soon as I got into my van. I lit a joint on the way to meet two cops at a cop bar. I said fuck it and went with the cologne. I was not in this place but 30 seconds before noses started turning in the air. I walked over to the bar and ordered a double Martel with a chaser of coke. Sitting around this many policemen made me nervous. They all had guns, but mine was in the van.

My party arrived just before boredom hit. These two corvette driving assholes walked in like they owned the joint. Hold on a minute, somebody needs to look into this shit. How the fuck is it that so many cops own a GODDAMN Corvette? But I was about to burst their bubble. They wore more jewelry than a detective could afford. They may have started out good, but these assholes had taken a wrong turn about 10 years ago when crack first came on the scene. Or shortly thereafter. Just looking at the two pieces of shit walking my way pissed me off, because they made twice their salaries by not doing the job and turning the other way.

Officer Curtis Ptacc, 16 years on the force and as hard on a young black man as they come. They didn't always work as partners, but on this shit, they were joined at the hip and wallet. At just over 6 feet tall, this gave me a chance of building a sense of false security on his part. Stroke the ego until later when I kick him in the nuts. Straight black hair and the goatee completed his tough guy look. This white boy loved working in the hood. He didn't give a fuck. If it was beating the shit out of a black man or fucking the three or four black women that he had on the side.

Now, Officer Finney was something different. He was one of the few in his family with a high school diploma, but he couldn't advance further because he was the most ghetto piece of shit I had ever laid eyes on. He wore a perm in his hair and in the style of finger waves. He also was wearing about eight rings, and yes, before I forget: Don't ever let this big mother fucker hit me with those rings on. He had girth and height, and even on a hot sunny day, he wore a leather jacket, mostly to hide his gut but also to hide all the hardware. This man was street certified, and if I was going to be there, I needed to play him just right. A few "yes sirs" and grinning would stroke his ego enough to keep him off balance.

I couldn't change shit at that moment; I was here on J Roc's behalf. I had told the waitress that I was paying for their drinks. I didn't have time, so I explained my part up front that J Roc was not testifying in open court because it was a death sentence. Trying to explain how this was asking too much; putting the squeeze on a teenager was one thing, but he was not there, and I was. It was simple to me. I wanted both officers to understand that this kid would be on a bus going to a welding school in Tennessee. There were only 25 more hours needed, and he would be ready for his GED.

These crooked-ass cops still wanted to play hard until I gave them the goods: a list of 10 cops in their precinct who were crooked. I asked them to look at the last two. It wasn't names; it was initials. Their initials. I was asked where I got it. The look on Finney's face told me he wanted to use those rings. Putting both my hands palms up signaled to them that there was more. I told them about a stash house that would be unprotected at a certain time and that I was in for 20 percent because I had to pay for the info. Plus a notarized statement from J Roc as long as he could stay out of it with immunity. After these greedy assholes squeezed me for two more rounds of drinks, a deal was reached, and I was reduced to 10 percent of the stash house take, and the confession by J Roc would be videotaped with immunity. Again, they asked where the list came from until there was just silence at the table. I didn't know exactly what to think of this new partnership, if you could call it that. I was truly afraid, and they were overconfident. They knew I would not say where the list came from.

To make a long story short, his case was dismissed. Just remember if you help people, then people will help you. The neighborhood gave me the list, not even knowing it.

This negotiation shit was over, so I had to hit the door. One more asshole turned his nose up at my smell. I wish I could say that it didn't matter to me, but it did. I really wanted to beat his ass with the pool stick he was holding, so I played country dumb and then threw on a little country twang with a stutter and asked him, "Wwhhooo hhaadd nnext?"

He responded as macho as a man could be and stuttered back at me tthhat ii hhad next if I had twenty dollars and a straight eye. I had $60, and I told him I needed to by lunch tomorrow. I walked over to the officers Finney and Ptacc, who I'd just met with, and asked as nicely as I could if they would circle back around in about an hour or so. They agreed. I knew this was a way of checking my new position. Considering the info that I had, the looks on each crooked face told me they didn't have a leg to stand on. As they were leaving, I noticed Ptacc had a limp in his left leg.

Now back to the pig with the turned-up nose and plenty of money in his pocket. At $60 a game, I needed to make quick work of Mr. Pork and his friends. My protection was only going to be gone for a short time.

They did return but showed up about 20 minutes too late—as I was at the back of the bar in the alley being stretched out, four cops hellbent on getting their 600 bucks back. I don't know if it was the seventh or tenth shot to the ribs and midsection. This old boy knew how to spread the punches around. I think it was just from punching all those innocent citizens. I am sure that this whole thing may not have happened if I would have just made that last eight ball straight in the corner, but no; I went four rails in the same corner with a little Tom Cruise stick twirl at the end.

When Mutt and Jeff came around the corner to ask what the fuck was going on, I was promptly released and fell to the ground like a bag of potatoes. I guess it was only fair in their minds to kick me one last time on the way to leaving the alley. After being helped up, I explained that I needed to go to the bathroom, and one of them told me to piss in the alley. Only after I explained how many gut shots I had taken, they escorted me inside to some dirty looks from the cops who had taken me out back and the ones who watched out the back door. So fucking much for SERVE AND PROTECT. But I limped to the bathroom, giving the best acting job I could to look hurt. Once in the bathroom, I retrieved the stash of money.

Quickly retrieving all $600, I thought to myself, *A couple of you together might kick my ass, but you are not getting your money back.* Plus I had a surprise for two of them. They were on the list, too. Besides, I had plans for a hard workout and run in the morning. I had been hit in the ribs before, plus it made that macho shit kick in.

Arriving home, shit was back to normal. Deon was the oldest kid in the house. He was my nephew. He was my legally adopted child. Something my oldest sister hooked up. She was a paralegal for the military, and she saved my undisciplined ass a few times. Deon was really rough around the edges but not like some people. This kid had vengeance in his heart, but I didn't understand how so much anger could build up in a child so fast. I guess if you had two sisters to watch over and my house was not your first stop as foster children. He was on top of things around the house.

Deon knew it was Tuesday: The house was clean, and they wanted to go skating. It was family night at St. Anselm. They had a skating rink at the church. After showering and going through that usual shit about not being able to find my shoe, I need some more socks, and the obligatory "I spent all my money," one hour later, we were in the van. I decided that police money was as good as any, so I started passing out twenties to the kids. Lots of yelling and thank you from all the kids ensued. There were 13 of them in the van. All I hear is fart jokes and "you a doo doo head," and yes, at their ages, they thought that shit was funny. I didn't mind even the extra friends that tagged along; no one at home gave them a dime.

I got on the skating floor with the little ones and tried to show off for the older ones. You have to remember, I am a Chi-Town man through and through, so yes, a little showing off was in order for the older children. This wasn't the first church floor I had skated on. They also had one in Altgeld Gardens where I used to live. If you can't skate there, you just get run the hell over. The smaller ones were amazed at how their older siblings could hold on to the back of my shirt as I flew around the rink.

The adventure was short lived as my ribs spoke to me in the language of pain.

Once back in the van, I didn't know who would go to sleep first, me or the kids. All I knew was we were all beat. Working the swing shift, I would have to be in by 3:00 p.m. tomorrow. This would give me some time to get a few things done before work the following morning, and get my run and workout in.

Just as I had gotten the house settled down, I started chewing four Tylenols. I needed this pain to stop. I walked out back and lit a joint. A few puffs later, I heard the most blood curdling scream, something almost out of a horror movie.

It turned out to be my neighbors three houses over. I didn't know what was wrong, but it had to be serious as I approached the front. There was a military car out front. Two officers were leaving the steps. I asked what was wrong. One of the officers looked at me, and I knew their son had been killed in action. It wasn't the right time for me to say anything but offer my condolences and move on. As my mother always says, "There is a dead cat on the line." Either this was dumb luck, or I really fucked up. I stole Clarence James Martin from his family and friends and this neighborhood.

Clarence was one of three young men that I enlisted into the Marines. I recommended the Army, but these were tough boys, and they signed up on the buddy-buddy plan less than two years ago. I didn't know how this would play out with my new batch of students. I was trying to help them all get out. Clarence was just a kid who needed help and guidance. He stopped going to school at age 15, figuring he could make more money on the streets. Moe Town was the place to do it.

I met Martin on the basketball court where I was a regular. He started talking to me after breaking up a fight amongst a couple of kids in the park. His first question to me was, "Why didn't you let them fight it out? That's the only way that they are going to get tough and survive in this neighborhood."

Even though his statement was probably par for the course, it just didn't sit well with me that an 18-year-old thought that children should be fighting. I had no fucking clue what to say to him at that moment, but, "Hey man, do you sell weed?"

He said yes and I gave him 10 bucks and asked him to roll a blunt and meet me at the bench where the OGs sat. There was no game plan, but I knew that I had to reach this kid, and that was my introduction to Clarence James Martin 26 months ago, and now he's dead. Mrs. Martin, I knew was working and would be home soon. I didn't want any part of that scene.

Due to the military being involved and the media, the service was first class with all the bells and whistles. I didn't spend much time with my neighbors because of the swing shift at work. On the day of the services, I took off work; I needed time to be right. I was going to bury a young soldier. I wore my old uniform, which was a little snug from my increased size due to the work outs and all the fucking cooking and eating I was doing. His two buddies were allowed to escort the body home. I had met with them in my basement where they studied for their GEDs. We all hugged a lot and cried a lot, and I expressed my sorry and guilty feelings. They tried to assure me that this was not my fault; that Clarence loved being a Marine, and that they each had reenlisted for five more years.

James O'Dell Tucker was a very close friend of Clarence. He looked almost as if he was a mistake; very small in stature, 5 feet, 3 inches tall and 135 pounds with bricks in his pocket. He had braces that the military paid for and a bad case of acne. No one fucked with him because it was rumored that he used to be a shooter in the town with a bad reputation. After speaking with them, I felt better about my decision to enlist them.

On the morning of the service, I walked out my door stiff as a board with this tight ass uniform on. Greeting me at the bottom of the stairs were the faces of two marines who saluted me even though they knew that I was not an officer. I returned the salute and proceeded with my head held high and proud. We were there at the bottom of the stairs, hugs and pounds exchanged.

Mrs. Dee, my neighbor-slash-housekeeper, asked us to pose for a picture in our uniforms. This lasted a few minutes, and we were all smiles until reality hit. We all looked up to see two limos there to pick up the family. There was a knot in my stomach that was not right. I was not comfortable watching the family march in and hearing from neighbors who never knew that I was in the Army at all, who thanked me for my service. But still I knew something was wrong.

The service ran long, and I cried a lot, which may have helped me more than I know. As I started to walk up to view the body, there was a loud scream and cursing. It got closer and closer until it was right in my face. I was frozen, rooted to the floor like a mighty oak, unable to move until I started feeling pain. Mrs. Martin was digging her nails into my skin; she was clawing at my face like a wild banshee, all the while saying over and over that I killed her son and that if it wasn't for me, he would still be alive. Luckily for me, there were people around who quickly grabbed her, but the verbal assault did not stop. She screamed more obscenities at me and again blamed me for her Clarance's death.

I used my handkerchief to wipe some of the blood off my face as I headed to the exit. I was grabbed by two female ushers from the church, who gave me what I needed—not just clean towels and some ice for my face for cleaning the blood, but words of encouragement. They held my hands and prayed with me and for me. My face being wet from tears probably saved me a few more scratches. Either way, that kind of an attack is very hard to get over because this was on her heart to say to me. I didn't proceed to the cemetery with everyone else. Partially out of pride and partially out of embarrassment, I just felt I didn't belong.

The day after the service was the first day back in class with my group. Things started out slow, and on this day, I was surprised by a visit from two soldiers in full uniforms. I didn't have to say one word about what was happening. It was broken down for the class: Don't be afraid to leave the hood; it is a big world to explore.

Perry was on his game. He almost sounded like a motivational speaker. Perry was very different. Perry was a fighter, like me. He once told me that he thought he could take me in a fight. Envelopes, yes. This was my second shock. Perry and James handed out bus tickets to travel to their base to visit. I thought this was a brilliant move until Toya said, "Y'all gave us bus tickets. Why are we not flying?"

Perry stepped in with the confidence of a real soldier and said, "We are Marines; we are not rich. We just got out of the hood 18 months ago."

We all laughed like hell. and I knew that my new crew was going to be alright.

CHAPTER TWO

DARLING NIKKI BACK ON THE BLOCK

I guess everything was going well if you let the natives tell it. This wasn't their story to tell. After the last two weeks of the swing shift at the foundry, my face was healing nicely, and I had about all of the jokes that I could stand about the scratches from the work crew, but I had to take it as good as I gave it. Even Mr. Carter asked me a couple of times, did I have cat scratch fever? Even though I didn't like his half-breed ass, it was funny. He got some laughs in the locker room.

I had worked all the overtime that I could get, and my vacation was about to start, and after that, I was out of there. I was ready to start a new business, and Mr. Carter was going down for selling out his union brothers.

First on the agenda was getting home and getting the kids ready for Great America, packing up the lunch meat, juices, cookies, and any damn thing else that I could think of to make my day go easier. At 7:00 a.m., all the kids were dressed, and we were ready to load up the van. The youngest two, a set of twins, clung to me like a second skin. It was obvious that they were still sleepy and grouchy. I didn't worry my nephew, and I had packed plenty of snacks and whatever they could think of.

As we filled out the door, the entire line stopped. I was yelling orders to keep it moving, but there was no movement from the front of the line. My 12-year-old niece yelled up the stairs, "Unc, there is a lady out here. She's blocking the door."

I yelled down, "What do you mean she is blocking the door?"

She yelled back up to me that, "The lady is blocking the door!"

Now shit was getting messy. I was trying to pass 12 children on the stairwell carrying bags, blankets, pillows, coolers, and any damn thing we had packed. After navigating my way to the front of the line, sure enough, there she was, just lying there on the porch with a small blanket that had seen better days. I could see her clearly through the screen door just lying there. I didn't know if she was hurt or just asleep.

After banging the door a couple of times, she started to stir. From the disheveled look of her, I didn't know what to tell the kids at first. Slowly rising and moving from in front of the door, I was able to step out and halt everybody in place.

"Hello ma'am, how may I help you?"

Wiping sleep out of her eyes and yawning, a whiff of alcohol hit me right in the nostrils; now I was really awake. She was still apologizing for being on the porch and trying to get to her feet at the same time, me looking and trying to pay attention. Extending my right hand was the best solution because I didn't want to get too close; I was still trying to assess the threat level. There were still 12 children inside the screen door that I loved dearly.

I asked, "What are you doing sleeping on my porch?"

The answer came in the form of an old school photo.

"THIS NIKKI, MY GRAND BABY." She held the photo so close to my face that I couldn't see the face clearly. After grabbing her arm and moving it back I could tell that the photo was one that you took in school on picture day. Even though I was holding her arm, the photo still moved frantically. I spoke as calmly as I could to the panicked woman.

"What does this have to do with me and my family? Because we are on our way out."

Calm and desperation came to her face at the same time. She told me that Nikki was gone, "And she ain't been home for three days. She was with her aunt, and nobody has seen her since." Even as she spoke calmly, she had a death grip on my t-shirt, which was the panic part because all I know is to protect me and mine. There was no danger on that porch other than me not sending her away. Other than that, we were good.

Asking her name was a good place to start. She said her name was Myra. Myra Links, and she lived on Laflin Street next door to the Muslim Center. Now that she was a little calmer and both of our heart rates had changed, I asked her to please step aside so that I could load my family in the vehicle, and I would hear what was on her mind. Signaling the kids to come on out and load the van, I took Myra to the side and proceeded to instruct my crew about putting everything where it belonged. Now was not the time, and I didn't have much as my patience was running thin, and I knew this was a matter for the police and not me.

Once out of earshot of the kids, I asked, "What was this about?"

Myra took a deep breath and then told me that her other daughter was in jail, so that's how she got Nikki. Another deep breath and she said, "Nikki has not been home for three days."

Placing my hands up for her to be quiet, I asked, "Did you call the police?"

Myra did this crazy spin and asked me, "Are you a zip damn fool?"

I didn't know the difference between a "damn fool" and a "zip damn fool," so I just looked at her, waiting for an explanation.

Myra's voice went up a couple octaves as she said, "Hell yeah, and they came out and told me she had to be gone for 48 hours and to come down to the station to fill out a missing person's report. I did all that shit, and now I'm here. CAN YOU HELP ME OR NOT?"

As loud as she said it, all the kids turned to look over to see what was wrong. I didn't know what to tell her and didn't want to get involved. Stepping back was my only defense since I knew that she meant me no bodily harm. It was the smell of her breath and the stench of drinking that caused me to retreat more than anything. Backing up to the wall, I was out of real-estate, my back up against the side of my house. Her hands rose to the side of my face, as she grabbed my face with both hands. Her eyes changed into something I had only seen once in my life. It was a look of not just desperation but a look of knowing.

"I KNOW WHO YOU ARE."

Trying hard to pull my face from her hands was not working and getting violent with her was not in the cards. Yes, I thought about it, but one of the kids had walked over to see what was taking me so long, and I had to stay cool.

"What do you mean you know who I am?"

A low guttural growl started somewhere inside of her, but when her voice came to the surface, I could not move. It was plain and clear. She simply said: "YOU ARE A NOBLE MAN." Her eyes closed, she took one last breath and walked away, leaving the photo of Nikki on the ground. She touched my niece on the head as she walked off and said, "NIKKI DON'T GOT LONG."

I finally got into the vehicle. I was confused as hell. There was something about Mrs. Myra…

What made her come to my house? Who sent her?

Getting gas and ice for the coolers on 55th and Halsted gave my nephew a chance to ask a few questions, and the first one was, "Who was that lady?"

Even only at 14 years old, I didn't have a chance at deceiving him. So I told him the truth.

"I don't really know her. She can't find her granddaughter and maybe thought I knew her or something, or could help her."

He looked me in my face and asked, "Well, where she at, Unc?"

I just gazed at him for a minute and replied, "I don't know."

He said, "You better know something because she's gonna come back."

"What makes you think that I know where her granddaughter is? Besides, I think she was a little drunk from the night before."

I didn't know what else to say and tried to change the subject by asking him to check to see if any of the kids needed anything from the gas station. And just like clockwork, three had to use the bathroom. I was glad it was three boys because they had to go around the corner behind the gas station to piss, because the station don't have a public restrooms in the hood.

All tasks completed, we are on the expressway at 7:45 a.m. Music playing and the little ones drifting off to sleep, my mind drifted to Mrs. Myra. I couldn't get it out of my head how strong she was as she held my face. It was not the type of strength I get from lifting weights, but the kind of strong from a possession or ownership of someone.

I snapped back to reality when my nephew called me loudly just in time to avoid hitting the semi in front of me. Even after I slammed on the brakes and checked to see if everyone was okay, I still felt the heat of those hands on the sides of my face and her voice saying, "I KNOW WHO YOU ARE." This shit had to exit my head fast, because in 40 minutes, we were going to ride every ride they could get on. Height requirements and fear for others.

I tried to stay alert by having a conversation with my nephew again and another curve ball came, because he wanted to know exactly why they all lived with me all of a sudden. Before I could say that their parents were sick and could not handle the task right now, he said to me in an adult tone, "OUR PARENTS ARE NOT SICK." Now we had to talk for real, and I just told him that they had drug problems that did not allow them to function as adults at the moment. This was only a stop gap measure, even though it was the God's honest truth.

He let up for a moment to tell me about a girl down the street that he was interested in. He told me her name was Tiffany and that her father was a bus driver, but her mother was more like his mom—not all there at the moment. I knew that his heart was in the right place, because he wanted to know if people ever left that neighborhood with a girl and never came back. Yes, this was a true romance story from a kid who knew that living there in that manner was not good.

Around 11:30 a.m., we took our first break for lunch. Excitement and contagious smiles and laughter about rides being scary and fast; the twins somehow got tangled up with some extra cotton candy, but it was not a problem. I had extra clothes in the van and sandwiches, those little blue, green, and red juices, and chips that flew around fast, so they could go back to ride. And ride, they did! They even rode my ass to a complete zero.

As we were getting ready to leave, my son Christian saw one of those games with the hammer. He wanted to know if I could ring the bell. I told him that I was tired. The kids talked me into it. I paid for three swings of the hammer. On the first two, I wasn't even close. At this point, a lady yelled at the operator to quit cheating people. We all saw him stick his hand behind the machine a second time. I still had one more swing left. I handed him a $20 bill. I told all the kids to get in line. I took off my jacket and started swinging that hammer like I was at work in the foundry. We swung a lot of sledgehammers in the gate knocking department.

Eleven straight swings. With each swing, a crowd started to gather. Each kid pointed out a prize. I only had one kid left to pick a prize. Talking to the kids, I didn't see the slick operator reach behind the machine again. I never did get close to that bell again. My baby girl Winnie was the last in line. One of her brothers gave her his prize.

All I had to do was navigate back home 64 miles before my clock expired and I turned back to a sleeping zombie. Seven of the 12 had to be airlifted up the stairs and to bed. This was not a night that I worried about them getting a bath before bed. It wasn't necessary.

The house was quiet within 20 minutes. I was sitting in my backyard with a bottle of Martel, two freshly rolled joints, and neighbors floating by. My house was on the corner of the block, a standard two-family flat with the sweetest landlord you would ever want to know. It was a large, four-bedroom apartment. Mrs. Hubbard was a state worker who, for the most part, would mind her business, but she knew all the residents and all their business. Just before, I poured myself a shot, and then I set the trap, with a little music and a couple extra beers for the neighbors who just happened to be walking by. A few passersby came from the park with chairs and blankets, some even with children as the mosquitoes were torturous in the park.

After sitting for about 15 minutes, target number one walked up and spoke to me with a wide smile that grew even larger after I offered a cold beer and a hit off my joint. This was a big boy, maybe 6 foot 3 with girth. I wasn't sure at first who I was talking to because he had a twin, and yes, they were both big, both gangbangers, and both gay. Keith and Kevin were known by everyone. After about 30 seconds, I knew this was the tough one. Yes, this big gay boy was as tough as they come. This would not be the first pair of lips that a drink and a smoke loosened up for conversation.

After about five minutes of very small talk, I offered a shot of Martel, and the flood gates opened. I found out a few things about Mrs. Myra, who lived about two blocks away. She worked in the school lunchroom for about 20 years. All Keith knew was she was there when he was a little boy, and she still worked there but was off for the summer. She had three sons, one in jail, one working for the city as a garbage worker, and the other one was smoking crack like the rest of the neighborhood. There were two daughters; the one she told me was in jail and Deja.

Enquiring a little more and offering another beer with Earth, Wind, and Fire playing in the background, talk flowed, and I found out that Deja had recently returned home from living with relatives on the east coast. It seems that she was quite attractive. Other people's husbands, checks, and credit cards were her thing; now we could add a little crack to the list. All info stored, and I had no idea what I was going to do with it and why I really cared. Well, let me stop lying to myself that I did not know. It bothered me that a child was missing, and I had a house full of them that I would go to war over. I didn't need this mother fucker to talk my ear off, so I turned up the music, which was the signal for my other neighbors to come on out and have a beer on me or smoke on me. It was Saturday night, and I knew that they would not go home until 2:00 or 3:00 in the morning.

First things first, I grabbed my friend and cleaning lady Mrs. Dee. She got a great big hug and a pint of Mad Dog 2020 fresh out of my cooler. As I hugged her, she whispered in my ear, "How was Great America? How are the kids?"

I took two of her grandkids, too. I told her that I was dead-ass tired and needed a bed, and the kids were all tucked in. She looked into my eyes and told me that I was a fool for believing that, and the look on my face changed. She nodded toward the second floor on the enclosed back porch, where her grandson and my nephew were sitting listening to the music and probably getting a contact high off all the weed smoke. Isn't that how all kids in the hood learned to be grown?

As she released me from the hug, she told me that Mike and Veronica and a couple of other neighbors would be over in a few. I knew that this would extend my fatigue because Veronica was a stepper, and so was 75 percent of the people there. Shit, this was Chicago; everybody could step, but Veronica was something different. She was a heavy-set, dark-skinned woman who was light on her feet and did not miss a turn. She could damn near be drunk and would make sure our rhythm was on point. It was one of the true pleasures of Chicago, steppin' to that beat that belonged to us alone, and we cherished every spin, every dip, and every move of footwork, which is what distinguished each stepper from another. When I had time on my hands, I stole away to a neighborhood joint. They had a great floor at ET's Lounge.

An hour in, I was showing the fuck out with Miss Veronica, and that was because there was maybe 20 people in the backyard, and Big Fred and his wife were letting it loose. They had just walked the side of the makeshift dance floor, which was a concrete slab with a series of spins that had a mean dip at the end, and Big Fred yelled over the music in his big bass of a voice, "YO VERONICA, I BET YOU CAN'T TRAIN HIS ASS TO DO THAT."

Laughter erupted as he told her to have me do something I was good at, like get him and his wife another drink and roll a joint, because I didn't know how to roll on the dance floor. This got another round of laughs from the crowd. Ms. Diane, who was another neighbor, held up her glass and yelled out, "Hey barkeep, get on your job!"

After telling Veronica, "Thanks for the dance, I got to get on with my job," I made sure everyone had what they needed. Most were working class folks and good people. I had nothing to worry about; Mrs. Dee was on the case, was refilling drinks, which some had brought their own bottles. Pulling me to the side, Mrs. Dee handed me a glass and said, "This is for Ms. Diane; she's waiting on the front porch. Why don't you take it to her?"

I did as told, not knowing that Dee knew that we had a thing going on. I can only describe Mrs. Diane as left behind by society. She was incredibly intelligent and attractive. Around 5-foot-10, which is tall for a woman, her body is what some would call thick. Size twelve jeans. She has two children by one of the local bangers who has been in jail for over 10 years. Her children were in high school, and she felt trapped by her situation. If she left for greener pastures, it would be better for her, but she, like others, have been here for so long that this was all she knew, and now her son was following in his father's footsteps. Her whole family was here in this death trap of a city, and she felt trapped.

Coming around the corner, before she could see me, I saw her with her hair hanging down, and so was her face. I could see the despair that drained her on a regular basis. This fucking neighborhood was an oasis for some and hell for others. When the sound of the gate struck, she looked up, and her demeanor changed, face smiling, eyes dancing. I nodded towards the screen door that it was open. She stood turned to the door, holding it open for me as well.

The split second that the door closed, I almost spilled her drink as she crashed into me with a full body hug that felt as though it came from Mississippi. We kissed and embraced each other for what seemed like an eternity. Pulling back to catch my breath, I had to take in her beauty. I could tell that she took some time on her makeup and her outfit, and I let her know that she was looking good. But in true woman fashion, she put her hands on her wide hips and asked me, "Do I really look good, or are you just horny?"

We both broke out into laughter because we knew it was all the above. She looked amazing, and the erection that came up while we were kissing told the whole horny story for both of us. We had made plans to meet up later after everyone had left. I put the offer on the table that I could send all of them the fuck home now and grabbed my package to emphasize the word fuck. We both laughed, and then Diane said, "If you are eating some pussy tonight, then I will help you put all those mother fuckers out."

After a little more making out, we returned to the makeshift party. Ms. Diane walked back around from the front, and I went up to check on the kids, so I could come down the back stairs as if nothing was amiss. I made a show of holding up the last of the beer as I put them in the cooler with the announcement that, "When the beer is gone, I want y'all's black asses gone."

There was some laughter and jokes, as a voice said, "I BET ALL OF US AIN'T GOT TO GO."

I replied to the voice, "You are right because I live upstairs." I gave a mean look to the nosey ass neighbor, Lisa Gibbs, who knew at that point to shut the fuck up. She lived across the street and saw and knew everything. At that moment, a light went off in my head. She's been here for years, and I needed some info. After gathering myself, I walked over to Lisa, leaning up against the fence so that her nosey ass could see all of the partygoers. Maneuvering my way over, I asked her to dance with me. She turned me down, as expected, so I just leaned into the fence with her and explained that she was going to get me in trouble. Her face changed to a serious look, like I had busted her out, because she thought I was talking about Diane. Then I told her that Mrs. Hubbard was going to be mad as hell because we were leaning on her new fence. We both got a laugh out of it.

Passing her a joint on top of the joke made things go a little bit smoother. Now directing the conversation where I wanted it to go, I told Lisa that I was worried about having my nieces and daughter in the neighborhood. Just as I expected, this was gossip time for her, and it was just like putting a $20 bill into a jukebox. She was going to go for a while. I found out that even though the teenage pregnancy rate in the hood was high, it was not always planned or consensual. What the fuck did that mean? We all know that young people get hot and have unprotected sex all of the time. So what was she talking about?

Leaning in a little closer, almost as if I was trying to holla at her, she just grinned and looked over at Diane and smiled. Now I'm thinking to myself this bitch was a piece of work. She wasn't bad looking, but she wanted to rub a little salt in Diane's wounds; nothing romantic here at all. This was not the case, but I still needed the info. So I kept giving her my best gapped-tooth smile as she told me about shit that went on in Moe Town since she was a teen. Sometimes as a part of the initiation into the gangs, some of the girls are made to have unprotected sex with several gang members. I wasn't born yesterday. I knew that this shit happens, but it sounded to me as she was describing something else altogether different. So playing stupid, I asked her more questions, and I got more answers.

"So you know that half of the kids in Moe Town are Nation Babies."

"What the fuck is a Nation Baby?"

Lisa looked at me and then looked at Big Fred with almost fear on her face. Yes, I knew that he had been a part of this gang life, but he always treated me with respect. The look on Lisa's face told me he was the next thread. I just didn't know how hard to pull this thread. I had to make a mental note to speak to him later, but in a much different manner. Mike, who took care of the music, walked over and told me that Veronica wanted one more step before they went home and that she didn't have all night. Just at that moment, I thought I would give this shit a twist.

"Yo Big Fred, can you please warm up Veronica for me, because I have to check on the kids."

I walked up the stairs for a minute and stood at the top of the stairs for about two minutes and returned to grab Fred's wife Minnie on the dance floor. She was startled at first but then happily grabbed my hand and said, "Let's make Fred jealous!"

Nothing else needed to be said as Marvin Gaye played on the box "COME GET TO THIS." It was a smooth number, so it was easy to get Fred's ire up now that his wife was in the hands of a better stepper and someone who was a complete gentleman. As soon as the song ended, he was back dancing with his wife, but not before I got a chance to ask her what the fuck was a Nation Baby. She tensed up in my arms and said that she couldn't and wouldn't talk about it here. I asked when we could talk about it, and she said never with a look of slight determination, which told me that she may talk about it later. That's when the song ended, and Minnie was gone as if the conversation had never happened.

When the next song was over, I turned off the music and wished all a good night. Just a few hangers on were left, and Lisa was one of them, more interested in which way Diane was going than anything. Knowing the streets and people as she did, Diane left with the rest of the guests. It took about 10 minutes to get rid of all the people in the backyard.

I quickly jumped in my van and went straight to the park, where I knew that she would be waiting. I let down the window and spoke loudly: "Is this the place to meet lonely women for the night?"

Diane replied, "It is if you are going to eat some pussy and fuck for at least 45 minutes."

My response was to pull over. I exited the van with my hands behind my back. I kneeled in front of her and presented her with a white teddy bear that one of the kids left in the van earlier in the day. This produced another one of those 100-watt smiles that she gives.

Escorting her back to the van, I opened the passenger door, and she immediately closed it and said, "We are getting in the back."

I offered a hand to assist her on getting up the step. She placed a piece of cloth in my hands, which I found to be a sexy pair of lace panties, and they were still warm and moist in the middle. What was a man to do? Well, I did my job.

She stopped at the very first captain's chair in the van, and I got down on the floor like the kids sit but facing the chair with my legs under the chair. No panties on, all I had to do was slide her to the end of the chair and have a late night snack. The problem is, I'm a greedy man. Before I finished, my face was wet from ear to ear. She was laid back in somewhat of a small coma, and her thighs were still on my shoulders. As any real man can tell you, there is no better feeling than to have a thick sister with warm thighs on the sides of your face. This shit is inspirational, and I wanted to take full advantage of the situation: Two fingers inserted and turned up, with the tightest assault grip that a clit had ever seen. Yes, it is an advantage to being a gapped-tooth person.

After about five minutes of this, Diane shot straight up in the chair, both eyes wide open, which rolled back in her head, mouth open sucking in air, thighs locked on my head, and the sweetest nectar flowed from her center. Both of her hands were on the back of my head, digging in those long nails. Yes, this was my pleasurable punishment for putting in that work for 49 straight minutes. It took four or five smaller ORGASMS to get her to this point, but it was well worth every lick.

Looking up, I could witness the facial expression change as Diane came down one breath at a time, and all of a sudden, she was gone. No more warm thighs, only feet kicking my direction as she retreated to the back of the chair. With her legs curled underneath herself, she said to me in an asking but commanding tone: "Back the fuck up, and don't touch me."

Raising both hands, I did as told, sliding back to her next question of: "What the fuck are you grinning at?"

It was not a surprise as I loved her attitude and brashness about life. So I answered her by explaining that I was looking at the spot where her pussy used to be. With another large intake of air, she wanted to know what that meant, and I explained that I think I ate the box that it came in. We both got a good laugh, her more than me. She thought that shit was really funny.

Getting up, I changed the music from Luther to The O Jays, grabbed what was left of the weed, rolled a fat one, and lit it. Walking toward Diane, I reached out in her direction, and she drew up in a ball and said, "Get your good pussy-eating ass away from me." Then she smiled as I offered her a choice between a joint and a snickers bar. It was almost comical to see how fast the candy was grabbed and consumed. This wasn't our first rodeo, so I knew that in a few minutes, I would have a fully grown woman coming at me with a fire burning down below that I had caused. I knew what I was doing because I sat and smoked my joint. I was slowly stroking a double digit hard on in her face, and she was falling for the bait. Only pulling her dress up a little bit for me to have my snack was a good thing, because now I was scrambling for my clothes, as I was butt ass naked when the police lights hit the back of my van. It turned out to be nothing. The officer just banged on the side of the vehicle with his night stick and said, "The park is closed, folks!" as it was 2:36 a.m. After getting dressed, we decided to drive to her place until morning.

It was Sunday morning, and the blues were playing on WVON in the kitchen while I prepared dinner. All the kids were busy doing other stuff.

Even the twins vacated the kitchen, which was a miracle. Yelling up front that I needed three volunteers for cooking duties, a large number of feet came towards me, loudly volunteering for the task. I never had a shortage of help in the kitchen, and today was no exception. I picked four kids for the task of picking greens and cutting up vegetables; only the older children were picked because of less instruction, and yes, I love being in the kitchen with all of them, but I only had so much patience.

At 2:00 p.m. exactly, I was pulling the pot roast with extra vegetables out of the oven and putting the cornbread in, going to the back porch to call out for Mrs. Dee, who was sitting there with a tall glass of ice and water, trying to soothe a hangover. I inquired about the chicken to see if she was finished frying it, and she laughed as if I had told her a funny joke.

"Boooiii," she said to emphasize the difference in our ages. "The chicken was done an hour ago, and these kids are ready to eat and me too."

Calmly, I reassured her that the cornbread would be done in 45 minutes.

My phone rang, and it was a foot race to it, as all kids like to answer the phone.

"Uncle James! Telephone!" was the next thing I heard. Yes, that's my name. James. James David Madlock.

Walking to the phone and telling the boys in the weight room to be careful, I asked, "Someone please turn down the TV, so I could hear on the phone. Hello, this is James."

The voice on the other end said, "Hello, this is Pokey," in a female voice that had more street to it than was needed. Pokey was a street person, yet at only 17, she didn't play, knowing what life had in store for a 17-year-old openly gay girl in this neighborhood.

"Hey Pokey, what's going on? You're giving me a call."

That's when I heard it, a crack in her voice.

"WE NEED TO TALK NOW."

I quickly walked over to the back porch, grabbed Dee and told her I needed to make a move, and she came right over to finish dinner. Going down to my van, I made a show of retrieving a cooler, so Pokey could see me out there. Once we made eye contact, I placed the cooler on the porch in my yard and started walking the half of a block to the park.

Not long after my arrival, Pokey walked up, looking only as Pokey could look. She was always in the latest hip hop fashions: her signature braids to the back, pants way too big and sagging, and a fresh pair of Jordan's. Because of family structure, Pokey was grown three years ago when she graduated from eighth grade. The local high school saw her for the first two semesters, and that was it.

She handed me a blunt, and I passed her one of the beers that I was holding.

"Hey Unc, what's up?"

We gave each other a pound and a hug, and she held on longer than I thought was necessary. I felt her body shake like a small burst of thunder, and her grip became more intense, and she did that thing that tears a man up inside. She was crying hard. All I could do was stand there and hold her and tell her it would be alright. Stroking her back and her head, she looked up at me and said that it won't be alright. So now was my chance to get her to talk. Doing my best to soothe her, all I had to do was shut the fuck up and listen.

"She pregnant, Unc. She pregnant. My girl, they got her pregnant. I didn't know what to say or who the hell they were." After some more tears and more body shaking, we sat down on a nearby bench to try and make sense of this info I was given.

"Who are they, and what happened?"

Pokey looked at me and made me swear not to tell what she was about to say. I only nodded, not giving a nonverbal commitment to what I was about to hear, and that was good enough for her.

"She having a Nation Baby." There was this damn term again, and I still didn't know what it meant. Pokey said to me that she was a member of the local gang, but she wasn't telling me nothing new; this was common knowledge to everyone. So she told me that she was gay, and this was common knowledge. She saw the confusion on my face and took a deep breath as though she had not been breathing all day. "Look Unc.

She is a Stone now, and she had to go through like all the rest." Pokey jumped up from the bench like new energy hit her as she pounded her fist still crying a little. "THEY FUCKED HER. THEY RAPED HER UNTIL THEY GOT HER PREGNANT!" she yelled at the top of her lungs. I could only hug her again and wish for calm.

About two minutes later, she was calm, and I told her to start from the beginning. She did, and I listened and listened and listened, then headed back home with a head full of fucked up knowledge. I climbed the stairs to a quiet apartment while all the kids were eating and Dee was sitting there looking at me as if she knew something that I didn't know.

"SO WHAT ARE YOU GOING TO DO?"

I didn't answer at first, so the question came again, and I answered, "I'm hungry," and headed to the kitchen and proceeded to fix myself a plate and eat. That didn't last because Pokey had fucked up my appetite. Retreating to the basement, which was my sanctuary, I had to think, and think fast. I didn't exactly know what I was dealing with, a GANG or a CULT. There were footsteps coming down to the basement. It was Dee. She yelled out, "Woman coming down. Is it clear?"

I told her yes as I laughed.

The small woman came around the corner with a large cocktail for me and a smile on her face. This lady was my neighbor for only 20 months, but she was a real friend. Sitting down and offering me the cocktail, which she knew that I would take, upon my reaching for the drink, she grabbed one of my hands to get my attention. All else in the world had stopped. It was just she and I.

"James, you need to make a decision one way or the other."

"Dee, I don't want to be in this shit. I'm a factory worker, and I'm not the police." Trying to apply a little humor, I told her that calling the police would be a novel idea, but I guess sarcasm don't work around here because Dee rolled her eyes and then told me to pay the fuck attention to what was going on around me.

"This basement has thick walls," Dee said to me, "but if it was more than just us two down here, the walls would leak. That's what this neighborhood does; it leaks, and everybody has plausible deniability because everybody knows what's going on."

"So what are you saying to me, Dee?"

"It's you. You are the outsider. They don't know you, and you go to work, you mind your own business, and you aren't dumb or scared. Before you ask about the police again, the last time four boys went to jail for rape—18, 17, and two 16 year olds got all of the charges. They were told that they were 'taking one for the Nation' and they would be taken care of by the Nation. This was hood shit that went on for years, getting younger guys to take the charges and promise rank and money when they got out. But didn't do shit for the families while they were locked up. Maybe gave the mother a ride every now and then to the many prisons in the state. Most of the time she was in a vehicle with three or four others who were going to see their children, husbands, boyfriends, and brothers who were locked up." Dee told me that she wanted to see the real mother fuckers go to jail—"Not no damn kids!"

Trying to calm her down and formulate a plan was where my mind was as she got up to leave. She looked over her shoulder to tell me, "Mrs. Myra is on your front porch, and she has been there for about an hour."

Shit, anybody want to be me for the next twenty minutes? Because I sure as hell wanted to be somewhere else and somebody else.

Doing my dead man stroll up to the front porch, this was not the Mrs. Myra that I had only met yesterday morning. She was wearing a church usher's uniform, hair pinned up with a touch of makeup. She rose to her feet and shook my hand with the most refreshing greeting ever. I started smiling because she brought that kind of a spirit with her. I immediately opened the door and asked her to join me upstairs for a minute, so we could sit down and talk. The first thing she noticed was all the children scattered about doing different things. I believe that curiosity got the better of her, and before anything else, she wanted to know, "How many children do you have?"

I told her six and that the others were my nieces and nephews. This satisfied her for the moment as I led her to the kitchen, and being my mother's child, I offered her a plate. She originally told me no, but I insisted, and she said she would take a plate to go. This made me smile inside because I'm always trying to show off my cooking skills. Mrs. Myra sat down and asked, "Did you find my grandbaby?" Which she knew the answer to, so she told me to get her plate ready as she asked to use the bathroom. Being a gentleman, I was trying to show her where it was, and she banged on the table and got my attention, then walked to the bathroom like she had been in my house before. Her banging on the table was not lost on me. There was a small piece of paper lying on the table that was not there before. I waited until I heard the door close to retrieve the note. It was simply an address in the area. I knew of this block and its propensity for being a stronghold for the Nation. There were three sets of initials on the note as well.

I placed the note in my pocket and started making that plate I promised. Hearing the door open and water, I knew she was finished. Trying to steal a little more time, I asked her if she wanted dessert. A blank stare and a remark of, "Boy, you young folks is just slow. Yes, I need everythang."

Loading the plate up and wrapping it up in foil, I handed it over. Mrs. Myra grabbed me by the face again. It wasn't that same intense feeling; this was more like a grandma type of thing. She gave me a peck on the cheek and said, "You stronger than them. You just got to fight hard."

With that, she turned to the door and spoke to all the kids on the way out. They all spoke, and a couple of them came over and gave her a hug. Walking her down the stairs to the front, she only had one word for me: "NIKKI."

Ninety-four degrees out, and I was exiting my back door on my way to get in a few miles. Even as I walked to the park, I knew that today's run would have a slight detour, just to have a look at that address I was given. Normally I would have some of the kids out running with me, but today was different, and I needed to see what the fuck had all these people so scared. Three laps around the park, then off the beaten path to see the mystery. Thinking is critical, and most people don't want to do that because it takes too much effort. An idiot would have run straight over to take a look. Not me. I needed to run for a while to build up a sweat. You don't want to go jogging, and you are bone dry. You'd stand out and be mistaken for the police. Again, this was all about thinking.

I kept straight on 52nd Street until I got to Justine Street, making a right turn to head north. I notice that there is a lot of traffic and security. Not uniformed security, but these boys were the kind that spray bullets everywhere without conscious or remorse. Slowing my pace a bit gave me a chance to look at the address and some of the gang ways to which I might have to run. I'm not a superhero, and my mind was dead set on giving all the information to the police, no matter what I saw.

About midway through—*bam!* There it is, and all its horror. It was obvious what I was looking at. Then someone called my name in a big-ass bass voice. Trying not to be startled, I wanted it to look like I ran this way all the time. Coming to a complete stop, Big Fred stood there as if he was the mayor or something. Within 30 feet of him in either direction stood maybe 25 goons, some serving crack, some on look out, and some were just there for the life of it. Walking across the street, my head was on a swivel and my eyes on record. A small amount of relief came in the form of two of my students standing on security, each giving me a slight nod as I passed.

Keeping my eyes on the prize, I never turned my head from Big Fred for nothing. He was maybe 6-foot-5 and well over 350 pounds. I heard that this son of a bitch was particularly nasty when it came down to money or product being short. He wanted to strike fear in people. I had never seen him in this setting before, and he commanded it well at first glance.

I was there to find the cracks in the foundation. Quickening my pace, I needed him to feel as though I couldn't wait and was delighted to "kiss the ring," so to say. I was greeted with a big bear hug and literally lifted off my feet. That's when I saw him over Big Fred's shoulder—the Prince. A man of small stature but a face of blanks; no tell signs, no movement. He didn't even flinch when I told Big Fred to put me down or I was going to kick him in the nuts. There was laughter from others but not the Prince; he didn't budge. Just as I thought, all this security was here for Fred. No, Fred was security for the Prince.

After setting me on the ground as gently as you can set down an egg, I was on my feet with my head on a swivel again as I was introduced to a few of "the generals," as Big Fred described them, and he shocked me when he said to his people, "This is who I was just telling y'all about. Me and Minnie were steppin' his backyard last night. Oh yeah, the boy is cold. He can spin a little bit." Everybody knew that that meant I could step. Just the mention of stepping, and a couple of the brothers hit a few moves. We all got a kick out of that.

Before I knew what was happening, Big Fred grabbed me by the arm. He was trying to introduce me to the Prince. I straightened a little bit and put on a harder breathing than was necessary. Putting my hand out first, trying to show a sign of respect. The young man got out of his chair and extended his hand. We both smiled at the same time with a look of familiarity. He didn't know my name, but he knew my face. We hadn't seen each other since childhood. A friend of my family from the Projects used to babysit him when I was younger. I was about four years older than him. He asked me, "Where do I know you from?"

And I quickly replied, "Maybe the basketball court or Fast Black."

Just the mention of Fast Black got some attention, as her brother was standing less than five feet away. I look over at him and give him a nod and a pound. He went by the name of G. Black; yes, the G was for General. I don't know who gave these clowns these names, but his fit like a mother fucker. He was jet black with a set of eyes that said "you wanna be the first or the last one I kill?" They were red from him being high, but they also had a yellowness to them, almost like jaundice, as if he was sick. Of course he had that damn curl shit dripping on his shirt

Again turning my attention back to Big Fred and the Prince, we chopped it up for about another two or three minutes before I made my excuse of finishing my run. As I left, the soldier in me spoke up and said this was a good recon mission. Now all I had to do was figure out what the hell I was doing and how I got into this shit. One thing was clear, there was something in that building worth them protecting.

Finishing up my run and getting back on the block, the kids were in the backyard playing with a water hose. Just as I got to the fence, I slowed it down to a slow walk and just prepared to get wet. Hell, they didn't know that after six miles that water was what I needed, and they laughed as though they had pulled off the caper of the century. I didn't care where the sweat started or where the water ended. This was going to be fun.

After getting soaked, I politely walked into the yard, locked the gate, and gave a huge yank to the water hose, which was now in my possession. I chased them until everybody was tired. We were muddy and wet. It was time to start putting some kids in the tub. As soon as the announcement was made, one of my nieces started to get the bathroom ready for the girls. I stopped at the door of the bathroom, I asked if they needed anything.

"No," was the answer. "We got our basket." It was a basket of soap, oils, and other sweet-smelling stuff for girls that was put together by the neighbors. I smiled at them as my baby girl ran up for some hugs and sugar. I stayed in the doorway talking to them until the bath water was finished and closed the door. I was trying to get a line on my oldest niece. She had been through a few things in life, and I wanted to know where her head was at or if she was the Nikki that I was asked to find. What would be my reaction, and what would I do to get her back; or my baby girl who just sat in my arms and sugared me up for five minutes while the bath water ran.

I needed a distraction, and fast. I didn't want this shit to hit home in my head. Keep reality where it needs to be. Going into my bedroom to make a phone call, it was easy to get on the phone when my niece was in the bathroom. I waited for someone to pick up. A rough voice said, "Hello?" into the receiver and my heart warmed. It was an old friend of mine.

"Ajaumu, hello sir, how are you doing today? This is James, and I need a place to squat for a few hours." I was told to hang on for a minute as he retrieved what info that he needed. His smooth baritone voice came back through the phone.

"IT LOOKS LIKE WE HAVE SOMETHING GOING OFF IN TWO HOURS."

"Where do I get a pass?"

He replied that I didn't need one; his wife would be at the door. Wanting to look good for my appointment, I went into the weight room to get in a quick workout, maybe 45 minutes or less. Sitting on the edge of my weight bench, I could see the crowd start to gather around the doorway. Just my sons and my nephew. By now, they had gotten used to the scene about to unfold in front of them.

After putting on my gloves and my belt for my back support and some stretching, 225 was the start out weight for the bench press with some lat-pulls curls followed by dumbbells, push-ups and sit ups, and a few butterflies with the dumbbells. For some strange reason, I went past the rest of the workout and went straight for the bench press strictly. I had a captive audience. This was my chance to hold court with my sons.

On my third set of bench press, I put 350 pounds on the bench. I knew that this was a little risky not having a spotter. Going into my pre-lift routine, I joked with the boys that if the weights fell on me, they would have to help me get it off. They all yelled emphatically and started doing muscle poses to show me that they had my back. I decided to make it interesting and started talking to them about their homework and book reports. I heard a groan from someone. Laying on the bench still running my mouth, they didn't know that I was in lift mode.

Silence filled the room as the weight started to move, and no one said a word so as not to break my concentration. This was not their first weight room experience.

The first three repetitions went smoothly; the fourth went up, but now it was a struggle. I could hear my two oldest sons whispering to my nephew that the bar was bending. As this fifth rep was on the way down, I was trying to get a good bounce off my chest. My upward motion was slower than the first four, and all the sudden all I heard from the boys was them cheering me on, saying that I could do it and keep pushing. They got louder and louder. They all went up in applause and cheers when the bar hit the bench. They made so much noise that the girls, who were in their room getting ready for bed came, running to see what all of the fuss was about. Now I got three kids on my chest after that struggle. Air was what I needed.

Once I caught my breath I had just one question for the peanut gallery.

"Why didn't nobody run over and help me?" With a straight face I reminded them that they had just promised to help me.

There was plenty of laughter as one replied, "We knew you had it!"

Again, I was trying to do what's right. My brother was coming over to sit with the kids for the evening. Looking at the time, I knew that he would be here soon. Deciding that my time was short, I decided that I would skip the boys for the bathroom. They didn't mind because it allowed them to stay up later. I gave them a small speech to inform them that Uncle Bonny was coming over to sit with them for the night, I added: "Yes, before anybody asks. Tasha and Becky are coming over." The whole house was cheering for a long time.

Tasha and Becky were Bonny's two daughters; they were in the same spot with not one but two crackhead parents. They ended up staying for the summer. It was only June 15; that gave me and Dee more work, but they were a blessing. Tasha every day helped with the younger kids. Becky was one of the younger ones but was a joy to have around. Now I had 11 permanent children living in my home and another nephew who came and stayed when his mom would let him. He lived in a stable household and just missed his sisters and cousins, maybe even his father.

Grabbing my toiletries, I headed into the bathroom to start undressing. Just then, there was a knock on the door. It was James Jr. Hell no, we didn't call him JJ. He came in before I could answer. He was talking to me with his head down. I stopped him immediately.

"Why are you talking to me with your head down?" I went on to say, "Proud men don't talk like that. Hold your head up and say your piece."

He looked at me like a young man should. Then told me that his sister called him last night on the phone at 1:00 a.m. I remained silent and listened to him explain that his mother had a lot of people at the house, and they could not go to sleep. I told him I would check on it. Then he asked me if everybody else was at the house why his sisters couldn't be there. Again, I told him I would check on his sisters.

"And Mrs. Hubbard might put us out for having too many people in her apartment," I added.

I turned off the water and grabbed my bathrobe, put it on and headed for my room, grabbed my stash of weed and what was left of my bottle of Martel, and headed for the back steps. It was nighttime, so I headed for my van. No one noticed. This was not the block where people hung out anymore selling dope. I'll tell you about that later, but it involved me sitting on my porch with a shotgun and a 45.

Closing the door and trying to take a deep breath, I sucked in a lot of air, and what came out was not dry like air, it was wet like water. Tears, tears, and tears. I just sat there in a moment of weakness. I think this was the first sign of depression, BUT BLACK MEN DIDN'T GO TO THERAPY. As a man I was growing into my role, it was becoming difficult. I made a mental note to buy a deep freezer. I already had two refrigerators and an electric bill that was about to explode. I sat for maybe 10 minutes, just trying to think. Finally realizing that I had a bottle and weed, I opened the bottle and took a bigger swallow than usual. It was burning on the way down. It grabbed a small amount of my worries and problems and took them down too.

Don't be too concerned about me and the drinking. You see, I come from a long line of drinkers. In fact, both my parents were alcoholics. My father passed my freshman year, and Mom, Brivion Madlock, is still around.

It's a nice thing to be able to think, and that was my advantage over people. They only saw what their eyes showed them at a first glance. I know what type of a picture I present to people. Muscles; a jock with no brains, and a scowl on my face that was put there by LIFE. That's my hold card on anyone. If I walk into a room, I have to know how to get out of that same room. I'm just paranoid that way.

While using my robe to wipe my face... *Boom!* A loud crash hit the front of my van. I looked up to see my brother standing there laughing his ass off. Coming around to get into the vehicle, he was still cracking up because he thought he got one over on me. I gave him a pound and a hug. Noticing his odor of stale beer and funk is not a good combination. He was still amused about his attempt, but his face changed when I told him he was about to get shot.

"With what, you dick? Your ass is in a bath robe," he said with confidence.

Raising my right leg, I showed him the 38 revolver I had retrieved as he banged on the van.

"Mannn. Whyyy the fuck you always got these damn guns around? You gonna fuck around and shoot somebody one day."

"Hey bro, calm down. Just hear me out. If I can raise my right hand and swear to defend this country, I sure as hell have a right to defend my BLACK ASS!" I handed him the weed and told him to roll up a couple of joints. I asked where the girls were, and he said they ran straight up the stairs. I took another swig and passed the bottle to him. After a healthy gulp he passed it back and started rolling. I had a few things that I needed to discuss with him, but the stolen jewelry was not one of them because I didn't want him in my house helping me look for something he stole and pawned already.

"First thing's first. I need to know what's going on at my ex-wife's house," I told him. He gave me a dead look, but he knew I was not amused. They got high together on occasions. I stopped him before he could lie to me. "Hey man, I'm only asking because of the girls. One of them called James at 1:00 in the morning. He told me she hosted a little action at her house so that she could smoke for free."

I changed the subject to something a little less depressing. I needed him to know that I would need a little more help with the kids. He had a full-time job as a messenger in Downtown Chicago. He was a beast on that bike. He made decent money, but he was working to get high. Oh, another thing about him. This mother fucker was a crackhead athlete. He didn't lift weights, but the dude could run and play some basketball. He used to play tennis and soccer, too. He wanted to hang out and get high more than go to school. Yeah, he used to be something like my hero. I would watch him ball out in basketball tournaments. One day I saw him score 22 points and dish out 18 assists.

We came from the Projects; well, a lot of Projects. By the time I graduated from an alternative high school, we were living in our fourth housing project. Yes, two in the city of St. Louis and two in Chicago. In two of those housing projects, the government Sprayed us with chemicals on more than one occasion. I don't know if this is a badge of honor or a cloth of shame. You see, we were not well rounded and definitely rough around the edges. If we could do nothing, we could play sports, fight, and fuck. I know that might not be a great resume for some, but in our part of the world this shit was vital. It wasn't like we were going to run into a Rhode Scholar in the hood to match wits with.

Bonny told me about a new guy at his job who lived up north that was a Hooper, an ex-college player who had a good spot on the lakefront where some ballers came to get it in. I let him know that I was down. It didn't matter where a game was. We just packed up the kids and some food and let them play in the park while we did our thang. My brother was the cog that made it all work. He was the point guard, and when he walked on the court smelling like liquor or still had the 40 oz. bottle in his hand, it threw off a lot of people.

But basketball was also his downfall he started getting high, hooping in the summer tournaments. There were pros and amateurs there, but a few of the pros let him tag along, and that was his first time trying COKE. I guess he liked it.

Passing me a joint and rolling another, he said, "Man, I talked to Denise yesterday and she is coming to Chicago in two days. She said that Uncle Pappy and Uncle Horse were coming with her."

Shit, this was way too big to me, because she lived in Maryland, and they lived in Mississippi, and I have not known them to travel much other than for a family reunion. I was glad that I was on vacation when they came to town. These were my mother's uncles, and proper respect had to be shown; maybe I'd have barbeque and invite over some family. Yeah, that sounded good. My brother was the first person that I told about my plans to leave my job, and that I was going to start my own business.

He looked at me and asked, "What type of business?"

I told him that I was going into the EXTERMINATING BUSINESS.

"Mannn, youuu going to kill some roaches." I responded with an emphatic, "Yes!" and he said, "What about your job at the steel mill?" I told him he was welcome to go apply for it because I was leaving within 30 days. Now his expression changed, as he knew that I was serious. "Man, good luck with that."

I told him that he could join me, and there was a spot for him if he was going to be for real about it. He said that he would help if he could. Realizing the time, I had to get my ass in the tub and get it moving.

One hour later, I was shit, showered, and shaved, dressed to a T, smelling good and back in the meat wagon—yes, that's on my license plates, only wagon is abbreviated as "WGN"—headed to what was supposed to be a secret location. *Man, I love this fucking city,* was my thought as I drove down Lakeshore Drive to my destination. Slowly creeping my way north, looking at all the boats and people out, the city so alive. I felt rejuvenated, if only for a moment.

Getting closer to my destination, I had to put on the mask. It wasn't a physical mask, it was an emotional one. Because even though they can see your face, you didn't want them to be able to read you. It was supposed to be about satisfaction and getting yours. These people played games on a whole different level. They could put enough I.Q. in one room to mentally move a tree, but this group was all about the pleasure of flesh, and at this point, I had to be careful not to slip.

Here came my exit near the Evanston border. Yeah, North Western University was my destination. I know; what the fuck was I doing there, at an Ivy League School? It took about seven or eight minutes to find the address. It was a sprawling place with a large, circular driveway. I guess that was for those who didn't belong to be able to drive the fuck out of there.

Pulling up to the door I needed to remind myself to shut my mouth because it was open as I gawked at what I could not afford. My van looked like it was just dumped into the wrong neighborhood. A middle-aged white man met me at the door, took my keys, and directed me to the foyer. Just as promised, Ajaumu's wife Lola was at the door to greet me. A full hug from her was something to behold, welcoming me with both arms open, and she smelled so damn good. I was handed a bag that contained a few things I might need for later. I thanked her for the plug for the night and slipped her a $50 for her troubles. I had no cover charge where a single man paid $500 or more to get a peep at what was going on. I signed the customary waiver and was waved through by Lola. She gave me another hug and said, "Good luck." I think I held on too long, because she sort of stepped back and looked at me funny.

Still with my mouth open, looking at more opulence that I can't afford, I stepped through the first lounge, which was decorated with plush red and white everything; even the server girl was dressed in red and white fur. Upon arrival at lounge number two, I was approached by a scantily clad older woman who seemed to know me, but I had never seen her before.

"Are you James?"

"Yes ma'am, I am."

She took my arm and told me that Lola had something special for me if I was interested. I gave her a nod, and she led the way to another direction, and I thought she was taking me to a dungeon of sorts. I was right, but this was different. Dark, but well-lit by colored lights, and luxury couches formed a sort of a circle around what looked to be a small stage with a large, round bed at floor level for viewing. I could see people lounging around with the lights doing their job because I could not see any faces clearly.

Asking my escort where the changing room was, she smiled politely and said, "It won't be necessary." Stepping over behind the bar, she held an envelope out and said that it was from three couples who wanted something special for the evening, adding, "Ajaumu said you could take care of things from here." She told me that Ramon was not going to show. Ramon was a good work partner; he was good for keeping shit flowing with the couples.

After placing the envelope under the bar, the escort winked and said, "Good luck."

These people had no fucking idea what they had gotten themselves into. Strutting over to the three couples, I introduced myself as Ace and shook every hand. I could see the looks on their faces. Just the handshake alone, it told a story. The men could feel the strength in my hands. It was intimidating. The women saw something different altogether. For them, it was the size of the hands—part excitement and part concern. Well, let's be truthful. I was not some Pretty Ricky. Again, I had buck teeth and big-ass lips.

These were not the type of people that you meet every day. This was old money; the kind that had dust on it from slavery and beyond. Keeping a watchful eye on their activity, they already appeared to be coked up and wound up. The petite ginger with a short bob haircut and the nipple rings showing through her silk dress was all over her male companion, and there was a tall blond with huge breasts. She wore a two-piece bikini and sat with her legs wide open as though that thang was on fire. The third couple was somewhat standoffish, so it would take a little longer to get a read on them. The wife herself was something altogether different. She looked like she just left a beauty contest, and the other contestants all lost. She was a stacked brunette with everything any man could dream of. I got excited from just shaking her hand.

All I had to do was put down my distraction until it was time, and my outfit was taking a part in that. I was dressed in a pair of white leather sandals, some white leather Bermuda shorts, and a Miami Vice jacket with the obligatory sleeves rolled up. The first thing I did was refresh all the drinks even though we had a server for that. I wanted them all to be comfortable. While making drinks, I slid off my jacket and gauged the reaction of those gathered around as I made small talk. Coming back around to deliver the drinks, one of the men in the room asked how much I worked out and what I bench pressed. I didn't want to smile too hard, but they had gotten over the looks thing and were stuck on the body. The husband of Mrs. America pulled me aside and said that his wife had an interracial fantasy and she wanted to pretend that she was being taken by a strong young buck. This fine bitch would not have to pretend tonight. He even hinted at some private work if tonight went well. CHA-CHING.

Turning back past the bar, there was Lola, asking if I would mind a spectator or two. She knew that I was a showoff and plus I was 45 minutes late, so I told her that I didn't have a problem with it.

Two of the couples must have been in the Jacuzzi because their hair was wet, so I figured I'd start with them. Going over to the first couple, these people smelled like money. Asking the missus what would be her pleasure, she replied that she needed to forget about her children and life's problems. Extending my hand, I led her to the round bed and held up my arm. She understood and took off my white silk tank top. The look on her face was priceless. There was no time for her to waste; her hands everywhere. I didn't mind; this is what her husband was paying for.

Not missing a beat, I saw light coming from the back of the room. Lola was bringing in about six couples who wanted to see a live SEX show, and that was what they were going to get. In a loud voice, I asked all of them to move forward to sit as close as possible. Me being a man, I know what we like, so I asked all the men in the room to take off their clothes and get cozy with whoever they came with. I needed to strip away their egos. A naked man only has as much pride as he has dick. They had no idea that I was about to make nine white men subservient to one black man. It was like a race as to who could get undressed quicker. Yes, men are freaks for anything as long as there is pussy in the room. And I had a piece in front of me that got their attention. She was wearing a two-piece bikini that barely fit, and she needed it off ASAP. I could have done my own dirty work, but I decided to enlist another woman into this to get things moving. I politely asked the reserved young couple to please join us, and the second woman stepped up to the round bed. I retrieved a knife from the bar and instructed her to cut off the swimwear.

Using what was available to me, I started squirting baby oil all over our swimsuit victim. This got a little gasp from the spectators. Right after the first strap was cut, I took one of those breasts into my mouth and made a show of biting her nipples. I could feel the nipple hardening in my mouth. I stopped the knife lady from cutting the bottoms off, wrapping my hands in her long brunette hair and sliding her head forward. She took the other breast in her mouth like it was her pacifier. I saw her submissive side right away and knew she could work to my advantage.

Needing just one more prop, looking around, I summoned one of the males to come up and kneel next to the bed. I told him to feel free to masturbate as free as he wanted. A light went off in my head. It was the speed that he ran down to the stage with. I decided, why not put all of them on their knees? I summoned the rest to come down. I gave them instructions like they were kids. I looked around to see nine white men on their knees waiting on a black man to literally punish their wives. I know that most people don't know what's going on here—it's called HOT WIFING. It's when you marry a beautiful woman, and you want to watch her get satisfied. He can buy her diamonds, a big house, a fancy car, but he only has four or five inches of DICK; now he wants her satisfied, and that comes at a cost.

The nine volunteers got in place and stroked themself to the two women making out. Our bathing suit lady decided to make it interesting and got the knife to cut off the dress off nipple ring girl, who ran up awfully fast. I guess she didn't want to waste her husband's money. She took possession of her new make out mate and laid her down right in front of our masturbators. She was laying so close, they could smell her arousal, and all those little dicks were hard as a brick. I didn't make things any better as I stood next to them and slid down my shorts to show the crowd 10-and-a-half inches of hard dick. This got a gasp from the audience.

Now, stepping into the middle of the bed, I pulled bikini lady on top of me so that she could straddle my face. Within 60 seconds, I felt Mrs. America gently slide onto my cock. She couldn't go fast; she had to take her time. In case you don't know, length x girth equals slow and easy. These two women rode me while facing each other. Nature took over, and they gave an impromptu full lesbian show to the audience.

This show went down for slightly over two hours, in every position you could have imagined. It wasn't just the visuals; it was also the sounds—sounds of passion; that's what the husbands were paying for. They'd seen their wives have sex before. But to hear them having an ORGASM with a dick that was five/six inches deeper than they have ever been or will ever go makes a different sound; it's guttural and animalistic. The shaking of the body where his wife's legs shake uncontrollably and her midsection trembled as she tried to catch her breath, this was why they were there. By the time it was over, no one was wearing clothes. Some even jumped in to either get a taste for themselves or a better view. Two of the spectating husbands that Lola brought in wanted to at least let their wives sit on the dick, just to try it out. I didn't mind; it was all about pleasing the customers. You could just imagine later, in a line right next to each other; it was like a classroom. Every one of those FREAKY WHITE MEN jerked off. Some at least three times. It was a nice touch to involve the spectators.

The envelope was placed in the center console with my pay and another several hundred bucks from the spectators. I just smiled because, truth be told, that is some shit I would have done for free just to get my rocks off, and I needed to unwind and get a little stress off. But the money was nice. Listening to some LL Cool J on the way home with the windows down getting that fresh Lake Michigan breeze, I felt like a million bucks, but the main thing was to keep my stress level down.

Back to life and back to reality, pulling up on the block all was quiet, and that suited me just fine. My brother was up, sitting on the back porch with a small radio, listening to some music as I came up the back steps. Even in the dark, I could see his face light up. He slid over as I came up the steps, turning sideways to get by him, which made us both laugh, because he just told me last week that I was getting too wide to slip the pics on the court. I told him, "Don't worry, I still set the best pics in the city."

He asked me if I was going to watch the game tonight. That's when it hit me how to get Nikki back. I started clapping my hands and saying, "I got that ass now," over and over. He didn't know what the hell I was talking about, but he followed me up the stairs to find out. As I talked, he plugged in the light over the pool table and said, "Let's go." He got us a few beers while I racked the balls. It was customary that he broke the balls up because he would be racking the balls a lot. Midway through the second game, he wanted to know who I got and how. I could not explain all things to my brother because I knew that he and the Crack Rocks had a different mindset. I said that I was talking about my night. A big grin came across his face as he asked, "MANNN, you are still getting down with all them fancy as rich people?"

I replied, "Yes," and that I made about $900 tonight plus tips.

"So that's why you got that gay-ass outfit on?" Before I could answer, he said, "I know that they smacked you on the ass in those leather panties you got on." I still didn't get a chance to respond because he was on the floor laughing rolling around like Richard Pryor was in the room telling jokes. Once he stood up, he never stopped being the court jester. While he was lining up his next shot, I dropped the contents of the envelope and the tips on the table. His concentration was broken, and he wanted to know if he could go with me next time and grabbed his package to indicate that he also had a big dick. This wasn't lost on me. We were brothers, but the mother fucker had no class. He was a scoundrel of the first order. My brother would leave me entertaining customers while he went in the back to steal all of their shit. Now tell me, would you take that risk? My brother was good for simple shit, like the next mission I was putting him on. I needed the house to be empty for tonight, and the Chicago Bulls had a chance to close out the Charles Barkley Phoenix Suns. Nothing like a championship game to send a man for a loop. I needed to scare the shit out of big Fred and G Black. Maybe even the Prince. The police would do it, but this was not the time for that.

I explained in slow detail what I needed my brother to do for tonight. After that, I had to get some sleep. It was going to be a long day, and I needed to get Nikki home. Tricking slow people is easy, but when you have to pull the wool over a dozen eyes at one time, that takes planning, and I didn't have long. I went all out on the food and drinks for some gangbangers I didn't give a shit about; I just needed shit to look as normal as possible. Rolling down on big Fred earlier in the day, I told him that I was hosting the game tonight with food and drinks on the house. I asked him politely to bring the Prince with him. Fred didn't have many intelligent friends, and he knew that this was a chance for him to score some brownie points.

The kids were going to my cousin's crib in the Robert Taylor Projects for the night, and all the girls would have their hair done. My cousin Jug and his wife Poochie were the best. He was my gambling buddy. We started on 38th and Cottage Grove, pitching pennies. By the age of 11 years old, shooting dice in the back room or one of the stairwells was nothing to me. His wife Poochie felt sorry for me sometimes and helped with babysitting when she could, especially when we were out gambling. She also did a lot of braiding for me.

Before I took the kids over, I had one other stop to make at my ex-wife's house. Delilah and Christina had to be removed from that house. It didn't take long for my ex to throw their shit in some Aldi bags and off we went. She didn't give a fuck as long as she got a check.

Getting out of the shower, I heard my brother coming up the steps with catered food and drinks. It took him a couple of trips before he got it all upstairs. Dee had done a great job at getting the house together. Now, it was showtime.

A few of the neighbors started arriving, and the game was on two different TVs. There were a couple pans of fish and some party wings, fries, rolls, and corn on the cob; two coolers of beer and some alcohol. Big Fred came about 10 minutes after the game started. We exchanged a pound and a hug as he wrapped his arms around me. I knew that he was going for the lift, but sliding a little closer to him, I put my leg between his and raised my knee and was immediately released. Now he understood about me kicking him in the nuts. It didn't have to be done; just shown it was possible. Leaning down to whisper in my ear, he said the Prince would be there at half time. This was great—less brain power in the room to help him think, and the timing had to be just right.

Speaking of timing, player number one was in effect. One of my students came into my apartment and didn't even speak. He rushed to G Black and whispered something in his ear. Observing from across the room, I could see a look of concern on his face. My student put the photo of Nikki back in his pocket like a family heirloom. As one of the guys missed a shot on the pool table, it was G Black's shot, but he stepped around the table to Big Fred to have a sidebar. They hooked arms and walked to the back porch. I knew that my student couldn't talk to me, but his eyes relayed flat out fear. I sent him into the kitchen to get himself a plate. While fixing his plate, the porch meeting ended, and they gave my student a nod and sent him on his way.

Returning to the pool table for his shot, G Black asked again, "How much am I about to kick your ass for?" Everyone laughed and returned to watching the game.

At the end of the first quarter, I invited them all into the kitchen to make a plate and get a drink. Like she was invited, Lisa from across the street came walking up the stairs and straight into the kitchen. We all spoke to her. She was a welcome distraction as Mrs. Dee walked in the back door, cussing loud and saying, "This shit has to STOP." Everybody stopped what they were doing as Mrs. Dee held up a picture of Nikki and said, "Another girl done gone missing. What the fuck is wrong. Has anybody seen this little girl? The police done been all up the block today, and they said that there were two more girls missing, but they didn't have their picture yet."

Standing at the kitchen door, I had a clear view of the room and Big Fred. This was a thinking man's game, but they didn't know that we were playing a game. Most people like to put their two cents in, and right on cue, Lisa chimed in that the police asked her daughter if she'd seen her. She wasn't even in the game, but she was more convincing than the players in the game. We all turned at the sound of people coming up the steps. It was Big Fred's wife Minnie and a few of the ladies in the neighborhood.

People soon filed out of the kitchen because the game was back on, and Pippin and Jordan were must see TV. I saw G Black and Fred huddled up in a corner like rats, all I had to do was be patient and follow the worry.

Maybe five minutes before halftime, the front doorbell rang. Dee told me she would get it. In walked Pokey with her head down and her hand in her pocket. She made a straight beeline for Big Fred and asked him to follow her. They walked into the bathroom. I don't know if she practiced her lines, but she'd better be convincing as an Emmy Award winner. Pretending that nothing was going on, I continued to play host and try to fuck one of Minnie's friends. Shut up, I know what I did last night, but I was horny again, and I think the two of them are together. Hell yeah, that would be a good coup for the night if they would both go.

While being asked was this my apartment by one of my intended targets, I noticed Big Fred come out of the bathroom and go straight to Minnie. Squatting down, he whispered in her ear and showed her the photo of Nikki. Minnie shook her head up and down like a bobblehead doll, then she leaned up to say something to him, and that was it. The party was over. All members of the Nation had to roll, and that meant Lisa, too. I didn't even know that she was a member of the Nation. Minnie had to roll, too, but she wanted to fix herself a plate, which gave me time to make my pitch at the undercover couple, Minnie's two friends. Dee laughed at me as I was trying to close the deal. She knew them from the neighborhood and told them both to my face to, "Be careful. He's a big ass whore!" but in the same breath, she asked, "I know one of y'all have been thinking about getting up on that pool table."

The two targets looked at each other and started giggling like schoolgirls. Minnie yelled from around the corner, "Hell yeah, I have been thinking about getting up on that mother fucker and spreading out." To me, this sounded more like an endorsement than anything. Minnie told them that she had to take care of some business for Big Fred and that she could swing back around to get them. Dee stood in the middle of the floor and shook her head like it was going to come off her shoulders. She yelled, "YOU SLY MOTHER FUCKER, YOU GOT THE WHOLE NEIGHBORHOOD TRYING TO HELP YOU GET SOME PUSSY!"

Trying to keep a straight face because she was funny, I bent down and retrieved a fresh cold bottle of Martel that was intended for persuading the Prince. I asked, "Would you ladies like to join me in a cocktail and a meal plus a little herbal refreshments while we finish watching the game? Mrs. Minnie can pick you all up when it's time to go."

Dee threw up both her hands and then she dug her MD2020 out of the cooler. With an exit statement of, "If y'all fall for this shit…" she left, stomping down the stairs.

We all laughed, as we knew that she used to be as hot as a pistol back in her day. Needless to say, Minnie never came back, and I dropped them off at home about 4:30 a.m., lying, saying that I had to be at work. In an hour. And yes, they got on the pool table.

Doing a little recon after the drop off, I drove down the block where the fortress of a building was, and there was no security, no sellers—nothing. The block was like a ghost town. I guess that a missing girl in your dope fortress that the police are looking for would scare a coward to shut down shop because it was their neighborhood. The Nation had 20 spots more just like it all over the city.

It was 5:15 a.m., and I was tired as fuck, but I was already up and put on my running gear. Getting to the park this early was peaceful. It was a small park, so my run without the kids extended out into the city from Ashland to Halsted from 59th Street to 39th Street. It was on concrete that I pounded out every mile, which gave me time to think. I know that this might sound crazy, but I do my best thinking when I'm running, working out, or fucking; it doesn't matter. Get that fucking frown off your face. Hemmingway is not writing this shit; I'm a kid from the Projects.

Rounding the corner to end my run, there was Mrs. Myra sitting on my porch, smiling, and I barely got the gate open before she came down the stairs at a rate of speed that I had no idea that old Myra was capable of. Her light frame hit me in the middle of my chest. We hugged like old friends as she told me that her baby came home. Nikki was home. She didn't care if I was sweaty or not; she just felt joy. Myra made me feel self-conscious as she kept talking about it, saying she knew that I was gonna get her Nikki back.

Just in case you missed it, we only had one picture of Nikki that came back into the apartment with each player. The picture of her was passed on from one person to the next. My student confirmed that Nikki was there at the building. Lisa's story added weight even though she was not involved. I'm glad she wasn't because I had no idea that she was a part of the Nation. That would have been a major fuck up. Plus I sent Ptacc and Finny to see Minnie to let her know that Big Fred might be in trouble if this girl was found in his possession. That was enough to scare a ghetto coward. He shut down the whole building and moved the operation to another location.

CHAPTER THREE
THE VISIT SAVED HIM

Now was not the time for me to get put out. Mrs. Hubbard had sent word to my son that she wanted to see me. I stopped washing my raggedy-ass van to go see what she wanted. Sitting in her kitchen looking out the window, Mrs. Hubbard sat smoking a Virginia Slim.

"Hello Mrs. Hubbard, how are you doing today?"

"I'm fine, James, but what I need to know is how long are you going to run an orphanage in my building?"

I apologized for the inconvenience of extra noise and just sat down the envelope. There was nothing to discuss. My rent was paid for the next two months, and she was going to take the extra money, or I was going to have to find a new place to live. Before leaving, I offered the most humbling apology I could give. I told her that they were my family and that I was between a rock and a hard place, and this was the only soft spot that I had for us to be. She told me that she understood as the envelope was scooped up and placed in her purse. Man, that went smoother than I thought!

Stepping out into the sunlight just made me feel good. I had to get to the store for some grocery shopping; now it seemed like I lived in the fucking store—never enough milk or cereal. It always appeared that I was buying the short loaves of bread. My siblings stealing didn't help. I was almost sure that it was my brother and not my sister. This trip was for the barbeque tomorrow. Two of my great uncles and my cousin would be here in the morning. I sent the smaller kids over to Dee's yard and took the three oldest with me to help with shopping and loading groceries. Now I had to stay on budget, but I wanted to splurge a little. These were my elders coming to town, and I was going to meet up with Ptacc and Finney to get my cut of the stash house.

Moo and Oink was crowded as hell. It was where the hood shopped for meat. Bring a jacket; it was always cold as fuck in that meat house. I got my shit and rolled, knowing that my brother was on his way to the house to sit with the kids while I went to my meeting. I felt safe that the meeting was in the daytime. There was a little anxiety about the area—Bridge Port; not a good place for a black man after dark. But it was still daylight, and I didn't want to get pulled over for walking, or being a black man walking, on a sunny day. So I left the pistol in the van. Walking the block and a half to the meet with my head on a swivel, I got to the address and entered slowly. It was a warehouse/car wash with large windows up front. Another on my safety list: I could have at least a visual on that side.

Ptacc walked in to tell me that Finney was called out on assignment. Red flag number one. There was no small talk. He tossed me a bag that contained $26,000 in cash and dope. Red flag number two.

"Stop—hold on. I didn't ask for any dope. I told you and your boy to keep all the dope."

He looked at me and said, "10 percent is 10 percent." Reaching into the bag to get the dope out, he stopped me to say, "DON'T LEAVE THAT SHIT HERE." He turned to leave just as I was headed for the door. Ptacc stopped me and said, "If you are going out the front, wait five minutes or go out the back." Red flag number three. I was fucked no matter what I did. There could have been police out front waiting on me to walk out with a bag full of dope or someone coming in to rob me before five minutes was up.

Quick decision time—and I mean quick. Spotting a dumpster between me and the back door, I had just found a new home for the dope. Now that the dope was gone, this bag was awfully light—maybe not even $5 grand. I was not walking out that door with a kilo of dope on me. Sticking my head through the door to make sure that the coast was clear, I started walking with a brisk pace. I was in the clear.

DARKNESS. DARKNESS. There goes that damn word again.

It's not dark; there is a big-ass light on, and where am I? I'm not dead because I can feel pain. There are images around me, so I'm not awake. What the fuck is that bright-ass light?

Oh, it's over the hospital bed. What am I doing in a hospital bed? Why can't I talk to anyone? They can't talk to me. Who's in this room? I can't see any faces, but I feel love, man, and it's strong and warm; not like hot warm, but like comfort warm. I know that I'm thinking about my kids, but I have no worries. They are fine. How do I know this? I just know.

But this damn light has to go. People are in a fucking coma and think that they saw a bright light and went to heaven and back, and all this damn time they won't turn off the light over the bed. That's why all you hear people say is that they "saw a bright light" and felt a chill throughout their bodies. That shit ain't true either. It's cold as hell in this hospital. If they turned off the lights and gave me a blanket, I could probably get some sleep in here.

Even in a coma, your mind talks to you: "NOOOOOOOOoooooo—you don't want to go to sleep. SLEEP IS THE COUSIN OF DEATH. You are still a soldier, you can't die."

I had no idea what was wrong with me, but I know that it was hard to breathe, and something was wrong with my lungs. My head hurt a little. But this morphine shit was the bomb. Oh yeah, I guess I don't know every DAMN thing, because if they turn off this big-ass light and you go to sleep, that means it's goodnight IRENE. You can only think about the past and things you already know or have experienced. You don't get to see the present or the future, just what you know.

What I'm going to tell you now is related to me by my Uncle Robert. He was my mother's brother, not the oldest but a noble man. He told me that we needed to be alone, so we could talk. I agreed so we left for the lakefront. As I drove, he didn't say one word; it was as though he was formulating his thoughts. This worried me because he was a man of few words, and he made them count. Even his jokes were sharp and straight to the point.

After finding a parking space, he pointed to my cooler and asked me to grab it and bring it along. I started to ask him why we were taking a cooler that felt to me to be just about empty. I was getting ready to look inside, and he stopped me. I just followed orders and brought it along with me.

We walked maybe a quarter of a mile in silence. Every time I tried to engage him in conversation, he would ask me to be quiet. Picking a spot that faced the water, he sat on the cooler. I felt like a sucker because he just tricked me into carrying that cooler for a seat. I sat on the grass and sort of looked up at him as he started to speak.

"James, we are not crazy," he said to me.

"We are two of the most stable-minded people I know," was my quick answer to him.

"JAMES, SHUT THE FUCK UP." (I TOLD YOU HE WAS DIRECT.)

Now I was silent. He started again with the same statement that we were not crazy. I didn't say anything, did not even bat an eye.

"You and I just left the hospital 20 minutes ago." I said nothing, and he indicated that he wanted me to answer.

"Yes sir," was my reply.

"Well, do you know why we were there?"

"No."

More silence, then: "But you do know who I am?" Again he signaled for a verbal answer.

"Yes sir, you are my Uncle Robert. My mother's second oldest brother, and you have seven more brothers and four sisters. Shall I name them?"

He gave me a look of *don't be a smart ass*, so I was quiet again, and he gave me this long spiel about our family history and how Uncle Horse protected the family back in Mississippi and how he had lived there all his life on the Lee Plantation. He said, "That's where I was born."

I wanted to ask a question, but I knew this was not the time. Here was my uncle telling me about his uncles, so I paid attention. As the history lesson continued, he started to tell me about violent stories of Uncle Horse and my Uncle Chester. That didn't surprise me one bit because I spent a lot of time with Uncle Chester, and I saw firsthand that he was a beast of a man. But he had a drinking problem that was out of hand, and that's how most of his brutality came about. Uncle Robert said to me, "No, don't focus on him. I want you to focus on me and Uncle Horse." Again, I gave him my undivided attention. He went on to say that I had some very respectful kids, and he had been at the house with them for the last three days with my mother. Now he was lying to me, and I knew it. How was he at my house for three days, and I just saw him for the first time when he met me at the hospital in the lobby? He saw the confusion on my face and raised both hands to continue my listening.

"James, you have been in a coma for three days." I knew not to respond; just listen. "We thought that you might die."

I started going over my body with my hands feeling for bruises or injuries. I felt great, maybe the best I've felt in years, so what the hell was he talking about? Out of the blue, he asked me, "Are you a noble man?" I didn't know exactly what he was talking about, so I asked for clarification. He looked at me with a look of *I'm losing my patience*, but he knew that this would be a lot for any person to take in, regardless of their mental capacity. He looked as though a light had come on in his head and he asked me, "Are you thirsty?"

I laughed and said, "Hell yeah, it's hot as hell, but you wanted me to bring that empty ass cooler." Now it was his turn to laugh as I told him, "We could have gotten a couple of beers out of the small fridge in my van." But he wouldn't stop laughing, so I told him to hold on, and I would run back to the van and get us a cold beer.

He handed me my keys and said, "Be my guest."

A short run is a short run to me. So off I went, and when I returned, he was standing there with an amused look, and the top to the cooler was open with a full case of beer, ice, a full unopened bottle of Martel, and a two liter of coke (because that's how he likes his drinks). I have known this man all my life, and I have never known him to be a magician or a liar. Now he had my attention, and I sat down on the grass and asked as seriously as I could, "What just happened?"

He asked me, "Are you ready to shut the fuck up and listen?" I didn't give him a verbal response. I just nodded like a kid in school. The first thing he said was, "It took you a little less than four minutes to run to the van and get this beer, which included stopping to open the van, get the beer out, lock the van, and run another quarter of a mile back to me. Do you know that you just got out of a coma less than two hours ago?" He kept going as if he was on a roll. "You just carried a cooler with a case of beer and ice more than a quarter mile and you thought it was empty."

So I said, "Can you please explain this to me without riddles? I'm a big boy and I can take it."

He said, "Okay, if that's how you want it. But you have a choice: You can stay here in Chicago where we don't know what might happen, or you can go down to Mississippi where we can keep an eye on you at the farm."

I was getting frustrated because here he goes with these damn riddles again, and I wasn't moving to no damn Mississippi. And I sure as hell didn't need anyone to watch over me. There was a RAGE building, and I didn't have time. I wanted to get back to my kids.

As though he was reading my mind, he said, "Your kids are fine. Tee is at the house with the kids." That was the pet name my family had for my mother. I asked him how long she had been here. He said, "Three days like the rest of us."

Now I shut up again.

"Look, James, shit will never be the same for you again. You have been changed, given a nobleman's chance at life." I still didn't know what that meant, but it sounded like some sort of a do over. He told me that I was attacked in an alley the day before they came into town, that I had a fractured skull, some broken ribs, and a punctured lung with a lot of other bruises from kicks and punches. "There were a few burn marks on your back and chest, like some type of electric shocker was used," he said. He told me that I was in bad shape; I was not breathing on my own.

I started touching myself again, looking for all of these bruises that he was describing to me, and he stopped me and said, "It's okay. HE TOUCHED YOU. It will be fine."

And I said, "Thank you, Jesus!" This had to be a miracle if all of that happened.

Now, we both poured a plastic cup of Martel and coke. He continued to talk, and he had my attention because he was talking some Biblical shit, and I wasn't buying any of it, not even wrapped in a pretty bow. A stab wound with a punctured lung? A fractured skull, and I didn't have a scratch on me? Uncle Robert put his hand on my shoulder, and this brought about a level of calmness that was not there before. He started telling me about the Madlocks in my family a couple generations before Uncle Horse. Uncle Robert tried to explain to me how they lived. They put on their Sunday best and went to church. The land was cleared and worked, and they built cabins from the timber they cut down. PROUD PEOPLE.

He told me about how the white folks treated our family down in the Mississippi Delta on the Lee Plantation. He said, "The violence was horrific, and they just came and took what they wanted. We worked the land, and they would come and harvest what they wanted, even our women.

"On a particularly hot Sunday in late August, they came with four wagons to harvest our crops for their winter and to take some to market to make a few dollars. Actually, they told the Madlocks to fill the wagons. He told me that black folks couldn't have guns, and these white folks did what they wanted to do to black folks. One of our relatives, Moses stood up and said that they could have only one wagon full, 'cause we need the rest to live off.' Well, they beat him within an inch of his life. The white folks told the women and men to fill the wagons, or they would be next. These blond-haired, blue-eyed devils took what they wanted and burned the rest saying that the next time A NIGGER SPEAKS UP, THEY WOULD KILL EVERY NIGGER IN THE COUNTY.

"Just as they were leaving, one of the white men decided he would do something even worse; he took Uncle Moses' 15-year-old daughter. He explained again that there were no guns and no way to fight back. Uncle Moses' wife Maingo Pink Madlock tried to grab her daughter back, but she received a boot to the face for her trouble. These were proud people, and later that night, the men had a meeting and decided that three of them would strike out in the morning to these white folks' property and risk their lives to get her back. The only weapons they had were farm tools, and they worked throughout the night getting them sharp for the next day. It would take a full day's walk because the two horses that they had had been taken back in the spring. All they had left was a mule, and they worked him from sun up to sun down. He was no good for riding.

"Back in Uncle Moses' shack, three of the women worked on him and used black thread and rags to sew up his wounds and to clean his wounds. Tears flowed and anger built. Maingo Pink was a beautiful woman, but that Gee Chee inside of her was boiling over. The hurt of losing a daughter and a husband on the same day was too much for one heart to bear. Maingo Pink was hurt and furious with rage. She wanted her daughter back, and she wanted her husband to live. One of the men that was to go on this journey was Maingo Pink's brother Nathanial. They were from the swamp in Louisiana. Nathanial knocked on the door to the shack. He saw his brother-in-law lying there, gasping for air. His sister was just torn apart. He consoled her and told her of their plans to get his niece back at nightfall tomorrow. Nathaniel knew that they didn't have a lot of time. A pretty 15-year-old black girl would suffer a mean life at the hands of those white folks.

"Maingo Pink held her brother and begged him to not go. She couldn't bear to lose the last thing she had. Maingo told him to go outside and to wait for her where the old farmhouse once stood before that day's fire, which is now smoldering ashes. It was a testament to the pride and hard work of her husband and her brother. They had worked hard to build up the Lee Plantation.

"Walking fast, she didn't need light to guide her way. She walked those steps for 12 years. It was where she came to get the smoked meats that came from their farming. Nathanial reached out his hand to help guide her, but she never stopped, just marching forward to where the back of the barn used to be earlier that day. Stopping at a particular spot, she handed her brother a shovel and screamed, 'DIG!'

"Nathanial stood there, shaking his head no over and over. Maingo grabbed the shovel and started to dig, sobbing harder and harder with each dig. Nathanial held onto his only sister and begged her to stop. She fought him hard and seemed more determined than he was. With the thought of his niece and brother-in-law, Nathanial's rage grew. He took the shovel and started digging. Maingo Pink talked and cried as he dug. She knew that she would need his help. She told him that her baby was gone, and her man would be dead by morning. If they didn't take this chance, they would be all dead soon. Because they had nothing else to give them white folks, but their lives.

"A hard sound was heard, then silence. The siblings froze in place as they looked at each other to confirm this last step. They knew that there was no turning back. Nathanial started digging with his hands, not wanting to damage the box he was retrieving. The box was old and hand carved from wood of their home land in West Africa. Maingo Pink Madlock knew that her daughter would be home soon, and those white folks would be dead. There was just one problem. Moses was not of their bloodline. Maingo Pink didn't care; she wanted revenge, taking the retrieved box covered in a cloth that belonged to her grandmother. It was used to protect the box from the dirt and mud.

"The siblings returned to the shack where Moses laid, believing he was on his dying bed. Maingo told the other women to go home; she wanted to spend her last hours with her husband. The women all filed out one by one, knowing that the pain their sister felt was crushing. They themselves were not strangers to the cruelty of those same white folks.

"The door was closed, and they started to pray and open the box. I wish I could tell you that they were praying to God, but I don't know that," my uncle Robert said to me with a straight face. "Maingo Pink Madlock had to clear her head, and fast. She needed to remember the ritual and the words that she heard her grandmother utter some 26 years earlier. She placed a hand carved mask on her husband's face. The mask was made from baobab wood. These were the oldest trees in Africa. Five hours later, with the rise of the sun and some of her and Nathaniel's blood, NEW LIFE BEGAN. OR WAS IT LIFE AT ALL?

"First light came, and the men with their sharpened tools were ready to strike out. Only two shacks remained on the property from the fire. One was Uncle Moses' and the other belonged to Jimmy Tyler. He was going on the mission, so they met at his place. They were all scared to death and wondering where Nathaniel was. He knew the way because he had been there to work the fields before. The door opened, and in stepped Uncle Moses without a scratch on him, looking fit as a fiddle. No one knew what to say. So he said it for them: 'I'M BACK FROM THE DEAD, AND IF YOU DON'T WANT TO BE DEAD, STAY THE HELL OUT OF MY WAY. UMM GON KILLS ME SOME PECKERWOODS.'"

I hadn't said one word and sat there with my mouth open. He looked at me and said, "You wanted to know." There was not a clear thought in my head, and he knew it. Instead of passing me a plastic cup, he passed me the bottle of Martel and said, "Your mother and kids are at home waiting on you." He said it so calmly, like he was telling me to take out the trash. I turned up the bottle and drank more than I ever consumed in one gulp before. He instructed me to pick up the cooler, and I stood there, waiting for him to get up off of the cooler. And that's when he yelled again, "Pick up the fucking cooler!" I walked around to the back of the cooler. I did my best at work lift position and again he yelled, "Pick up the fucking cooler!"

I braced myself and started to lift. My Uncle Robert rose to eye level, only I was looking at the back of his head. I quickly put the cooler back on the ground, almost dropping him. I was afraid of what just happened. I also had a grin a mile wide because I was into the physical strength shit. I wanted and needed to know about this being dead. He said that we needed to get back and he would answer any question that I had on the ride home. My first question was why me, and what I was supposed to do now because there were no white folks coming after us in Chicago like that. Uncle Robert said, "ENEMIES CHANGE AND ENEMIES STAY THE SAME." Then he asked me, did I think some black boys jumped me in an Italian neighborhood? He had a point, but that was not some shit I was trying to pursue. Hell, I don't even remember what happened.

As we approached the van, he asked for the keys saying that he would drive; just give him directions. Again, I carried this heavy-ass cooler, and it felt empty.

Uncle Robert didn't start the vehicle right away. Instead he handed me a large envelope and said, "Please, take your time; it will explain a lot."

Taking it and looking at the contents just took my breath away. I had no clue as to what I was looking at combined with the crazy shit that Uncle Robert told me. There were photos of a man who looked as if he was on his dying bed. It was me in the photo, and I looked bad. Head bandaged, tubes in my nose, and one eye was swollen shut. I asked my uncle, "Did I die?"

"No. No, no," was his answer, and he was very quick to point out that things did not get that far. Looking at the next page, it was the medical report. Shock and amazement was an understatement: broken ribs, fractured skull, possible vision loss, and a collapsed lung due to a knife wound. Eight electrical burn marks. Not to mention the bumps and the bruises.

I didn't have words other than, "How? How could a person heal from all this in three days? I feel no pain or anything."

Again I was told that I was being told the truth. Why me? Just a short and direct question. He said, "We didn't get to choose, and life makes the choices, not us. You were picked, and it cannot be reversed."

Knowing that I was going to my mother and children, I needed to calm down. I started to search for weed. I needed a joint now because I didn't know what was coming next and wanted to know and wanted to be ready.

While riding and smoking, there were other things to fill me in on, like the fact that I would need to be looked after. I didn't know what that meant either, but I decided not to interrupt.

"Young man, you need to get that vengeance and anger out of your system." Trying to reply that I had no vengeance against anyone was cut down with a swift reply of, "Are you going back over there with those mob boys? Or are you going to forget about it when you can snap a man's neck like a toothpick?"

Stopping at a red light, he turned in his seat to look at my face and said, "You have been given a gift that comes with responsibility and compassion. James, you have to know the difference between a man who steals meat from a supermarket and why he stole it, not just that he stole it. A CEO of a company steals, you have to have the same empathy and compassion even though you know it was greed."

"Uncle Robert, why didn't they give this to you?"

"Because that's how you live your life. You are a fair man." His answer was to tell me that he was not a violent man, so what the hell was he saying about me? I'm a family man. I haven't fired a gun since the Army, and the only thing that I was beating up these days was PUSSY. That's true because I got my ass whooped twice in the last month. DAMN, that wasn't a good look. Knowing that we only had a short distance to get to my house, I wanted to know where my Uncles Horse and Pappy were. He said that they were at a hotel and that Uncle Horse had to rest for a couple of days before he could travel. Uncle Pappy had to be there to look after him. I gave him the last turn of directions and asked him to park on the side of the house.

He put the van in park and said, "Some people are going to ask what happened and how you recovered so fast. Just tell them that people exaggerate shit. It was a very bad 48 hour virus or something." Before the van could come to a stop, the kids were on their way out of the gate. My Uncle Robert asked me, "Are you running a fucking daycare?"

Getting out of that van was the coolest shit that ever happened to me. All the kids rushed me, and we hugged, laughed, and cried even a little. There goes that macho shit again, okay? I cried, too. While all the love and hugs were great, we rolled around on the ground.

"GET UP OFF ME RIGHT DAMN NOW, EVERYBODY MOVE." My voice was loud and full of warning. The kids were scattering and screaming.

My mother, who I had not had a chance to hug yet, stepped forward and grabbed the front of my shirt as she asked, "What the hell is wrong with you? Don't you see these kids out here?"

I tried to calm down and explain that the neighbors walked their dog over here, and I was rolling in shit. This took my family to a whole other galaxy. The laughter went on forever and forever. The shit would not stop. Pun intended. Uncle Robert chimed in that it looked like I got the shitty end of that deal. Again, the peanut gallery went up in laughter. At this point, I made serious eye contact with my mother, and we both started to walk towards each other with our arms out. I missed her and wanted to hug her, but she had her arms extended in front of her to ward me off and told me that she was not getting caught up in my shit. Again, the peanut gallery went off in a belly shaking laughter.

I'd had enough of this shit. Now they had me doing it! So I decided to chase all of the kids around to put it on them, and they all turned into track stars, running around to the front. My nephew Deon asked me to stand still as he got the water hose and blasted me with water. After removing the shirt, I felt the power of my mother come at me with full blast. She hugged me hard and long again with tears. My mother held my face and kissed my forehead. This went on for a couple of minutes, and the kids who had come back thought it was cool that they got a chance to wet up me and Granny at the same time. Who were they fooling? It was summertime, and the water was on, so now we are all wet.

I went upstairs for a real bath; Moms and Uncle Robert were in tow and close behind. No sooner than the door closed and no children were around, Moms ran up and just held me and we sobbed some more. Unc quickly broke that up and got down to business about this thing that has happened to me. He told me that I needed a lot of rest because I would burn a lot of energy. We were back to the riddles now. Moms stepped in and broke it down.

"Look James, you are not like other men anymore." She said, "Whatever a man can do, you can do three or four times over so you're gonna need more sleep to recharge your ass back up."

That was plain and clear, but just as she said it, something happened. I stopped talking and started walking to the kitchen. There were bags on the table, and there was meat in one of them. Turning to my mother, I asked where those bags came from. She replied that she and a couple of the kids walked to the neighborhood Arab market on 51st and Racine and got some meat for dinner. I told her that the meat was bad. She asked how I knew, and I replied that I could smell it. Uncle Robert looked over at my mother and nodded a confirmation of some sort. Moms explained as only she can do, "See you can smell shit." She said, "And no I am not sorry about that shit joke." Uncle Robert was already grinning.

I don't know how many hours later it was when I awoke, but it didn't seem long to me. I smelled breakfast cooking, and Mom was saying good morning. I rushed over and hugged her hard. She gave a big grunt and told me to put her down, as she was not a big woman. I asked what time it was, and she said 10:30 Saturday morning. I could not grasp that I came home on Thursday afternoon. Seeing the confusion on my face, she said that my body had a lot to heal from. The house was really quiet, so I asked where the kids were. Moms informed me that they went to the zoo with Denise and Uncle Robert. She said, "He had to do something with his time while you slept." I was surprised that Denise was still in town, but Moms said that they all would be leaving tomorrow and that there was a meeting set for tonight, so Uncle Horse could talk to me. I was looking forward to this talk, so I could get some clarification.

In the meantime, I needed to get in a run and a workout, going into my room to change. I felt great. I looked into the mirror on my dresser. I looked physically amazing to me. I would usually walk over to the park and stretch before my run, but today, I was running right out of the back door. I'm more of a jogger, not a runner, due to my size and weight, but noticed that my pace was quicker and I wasn't as winded after my first couple of miles. Now that I was headed up the back steps, I was a little tired, but I felt great, plus the house was still quiet, and my next stop was a workout.

Moms asked, "Did you change your mind and go for a shorter run?"

I didn't know how to explain to her that I ran four miles further and in less time.

The workout went above and beyond anything I had ever done before. There was not one break in between reps. I needed a shower because I smelled like I wanted to be alone. I woke up with five kids on the bed, wanting to wrestle with the champ—yes, I was the champ. When we wrestled, I would literally pin their asses and get a three count, and so far they wanted the title. Man, I felt alive and well.

Moving through Downtown Chicago with my uncle, the city was lit up, and all I could smell was all of the different smells of food. Not having gotten used to this new sense of smell, I was like a dog in a butcher shop, just hungry. Arriving at the Holiday Inn where they were staying, I started to get scared and nervous because I was still in some sort of disbelief in my head, but I didn't want to be dead either. I needed to see Uncle Horse's face to know the truth, and was I really ready for that?

Room 1122 looked back at me as we waited for the door to be open. The first person I saw was Uncle Pappy. He was a big man, maybe a little over 6 feet, but as wide as a door. He had worked in the fields of Mississippi all his life. We hugged, and he lifted me off the ground like Big Fred but less threatening. After the hug, he stepped back, and we all exchanged greetings. My cousin Denise took after her uncles because she was tall for a woman, but she was a pretty chocolate brown that only God could produce with a pretty, full, white-tooth smile. After our hug, she slid over out of the way as if she was revealing something to me. Yes, she was revealing something to me: my Uncle Horse, sitting in a cushy hotel chair, looking a little worse for wear. He rose slowly and reached out to me. I advanced fast to hug him and to hold him up. He was maybe 5-foot-11 and not of a large stature, but when his arms wrapped around me, I felt his power. It was EUPHORIC. Strong, but nothing to fear. It was warm, but not hot. His grip felt like something permanent that you never wanted to lose. I wanted to step him back a little, so I could help him sit back down. Nothing happened; no movement at all. It was as though he weighed a ton. Pulling my head back to look at him to try and gauge what was going on, he was smiling saying that it was the POWER.

At this point, everyone else cleared the room. He stepped back and sat in his original spot. He motioned for me to take a seat. It started with a look. One of knowing. I didn't have to tell him that I was confused. He knew it. He was one of only four men who had been in my shoes before, and he wasted no time telling me all the do's and don'ts—don't drink too much, stay in control of my emotions, and accept the truth as you see it. In people, there is good and bad, so look and pay attention. Don't do nothing out of vengeance… The list was so long, I thought that I was going to have to become Mr. Perfect or a priest. Then he looked at me and said, "Don't forget to have fun."

Some of the things we discussed in that room for the next two hours was mind blowing. Most of it, I will take to my grave because no one will believe me any way I tell it. I had two questions for him. The first was, with all this going for him, why stay in the country? He told me that power would kill a man if not checked. There was less danger for him in the country, and he could live in peace.

"This was not something I asked for, James, and neither did you," he said. "It just fits, and before you ask, yes, there are other good men in our family. IT'S NOT THEIR JOURNEY TO WALK."

My last question was, did I die? He stood and touched the top of my head as if he was a minister in church.

"No, James. You did not die. You were close." He told me that they were all coming to visit me as a candidate for the power and to interview me to see if I was a noble man.

"But when we arrived, your mother was already here, and she knew of the power, as she is the family historian." He said, "As we walked into your hospital room, we saw your condition, and your mother, with tears in her eyes, told us as only a mother could say: SAVE HIM."

CHAPTER FOUR
A NEW BUSINESS FOR THE FAMILY

Packing up my locker at work was bittersweet for me. It was where I was cutting my teeth as a man. The military teaches you responsibility, but the foundry taught you how to make ends meet and bring home the bacon. There was no fanfare or retirement party. One of two things happened: Either you were one of the men the foundry chewed up and spit out; or you were one of the men the foundry made stronger. I would like to say that I was the latter.

Some of the old timers stopped by the melt deck in the control room to say goodbye. Harry Reed grabbed me and hugged me real hard. I felt the tears hit my face from his cheeks. Harry was the second man on the melt deck with me. I learned a hell of a lot working with him; his 30 years of experience and my macho shit made for one hell of a team. We poured more iron than any team in the history of the plant. At some point, we had to let each other go or this was going to look gay. His eyes and my heart told me everything that I needed to know. Harry told me to say hi to my Uncle Big Bill Madlock for him. Oh yeah, that's how I got this job. My uncle was a legend in this shit. I showed up at the plant and told the people at human resources that Big Bill Madlock told me to come there because they were always looking for good workers. The young lady took my application and walked off as if she didn't give a fuck about no Bill Madlock, but while walking to my car, trying to figure out my next move (I needed a job), Harry walked out and shouted, "HEY."

I turned to see a burly man looking at me waving his arms as if to get my attention. His white skin would have looked pale if it wasn't so dirty. Quickly walking back to him, we reached out our hands to greet each other. His grip was strong like a man who had been working all his life. Before I could get my full name out, he was telling me about Big Bill and their years together. Harry said, "You got big shoulders, you might be a good worker, and besides, Bill wouldn't send you here if he didn't think you could handle the work. He also knows that I chew up mother fucking green horns and spit 'em out."

He took me into the locker room and hired me on the spot. A legendary team was formed.

Walking through those doors one last time, I kept my face shield and helmet for some reason. Knowing I would never come back this way again, there was only one last piece of business to handle. I went by Mr. Carter's office and knocked on the door rather loudly. After yelling, "Come in!" he smiled as he saw my face and let me know that he was glad to see me go. I spoke and told him that it was nice knowing him and that I needed him to put in his paperwork and leave the plant today. His size and height stood ominous in such a small office, but I wasn't there for that. I had already won the fight before I came into the room. Throwing the photos on the desk and stepping back a safe distance, he was in a desperate situation. You never know how a man will react. It was right there in living color, Mr. Carter smoking that crack pipe while getting his dick sucked at the same time. My cousin told me that it was how the young girls tricked them old men to keep spending money all night long. I informed him that Stanly Jackson and Danny Chavez should run the union. He nodded in agreement, and that fight was over.

I don't want you to miss something here. Crack cocaine hit the poor community hard, not just black, but white and Hispanic as well. This shit was crushing us from every side. The men that used to work with me didn't just decide to fuck off their pensions and retirement money; this shit was strong. We now had people living with relatives, and no one knew what the lasting effect that it would have on the children who were being born. No one knew the economic effect. The prisons would burst at the seams with our young people. No one knew that great-grandmothers would have to raise multiple generations of children.

There was no immunity from crack. Even if you didn't use it and your relatives did, you were still involved by some sideways effect. The hardest part was the pipe dream that it fed to our youth about fast money and riches. One or two summers was the average amount of time someone sold crack before jail, death, or using it themselves. The young ladies who got high turned into something unrecognizable, and the young men became predators in their own community. Drive by shootings; sorry-ass mothers fuckers who never worked a day in their lives were buying luxury cars and phat-ass gold chains. They had more money in one pocket than their parents made in six months, but they had money in all four pockets. Know who ran the house? A hard-working man that drove a Chrysler and went to work every day was no longer a role model.

You must know that a drug dealer can't understand a man with short money. The idiot down the street whose only claim to fame was that he slept late every day and made plenty of money was now on the block, preaching his brand of death or jail economics to your child while you were at work. Don't worry, you will find out like the rest of us when it is too late. My oldest child was born with coke in his system, so yes, this shit was personal to me, but I was just caught in the middle, looking for a soft place for me and the kids to land. Well, this ain't no fairy tale, and that's why you have to look closely at what happened to your aunts and uncles who just changed their behavior. Uncle Zo had not missed a day of work for 21 years. Now he is unemployed and SMOKED UP 21 years' worth of vacation money and pension money, and he lost his family.

You think that you understand what's happening, but you don't see the way people are changing in front of your eyes. Theft from older family members was the worst. It could have just been strong arm robbery. They took what they wanted: TVs, VCRs, and anything that could be pawned for fast money. One of my cousins had an apartment that was stacked with pawned goods from floor to ceiling. I personally saw guns change hands with dope and money. Now, the murder rate in Chicago is sky-high. It was this way all around the country, places like Little Rock, AR, Lima, Ohio, Columbus. GA, and Phenix City, AL, started to triple and quadruple in crime and dope fiends. There was really fast money to be made. Diploma rates were dropping, and prisons were being built and filled at a rapid rate.

Now was a time for grandmothers to pray harder than ever. People who never did hard drugs in their lives were being offered rocks by family and friends just so that they had someone else to get high with when their money was low. I even saw my first cousin sell rocks to his mother. Yes, he introduced her to the drug. So now who can you trust?

This game was deep; there was trickery all around you. I showed up at a relative's house, and the older brother was teaching the younger brother how to cook this awful shit. But when it got done, he started to teach him how to break up the crack into smaller rocks. I noticed how hard he was smashing them to reduce the size. The only reason he was smashing so hard was the fact that he was stealing a part of the dope by somehow wedging the smaller pieces underneath his fingernails. One brother teaching another brother. Where is the love?

You have to be me to understand my world, because it's complicated. I'm sitting down talking to my six-year-old Corvell about our schedule for the day, and he asked me why he didn't have to do a book report or math problems today. I explained that we were going to do flyers for the new business. Again, he had a question about our schedule and the work for the new business.

"So Pops, do we all work for the new business?"

With my head held high I repeated the name of the new business.

"Yes, it's called MADLOCK AND SONS PEST CONTROL SERVICE."

With a renewed vigor, he repeated what I said: "MADLOCK AND SONS PEST CONTROL." He had a little trouble getting it all out, but he said it correctly.

"Yes!" I screamed in response to his getting it right. Now all of the kids were chanting, "MADLOCK AND SONS PEST CONTROL." We were elated jumping and dancing. This went on for about 30 seconds. We had to stop jumping because Mrs. Hubbard lived downstairs, and we couldn't afford to get put out. Speaking at a normal tone again, Corvell simply asked, "If this is our job, how much do we get paid?"

I guess the term is flabbergasted because I didn't have an answer. That's when I saw the smile on his face. The little lawyer was framing his case the whole time to see if he was getting paid. When I told him that they would be getting paid, now they were cheering and stomping again. These kids were going to get us put out. That was my last thought before chasing them all downstairs to pack up the van.

At 8:30 a.m., we were on our way to do flyers for the new business. I had everyone stay silence while I explained how we were to do things. The twins and Becky would stay with me at all times, and each girl must have a boy with them at all times; do not cross over to the next street unless the others working with you were ready, and go together. I kept four smaller kids with me. Corvell, only six, wanted to earn his money and go with the bigger kids. Reluctantly, I let him go and told them to keep an eye on him and not give him too many flyers at one time, or they would be picking them up off the ground.

We all learned lessons that day. It was not a disaster, but it was a learning experience as to which kids were interested or not. I found a sitter for the twins, Becky, and Delilah. They were too small to reach some mailboxes, and they dropped a lot of flyers on the ground. It took a while before I got my first customer, and I think it was set up by a female friend.

Before school started back in August, we were well on our way. Calls were coming in, and I was learning the business. The kids could literally do 4,000 flyers per day. This was enough volume that could take me through the winter. We did the exact same routine every day. I just had to budget my money for the winter and pray. Oh shit, I did say that things were going well? Okay, if you look with some real rosy colored glasses. I still lived in the Town, and this shit was getting out of hand.

After finishing my last job of the day, I got home, and there was a police car in front of my house, so I pulled around to the side, and there were more police cars. I told my nephew and two sons to, "Stay in the van while I see what's going on." I walked to the alley, and there was an ambulance. One young man was in the back, and the other was still on the ground being tended to. Mrs. Dee walked up next to me and put her arm around my waist. She squeezed me tight and said, "We have to talk."

I went over to get a closer look and saw one of my students in the ambulance. I was lost and stunned. This kid was waiting on the results of his GED. You have to know his name is Melvin Cummings. He is important; he is someone trying to make something of his life.

Dee grabbed me and held on for dear life. Her legs were scissors between my legs; I could barely walk, and she refused to let go. It may have looked as though we were having an altercation, but nothing could be further from the truth. Getting me out of that scene was her goal and to keep me calm. Sitting on my back porch, crying, and talking to Diane and Mrs. Dee, I was told what happened out in the alley today. Two young men were short on their money or drugs, and an example was being made of them. Melvin Cummings will never be able to join the Military because of the damage that was done to his right eye. The other young man I didn't know at all. I heard he was from the other side of the park. I asked, "Who did the work?"

And the response was slow coming. Sitting through a moment of silence, Diane said that Big Fred was in the alley, but she didn't think that it was him. She told me that she arrived as he was leaving the alley. His appearance was still neat, and he was carrying the bag. I'm assuming that meant that he was carrying money. This was confirmed by Diane.

"So if he didn't do this, who did?"

"Sun Down," was her reply. This wasn't good, because he was an old head that had been around for quite some time. He was already a legend when I was a boy in the Projects on 38th and Cottage Grove. Madden Park homes to be exact. We called it the Low End. That wasn't a made-up name. Stay the fuck away from there, and you won't end up on the Low End. Sun Down and his crew hung out in the park; they worked out all day. Mostly a bunch of cats who had been in and out of the joint a few times, and they were generally muscle for the Nation. Staying to myself was working out just fine, but I was going to take a stroll in the park tomorrow. Even if it killed me.

I took off work the next day to take the kids school shopping. Who the hell was I kidding? I was the boss now, and I could take my kids anywhere and anytime I wanted. When the torture was over, I had to apologize to myself for bragging earlier. Those kids wore my ass out. Yes, they were the bosses. I was just the adult and the wallet.

Getting closer to home, the anxiety was building inside of me. It was 3:45 p.m., and the sun was out, maybe 90 degrees. I took my nephew and the older boys for a walk in the park. I figured that if I had kids with me, maybe it would be easier to control myself. Getting into the park was nothing different than usual. Gangbangers all around innocent families trying to enjoy the park and pray that nothing went wrong. Being as astute as he is, my eight-year-old said, "We don't go this way."

I assured him that it would be fine.

Slowly walking past my intended target, I knew with my tank top on, they couldn't help themselves. I heard Sun Down calling me. As I turned us all in that direction, my nephew wanted to know what we were doing over there. He was mumbling under his breath as not to be heard. I told him to speak up, and he said, "You told us don't come over here. Because of the Nation." Just as he was saying it, I was just in the process of exchanging a pound with Sun Down. He acknowledged what he heard and said, "I understand, bro."

One of the members of the Nation wanted to know if I was lifting or visiting. This was too easy, so I gave him a chance to get back into his own lane. Because he was about to have his plow cleaned, as the country boys say. Sun Down noticed the error of his ways, set him straight, and dismissed him. Now he was asking if I wanted to get in on a set with him. I told him, "Yes, let's go." The bar was currently at 265 pounds. He and I both knew that would be child's play for us. We originally agreed to 325 for a four-rep set. It was no problem until one of his guys wanted to get in, and he had money. Just a friendly wager. All the money was on the Nation boys, even having prior knowledge that they saw me running all the time. That shit wasn't a problem to me, plus I couldn't get the kids to stop laughing.

Before the first lift there was over, a grand was on the ground, and I needed that money. This is what I call CURVEBALL COMING. Since we were betting, the rules had changed. It was heaviest lift wins or most reps of the same weight. There were two others besides Sun Down. I wanted it over with as quickly as possible, so I started the first lift at 375 pounds, and you needed at least two good reps to move on to the next round. Well, everybody made it.

Sun Down yelled out, "Fuck y'all, give me my money!" and asked for 425 pounds. I have never gone past 375, so I didn't know what to expect. It was his call and his first lift. The first rep went smoothly, the second was a struggle, but it was a clean lift. This mother fucker was nothing to play with. Thug Number 2 went down swinging and was short on the first lift. Thug Number 3 was the real deal. About 6-foot-3 with a body that looked like he picked it himself, once he removed the T-shirt, the park went up in a roar.

Now the kids were looking at me, and they were no longer laughing. In fact, they looked as worried as I felt. He did an extra rep just to prove a point. Now it was my turn, and I had never tried this much weight before, but I was going to give it the old college try. Laying on the bench was the most relaxing thing that I could have imagined. There was nothing, no emotions, no people around me talking. It was quet, like prayer before a meal. And in that split second, I knew that these gentlemen were in for a treat. I got up from the bench and was told right away that if I didn't lift that I would forfeit my money. Now, I produced the silence by asking for an additional 50 pounds. They had to remove weights from a curl bar to accommodate my request. I waited and talked to the boys to keep them calm. Then I looked at the crowd and yelled, "SHOWTIME!" because I was about to get my sucker.

I can't explain the adrenaline from the power. The five reps went almost too smooth. Hell yeah, five reps of 475 pounds, and I didn't even breathe hard. But my adrenalin was on 100. I stood up, looked at Sun Down, and told him to bend down and pick up the money and give it to my sons. There were a few grunts and groans from the peanut gallery.

This man held sway over them with physical strength. I now had one on him that was both physical and mental. Making a couple of jokes about his new task, he complied like the good foot soldier that he was. I told the boys to head straight home and don't stop. They took off running as if their lives depended on it, as if I wasn't there holding court about my lift and talking shit, still keeping an eye out that not one person left that circle following them. Giving Sun Down lots of praise before I left, it threw him off a lot, and I asked him to take a walk with me, and we strolled about 100 yards from the crowd because I wanted my instructions followed to the letter. I stuck out my hand to shake his hand while I complimented him on his lifts. Once we were shaking, I leaned in to him and pulled him to me. I can't explain why; maybe it was a reactionary move that knocked him off kilter enough for me to get a grip on his hand. That's when the tables turned.

Sun Down was no longer a big strong man; he was putty in my hands. I lifted up on his arm to tell him that he must stand and make no reaction to what was going on between the two of us. The look in a man's eyes when they see real fear or death, it is something that will never leave you; it burns into your soul. The eyes are pleading without saying a word. The feel, the crunch of human bones as you look into the eyes of guilt. Sun Down had no idea what was going on or why. I said Melvin's name, and he now had a clue. It was too late, and a good five or six bones in his hand were already broken. The light was on, and he was going to pay for his cruelty. Asking him to remain silent while his hand was in a vice was asking a lot, but hell, he had done a lot.

Ordering him to bend down a little because of our height difference, he accommodated me without hesitation. I let him know that he was to pay attention. He was told to leave the Town and the city as soon as he walked out of the emergency room.

"Only take what you can pack in your car, and don't come back." I really think he heard me. I never thought he would call me sir, especially with our age difference. Now we had each other's attention. I told him we were having a pop quiz. "What do you think will happen if I let you go and you tried to hit me?" A little more pressure, and I saw his knees buckle again. No words came out.

Hoping to relieve the pressure, he stated with an apologetic tone, "You are going to break my other hand."

"Yes, you are correct." The cracking sound of a couple more bones in his hand. I told him, "Go straight to the emergency room and have your wife or someone bring you some clothes and get on the highway. Tell people that the car door slammed on your hand. If you tell someone about me, I will go to your parents' house and see who can stand this grip."

Upon release, this man made a beeline to exit the park, not stopping to say a word to any Nation members. I think he dropped his flag. That means he stopped gangbanging. The last I heard, he was getting a disability check in another state. It was because his right hand was nonfunctioning. Big Fred was still out there, and that cock sucker was on my radar.

Walking into the door, the boys were standing in the weight room with the money stacked on the weight bench. No one spoke at first until James spoke up and asked, "How did you pull off that trick?"

"It was a mental trick," was my reply. They were not buying it, so I told them the truth to see how that would fly. "Well, I have special strength that only lasts a short time, but I have to concentrate really hard to make it work."

Terrell, the genius of the group, gave me some shit about weight and body mass compared to my lift that did not add up. They didn't buy that shit but wanted to know how much of the money they were going to get. I gave the five of them a bill to split, and that's what they did. Split with the money. I knew the candy lady down the street was about to get a windfall. All was going well, and they had bought extra shit for the whole house. The sugar rush was coming, and something different was happening to me. I needed to lie down for a while, and I felt drained. Informing the older kids that I needed a nap, they knew to keep the noise down and to make some sandwiches if they didn't overdose on junk food.

Rolling over all I saw was a small light coming from the closet. Silence filled the apartment; this turned on a light in my head. The house was too quiet to have 13 children, so I got up and looked over at the alarm clock, which read 1:14 a.m. Damn. I slept over six hours and didn't know that I was that tired. My mother somehow popped into my head that I would need a lot of rest. Just strolling through the apartment, checking on the little ones, not a creature was stirring, not even a mouse. As things happen, when a young man wakes up, my wood was talking to me and asked, "Who are you going to call?"

I tried to ignore him and went to the fridge and drank straight from the milk carton. It was my house, and everybody was asleep. Or so I thought. There were two heads looking over at me. It was my two nephews sitting on the enclosed back porch, looking through the window laughing. I almost spit out the milk, and they laughed even more. After putting the milk back and heading to the porch, they couldn't stop laughing. I thought it was about me getting caught drinking out of the milk jug, but that was only part of it. My brothers' son Tony said, "You're gonna be sick."

My face scrunched up even more when the big announcement came that they were drinking out of that milk, meaning the kids. Oh shit. My first thought went to Christian. His nose ran all day, every day. No matter what the temperature was outside or the season. We all laughed a little more as I gave Tony a pound and a hug. I had not seen him in about a month, and he could not wait to ask me about the park adventure earlier today. Once I gathered my thoughts about it, I told him that I did that concentration thing I keep telling him about.

"It is all about focus and concentration. Once you master that, the world is yours."

We sat up and talked about all types of things: school, girls, gangs, and even their parents. We all looked at each other as a car came past the house for the second time. I didn't have to ask them to go in the house; they were already in motion.

After closer inspection, I saw it was one of the neighbors, but I had no idea why she stopped and parked on the side of my house. It was Ms.

Tanggy. Yes, that was her name, and it fit. She had a body that won't quit and a walk that would excite the dead. She was a bartender at one of the local clubs. Her mouth told you that in one minute. Looking at her get out of her vehicle and walk to my back door was a surprise. Upon opening the door, she spoke in her normal greeting, which was loud and came with a, "How the fuck you doing, James?"

I answered with a, "Hello Ms. Tanggy," and she told me to cut the proper shit because she didn't have a lot of time.

"The bitch that ran in the house when I pulled up is probably waiting for me to leave," she said.

"Well, what can I do for you?"

"I'm not sure," she said matter-of-factly. "All I know is you helped get Myra's granddaughter back and you don't like the Nation."

My first thought was, *Some of those Nation members were friends and family.* My second thought was, *Here comes trouble; put her loud ass out before she wakes the kids.* I didn't invite her upstairs; she just started walking up on her own. Stopping at the top of the landing, she took a seat and kicked off her shoes.

"WHAT THE FUCK YOU LOOKING AT ME LIKE THAT FOR?" Her question was loud, and she started rubbing her feet, saying that they hurt and she needed a real MAN to massage her feet, because she had been at work for 11 hours standing the fuck up and they hurt. I could only shake my head. I had no intention of rubbing her feet. "Where the fuck is the weed? I just got off work, and I need a joint."

Again, I had no intention of using any words in the dictionary to answer her. I opened the back screen door and walked into the apartment and retrieved her a joint and one for me. Coming back out the door, she was still rubbing her feet, and her skirt rode up and that thang was PHAT. Trying to avert my eyes before she saw me looking, it was too late, and she told me so.

"I see yo ass looking, and hell no, I ain't here for that." Reaching out for the joint, she said thanks just like she said everything else—loud and snarky. This was only the second time that she had been by my house and only in the backyard. Just the mention of Nikki was still on my mind and the fact that thang was phat. Okay, okay, okay. I'm a man, and I just woke up a little while ago.

Ms. Tanggy wasted no time getting to her point.

"I just found out that my niece is pregnant, and it's a fucking Nation baby." She stood in place as she continued talking. There was no reason for me to say anything. Ms. Tanggy stood on her soapbox and talked for the next 10 minutes about the Nation and all of the young women in the neighborhood who had been impregnated over the years. FOR SOME STRANGE REASON THE MOLE ON HER NOSE DIDN'T SEEM DISTRACTING. HER CONFIDENCE COVERED IT WELL. That's when the cover flew off the wagon. TEARS, TEARS, TEARS, AND MORE TEARS. This was where I didn't want to be, but like any man, I stood to comfort her. I don't know if I had the right words, so I did the obligatory, "It's going to be alright," and rubbed her back. I let her get it all out as best I could. I wasn't a fucking GUM SHOE, but here I was with a damsel in distress.

I don't know if she rehearsed her lines or not, but the part where she pulled away from me and looked me in my eyes and said that two of her three children were Nation babies... I didn't know what to say, so I just coasted her back to her seat. We didn't make eye contact because she had her head down and mine was in a fog. Ms. Tanggy frisked her oversized handbag for a lighter and lit her joint. After several pulls, she told me to pick up my fucking head and quit looking at her stuff. She was 100 percent wrong. My head was down due to the fact that I was hearing some more shit I didn't want to hear and I didn't want to be involved in.

"So what do you want me to do?"

Her response was, "I really don't know. But you the one out here running around the park and the neighborhood like some fucking SUPER HERO." I knew right then that she was going to be okay, because she had that smart ass twang in her voice, and she was loud again. Over my shoulder, she saw one of the boys moving around in the kitchen, and she said, "I think yo bitch in there getting restless."

I'm not in the mental health business, so I don't know what to say to crazy people. So I started with the truth.

"Those are my nephews. We were on the porch talking when you pulled up."

"OH, my bad. I thought a stud like you had bitches crawling out the walls."

"No, Ms. Tanggy, I live here alone with my children and that's all."

"How many you got?" she asked. I replied that I had 12 no13. Ms. Tangy stood again and added, "No wonder you don't know how many you got. It's too damn many to count. And what kinda dick you got to have all them damn many kids?"

I was worried about running out of wind just trying to get her to sit down and listen. Once I explained to her about the extended family, she was a little calmer about it. Yet still worried about her waking the kids, I asked her to join me up in the attic, there there's much less noise to wake the kids, and this was my smoking and getting away spot.

On the way up to the attic, she wanted to know if I was trying to choke her with this dry-ass joint and nothing to drink. I told her to hold on. Once I turned on the lights in the attic, I went back down and grabbed some Martel, ice, glasses, and a few beers. I needed info from her, and I needed to get her out of my house. This was not something I needed to rush but be firm about whatever we talked about. That shit went out the window as soon as I walked in the door. She was sitting on a short love seat with one leg propped up on the cushion. Just coming into the room I saw her sitting with her leg up, and by instinct, my eyes went to the middle of her body where she had her skirt pulled down in front of her to cover herself. I wasn't trying to be a pervert. But it did not escape Ms. Tanggy.

"What the fuck is wrong with you men? Do y'all got pussy on the brains or what?"

No answer again from me. I just handed her a glass of ice and tried to keep my eyes focused on her eyes. That didn't work so well because she was coming home from work and dressed to get tips with a pair of 38

DDs with a push up bra looking at me in my face. She spared me the comment, knowing that I was at a disadvantage.

"Ms. Tanggy, what can I do about this Nation Baby thing that the police can't do?" Before she could speak, I was talking again. "What about calling the police and telling on these dudes? All it takes is a few sisters who want to leave this place to speak up." I was sitting in a chair across from her, and she reached out and grabbed my hands.

"Mr. James, that's not how it works. If your family is still here, then they become the targets." Her response was calm and direct. "We can't do it that way. We need to find another way. It's got to come from outside the Nation. Somebody they can't do nothing with." This came out like it was some type of plan that she had. This was not the first day this shit had crossed her mind. She was waiting to dump this pile of crap in someone's lap for a long-ass time.

I listened to her talk and talk. By now, we were on our second drink, and we had not touched "that cheap-ass Martel" as she put it. We were drinking a 20-year-old scotch she had swiped from work. It was pretty smooth. Now lighting the second joint, we were getting down to the history of Nation babies.

Ms. Tanggy told me, "Back in the day, the founder said that we needed to be populating the Nation by producing children and raising them and later educating and indoctrinating them into the Nation. The men in the Nation would pick a woman and take care of her and the Nation baby and make more." She said that it was going fine for about 15 or 20 years, and all the sudden it just became free pussy with no responsibility. "This was a part of the bylaws," she explained. "We all swore to this and now look where the fuck we are. Our girls are being robbed of their youth and their futures. Now, Mr. James, what are you going to do?"

SHIT, I didn't know what to say, so silence was my response, and I just let her keep talking. Eventually she got off the subject and started telling me about shit that happened at the club that she worked at. Still with a yes and no mixed in with a little uhuh, at some point, my eyes drifted to the center of her body again, but she had stopped holding that skirt down, and yes, it was still PHAT. Now there was some moisture in the center of those red panties, and her leg that was on the couch was shaking, and she said nothing about my reckless eyeballing. I slid over onto the loveseat before she could put that leg down, and she just wrapped that other leg around me and pulled me in for a kiss.

An hour and a half later, as I was getting dressed, she asked me to leave my shirt off because she wanted to look at my chest and broad shoulders. Talking about stroking a man's ego. Shit, I thought I was on cloud nine.

Going down the steps, she kept talking, and this thick sister loved to shock people. I guess I was no exception. That bitch twang came back to her voice as she said, "HHMM. Well, Diane didn't lie."

Now was my turn to have a shocked look on my face. She told me to close my damn mouth, because she and Diane had been hanging together for years.

"Diane wasn't lying, she said you were the best PUSSY EATER ON THE SOUTH SIDE." I wasn't going to argue with that. "She said that you fuck nice and smooth until you get fired up, and then you be like an old mad gorilla. That's why you haven't seen her all week. She is at home letting Ms. Kitty get a rest." Her parting words getting into her car were, "Don't worry, I will tell Diane you took good care of this PUSSY."

Well, I had a little time to think and realized that I just got fucked in a major way. I just let a woman I barely know play with my dick and ask for a favor at the same time. Even worse, a woman that I thought I could trust sicced her on me. Just believe me, we can't outthink women to save our lives. Plus, I need to learn how to use this new power shit to my advantage. I smelled her arousal 20 minutes after she got to my place. Yeah, I wanted to slow play it, and I got slow played.

Sleep was my next move, and clearing my head of the carnage that these young black girls go through with these Nation Babies. How many of them populated the city of Chicago? I didn't know exactly how to start. From what I was told about the initiations, it always involved underage girls having sex with adult men under the auspices of keeping the Nation going. It ruined some lives, and it crushed others knowing that you were stuck in a life of violence with a child or two and no father because these COWARDS wouldn't step up to their responsibility.

Now there seemed to be a group of women who wanted to change some shit, and they meant business. Just getting a vibe from Ms. Tanggy, she broke it down there were 23 of them, and they were mad as hell. Diane had also sent a message to me that her oldest son was a Nation Baby. So how do you remove your emotions? This also affected people that I knew and also called FAMILY?

Understanding the beast was a little difficult for me. I had never tried coke, rocks, speed, or anything other than weed, so it was time for a little crash course in Drugs 101. I called up my cousin Coon—yeah, that was his nickname from the family—also inviting my brother over. I needed to know as much as possible in a very short time. When they arrived, we went into my bedroom, and the lesson began. I had a million questions and seemed to be going a mile a minute. Learning about drugs was one thing, but learning about my NEW body was a greater challenge. Drugs were put in front of me, one small pile was coke, another pile was heroin, the last two were crack and methamphetamine. Something was going on with my nose because this shit was strong. I mean really strong. I had to leave the room, and when I came back into the room, they had put up the drugs, but the smell was still driving me on a strange level. I wasn't high or tripping, but this smell was putting me in a tailspin. I couldn't put my finger on it at the moment, but before I knew what was happening, I walked over to the other end of the room and picked up Coon's backpack. They both looked at me to figure out what I was doing. Boom, it hit me.

"You have drugs in this bag!" was my loud statement. Again, they both looked at me in a strange manner. I told them again that there were drugs in the bag, and now it was like I had two heads.

My brother put his hands on his head and simply stated, "This mother fucker is a certified genius."

The two of them laughed at me because I saw Coon walk in with the bag. I had to know what was in the bag. They were both wrong. I smelled the dope in the bag. Now how do I explain this new shit to a couple of seasoned veterans in the dope game—one a user, the other a dealer. Not even 20 minutes ago, I was getting my first lesson in drugs, and now I could smell it through a bag? They were not buying it at all. I told them I would walk outside for two minutes and told them to hide the dope in the house, and I would try to find it. Well, I was gone for maybe 20 minutes running my mouth with one of the neighbors, Eli Banks, who was getting off work. I handed him a cold beer out of my van, and we talked for a few minutes. I had to leave because I thought that my nose was still playing tricks on me, but no, the city garbage worker was actually holding some crack in his shirt pocket. Now I was fucked up on a mental trip with this drug smelling adventure not even one hour old.

I had four bags of dope in my hands only two minutes after walking back into my apartment. These were guys that had been involved in this shit for years, and there was no way for me to explain what just happened. All I could say was not a fucking word. Without me explaining what really happened at the hospital, my brother was extremely confused. He saw me at the hospital, and now this. I didn't know if this would shake his belief or send him deeper into drug use. This was not the type of secret that you trusted a crackhead with.

Noticing the time, I realized that I had a 4:30 p.m. appointment to put down some rat poison in a four-unit building. Ushering everyone out and getting on my way, it would not have mattered if I smoked a box of weed. My mind was in outer orbit somewhere. I could actually smell drugs like a fucking DOG. I had to analyze this the way that the military taught me. If this problem was a glass jar, I would pick it up and look at it from every angle to ensure that it did its job effectively without leaks. My new problem had too many tentacles and leaks. There was the fact that I might be the strongest person walking. I'm three times as fast as I used to be, and I'm smelling shit from a mile away, and that's why my van is in a Gyro Shop parking lot. I smelled this shit, and now I'm hungry again.

Oh Lord, don't mention the sex drive shit! It's like there is some type of spray on me or something because I have been getting pussy like running water. No, I'm not hitting on these women; it's the other way around. It's like in the daytime, at nighttime. It's like it didn't matter to them. I went to the DMV two days ago, and one of the tellers picked up on something and pulled me out of line and said, "Mr. Madlock, could you please follow me?" I was led to a small office in the back, and we fucked for 30 minutes. I don't know her name. Plus my license was renewed; I didn't even have to take the test over. I had to fight off one of the nuns at my kids' school where I work part time as a janitor to offset the tuition payments. I had a lot of kids in private school. I ran from that nun for six straight days. On the seventh day, she got nailed to the mattress. I hope GOD forgives me.

After finishing up the four flats for rodents, I was back in the van and heading to pick up the kids and getting in some hoops with the "point guard" as I call him. Pulling up to the house, everyone was ready and waiting on me. Getting to the park was a release of stress. The kids, mostly all of them, went straight for the playground, and the older boys just followed us to the court. After some warmups and shooting around with the kids, it was our game. My brother, who was the master of trickery, talked up a $100 bet with some dudes while standing there killing the last of a 40-ounce of OLD ENGLISH 800. Coming to the sideline, he told the boys to "watch this" and waved over his 6-foot, 5-inch coworker I didn't know was in the park. All I could do was shake my head and laugh.

The game started, and on the second pass of the game, I shot the gap on a pass and was off to the races with a wide-open lay-up. On the way back down the court, my brother gave me a funny look. I didn't know what for. All I knew was I was feeling a little pain in my pinky finger, and that's when I realized that I hit my hand on the rim for a basic lay-up.

The first game was a blow out, and so were the next two. Out of the three games, Slick walked away with $400. He told us that he only had $12 when the game started.

It was getting dark, and I needed to collect the kids. Before I could head to the playground, my brother told me that he had sent his son to go get the kids. I knew my brother and his friend Terry Spencer wanted to talk about the game, but I didn't. How was I going to explain all the steals and the one dunk? I couldn't and didn't want to try, but the questions came. I told them both that I had been working out and running five days a week for the last eight weeks. Terry, being an ex-division one ball player, knew the power of workouts. He was like, "Hell yeah, man, it shows," and Uncle Bonny wasn't going. He didn't believe that shit for one minute. Terry told me that he had played on a couple of travelling squads and played a couple years overseas in Europe and had never seen a guard play defense like me. I didn't know what to say but thanks and kept it moving, and the kids running over asking if I won was the distraction that I needed. Melting into the kids got me out of that for now.

On the way home, I asked what was for dinner, and it was the same old favorite cheer—Kraft macaroni and cheese with Polish sausages cut up in it. I just agreed since it was a quick and simple meal. Later on in the evening, I was summoned to Mrs. Hubbard's apartment and went straight down the stairs. To my surprise, there were her two nieces I had met a couple of times and even drove one of them back to school last year. Mrs. Hubbard was sick, and their mom was away on some assignment. They both gave me a hug, and we started to talk about school and their careers in the future. Surprising me again, I heard the toilet flush, and I turned to see Mrs. Hubbard's sister for the first time ever. I always heard them talk about her, but we never met in person. The introduction was being made, and I moved swiftly towards her with my hand out and side stepped her to quickly bend down to remove some toilet paper from the back of her shoe and remarked that I didn't want her to trip on that. There were a few giggles and her hiding her face.

And that's how I met FBI agent Nora James who was small in stature, but it only took about one minute to see how big her brain was.

After discarding the tissue in the garbage, we shook hands, and she pulled me in for a hug. She said, "Thanks for taking care of my baby and you didn't even know us."

I just told her the truth: "If your landlord tells you to do something, you do it, and don't ask questions."

Nora's daughter Jenelle said, "Momma, you can let go now," and like a lightning strike, we broke apart, and now there were more giggles. I stayed there talking to them for the next half hour and had a great time. But the bullshit didn't stop. I figured out Nora was carrying crack in her purse. Jenelle was holding weed, and every woman in the room was horny as a female dog in heat. What the hell was I going to do with this nose of mine?

Exiting as fast as I could after exchanging info with Nora, I went upstairs to a somewhat quiet house other than a couple of the older boys shooting pool and standing around leaning on pool sticks, talking shit like grown men minus the profanity. The only thing on my mind was sleep. I didn't eat or shower; I just took my sweaty stankin' ass to bed.

Getting up the next morning for work, the house was hectic, and kids were everywhere and loud as hell. Man, I was glad Mrs. Hubbard was at work and could not hear this racket! I whistled to get their attention and some quiet. All motion stopped, and everyone stood in place as I barked out orders for the boys to get ready to go do flyers with me. We had two apartments to do. The whole house went up in laughter. This shit was funny to them because when I whistled the second time, no one stopped laughing. Sitting down in the nearest chair, I got my answer. *JEOPARDY* was on television.

It must be after 3:00 p.m. Shit, what happened? I had literally slept the day away, and the kids said that they had been trying to wake me up, but I just rolled over and kept on snoring! This was not good. I needed to be able to watch my kids. I needed a solution, and fast. Calling my mother to move in for a while was an option, but I didn't want to wear her out toppled with her drinking, so I went with Plan B. Walter to the rescue!

Walter Jackson was my first cousin from St. Louis, and my phone was ringing off the hook. It was the third call from a neighbor asking who was on my porch and then Mrs. Hubbard called with the same damn question. It was 7:30 in the morning, and I didn't have time for the bullshit. The landlord was on her way out for work, and I knew that she didn't play games, so I got out of the bed to see what all of the fuss was about. Boom, on the front porch was my first cousin Walter, a full-fledged homosexual, and he was flaming. I called him yesterday, and he got on the next bus leaving St. Louis. I picked him up at the bus station at about 2:00 a.m., and now he was sitting on my porch with a knee length gown that looked like a hospital gown and some green and pink rollers in his hair. He had his legs crossed and was smoking a cigarette with a cup of coffee in his hand. Oh yeah, and he had the gown hanging off of his shoulder. Whatever picture you could conjure up in your head, that is what it was.

And now I'm telling my landlord who Walter is, and that he was here to help with the kids. She grabbed me by the collar and pulled me into her apartment. In a hushed whisper, she said, "I almost killed that nigga on the porch," and then she produced a .380 Magnum from her jacket pocket.

Walter didn't make things any better by announcing, "I DON'T CARE WHAT Y'ALL IN THERE WHISPERING ABOUT. I JUST GOT HERE TO CHICAGO, AND I AIN'T READY TO GO BACK YET."

I just stepped forward and hugged her and said, "Let me speak to him, it will be alright." I held her for over a minute and apologized for Walter's mouth.

Mrs. Hubbard calmed down and said, "These bullets are one size fits all."

At that point, I knew that Walter and I needed to talk, and fast. Asking him to join me upstairs and to shut up was the next order of business. The kids were getting up and discovering that one of their favorite people in the whole damn world was here. The girls had someone to do their hair whenever they wanted. The boys knew that Walter was the toughest faggot you will ever meet—his words, not mine—and that was backed up by the straight razor that he carried.

After a short conversation, Walter had a better understanding about the respect that is due Mrs. Hubbard and that he needed to cool his heels a little bit.

Work went well. We got out over 4,000 flyers and stopped to play a little basketball. When we returned home, dinner was done, and Walter was in the backyard with Dee, Lisa, and Kenny, the big-ass, gangbanging, gay dude. Well, I guess I didn't have to explain Walter anymore.

I spoke to everyone and tried to go upstairs, but my way was blocked by Kenny. I stepped to the other side, and he moved in front of me, blocking anyone seeing him hand me a small piece of paper. I tucked it away and went on by as though nothing had happened. It was a note with a phone number and no name. Waiting for the phone to ring, I had no clue who would send me a note through Kenny of all people. The twang was enough for me to get a positive ID of the person on the other end of the phone. Ms. Tanggy.

"So you get some pussy and don't know how to call a bitch. Is that how you get down?"

"Hello Ms. Tanggy, how are you doing today?"

"It ain't about how I'm doing. It's about how the fuck you doing. Are you ready to get to work?" She said it in her "you're getting the fuck on my nerves" voice.

"Exactly what do you mean 'get to work'?"

Ms. Tanggy said, "Well, we got some women who want to meet with you, so we can find out what it is that you plan to do."

"Do you have the information I asked for?" I asked.

She said, "Yes, and we got a lot of folks coming to the meeting."

As soon as I heard about a meeting, I put on the brakes on that shit right away, having to scream into the receiver over her, but she still would not stop talking.

"LOOK, Ms. Tanggy! There is not going to be a meeting like that, and some of these women are still loyal to the Nation."

She assured me that these women all wanted it to stop. My last salvo before getting off the phone was to inform her that I would meet with her and two of the women, and we would see where it went from there. In true Tanggy style, she let me know that would be cool, but she didn't have time to fuck with me if I wasn't going to get something done. I hung up the phone with a mental note that I had a late-night appointment with some Nation mothers.

It was 4:00 p.m., and my doorbell was ringing, and then there was a frantic call from my nephew Tony. Uncle James his voice was loud and repetitive. Rushing as fast as I could to the door, I found my sister at the door with the police and two social workers. I came down to try and put a lid on things because they were heading up my stairs and pushing past Tony. I told him to move and asked what this was all about. I was given a stack of paperwork that just basically told me that my sister finished some seven-day drug program. The state signed off on it. They were giving her the kids back. My sister spoke to me and gave me a fake hug, like we were close or something. She didn't bring the police; they just accompanied social workers on domestic cases.

There was no fight in me. I sat where I was on the steps and let them walk past me into the apartment. After 10 minutes of grabbing clothes and other shit that she didn't buy for them, I was still sitting on the steps, not moving and not responding. The police tried to talk to me, as well as the social workers. I had no words for any of them, and then they were gone to their new apartment in the Robert Taylor Projects. My nephew went with them even though he was my adopted son. I knew that it was where he wanted to be, there for his sister's protection.

The rest of the kids gathered around me with Walter and Dee in tow. I sat there numb and did not move for what seemed like forever. My youngest son, who was almost four, said that I still had them, and he was going to make sure that they had bus fare, so they could come back to visit. I know that it was not funny, but the bus fare part kind of brought us out of our funk for a little laugh.

Asking them to give me a few minutes to compose myself, I was left alone and had a chance to reflect on all the things that were going on around me, and I wanted to punch GOD in the face. I knew it wasn't possible, but I was mad, and I wasn't going to apologize for my thoughts. They had lived in five or six different places and with my older sister and Mom in Kentucky, where my oldest sister was stationed as a soldier. You could only imagine how much anger was building up inside of those kids, and how safe would my nieces be in the Projects?

Dee approached me from the rear and sat down behind me and held me. I don't know who cried the most, but one thing for sure, she felt my pain because she has been there with me all this time. The three children she was raising were her grandkids. She was also a victim of the crack epidemic. All the baby sitting, more overtime worked than I knew what to do with, and this was the thanks that I got? Even though this was not about me, it just hurt and felt personal. They were not the first kids used in this crack epidemic to get a check and a roof over someone else's head.

Mrs. Dee kissed me on the back of the head and told me that she would give me a couple more minutes, then she was going to sic the twins on me. That made me smile, and I didn't know that life would be okay, but I got up altogether, trying to get myself together.

Out in the backyard, I had to dodge the water hose, which seemed to always be on. Heading over to the park, I was ready for my run but made a detour to the basketball court. It was filled to the brim. Sherman Park. Two full courts running and nowhere to warm up and maybe not get a game in, depending on who had next and next after that. Surveying the crowd as I walked up, I could see these were the big boys out today. I wished I had my brother here, so I would have someone to run with. Our pick and roll was the shit. People were standing around the court almost shoulder to shoulder. The action was fast and very competitive. Now more than ever, I wanted to play. I had some aggression, and I needed to work it out.

Looking around to see who I knew could get me a spot on one of the next couple of teams, just like clockwork, there were Big Fred and the Prince just chilling on the sideline, smoking good weed. I made my way over to the two of them and got right to the point.

"Yo, who got next? I want to play."

Big Fred looked at me and said, "Come on, James, are you sure you want some of this shit out here?"

I tell him "hell yeah" with a lot of emphasis on it. He gives me a pound and says that I'm about two games down. Even the Prince was fired up because this was balling at its finest in the hood, and he was watching his Boy Lil UGG play. He was a point guard extraordinaire. Yeah, this baller was something to see. He used to be a stand-out at DePaul University back in the day. A half of a season and he was back home. He was now holding court. He had two big-ass book ends on the wings, and they were filling the lanes like you would not believe.

Now the Prince was making jokes: "Man, you don't want to get out there, these mother fuckers outrun greyhounds."

Of course all of the hoodlums in the ear shot were laughing, and I kept on coming.

"Can y'all get me a game or what?"

The Prince told me to hold my horses because the freight train was running over my ass next. More laughter from the faithful followers. He called over one of my neighbors, a young guy I had seen before but didn't really know him. The Prince told him to put me on his squad, and I could see his face was twisted. This was a big stage for the hood, and he didn't want to lose. We were introduced by Big Fred, and I was told that his name was Zoo Man. He asked me if I could ball, and I tried to ease his mind by letting him know that I would not hurt his team. Then he asked the real question on his mind: "Can you hold Lil UGG on defense?"

My immediate answer was yes, and again, who gave these people these nicknames? Lil Ugg looked nothing like his name. In fact, he was almost model material with a head full of wavy hair that he kept in braids, and striking features. As Zoo Man was looking at me, the Prince said, "It does not matter WHAT TEAM Zoo Man has, UGG is in a nasty mood and will destroy any player that comes on the court."

Big Fred saw this as a chance to make a few dollars. I saw it as a chance to make some headway for the neutron on the block. Neutron was a name given to those who traveled in gang circles but didn't gangbang. He wanted to know if I would bet and how much. I had no answer for Fred and walked right past him, stepping over to the Prince. That was a mistake on my part because two bangers who were not even of my concern stepped in front of me with the quickness of real security. Big Fred and the Prince waved them off and Fred said, "Speak your piece."

I told the Prince that I would make a bet with him. This got his attention, and he produced a role of hundreds that almost took my breath away. He asked how much was on the game. I told him not one dime because they had a stacked squad. Now the bodyguards were back, and waved off again.

Fred said, "James, make your point."

Now was time for my bullshit.

"I got two bills that I shut your boy UGG down."

This went from a private conversation to the Prince holding up his hands, and the court went silent.

"YO, YO, YO. I got a bet over here, and if anybody wants to join this fool who said that he's gonna shut down the king of the court..." The Prince was standing behind me and pointing, which explained all of the laughter and shit talking.

Fred chimed in that, "Neutrons don't do well out here."

I wasn't stupid. It was a warning that if I had the ball, come at me with something special. UGG never moved; he just stared at me like a second head was applied to my shoulders. Well, at least I knew that a target was put on my back.

Just before the game started, we had to discuss what constituted a shut down. UGG said that if he scored 10 points, I would lose the bet, and I wanted to be fair and said, "No, if you score six points, you would win the bet," and they thought that I was the dumbest ball player in the city of Chicago. Because it was hard enough trying to hold this beast to 10 points, and I picked six.

The Prince, being a straight-up guy, said, "Nope, we will make it eight."

Standing my ground, again, I said, "Six."

We all shook on it. After the bet was bumped up to $500, the game started with me playing tight defense on UGG. His squad set a double pick, and he was at the basket with a lay-up. After no one on my team tried to block the shot, I came to the realization that these cock suckers were still a part of the Nation and would sell my black ass out to impress Big Fred and the Prince. My squad lost by four points, but UGG never came close to scoring another basket. Every time he tried to even get the ball, I used the power to move him around and to physically intimidate him. At one point in the game, he stopped hustling because I beat him to every spot, and he swung at the ball so hard one time that I could tell his left wrist was hurting.

On the post up, I just moved him where I wanted him to be. One of their players quit, and UGG came and told me they needed a sub. I ran two more games. We won both in a blowout. This athletic performance today put me right where I wanted to be, and the fact that I was sitting there smoking let them know that I was not the police.

Sitting on the Ogs' bench, the Prince paid me by handing the money to Big Fred. To me, this was a sign of his street smarts. The young man would not exchange money in public. That meant he knew that the Feds could be watching. I was handed a fat-ass blunt, and a flunky was dispatched to bring a cooler with cold beer. Man, all a person has to do is be patient in life, and it will reveal itself to you. I damn-near choked to death on a blunt and kept my head down, choking. I didn't want to be identified by Officer Finney as he went by at a slow pace and gave the nod to Big Fred. I kept my head down but heard the Prince tell Big Fred to go. He and one of the security boys got up and started walking at a brisk pace. This was my opportunity to slide over towards the Prince. I passed the blunt back to him, and he said, "I don't know if I want this bitch, the way you were just coughing."

Laughter and jokes, because they all wanted to be in his good graces, but I took the time to bring up the game just to start some conversation. He said that UGG hadn't been held to two points since he was two years old, and I agreed but told him that UGG had a hurt wrist that he was covering for.

"How do you know that?"

I told him, "I saw him favoring it and played the strong hand on defense and pushed him around a lot." I could not help myself and threw in the fact that, "Pretty boys like him weren't built for that physical shit." He knew it was a jab at him, too, because he had hair down his back and almost looked like a foreigner.

I told him after another five minutes or so that I had to go. My nose was on fire with all the crack I was smelling in the park; it was almost driving me crazy. It was like they all had some in their pockets except the Prince. I now knew that he didn't carry, and he didn't make public transactions. We made a plan to play some bones. I had to go. The dominos date was just another chance to get info.

My mind was really on Officer Finney and Big Fred up the block. Walking to my house was killing my patience. As soon as I was out of eyesight, I raced up the block to the end of the park where they appeared to be having a heated conversation. The bodyguard was as animated as Fred. By my calculation, I wasn't sure if they could handle what Finney carried under that leather jacket on an 82-degree day.

I sat watching from a good distance away. A van pulled up, and the Prince got out and walked over to the threesome and waved over the second body guard. As he approached, the Prince walked off so as to not be in a transaction, especially in public.

The second bodyguard handed a fat envelope to Finney. He hefted the weight in his hand, and it must have felt right to him. Officer Finney said nothing else and walked off smiling. I know that I'm not a Gum Shoe, but at that moment, I could have used a camera or something because this just happened in my face, and no one would believe me.

Hold on a fucking minute here, who the fuck was I going to tell, and why the fuck was I all in these other people's business? I couldn't tell the cops because the only ones I knew were crooked as a winding road, and I was not some snitch.

Getting back home, I decided to stop in the alley to compose my thoughts before I got swamped with kids. Maybe standing in certain places makes you think about certain things. Like all the mornings that I saw the older gang members walk up to children at the school and present them with the Nation handshake and beat on their chest; I would watch as they would take up to five or 10 minutes just doing this.

It was starting to be a little clearer to me about the Nation Babies. If you raise them to believe in this type of life, they won't depart from it later. I know that's biblical. Don't ever think that a gang leader won't or hasn't read the Bible. Now we need to look at the real misconception. All leaders are just that, and it does not matter if he is a pastor, a politician, a community activist, or a gang member, there must be something there for people to follow. Remember, Jim Jones was followed. This had grown into a culture and had taken root in poor communities that had no chance of fighting back. At this point, their numbers were somewhere around 36,000 in Chicago alone. That was the size of the military in some nations around the world.

I was lost because I didn't want to get involved. Yet here I was, and I was involved even if I didn't want to be. Looking at the expanded Libby Grammar School across the alley from my house, My mind had to wrap around the fact that Ms. Tanggy said that 30 percent of the 850 kids that attended Libby were Nation Babies. There were mothers, daughters, aunts, cousins, and nieces who all had Nation Babies, all being indoctrinated at the same school and the same neighborhood, don't get me wrong, but this was all over the city of Chicago. You just had to pay attention. All gang initiations are basically the same. The guys get jumped in, and the girls get fucked in. The only difference with the Nation was they would keep up the sex until these young girls became pregnant. This sometimes take several sex sessions or rapes. Whatever you called it, IT HAD TO STOP.

Water drowning, water drowning. SWIM, SWIM, MOVE YOUR ARMS, MOTHER FUCKER. MOVE YOUR LEGS. SWIM, SWIM!

Giggling and laughter followed.

I looked up to see Mrs. Diane and Ms. Tanggy standing over me in my van and Walter standing there with his hands on his hips, saying, "Yeah, they got yo black ass. I told them not to do it."

This was almost like an attack signal from Walter. Ms. Tanggy was standing with her hands on her wide-ass hips, talking shit with that twang.

"How the hell are you gonna save us when a cup of water got you kicking and swinging your arms? You can't drown in no damn cup of water!"

Now the laughter wouldn't stop. I reached out and grabbed the two women, pulling them to me and wrestling and tickling them. Diane must have had a flashback of our earlier wrestling and yelled, "OH YOU WANT SOME WWF IN THIS BITCH!"

Both women turned aggressive and really tried to pin me to the couch that I had let out in the back of the van. I let them win for a little bit. Hell, what man wouldn't want two women on top of him? But just like with the kids, I was the champion. I was going for the pin and my three counts. Rolling Diane on top of Ms. Tanggy, I explained that when I stacked the kids up and pinned them, it was called a chump sandwich. A little more rolling, and I noticed that there was some touchy feely shit going on. Ms. Tanggy on the bottom was getting the least amount of air, so she started hollering first: "GET YO BIG COUNTRY ASS UP! WE QUIT."

Diane didn't quite agree. She was in a better position and said, "We can win this!"

I applied a little more pressure, and now she, too, wanted to tap out. I slammed my hand on the wet couch three times to count them out for the pin. It was over, and I was still the champ. We were amused and got out the last of the laughs. The two ladies sat in the captain's chairs, and I found a dry spot on the couch of my old van. Diane started off the conversation by stating that she was very disappointed about me blowing off their meeting earlier tonight, and she thought I was a standup guy until now. I did not have a leg to stand on, and she was right. I was not going to say that I had to recharge. Tanggy brought no mercy to the situation and unloaded on me that these women had no one to trust and they were ready to do something now. That was her message to me, minus the profanity. I didn't stop her. She had every right to feel disappointed.

I asked what time it was. The reply threw me for a loop. It was 3:01 a.m., and Diane explained that they had been at my house for almost two hours talking to Walter and found out about the kids being removed from my home earlier today, and they thought I just got drunk to forget about it. Who was I to argue with a good story line? Tanggy twanged at me about how much they thought I drank and offered her concern about the kids. Again, I knew that silence was golden. A few tears came from Diane about the kids. Diane offered me a stack of papers, which I took, but before we could start, Tanggy got real quiet and looked at us with concern on her face. No words were spoken. Ms. Tanggy grabbed both of our hands like a prayer session. I had even bowed my head. When she asked, "WHAT THE FUCK IS UP WITH WALTER AND WHERE THE FUCK DID YOU GET THAT BITCH?"

We lost it. There was not a dry eye in the van, and I did not try to explain my cousin, only said, "That's family, and my kids are safe."

And, just for the record, when they came to my apartment, he answered the door wearing a rainbow-colored, flowing gown with rollers and a scarf around his head. I was told they had come to the van twice to wake me, but I was out with no results. I thought the water was Tanggy's idea, but Diane said she had to work in the morning and had no more time to waste. This brought me back to the stack of papers in my hand. I was informed that it was a list of every house in the neighborhood within a one-mile radius that was Nation affiliated. It even had names of key players and ranks of higher ups.

Continuing to listen, I found out the young lady who made the list was no longer with us. She tried to use it to convince one of the higher-ranking Nation members to stop the practice of Nation Babies. She had given a copy to her sister, and they wanted justice any way they could get it. Trying my best to give them my undivided attention became a the problem. When I concentrated on them, I could smell their arousal. I didn't know what to do with that because Tanggy had already informed me that Diane was not ready to reveal the true nature of their relationship just yet.

We composed ourselves once again, or maybe I did, and we went on with some of the game plans. They had all types of information. Government names, social security numbers, and even info on how they bought their vehicles under the table. Having this much information gave Ms. Tanggy a chance to brag a little: "I TOLD YO ASS WE WAS READY."

"So what can we get done with this?" Diane asked. I tried to be as honest as possible and let them know that I wasn't sure. I told the ladies that we had a ton of information and we just had to figure it out step by step, and I begged for their patience. Tanggy was always on 10 and wanted a joint now that the business was over. Diane spoke up and informed her that she would have to take that joint to go. There was no argument, and she left with enough weed to roll a couple of joints when she got home.

Diane was fired up and ready to talk, only she wanted to be held while we talked. Undressing in my van was nothing new to us, and I turned on some soft music, and we cuddled in one of the captain's chairs while I just listened to her talk about the old days in the Nation before the Prince's father went to jail. She told me that it was like a big community where everybody was taken care of regardless of your level of status with the Nation. Her oldest son was born when she was 17 years old. One of the brothers stepped up and took her into his crib before she even had the baby, and they even had a second child together. Shortly after that, he caught a 20-year bid for attempted murder. I didn't ask if he was guilty or not. Shit, I thought he did a hell of a thing to step up like that, but I guess it didn't hurt that she was fine as a mofo.

That brother almost hit the lottery. She said that there were a few guys on the list who needed to go first, and that would cut down the IQ level. This would make them easier to deal with.

Now, let's take a pause for the cause. If you are a man reading this, please look at the thought process. Women are thinking when we are sleeping. I asked if we could discuss Ms. Tanggy. There was a slight frown, and she waved her hand to signal me to go ahead. My first question was, "Why sic her on me? And what made you think I'm the right person for this shit?"

Diane didn't answer at all; she just sat there gathering her thoughts. When she did respond, it was to turn a 180 in the chair and face me. Mistake number one. She didn't need to turn around to answer me, but she did. Now speaking in a low whisper, I had to pull forward to hear her clearly. This brought us closer physically, and she was already sitting on my lap. I felt something hit the bottom of my lip. It was the bottle of Martel that we had been sipping out of. Mistake number two. I didn't need another drink or the other joint that she was leaning back rolling. The view of her breast and bush was another distraction, and I didn't want to count it as mistake number three, so I tried to look the other way.

Once the joint was rolled, Diane started another story, only this one was about her and Ms. Tanggy—how they grew up together and both had Nation Babies in the same year. Their friendship grew out of being neighbors in one of the apartment buildings that the Nation owned. They had a choice if they wanted to work or not, but they were still supported by the Nation. There was a heavy government crackdown, and the Nation lost six of its eight apartment buildings. She told me about her guy going to jail and Tanggy losing her guy and two sons in a car accident. At that moment, I felt sorry for them both. We were just about finished with the joint, and that's when I saw mistake number three. She had pulled out my dick and was playing with it as she talked to me and I listened like the man I am. I had no excuse; but hearing the next part of the story was well worth the wait.

Diane told me that she did, in fact, send Tanggy over to see me and told her to do whatever she could to help bring me over to their side and way of thinking. I asked her straight out, did she tell Tanggy to come over and fuck me?

Diane put her head down and said, "Not exactly."

"What the hell does that mean?"

She reached up to kiss me, and I turned my head to avoid being suckered even further. Now was the come to Jesus moment, and I was playing Jesus in this scene. She looked at me and said, "I didn't tell her to fuck you, but I told her to do what she had to do, and that's what she did, and here we are."

Nothing came out of my mouth, just a stare that only meant "get on with the fucking story." One big-ass deep breath and 20 minutes of pulling teeth later, the whole story was laid out on the table where she and Tanggy started messing around on their trips to visit their guys in prison. They were two hot and horny young ladies, and one thing led to another, and 14 years later, they were still together but on the low, even though she didn't have to be because I understood. She told me how they had to depend on each other, and the relationship grew, and this was something that was frowned upon by the Nation.

Diane raised up, looked me in my face, and said she was sorry for not being honest and upfront with me as she was sliding slowly down on my dick. Hell, I was tired of counting mistakes, and I was horny as a bull. I was already being used, so I might as well get fucked because I knew that I was going to get fucked later with this Nation Baby shit.

The greatest lie ever told to man is "I'M GOING OVER TO MY GIRLFRIEND'S HOUSE." If you men out there think that they are telling me this secret that they have had for 14 years because they trust me, hell no; they are using sex and the hope of a threesome to help string me along. Even though I know this, I'm still in. So which head am I thinking with?

Oh yeah, before we get back to the story—75 percent of the time, it is her GIRLFRIEND exiting the van at 7:15 a.m. Mrs. Hubbard was leaving for work. We both said good morning, and she told me that my cousin Walter made the most amazing cup of coffee. Holding up her travel mug, she informed me that this was her second cup. Mrs. Hubbard expressed her sorrow for the loss of the kids and told me that she could never put me out with all those kids, and I was doing a good job for it to be so many of them. We both laughed at that part.

Then things turned serious for a second. I don't know why people like to grab my hands, but that's what she did and held me still until she had my attention.

"James, I don't know what's going on, but I came to the hospital to see you. It's been over two months, and you haven't said a word about what happened." As usual, I thought being honest was the best policy, but I had to shade the truth a little bit.

"Mrs. Hubbard, I don't know. All I know is that I have a praying family."

Her being a religious woman, she just looked at me the same way that I looked at Uncle Robert. Her last warning was the sternest: "Be careful of the company you keep around here. That Tanggy lady is a handful."

How the fuck is she up at these hours to see who comes and goes at my apartment?

Mrs. Hubbard walked off saying, "Alright, Mr. Miracle Man; or is that Mr. Indestructible?" Even I had to blush on that one.

CHAPTER FIVE

BECOMING ROACHMAN

My children started school in mid-August, and this was the first day of school. Scrambling and all that about the house had taken its normal course, but Walter had everything under control. No one was missing socks; all uniforms were pressed, and all book bags had all the necessary supplies. The only thing left to do was drop them off.

I slipped Walter an extra 50 bucks, and he grabbed me and hugged me. I told him not to get that damn lipstick on me. Walter told me in his voice that had a slight speech impediment, "DON'T NOBODY WANT TO KISS YO UGLY ASS."

Just as I relaxed and bought into the story, he leaned in and kissed me on the cheek.

We could hear Dee coming up the stairs yelling, "Knock knock!"

I yelled back, "Bring your little self on up here. Walter has coffee ready!"

She came around the corner with a coffee mug in her hand and started jumping up and down, screaming, "I got your ass now. I got your ass now!" No one knew what she was talking about, so we had to wait until the floor show was over. Dee almost slid across the floor to me and got right up in my face and asked how long had Walter and I been involved, pointing to the fresh lip stick on my cheek as her proof. Again, I knew that silence was best for me and maybe Walter would clear it up over coffee. I didn't give a shit either way, and she was laughing too fucking loud to hear any explanations that I had anyway.

Letting loose a loud whistle in the house, all the kids who were going to school filed in one at a time. Dee told me, "Stop that whistling at those kids! This is not the military, and they ain't no damn soldiers!"

The whole peanut gallery started cracking up because they knew she was right, and from what I had been teaching them, Mrs. Dee was too old for me to argue with.

Even though it was not the military, I gave the order to move out and we were off. We pulled up to the school lot, and everybody got out ready for their first day, including me. I assume they found their classes alright.

I went to the maintenance office, put on my uniform shirt, and went to work. My first stop was to make sure all the bathrooms had tissues. There was a fresh box of barf bags that I needed to get distributed to each classroom. (That's the orange shit you put on the floor when a kid throws up.) I ran into Big Red in the hallway, and he informed me that everything was going well. Big Red was one of my coworkers, and he was 6 feet, 4 inches tall, hence the name Big Red. We were a good team, but the man that made it all work was the boss Johnathan Gant. Not as tall as Red, but by the shoulders, he was a mountain of a man. Johnathan had a gimpy walk from a hip replacement. It was his brains and his knowledge of getting shit done and the way he carried himself. He was a man among men. I ran into him in the office as I was dropping off tissues and barf bags. We spoke and hugged each other like we hadn't seen each other for years. It had only been a week.

When breakfast was over, we all met up in the cafeteria to give it a good cleaning before lunch. The rest of the day went fine. I left the school twice to exterminate; there were no complaints. They knew that I would pull my weight, but they were both excited that I had started a business. Sitting in the maintenance office, we shot the shit for a while, and they both were telling me about all of the new teachers who came in, and of course Big Red had his eye on a big healthy one on the third floor. He was a thin man but loved a thick woman. He said that was his specialty. I listened to all they had to say but could not figure out how to throw in the fact that I was a new man in every sense of the word. Now my friendship with Red was on the line because he was holding crack in his shirt pocket. I just sat there and listened. This had to be my new way of life, to know something and have to shut the fuck up.

I told them that I would go up and start getting the cafeteria ready from lunch. Red went to put out the crossing barriers for the unruly parents who didn't care and would hit someone else's kid with a car just to pick up their own child. Mr. Gant came up to the cafeteria about 15 minutes later, and I was leaving. He looked around to find that all the work was finished and the floor was mopped.

"How the hell did you finish so fast?"

I told him that I was motivated and had to pick up the kids from the maintenance office. I had no way of reading his mind, but *What the fuck?* had to be one of his thoughts. It was normally a two-man job that took 30 minutes to finish, and here I was leaving in about 15 minutes. *Note to self: Don't let someone catch me moving that fast.*

On the way home from school, the kids wanted pizza. I knew that Walter had probably already had dinner ready or some type of snack for the kids. I voted down the pizza and got jeers from the peanut gallery. This was going to be the test to see who wanted to go running with me after their first day of school. I got the same volunteers—James, Christian, and Corvell. That was cool with me.

After we all took off our uniforms, we were at the park stretching for our run. We took off, and they did as usual, keeping up for a little while then falling back. I never got too far ahead of them and made sure they could see me. They did four miles that day. I know kids that young running that far are almost unheard of, but this was par for the course at my house. With the kids trying to beat me to the house, they almost ran into the mountain that was standing at the gate.

Officer Finney stepped aside, letting the kids pass and telling me that I had a good-looking family there. I didn't miss the innuendo that he knew where I lived. I said hello and told the boys to go upstairs and to close the back door. I didn't know why he was there, and I needed to gain the upper hand. He asked me if I was carrying, and I looked at him like he was a fool. I'm in running gear, so how could I be carrying? This was my chance to flip the script, so acting as if I was afraid of him put me in the right position and gave him an air of confidence.

I asked, "Can we please walk around to the alley and not do this in front of my kids?"

He nodded towards the alley, and I started walking. As we turned the corner, there was a shot to my ribs. I didn't expect it and didn't see it coming, and that cock sucker had those rings on. I laid on the ground for almost two minutes while he stood and admired his handy work.

Officer Finney kicked me in the back of the leg and told me to get the fuck up. I tried to get up but fell again. This made him reach out and help me up. I put out my hand, and the big man pulled to help me up. Nothing happened; not one fucking thing. He pulled again, only this time, he was trying to pull his hand out of a vice. I turned on the power. He had maybe five rings on that one hand, and I tried to smash them together as one. There was pain on his face, and I laid flat on the ground like a child and told Officer Finney to join me. He tried to resist and even tried to kick me. I didn't worry about that. Pain will make a man do funny shit, like lay down on the ground next to me.

He laid on the ground and didn't move, begging for his hand to be released. I squeezed again and heard the man scream in pain. Now I had his undivided attention.

"Look at me." He turned his head in my direction. I spoke slowly and low: "PLEASE LEAVE MY PROPERTY AND MEET ME ON 55TH AND HALSTED AT THE GAS STATION IN 10 MINUTES. Nod if you understand."

He nodded vigorously. I wasn't sure of his commitment, so I grabbed his elbow and gave it a squeeze. This pain was something new to him, and I knew he would follow directions. Slowly standing but not letting go of his hand, I asked what would happen if I let go of his hand, and his eyes told me that he would reach inside that leather jacket. He was holding many guns. Shit, I knew that he could shoot with his left hand. I couldn't afford that. He carried too much artillery.

Now was the moment of truth about how much fear you can put in one man, and a tough son of a bitch at that. Then it hit me. Reaching out to grab the back of his pants, I picked up all 300-plus pounds of him and placed him in the garbage dumpster. Still holding on to his hand, I informed him that I would kill him the next time he came to my house or if he told Ptacc where I lived. In under 10 minutes, we were both at the gas station lot. Finney was coming out of the gas station with a bag of ice he walked over to my van and asked what the fuck I did to his hand. There was no answer from me but a look that asked, did he want a matching set? What I wanted to know was what the fuck he was doing at my house. He told me that his lieutenant wanted to see me tomorrow morning for a chat. I asked him, "Who the fuck is he, and what does he want?"

Finney said he didn't know what this was about. And he didn't ask.

"Just out of curiosity, did he tell you to hit me in the ribs?" I asked.

"No," was his answer. He said he was just trying to soften me up, so I didn't go talking crazy about the list. I appreciated his honesty. It wasn't needed because I didn't trust any of those crooked cock suckers. Looking at his hand, I knew that when he went to the hospital, they would have to cut the rings off his fingers. They were smashed into different shapes, and he was standing close to my van. I started to hit that bitch in his face because my fucking ribs were hurting. Yes, I am a big-ass kid, and I wanted my fucking lick back.

Heading home was my second surprise and my second officer of the day. Nora James, the fucking FBI. She was Mrs. Hubbard's sister, which meant that she was not all that attractive. OH, I'm sorry. I didn't tell you that Mrs. Hubbard was not good looking from any angle. Her sister was a lot better looking. Her athletic body was something totally different, but she was still not my type. I got out of the van and asked her to state her business; I didn't have time for any more bullshit today. She got straight to the point that she was with her sister at the hospital. That was how they got in; she flashed her badge. That's how they gained entry, and she also saw me fucked up and damn near dead. It all started coming back to me, and that's why she hugged me so long when we first met; she was checking me out, and Mrs. Hubbard knew it. I told her what I thought. She confirmed my suspicion about the hug but told me that it wasn't a bad hug.

Agent Nora asked me to remove my shirt. At first, I refused, but she assured me that it was not sexual. Okay, okay. It's my ego. After taking off my shirt, she looked at my whole body and compared it to some photos from the hospital. She asked if she could get a couple of photos, and I refused her and asked that we not talk about this. Nora was not one to quit and kept right on talking. She said that no one in her department knew about this. I requested that she destroy the photos, and she said she would for some direct answers. I told her again that there would be no answers because I didn't have any. I just woke up and walked out of the hospital and came home to my kids and my mother. I didn't ask any questions. I just thanked God and hugged my babies and my mama. I walked off, leaving Agent James holding the wet shirt that I had taken off.

Instead of going into the yard, I picked up a few pieces of paper from around the fence and walked it around to the alley to throw it away. I needed time to think. A police lieutenant wanted to see me in the morning and a GODDAMN FBI agent was at my house. What the hell did I do wrong? Too many people knew about the hospital transformation. Shit, I needed to move, and fast. After throwing away the paper with Agent James on my heels, the wheels in her head were turning.

"So why did you have crack in your pocket when we met?" I asked her. You can hide a lot of shit with your face, but surprise is not one of them. STOP, FREEZE, AND TAKE A PICTURE. Based on my comment to her, she knew that I had some sort of proof, but she didn't know that the proof was her face. Plus, I couldn't tell her that I could smell it. She said that she took it off two young black teenagers who she was trying not to send to jail. Now she thought that would get her some answers about the hospital drama, but I just didn't have any answers and asked her to follow her religious beliefs and education in science and tell me what she thought. The shake of her head was one clue, but the cursing is what got my attention. When intelligent people run out of words and explanations, they curse.

Looking around, I noticed her government vehicle and realized standing there talking to her on the side of my house didn't look good. Before I could recommend that we talk somewhere else, Big Fred walked around the corner. Me standing there with no shirt on and her looking all official in her black suit and holding my discarded t-shirt, that must have made for a hell of a picture as his big ass neared. The observation of faces can tell us a lot, and the look on Agent Nora James' face said that she knew this rotten SOB. I just stood and observed as he turned on those subwoofers in the back of his throat and gave me the loudest most ghetto greeting that he could muster: "WHAT THE FUCK IS UP, JAMES, MY MOTHER FUCKING NIGGA?"

I knew that it was more for her benefit than mine. We exchanged hugs and a pound, and my left knee went up against his nuts just in case he tried that lift shit. So predictable, but my body didn't move, plus I turned on the power to swiftly lift him high in the air, and now I was watching his face as I gave a little bear hug with the lift. It was sheer panic on a whole other level.

When I set him down, I whispered in his ear, "Do you see what working out and running can do for a man?"

Big Fred was not buying it. He knew that being a big man himself, and he spent plenty of time with the brothers at the weight benches. He was convinced that he had encountered something different. In his experience of being a bad man, no one had moved or handled him that effortlessly before, even in prison with the big boys, and he liked a good fight. This all took less than 15 seconds. Now a new higher alert level was established. Not only by Big Fred, but this shit was not lost on our FBI agent.

Nora spoke up and said that she wouldn't want to put an end to the little dick measuring contest. Her observation was keen because she didn't miss Fred holding his back as he stepped back from me. I started an introduction but was cut off by her and Fred giving each other a big hug. She yelled, "IF YOU PICK ME UP, I'LL SHOOT YOUR BIG ASS!" It turned out to be a big but simple hug. I guess that I wasn't the only one who didn't like being picked up.

Big Fred said that they went to school together and that she was his people. (*FILE THAT SHIT AWAY FOR LATER…*) He stayed for only a hot minute and was off to the gossip mill or some other Nation shit. I didn't care either way. Nora and I talked for a little while before we noticed the time and parted ways.

I sat on my back steps to gather my thoughts. I needed to clear my head and get ready for my students tonight. There were only four of them now. Melvin Cummings did not return to class after the beating at the hands of Sun Down. Some parts of me wanted to inflict more pain, but I kind of knew it was wrong, and I am nobody's JUDGE. But I had done physical damage to two men. An FBI agent just left my house, and another cop was here earlier. Not to mention this Nation Baby shit that kept showing up. I was running low on money. Yeah, that steel mill check was hard to replace. My mama always told me to keep getting up and trying. You can't fail because you will make a little progress every day. I think that I went backward on this one. There was a lot of shit on my plate, and I needed to get some food together quickly. This was the last class, and the test was in four days, but they told me that they would study every day until the test. I threw Walter the keys to the van and a few dollars and told him what I needed to do and that I had to get some sleep. The house was put down after I played Connect Four with the kids. Yes, I am the champ; I don't give them any mercy.

My alarm went off at 11:30 p.m. Class started at midnight. It was only going to be a practice test and a quick meal to let them know how much I appreciated them. I jumped in the shower, but on the way, I passed the kitchen, and Walter and Dee were sitting at the table having a cocktail. The food smelled amazing, and Walter yelled out, "I have a surprise for you when you get out of the shower!" I could not get in the shower fast enough. Dee would not let it go: "So you come out here half naked, and he has a surprise for you when you get out of the shower?" Again, I had no words for her and shut the bathroom door. As I was closing it, I could hear laughter coming from the kitchen. It lasted too damn long for me. About a minute or so, there was a knock at the door. It was Dee, and she was banging on the door telling me that she had to piss. I didn't unlock the door, and I didn't respond. I just laughed to myself, hoping she didn't make it next door to her apartment.

Shit, showered, and shaved, and I was standing in the kitchen. The food was excellent, and Walter did have a surprise. He made a cake and put graduation decorations on it. I hoped that the students would like it. Class went well, and they all passed their practice test. We ate and talked. I let them know that leaving the hood didn't mean that they had to forget about the hood, making it clear that they had to reach back and help someone in the future. Latoya hugged me hard and fought back the tears as she told me that she would reach back, and all the fellas chimed in at the same time, sounding a little more macho than she did, but they were emotional as well. J Roc tried to hold it back, but it was just too emotional. We made a pact and a game plan to see this through. Now it was time for the exit of the same old drill, and they were gone like goons in the night.

After class, I decided to sit in my van and smoke my joint and have a sip of that 20 year old good shit that Ms. Tanggy left me, and it was a good idea. Speak of the devil, Ms. Tanggy drove by twice and didn't see any lights on, so she kept going. I knew that she had some more info for me about the Nation Babies or some good hot pussy. Either way, I was too tired and didn't want to put up with that twang in her voice.

Hold on—I know that I had a long day, but did I just say that I was too tired for pussy? I guess life has a way of wearing you down. Now I have a fucking crook in my neck…

It was 6:15 a.m., and the sun was coming up. I needed to get upstairs. Walter had his fresh coffee going, and I was heading to my room to get my shit for a shower. Man, this water felt good, and I just stood there and hoped that some of my thoughts and worries could wash down the drain with the soap and water.

Turning off the shower, I heard voices. Walter was turning this place into a fucking Starbucks. Now his nice, sweet ass was serving muffins and Danishes with the coffee. He said that Mrs. Hubbard started buying them about a week ago. Drying off, I could hear the conversation going on in the kitchen. It was Mrs. Hubbard and Walter, and they were discussing the kids and how I was having a rough time with the new business. I made some noise as I left the bathroom. They both looked up at me and said good morning before I could get it out. At least I knew that I was around people who loved me for sure.

Getting past them was no problem. But when I got to my bedroom, there were five kids in my bed who didn't look like they were leaving any time soon. I got dressed in the living room. Now heading out back to have my morning joint and coffee, with the timing of the police, I heard, *knock knock*. It was fucking Agent Nora James coming up the steps with a cup and telling me that she heard that Walter made the best coffee in town. I said good morning and waved her through. The short silk pajamas didn't hide one inch of her tight body. I asked her to have a seat and added there would be a fresh cup on the way.

Nora took this time to try and push for more information. She inquired about the bruise that she saw yesterday with my shirt off. I responded that it was from an elbow that I got from playing basketball. This didn't fly too well. Agent James had seen some of the marks that came from Officer Finney's rings and told me that someone on the court was carrying a weapon and that she was All-State in basketball for two years and she never had an elbow like that.

"It's cool," she said. "I guess you were playing with the big boys." After that statement, the screen door opened and so did Agent James' mouth. It was her first time meeting Walter, and it showed all over her face. Walter poured us both a healthy cup and went back into the apartment. I could hear him talking to Mrs. Hubbard.

"Is that your sister out there?" And she responded with a resounding yes. Walter said, "Well she needs to change that look on her face or she is going to be wearing her next cup of coffee."

Mrs. Hubbard reminded him that the lady was her sister, and her bullets don't have a name on them. Walter pointed to the kitchen table where his straight razor laid and explained that that was his razor, and it was blind and only had one job. He paused for effect and then said: "CUT SKIN." I thought I was going to have to come in and save somebody, but after hearing the laughter, I decided it was okay. These two now got along great. Walter just had that effect on people.

I had a question for the FBI lady, and I needed an honest answer.

"Do you know Lieutenant Sosa?" She paused and thought before answering. I didn't have a lot of time, so I went ahead and lit my joint, explaining to her that she was welcome to go inside to avoid the smell while she thought about her answer. I made the statement in a manner that told her that I was still waiting on her to say something. We went back and forth about why I wanted to know about him and whether I was in some type of trouble. Shaking my head briskly, I said, "No, no, no, there is no trouble. He sent word from a mutual friend that he needed to see me this morning. I just wanted to know what type of person I would be meeting."

"So the shot in the ribs was a reminder that you were going to act right?"

I turned my head to hit the joint and turned back around to pass it to her and throw her off a little bit, not wanting her to read my face. God damn, this agent was full of surprises as she reached out and took the joint and grabbed my hands. What the fuck is up with people grabbing my hands?

"Well, Mr. Madlock. You are in good hands. He is a fair man, and he cares about the community."

I asked if I was in any danger. She responded that I had already encountered the dangerous part and got past it. Walter appeared with the coffee carafe and topped us both off and gave her a nice-looking Danish roll with strawberry filling. Shit, I felt jealous. I didn't get one, and it was my apartment! Nora still had her mouth open at Walter's appearance. Fuck it, let me tell you what this queen was wearing this morning.

Walter had on a Kimono with a matching scarf on his head, and yes, makeup—all at this time of morning. And he wants to know why this woman has the gas face looking at him. He was a dark-skinned brother with rollers in his hair.

Walter went back inside and returned very quickly with cream and sugar. Agent Nora had a smile a mile wide, and she thanked Walter over and over for his hospitality. I guess he has won over another groupie.

Mrs. Hubbard came out the screen door with her coffee thermos in hand and said that it was her second cup, plus she had some sort of pastry wrapped up in a paper towel. She went down the stairs and grabbed my hand, and I quickly followed her. At the bottom of the stairs, she told me that I needed to go to church with her on Sunday and that she was not taking no for an answer. Silence and respect from me. She said, "Be careful with that Tanggy lady," and walked out the door. All I wanted to know was how she was up watching who goes in my apartment.

I said in my best "good little boy voice," "Yes, Mrs. Hubbard."

She was out the door, and I could hear the kids in the kitchen going back up the stairs. Agent Nora was borrowing one of my travel mugs. Really, what the fuck is this? Starbucks or Dunkin' Donuts? She saw me and said, "Back to our conversation. Stay calm and breathe. Lieutenant Sosa collects minds. He's always playing a game that pushes people, but he is a fair man, and you can trust him." With that, she was gone with half of a joint in her purse. I could smell it as she walked by.

Winnie was having some problems getting herself together this morning, and she and Walter were having some words. It didn't take long to figure it out, and they were having a cereal war; she got left out of the kind she wanted. Her brothers had beaten her to them, and Walter was telling her she needed to get her little but moving with the boys or she was gonna always get the last of everything, or get left out altogether. I started to step in and help my Winnie, but the problem was that he was right, and I might not have been able to teach the lesson better. It told me two things. One, that my kids were in great hands; and two, it was time to pay Walter, and my bread was running short. Winnie knew that Walter didn't play, and she knew that there was no winning with him. I felt sorry for my baby, so I went to the other side of the table to give her a hug to make her feel better. Before I could put Winnie back down in the chair, Nelson had already switched bowls with her, and she had the cereal that she wanted. Walter turned around with one last comment with his hands on his hips, saying, "Yo Lil Tail is lucky your brother felt sorry for you. I'm done telling you. You are a girl, if yo brother didn't give it to you, don't start no crying and carrying on. You gotta get up and get what you need."

Shit, after hearing that, I was getting motivated. But I had to give Nelson a hug for the assist with the drama.

Loading up the van was routine, and as we pulled up to the corner, Lisa was coming across the street, with a pack of cigarettes in her hand. I knew when she waved at me that she was headed up to "Walter's Café." I didn't give it a second thought and proceeded to the school and dropped them off and told Mr. Gant that I had to go up to the police station.

I had a nerve-wracking drive there to the police station and just didn't know what to expect. I parked in the back, and as I approached the station entrance, there was a sign directing visitors to go around to the front. Walking a little slower than normal to check out my surroundings, I smelled dope in more than one location, and I hadn't gotten in the building yet. It was a brand-new building from top to bottom. Well, we see what they would rather spend money on. Police stations and not schools, which we need.

I went to the front desk, and I was greeted by a young white female officer who looked to be just out of high school. I told her that I had an appointment with Lieutenant Sosa. At first I was told to go have a seat as she got on the phone and called Sosa. The young officer told me he was in a meeting, and he would be at the station in about 25 minutes. She walked over to me and handed me a pen and a yellow legal pad and asked if I wanted to leave my information for Sosa to get in touch with me later. I explained that I would wait there for him.

I could smell her arousal just before she told me that she could escort me to a better waiting area. I followed and noticed that it was complicated to get in or out of this place. She only used a key for the last room that we entered, and the rest we had to be buzzed in. Something hard and heavy hit the floor, and I snapped back to reality. It was her uniform pants with all that damn equipment on it, but I wasn't that damn slow. My pants quickly followed, and we were in a wrestling match until I picked her up and placed her on the table that dominated the large conference room.

That rag that I held in my hand used to be a sky-blue pair of bikini panties. Even though I figured our time was short, I went straight for my favorite shit. With both thighs on my shoulders, I had every intention to get my whole face wet. After a lot of moaning, my brain turned on for about 30 percent, and I asked the question, "Can anybody get in this room?"

She said no and grabbed the back of my head. OH shit, I had a dedicated officer, and she was ready to serve it up. Taking advantage of the extra-large conference table, she spun around, and we engaged in a wet and pleasurable 69. Then we fucked from one end of the table to the other and even slid off into a couple of the chairs for a while. It was great to be able to get that off my chest with no holds barred. Twenty-five minutes later, she was handing me a towel from a cabinet at the other end of the room. We both straightened up, and I was returned to the waiting area.

Okay, okay, okay, I don't know what to tell you. It was something about the power that has gotten me screwed six times by strangers since this shit started. Don't get me wrong; I'm loving this, but who the fuck knows when and how it is kicking the hell in. Someone needed to pinch me and wake me the fuck up.

"Mr. Madlock?" I heard a friendly and familiar voice call me. Coming out of the current thought, it was the young officer. I had to look at her name tag to respond. We just spent a remarkable 25 minutes together, and I didn't even know her name, but I rose anyway and followed her to the conference room that I just left. We both gave each other a knowing look as she told me that Lieutenant Sosa would be joining me soon. Again sitting and thinking, I had already figured out how I was going to play it with Sosa and how to deal with Agent Nora James. I told you a while ago when I do my best thinking, and I just had damn near a half an hour to think, thanks to Officer Pulaski.

Lieutenant Sosa walked in, and I rose to meet him. We shook hands, and it was a good, firm handshake. A wide smile appeared on my face because this man was nowhere near what I expected. In my mind, his name was Jessie Soft Hands, and I was trying not to laugh. He was taller than me, maybe 6 feet tall, and extremely thin, almost to the point of being a feminine person. I have seen my share of gay men trying to survive in a macho world. Apparently, he was making it work for him.

The lieutenant got right down to business about why I was there. He told me that he heard about Mrs. Myra's granddaughter, and it shut down a block that he had been fighting for two years. Then he added with some emphasis of his own that there was not one punch thrown and not one gunshot fired. I told him it was just luck. Sosa told me that he had heard my name in a few other situations. I wanted to know what this was all about, and he slowly played his hand to tell me about some other things going on in Moe Town. None of it was my business, so I wanted to move on to the next subject and get the fuck out of there. My impatience was worn on my face, and that's when the fireworks started. He let me know about the fact that he knew about the students in my basement and even about J Roc's deal. I was told that he could use a man like me to help him keep an eye on things in Moe Town.

Standing to leave, I let this fool know that I was not a snitch. Now standing, I could see the name on the top of the first folder that he had on his desk. His eyes followed mine, and we both looked at the folder. Melvin Cummings was the name with two more folders under it.

"Lieutenant Sosa, if you are trying to use my students to enlist my help, you must be out of your fucking mind. Do you understand that I have a fucking house full of kids, and you don't have a clue why there are so many empty lots in this neighborhood?" I didn't let him speak so that I could finish. "When there are people who want come out of their home, they are burned to the ground."

He sat silent for a few seconds; maybe it was to gather his thoughts or give me time to calm down. Agent James popped into my head: Just breathe, and he collected brains. I sat and started to breathe again. The folders were handed to me with an explanation that these three were arrested riding in a stolen vehicle three days ago and asked to call me for their one phone call.

He said, "So yeah, I took note of the fact that this name had crossed my desk three times in the last month or two, and it was all for doing something good, and I just wanted to meet you to see if you were the noble man that I had heard about."

I wanted to know what would happen to my students about the arrest.

"Nothing," was his response. "After they told me about the GED program and that they were going to take the test, I decided to speak to you first."

"Well, Mr. Boss-Man, what do you want from me? I ain't putting my family at risk."

I was asked to keep an open dialog with him, and we could work something out. I still wasn't convinced that this thin mother fucker would be straight up with me.

Okay, I said I had a plan from all of that thinking in the conference room. Let's see what he really knows about this area

"Yo Sosa, I just got one question for you."

The lieutenant nodded in my direction as he was waiting on my question. Remembering back to my military days, I knew that all officers liked to get their ego stroked, so I referred to him as "sir" before posing my question: "Do you know what a Nation Baby is?"

There was a blank stare and no answer. I knew that this was strictly a street term. He wasn't the macho type, so he just said, "No. But do you care to enlighten me on what a Nation Baby is and what the problem is in the neighborhood?"

For the next five minutes, he listened. After I was done, he said that it was quite a story; what could he do to help? The wheels were turning, and I just had one more test to see if he could be trusted. I stood to shake his hand and leave. I did have a real job after all.

The lieutenant decided to walk me out, and that was all the break I needed to test his loyalty to me and needing my help. We walked past a bench in the hall, where I took an unexpected seat and looked up at Sosa. He followed my eyes to two officers standing talking. I whispered to him to cuff me to the bench. Now he was really confused. I signaled for him to lean forward, then I informed him that the two officers were carrying a large amount of dope and probably a large amount of dope money. All that sweet shit in him came out at one time. His voice went straight the fuck up, and he gave me a twist mouth that Walter would have been proud of. Now Sosa was on top of me as though he was trying to rough house me, but we were doing the shouting whisper thing. He wanted to know if I knew who that cop was. And I shot back, "A crooked cop."

The lieutenant leaned into me again and said, "That's Robert fucking Canens, a 35-year vet set to retire in two months."

Well, if he can serve, I can volley.

"I don't give a fuck who he is. That crooked-ass cop is holding. Now if you want me to put my family and students on the line, invite them into the conference room and ask them to empty their pockets on the table." He took another look at the officers, and I asked, "Are you their boss or what?" Then I told him, "Get the hell off of me and uncuff me." For emphasis, I told him that I was already cuffed, and he could charge me with whatever he wanted if I was wrong or just feed me to the cops I just wrongly accused.

The lieutenant shook his head and said, "Your funeral."

Just sitting and watching the show, I had been cuffed to this bench for over an hour watching people run in and out of the conference room. First it was a captain and a higher-ranking desk sergeant, then Officer Pulaski with a roll of evidence bags. About 20 minutes in, the Brass started to arrive. I couldn't hear what was going on, but I knew that the shit had hit the fan. Pulaski came out and uncuffed me and led me out through a back door. I don't know how much dope they had, or how much money, but I knew that Sosa was either going to be on my team or an enemy.

Driving back to the school, I knew that I didn't feel like working, and I needed to tell Mr. Gant something. I told him that I needed the rest of the day off because I needed to meet with a social worker. He told me to take the rest of the day off, and if I lied to him again, he would cut my nuts off. I never could trick that old dude. Leaving the building, I went to the last place I thought I would go. To church.

I walked about 50 yards to the front door of the church. Parishioners were all over the place, and I was not clear why I was there. On my way to the back of the church, I saw Father Fitzgerald. He was a happy old fella who always had a joke for you and a smile. We exchanged greetings and a smile. Then he reached out and grabbed my hands. I knew to just go with it, as he said to me that my burdens were not heavy compared to the One we have to help lift burdens off of us. My face gave way to mystery. He squeezed my hands and said, "Don't worry about the kids. You just have to take care of what God has charged you to do."

Well, I know he was a priest and that he was talking about something biblical. I made my way to the back row and sat in the middle of the pews. Trying to process what went on today from Agent James to Lieutenant Sosa, even Mrs. Hubbard's with her church shit, I was really in a funk. I was doing shit that was out of character for me. I had physically hurt two people; a man's career and pension was in the balance because I wanted to prove a point; and I had two women on my back about these Nation Babies.

I sat there thinking for the next two hours, trying to figure out what my next move was. Okay, okay, okay, I fell asleep there on the bench; that's what took up two hours. On my way out, Father Fitzgerald didn't disappoint with the humor. He walked up to me and said, "James, my boy. LIFE IS LIKE A GREAT BIG SHIT SANDWICH. SOME DAYS, YOU HAVE TO TAKE A SMALL BITE, AND SOME DAYS, YOU HAVE TO TAKE A BIG BITE."

Wisdom from an old man. I took that with me and smiled on my way out of the door.

Waiting on the kids to get out of school, I was still thinking. When I gave Walter a few dollars, I had just $600 left in the box under my bed, and I needed money fast. When I got home, the kids' mom was sitting in front of my house. I couldn't take any more drama. We spoke, and she gave me a hug and was mobbed by all the kids. I was told that she would take the kids for the weekend. They all cheered and jumped around. I wasn't falling for this shit; I knew there was something going on. But it was Friday, and I needed some time to work some things out in my head. The first one was the money, period. I had called my ex-wife to see if I could get her to keep her kids for the weekend. To my surprise, she said yes.

Once the last drop off was complete, all I wanted was sleep and nothing else. Walter was given the keys to my van and told to go find himself some fun. Finishing my third shot of Martel and my joint, I went straight to bed. Do not pass go; do not collect $200; go straight to bed. I slept like a baby, and then there was sunlight. I felt weight on my bed, rolling over to see Ms. Diane smiling at me, feeling a warm and naked body next to me. We melted into each other like caramel and chocolate in a hot pot. Her timing was amazing, and so was she.

Looking over at the clock about two hours later, we both wanted something to eat and agreed that breakfast would be great after a shower. The sun was shining, and I was feeling good.

Holding the door open for Diane, we smiled at each other, feeling like we could do no wrong.

"SO THIS IS THE MOTHER FUCKING REASON YOU CANT GET THE FUCK UP AND GO LOOKING FOR AN APARTMENT FOR ME AND THE KIDS." This was being shouted at me from their mom, and she was loud as hell. I first looked around for the kids and then asked what she was talking about. Again, the speaker came on with more cursing and making claims that I didn't care about the kids; I just wanted a piece of ass. My neighbors came out to watch the floor show. I just sat on the steps and watched with all the people on the street. As the audience got bigger, so did the show, and now I was being told that I would not be able to see my kids again and kiss my ass. I never said one word because I didn't promise to go with her that morning, and I was not going to argue. After I paid no attention and didn't give a reaction, Diane was the target and was being told that I wasn't shit. It was not cool with me, but I was not going to pour gas on that fire. It eventually burned out, and she got in her vehicle and left.

Well, I didn't go to breakfast. I sat and drank my breakfast and lunch. I might have drank dinner if it wasn't for Walter there to look after me. I held it in while the attack was going on, but I could have killed her.

Monday morning, my kids were not back home, and I was losing my fucking mind. I picked up the phone, and it was dead. I know damn well that I had paid the bill, and my service was not turned off. Maybe trying the phone for the tenth time, I went to Ms. Dee's apartment to use the phone. I called my kids' mom and got no answer at her mom's house, and then I called the phone company and inquired about my service. The lady on the other end told me that the customer requested that the service be turned off. I told her that I was the customer, and I never requested to turn my phone off.

The lady on the phone asked my name, but she used my ex's name and said she requested the change. Only getting angry, I told the lady on the phone, "She doesn't live here anymore. She moved over a year ago." It never dawned on me to switch the name over after she moved. I just never thought about it. Thinking quickly, I wanted to know how much it would be to turn the phone back on in my name. I was informed that the customer put a hold on the number for one year in case she wanted to move back. I had no fucking clue what that meant and asked again how much it would be to turn it back on. This time, she spoke a little slower, and I understood that this was a lost cause. The number could not be reassigned because of the hold. I went home and sat on the floor for about forever. James Jr. and his two sisters were dressed and ready for school, but I wasn't ready.

Somehow, I dragged my ass to the van and took them to school. No sooner than they got out and went into the school, I made a beeline straight for my other kids' grandmother's house. When I got there, my kids and their mom were not there. I was informed that they had left the night before, going to her house in another state. A hole was created in my stomach. This crushed me, and her father came out the door and put his arms around me. He held on tight. If this man was not holding me, I would probably be on my knees crying. Custody battles were something he knew about, and he felt my pain. I think I wet us both up with my tears, but I couldn't get a hold on this new reality. I don't know how long it took me to get back in my van, or how long it took me to get home.

I was in a funk, and being around people was not going to work. I asked Walter to pick up the three kids from school, and I went straight to bed. I was a zombie and had not shown up for work and not seen the shower too often either. I didn't have a bottle of Martel, but I had a bottle of Paul Mason that was almost empty. On my way to the bathroom, Walter spoke and said, "Good morning." I mumbled back a response, and he fired back, "Well, fuck you, too. I DIDN'T SLEEP WITH YOU LAST NIGHT," was his reply. This was something people in my family said to you if you didn't speak in the morning. I think it's a southern thing.

Finishing my business in the bathroom, Walter was going down to answer the door. He was a little loud in asking, "Where the hell you think you are going."

I heard the commotion and raced to the steps. It was Lieutenant Sosa. I told Walter that it was okay. He moved aside, and the thin man walked up, straightening his uniform as he came up the stairs. Yes, he got roughed up a little by Walter. Already knowing that he was assessing my appearance, probably the biggest thing on his mind was Walter and the roughing up he was getting on the steps.

After Walter came up the stairs, I made an introduction. Walter turned his head and walked off, explaining that he didn't care if it was the police; he might get his throat cut. Sosa laughed until Walter spun around with his razor in hand and said, "Dead men don't fight back."

I stepped between the two and sent Walter to the kitchen, asking for some coffee and some privacy. There was no time for bullshit, and Sosa said he had been trying to reach me at my home for a week. Not even knowing how to explain my situation—I was just waking up—I didn't wait for Walter with the coffee, grabbing the bottle of Paul Mason and taking a big swallow, and just as uncouth as that. I passed him the bottle, but he denied it, and I took another swallow before sitting the bottle back on the table.

"What the fuck are you doing at my house?"

The lieutenant said to me again that he had been trying to reach me for a week. I asked why he didn't send his black retriever like last time. He said that Finney was on leave for a hand injury, working on one of the old school cars he has. I wanted to know what happened, and he said, "Something fell on his hand and smashed two of those rings into his flesh."

The frown on my face painted a different picture than what was in my heart about Officer Finney.

I offered the lieutenant a seat. He moved to a chair that was facing the kitchen with a view of the door. I didn't know if he was looking into distrust with me or worried about Walter coming out of the kitchen. Sosa wanted to talk about the inside information I had on his officers, but that shit could wait. He was more interested in what happened to the confident man that he met in the conference room.

Walter came in with fresh coffee and some fruit for us. They exchanged nasty looks, and this time it was different. In the back of my head, my fucked-up sense of humor kicked in, and I thought to myself, *IT TAKES ONE TO KNOW ONE.*

The eye rolling contest was over, and Walter returned to the kitchen for a brief moment. I had no answers for Sosa, but again, it was Walter to the rescue. He came out of the back with my robe, some toiletries, and a stern look on his face. He spoke clearly and steady.

"James needs a shower to get himself together, and if you want to wait, you are more than welcome, and your cooperation would be greatly appreciated."

I went straight to the shower, and curiosity got the better of me as I wondered what they talked about as I showered. Thirty minutes later, I was walking to my room with my robe on and feeling better. I stopped before going into the dining room to try and hear a part of the conversation. Crickets. They heard me coming and went to another subject, like they had been discussing the weather.

Lieutenant Sosa stood and said he needed to see me soon and that Walter told him about the kids. On his way out, he still hinted around about the dope and the shit storm that it caused.

On my way back up the steps, I thought about calling Mr. Gant at the school. Then I changed my mind as quickly as I thought about it. Two weeks had passed, and no one other than Walter and Sosa had seen me. Walter was the perfect watch dog, and no one was getting in my house, not even Mrs. Hubbard. Showers can make you feel good, but they can't remove what's going on in your head. I'm not gay or anything, but me and Paul Mason went back to bed. Two days later I was trying to get my head on straight. An idea had hit me like a ton of bricks. No one could call me because of the phone, and I had only a few dollars in my pocket.

I got up, took a shower, got dressed, and went to the west side of Chicago. I parked my van in K Town. I put my spray tank in my backpack with a couple bottles of chemicals and some rat poison. I walked to the end of the block and took a deep breath, knowing that I was about to swallow my pride and face some embarrassment. I cupped both my hands around my mouth and yelled at the top of my lungs: "ROACHMAN, ROACHMAN. GET YOUR HOUSE EXTERMINATED FOR $25 DOLLARS. ROACHMAN, ROACHMAN!"

Walking through the blocks of the Westside was challenging and entertaining as hell. But all day long, I hollered till my voice was strained. At the end of the day, I made $125. It wasn't foundry money, but I made an honest buck, and it was tax free. I made my way back to the Southside with a whole other thought process. I was thinking if I did this five or six days a week, I could cover all of the bills. Still, it's a blow to a man's ego to go from punching that clock with all the overtime I wanted and bringing home $1,200 a week plus hustle money. WHAT THE FUCK WAS I THINKING? SHIT. I could still be getting that bread. Well, it crossed my mind to call and see if I could get some part time hours, but that can't work for me. My name wasn't the only one on the business. It said Madlock and Sons, so for me to teach my sons, I had to make this shit work. Lead by example, don't follow. Now I was giving myself the same speeches I had been giving the kids for years.

With all that, thinking I was back home in no time. Back to life; back to reality.

I stopped in front of Pokey's house and spoke to her parents, Poly and Sconey Dog. I told you a while ago that these street names were wild. Yes, Sconey Dog. He was a lifer with the Nation and believe this or not, in the Projects on 39th Street, he used to be one of my baseball coaches. His little brother Frank also played on the squad. Now he was a shell of a man. Let that be a lesson to you: Anything that does not grow will die; nothing stays exactly the same.

Pokey ran up to the van and stuck her head inside, asking, "What's up, Unc?"

We exchanged a pound, and she blushed as I said, "What's up, nephew? Yo Pokey, I just got off work, and I need you to send Big Fred to my crib in 20 minutes."

She said, "No problem. He's at the park lifting weights." We exchanged another pound, and we both broke in different directions. I went upstairs and gave my keys to Walter to pick up the three remaining kids. I can't lie to you; it was a sad-ass household. I moped around a lot, and since I was the head, everybody else moped around. We had not been skating or to the park to play ball. I didn't have to ask anyone; I knew that I was in a deep depression. I also need you to remember that BLACK MEN DON'T GO TO THERAPY. I ran to the shower because I knew that Big Fred was coming, and if I was going to get out of this funk, I needed to put my mind on something that really mattered.

I heard the doorbell ring as I got out of the shower. I knew that it was Fred. I came to the door in just a pair of basketball shorts. I wanted Big Fred to get a good look at me and decide if we were going to be friends or enemies. I had already made up my mind this piece of shit was at the top of my enemies list.

Doing my best to slide over to let him past, he realized how wide I was. We dropped a small dap at the top of the stairs. I didn't get a chance to even tell him what I wanted before he threw a half ounce of weed on the table and said, "Rack 'em up."

Putting the pool balls in the rack, I noticed how he looked at me. My immediate thought was, *I hope this big mother fucker ain't gay…* I knew he did two stretches in the joint, but man, this dude was about to die in my living room. After a closer look, it wasn't a look of passion, but he was checking out the physique; sizing up the enemy.

Fred broke up the balls as I started rolling us a joint apiece. He was a decent shooter; he had three balls left on the table before he missed. I took my time shooting, so he could really size me up. We talked shit about every damn thing. We were both big Cubs fans. He even brought up Pat and Tracey. I didn't know who the fuck he was talking about. He thought that I was bullshitting him, but I wasn't. Then he said they were Minnie's friends. It hit me right away: the pool table girls. I told him that nothing went on, and I shot my best shot. At that point, the tides had changed, and he saw me as an honest man.

Fred said to me, "I thought you were going to lie and say that you fucked them." He went on to say that they were undercover lesbians. I could have bet him that weed he just dropped on my pool table that he didn't know that his old lady Minnie was the head carpet muncher. Just a little info that I got from Pat and Tracey. Going with his flow, I even told him I tried to show them the goods, but they weren't having it. I laughed at that pretty hard, and Fred confessed that he had hit on them for years without any luck. MAYBE I CAN DO IN ONE NIGHT WHAT HE COULD NOT DO IN A LIFETIME. Now I was trying to destroy what he was doing in his life and time. Nation Babies. We had played five games and he had won none. I wanted to dominate this piece of shit in every way possible.

There was still a look of concern on his face. I was not going to beat around the bush, so I asked, "What's on your mind, bro?

Big Fred paused from his shot and raised up and looked at me. There was an awkward silence before he asked his question.

"So you're gonna just let me choke to death and not give me a beer or something?" I apologized and with haste came back with the last two beers in the house. He took a long swig, and the words just sort flowed out. "Some of the boys in the park said you went straight 500 pounds five reps no strain, no slow down."

"Wow," was my reply, "you can't believe everything you hear, my brother. I wish that I was that strong, but it was over 400." Again, there was that funny look of trying to figure me out. That was all I needed to walk him into my confidence. I said to him, "I'm physically too small for my frame to support a 500-pound lift. Take a good look at me."

He did, and I explained to him, "It's a mental thing. I can teach you how to do it."

Once the next pool game was over, I invited Fred into my weight room. We put 450 pounds on the bench, and his eyes lit up in a negative manner. He said that 390 pounds was the highest that he ever lifted. He said that it was seven years ago in the joint. I made it clear that the two of us were going to lift this weight, and that it was straight about the mental. I laid on the bench and went through my pre-lift routine and a few more theatrics to make it look like I was about to struggle. This was a mile away from the truth. Three reps and a little struggle and acting, at the end, Big Fred was cheering me on like the kids do. It was just a male thang because we know that shit ain't easy.

A con job is a con job no matter who is pulling it. Big Fred got on the bench, and I started my speech about concentration and breathing. I wasn't telling him anything that he did not know, just reinforcing what was already there. Looking at this big mother fucker, he had way more gut than I thought as he laid down. Going through his pre-lift routine, he looked a little worried, which told me that he was not in as good of shape as he bragged about. I gave him the old high school speech on spotting: "I got you on the spot. JUST PUSH THIS BITCH." I screamed to fire him up.

I had two fingers on the bar in the middle. Big Fred had no idea what I could now do with two fingers. He gave a loud grunt, and the weight started to move. Up smooth as hell on the first lift, three reps; some problems on the last one, but all in all, it was a good lift. Fred sat up on the bench and took in damn near a room full of oxygen. I gave him a pound and pulled him up from the seat in one motion, handing him one of the joints as if it was his prize for a good lift. Our faces can't hide shit. A look of shock and accomplishment was on his face, and I went straight into a spill about confidence and believing. He concurred that it worked because he just pushed 450 pounds, three reps, and you could not take that away. I hoped he wouldn't try that shit in the park tomorrow and break his fucking neck.

The hook was in. I had his ass, now all I needed to do was change the subject to what I wanted.

"Yo, Fred man, you were right about Pam and Tracey. I tried to get at them on some freaky shit. But I got to be honest, man, all these old women around here. I need something young and tender." I offered a nudge in the side and the obligatory, "YOU KNOW WHAT I MEAN?"

Fred's lights turned on just from the thought of some young girls. He said, "Man, I hear you, but I have been with Minnie for 12 years, and I need a change of pace every now and then."

I chimed in with a little encouragement and gave him a pound. Fred told me he could get me a couple of them, and for me it could be on the house. I cheered him on some more and complained about the older women not having such tight bodies. He agreed and states that we had something in common. And we both yelled "TIGHT PUSSY!" in unison. I was feeling a lot better about myself, and I was behind the eight ball on a ton of shit.

Dropping the kids off at school the next morning, I needed to speak to Father Fitzgerald. I sought him out in the rectory when he was coming out of morning Mass. Before he had a chance to remove his robe and collar, I invaded his space. To him, it was strange for me to be up on him like that. Father Fitzgerald has always known me as a standoffish type of person; now I was in his personal quarters. Being the man that he is, he told me to get on with it, and "Why are you in my room?"

I didn't slow play it at all. In fact, I couldn't get my words out fast enough as I explained that I needed a classroom at the school for one night for a meeting of about 25 or 30 people in two days. He didn't ask what it was about. He just said, "Well don't you have keys?"

It was settled: Thursday evening. All I had to do now was inform Mr. Gant and endure whatever his wrath would be about my abandonment of the job. He wasn't in his office, and I just left a note about the meeting and that I was sorry for stepping out on him and Big Red.

Next stop was the police station. Officer Pulaski was not at the front desk. I didn't know if it was a relief or a disappointment. But the officer at the front desk asked me to have a seat. He got on the phone to call Lieutenant Sosa, then he told me to follow him to the conference room. I got a flashback of the carnage that went on at that table.

I was directed to take a seat by the young black officer, and he said that Lieutenant Sosa would be there shortly. I sat in a chair that I had previously occupied as Officer Pulaski slid down off the conference room table onto my lap. Being that caught up in thought, I thought that I could still smell and feel her. Oh yeah, I was smiling my ass off until Sosa sat on the desk and brought me out of my reverie.

The first thing I saw was that pencil thin mustache that he sported and a grin that almost reminded me of Ms. Dee when she got on her Walter kicks. The lieutenant spoke first.

"How are you, Mr. Madlock?" And before I could respond he enquired about "Walter the pit bull." That got a much needed laugh out of both of us and helped to break the ice a little.

I told the lieutenant I was getting better each day. Then it was my turn to dominate the conversation. Everything was put on the table about the Nation Babies thing and a copy of all the addresses and connections that I was given. When I was finished, he wanted to know how I got the info, and I simply reminded him of the conversation we just had.

"Come to the meeting and ask any question that you want," I told him. I had to remind Sosa that I needed him at the meeting as a cop and a father, and I wanted him to listen because these women had a story to tell. On my way out, I was sensing that he had a parting question, so I let the cat out of the bag: "Cars 9 and 23 have dope in them." Sosa gave me one of those "are you sure?" looks, and I repeated the numbers again. "Nine and 23."

I had a little while before picking up the kids. Agent James was my next contact. I stopped at a payphone to call her. There was no answer, so I left a message for her to either call me or come by the house later because it was important. Shit was shaping up. I already had a police lieutenant in my back pocket; now I just needed to see if an FBI agent would fit as well. Shit, I still needed money, and the "Roachman" shit was okay, but I had to have some real money, and it couldn't be dirty dirt work. So I called my guy Ajaumu to see if he had some work for me. It turns out, he did. It was a private job for a thousand dollars.

You just have to trust me on this, the more the money, the kinkier these predators are—yes, I call them predators. Even though I work in this industry, I know of others in this industry who do everything from child pornography to snuff films. Most of them just want a little excitement and to return back to their families. Some just want to be taken to fantasy land. I never did the man on man shit, but my boy Ramon did, and that was cool with me. We even had a session once where I fucked four wives, and he fucked three of the husbands. It was all in the same lounge, and one of the couples wanted to be side by side and hold hands. I didn't care either way as long as they didn't reach over and touch me. Ramon did that shit once, and I choked the shit out of him later in the changing room. Safe to say he didn't try to touch me again. This is the fake shit about the world, and I'm a part of it. We love to see two women together. It's like watching art. But two men, that shit wasn't right.

I had about four hours left, so I decided to do the ROACHMAN thing where I was and see what happened. I walked right out of the front door on my own block. I got a few laughs, and a few people wanting to know what I was doing. I explained to those who wanted to know and for those who laughed I was waiting on them later. Shit it was the hood, everybody had roaches. I never made it off the block and was late picking up the kids. There were four customers right away and a few asked if I could I get them tomorrow. One neighbor asked if I could do hers later in the evening, and I said yes. It was embarrassing at first. But now I don't give a damn what nobody says. Roachman was going to keep my fucking bills paid.

I walked back to the house and gave Walter the keys and told him that I had work to do. He cracked up laughing and said, "I heard yo ass out there screaming 'ROACHMAN.' What the fuck are you doing?" I told Walter I found a new way to make money, and he said, "Okay, what are you doing?"

For someone like Walter, showing was the best method to explain it. I strapped on my backpack and asked Walter if he didn't know me, would he know what was in my backpack? He said, "No, I wouldn't," with a twisted mouth that said, "why the hell are you wasting my time?" Then I put my hands up to my mouth and yelled, "ROACHMAN, ROACHMAN!

GET YOUR HOUSE EXTERMINATED FOR $25. ROACHMAN, ROACHMAN!"

Walter told me to get the fuck out of his kitchen with all that damn noise and turned up his nose as he walked to the stove. No, I didn't give a shit what Walter thought; I was making a legit dollar, and that ROACHMAN thing was starting to sound FLY to me. The only thing that mattered was that I was not out on the streets. ADVERTISEMENT. ADVERTISING. THAT WAS THE KEY, and Walter didn't get it. It's the same reason that women have worn short dresses with their cleavage out all these years. You can't sell anything if no one knows you are selling it, because you never know who your customers are. I can't walk down the block and tell which house needs my services, but they can hear me yelling and come on out.

Walter came back with a small box that was filled with my flyers. He said, "Take a look in the box, ROACHMAN." They all had the old number scratched out and the new number written on the front. He said that he and the kids were making them to help me out, and that they had been bored as hell. Things were looking up, and now I had numbers to leave for the neighbors.

It was important to contact Diane; she was not aware of the meeting that I had set for two days out. She wasn't home from work yet, and Ms. Tanggy answered the phone. She was extremely nice to me. I was a little surprised at her manners. Then she said she was sorry I had lost the kids, and she felt bad for me. I thanked her for her support because she did say that she thought I was a good parent. For a second the time, she said that Diane was not home. So I took that to mean "get the hell off the phone," but in true Tanggy fashion, she kept right on talking asking about the celebrity I lived with, Walter. There wasn't a person that came outside on my block who didn't know who Walter was. I told her that he was fine and just kicked me out of the kitchen. She laughed at that and asked if he had a knife in his hand when he did it. I told her no, and I had no reason for it to go that far; I got the hell out of the kitchen. I had to cut her off so that I could explain why I called.

"I need you two to meet me at St. Anselm Catholic School," I informed her, "in two days at 6:00 p.m. Bring as many of the sisters who wanted to come."

She started screaming into the phone, and there goes that damn twang again. I had to remind her that she had to make sure whoever she invited was with us and not standing with the Nation. That would equal more missing people. Before I got off the phone, Ms. Tanggy called my name, "JAMES," to get my attention. Then her voice dropped as she said that she and Diane would do something special for me real soon. I was silent at first, and then I asked why I couldn't come over now, and we could wait for Diane to get home, and they could give me whatever they wanted. Yeah, being a man, I fell for the bait. Ms. Tanggy's loud-ass mouth asked, "What the fuck is wrong with you men? I meant like take you out to eat or something. Ain't nobody trying to fuck you when they get off work. And who said we was going to do you anyway?"

I said bye and hung up the phone. Yes, she was laughing. I didn't like being played, but I was still hopeful. Shit, don't judge me. I'm still a MAN.

I went to do the later appointment and got more than I had bargained for. My buddy who got me in this game told me to always use twice the amount of chemicals than needed on a first-time job. It was called a clean out. This shit had roaches falling everywhere. They were crawling all over my clothes. It was bad, not just for me—hell, the residents all went and sat on the front porch. It was nothing new to them. They could sit there all day and watch "Ghetto TV."

After an hour and a half, when I finished and emerged out of the door, there stood another problem. It was in the form of the tenant downstairs. She wanted to have her apartment treated, fearing that all the roaches would soon invade her place. After explaining the pricing of $25, she told me she didn't have any money. She told me that she could pay me on the first. That was my first credit customer. The apartment was as infested as the first one. All I wanted was a hot bath. I even stripped down to my basketball shorts, trying to shake all of the roaches off of me and my clothes.

Walking into the door, I spoke to the kids while keeping my distance because I was not clean and went straight for the back, and BOOM, there was Ms. Dee making jokes about me walking around the house with Walter with no clothes on. No need for a response. I kept moving until I was in the backyard, where I dumped my work clothes and my backpack and sprayed everything. The cat calls from Ms. Dee and Walter got louder out the back porch window, and I realized it was more than two voices. Looking up, I saw Mrs. Hubbard and Agent James whistling and cat calling. I decided to play along. I spun around and hit them with a double biceps pose, and the crowd went wild. I took a bow and asked them to let me finish working.

Agent James walked out to start a conversation. There were pleasantries in the beginning until I told her my plan, and she told me that it could better be handled by the local police. I argued a different point, that the less locals the better, because we didn't know who was taking money under the table. She asked about Lieutenant Sosa, and I informed her that she was the one who told me to trust him. Agent James knew something that I didn't know. Trying to get her to understand that all these ladies were putting their lives on the line was my only sales pitch. Eventually she caved and told me the story of the lieutenant, who came from the FBI who couldn't get a decent partner or proper support at the FBI because of his sexuality, so he came to the Chicago Police Department about 12 years ago. Sosa had been fair but was a hard driving watch commander.

"Do you trust him to work on this with you?"

Agent James held up both hands and said, "I never said I was on board."

"Agent James, can you please bear with me for a few minutes?" I retrieved another copy of the list from my van and asked her to look it over and then give me her answer. Some people need to check their EGO at the door, but man, this shit was falling into place, and I was making it look easy.

By the time I finished my shower, Diane was on the phone. We exchanged hellos and the conversation went straight to the meeting.

"Look James, we need to keep this shit small for now," she said, and at least three of the ladies on the list, she was not sure about. She said we could use the excuse of limited space to keep the numbers down. I agreed with her and asked how her day was and if she was tired. Diane told me that her day went fine, and she was tired. I asked if she needed to get off the phone, and she replied with a resounding no. I felt good about that. Somebody just wanted to talk to me for me. We talked about the job, her meeting, and I even explained to her about the whole ROACHMAN thing. She laughed at first, but later on in the conversation, I was informed that she was proud of me for swallowing my pride.

Then Diane turned real serious on me and wanted to know exactly why I was doing this Nation Baby thing and what was in it for me. Diane thought there was some type of angle that I was playing. No angle; just caught up in a situation where I was trying to help some people out. I didn't think that there was a pot of gold at the end of this rainbow. Just misery and trouble. Again, Diane asked what was in it for me. Again, I replied that it was just something going on in my life. There was no way under the sun I could tell her about THE POWER and how it had given me a second chance at life. No, that would be a ridiculous story to tell her. All I knew was that I was going to do whatever I could to help without getting shot. Let those mother fuckers play cops and robbers.

"James, James?" Diane was calling me, and she asked, "Did you just fall asleep on me?" I tried to explain that I was deep in thought about her question. Well, she killed that by saying flat out, "WELL, I HOPE YOU AIN'T DOING THIS FOR NO PUSSY."

Before I even opened my mouth, I thought that Ms. Tanggy was behind that little inquiry. Now it was my turn to do a little reading of people.

"Ms. Diane, can you please be quiet for a minute. No, this is not about pussy, and if it was, we were fucking long before I knew about this Nation Baby shit. So what that really mean is that you were playing me from the start, and then I find out later that you sicced your bitch on me like she a fucking dog. Now you have the nerve to ask me if this is for the pussy? I already fucked your girl, and she waves it in my face every time she hears my voice. So, Ms. Diane, correct me if I'm wrong here. How was this not about PUSSY from the beginning? Now if you don't mind, can you please tell me about Mrs. Myra showing up on my doorstep with all of the fucking tears and shit. Where does that fit in?"

My next statement was a simple message to Ms. Tanggy. I told her she could stop holding her breath because I knew she was there and that I knew we were on speaker phone. It was the most lackluster greeting I had ever received from Ms. Tanggy, a flat-ass, "Hi James," was all she said. And it sounded like someone was squeezing her to get the words out.

My next question was directed at both of them: "So if the two of you wanted me to be smart enough to figure out how to help you, why didn't you two figure out that I would see through this too?"

CRICKETS.

"This ain't what you think, James," was the response from Tanggy. It took her a whole minute to come up with that. I stopped the whole conversation right there and told them that I would rather have my lies in person, and if they wanted to talk face to face and make a date, I would be there, like I was shot out of a cannon, bright-eyed and bushy-tailed.

I was on the block as soon as I dropped the kids off at school. First order of business was to knock out the two houses from yesterday. Then I was back on the grind: "ROACHMAN, ROACHMAN! GET YOUR HOUSE EXTERMINATED!"

It didn't take long. I was on 52nd and Bishop. Fast Black appeared on her porch and asked what the hell I was yelling about. I explained, and she laughed and said, "If you can kill them bitches up in my apartment, then have at it." I was on my way up the stairs to get started when she asked where my spray stuff was at. I tapped my backpack to indicate that it was in the bag. She looked at me and shook her head. "You young folks don't know nothing. Why do you have it in the bag? Can't nobody tell what you do if it's in the bag. If they see the tank they can tell." Common sense and wisdom are two different things. Fast Black just gave me both, and I took it. She has never told me anything wrong in all these years, so I would be a dummy not to listen today.

We didn't always call her Fast Black. Most of the time she was known as Fannie Girl. Even her children were all real dark, just like her and her brother G Black.

Fast Black came up the stairs to talk to me while I exterminated her apartment. I could tell how she started the conversation that she was up to something, and yes, she was the highest ranking female member of the Nation. Watching how I answered her questions was keen on my mind, and not telling her shit. She wanted to know about her ex-side man Sun Down. I told her that I didn't have a clue about him and that we were not that tight because of the age difference, and he spent a lot of time in the park with the Nation.

Fast Black stood in front of me to get my attention. She wanted me to know that she knew something. It wasn't something that she could just come out and say. I turned away from her direction and asked her to move over so that she didn't get Roach spray on her. Fast Black moved quickly but never took her eyes off me, trying to read my face. I made a mental note to let Diane and Ms. Tanggy know that Fast Black or any of her known associates could not come to the meeting.

There was nothing to read. I sped up my work pace and asked her to ask the people downstairs if they had roaches.

"Hell yeah," was her reply. "That's where they keep coming from because they are nasty as hell."

I said, "Can you go down and see if they want the service?"

While she was gone, I took the time to look at all the photos on the wall. It was everybody from the Nation who ever climbed the ladder of Nation rank. I saw two of my relatives, my sister's old boyfriend J.P. was even up there, and he was Poly's brother and Pokey's uncle. Another tragic story.

Heading down the steps once I finished, Fast Black informed me that they didn't have the money right now, but she would pay for their service. She didn't want them nasty MFs to keep sending the roaches up to her apartment. I knocked that out as fast as possible because Fast Black never stopped following me, and the questions never stopped. Finally, I gave her one of my flyers and told her that if he came back to town to call me. Something good did come out of that visit. Sun Down said something to Fast Black, and I never put the tank back in the back pack. It got me two extra customers that day. This ROACHMAN shit looks like it is going to work out.

I yelled until about 3:00 p.m. and made $200 cash, no taxes. Walking the three blocks back to my apartment was going to be a breeze. I made legit money, and I didn't have to work too hard. I was thinking about a cold beer when a police car swerved in front of me on the sidewalk. I didn't panic, but I was on high alert.

Officer Ptacc stepped from the police car with a shit eating grin on his face.

"WELL, WELL, WELL. Somebody has nine lives." I saw his hand on his gun, but there was no way he could get it out before I ripped his fucking head off; he was too close to me. I gave him my biggest gapped-tooth smile that I could muster. Ptacc walked closer to take a good look for himself. I had no idea how to put a lid on a volcano, so I just held my breath just to let him get as close as possible and to hear what he had to say. "HOW THE FUCK DID YOU WALK OUT OF THAT HOSPITAL?" No answer from me; he even walked up to touch my face, not understanding what was standing in front of him.

I didn't move or say anything. I knew that he saw me in the hospital, and now I was in his face without a scratch on me. He looked and examined me for more than a minute, and I was getting tired of this. It's a miracle game with him. Thinking fast I told, Ptacc that we could not talk right here; there were too many eyes and ears on the block. Not only did he fall for that, he thought he held the upper hand because he constantly kept his hand on his gun. I let him put me in the back seat with cuffs on, and now he was cocky as ever. Before he got in the vehicle, he was saying some shit about if you wanted something done right, you have to do it yourself. Officer Ptacc got back into the car and drove to the first alley that he saw, still cursing at the top of his lungs about not being able to hire good help. There was no doubt in my mind that he was going to try and kill me. Not trying to die, I could not give away the fact that I had snapped those fucking hand cuffs and was waiting on this son of a bitch to open the door. Not surprisingly, he got out with his gun in hand and attempted to pull me out of the vehicle. I turned on the power and snatched Ptacc into the back of the police car with all the force that I could muster. This did not relieve him of his weapon, and he got off one shot into the floorboard of the vehicle. There was no way possible he was getting another.

No time to waste, I reached out and took possession of the gun by squeezing it into his hand so hard that his thumb and ring finger broke with the force of it. At that point, I was frantic about taking control of the situation, which explained my left hand around his throat and making sure breathing was not an option. In my world, you have to try and do enough to make a difference, so now it was time to put my knee in his chest to apply a little more pressure. Well hell, I figured that I had maybe another 20 seconds to choke this cracker before I killed him, so I decided to choke on. Nothing came out of my mouth, but I made sure that our faces were close enough to French kisses. All this crooked cop could see was the kiss of death. Yeah, he was a good sized man, but he was no match for the power, especially after I balled his ass up in the back seat. I was sitting on top of his chest trying to assume the most dominant position possible. I had a message to deliver, and he couldn't carry out my orders if he was dead.

After about 10 seconds I got off him and sat him straight up in the back seat. Releasing him and sliding back, I knew that he wasn't going to try anything. Officer Ptacc was in shock that a supposed to be dead man just choked him and broke his wrist in several places, and his fingers registered an amount of pain that was unbearable. Mistake number one for him. I left the gun on the seat between us where he could see and reach it. Ptacc was no stranger to adverse conditions, and this was no different. He was looking for a way out, and the gun was one—if he could beat me to it with one hand. Yeah, he did his best to evaluate and do a risk assessment. My face and my mouth both told him to, "Sit the fuck down and catch your breath." I didn't say anything at all. I just sat and looked at him, knowing that at some point his mouth would start moving, even if it was to ask why I was not dead. Stuttering was always a dead giveaway about your negotiating position, and I wasn't stuttering. In fact, I wasn't saying shit. I needed him to start talking, and fast.

"Who's in charge, who's trying to kill me, and why?" Damn, I couldn't shut up for shit. Ptacc received a punch to the kneecap, which shattered it. I think I had his attention, and I raised my fist to hit the other kneecap, and I got a desperate "okay, okay, okay!" He wanted to talk and alleviate the pain.

"What are you asking me, sir?" A white cop in the middle of Englewood called me sir. He must be scared for his life, and I just played right along.

"Who told you to kill me?" A stern look from me, and he came with the truth.

"No one. No one," he said with desperation in his voice. I saw a chance when Finney was sent somewhere else, and I took a chance. Now I wanted to take a chance. I slowly climbed into Ptacc's lap like we were about to kiss, and I made it very clear as I leaned back and gave a little extra pressure to that knee.

"Bring me the rest of my money tomorrow."

"What money?" was his reply. I didn't have a clue who was making that growling sound, but I heard it just like Ptacc, and then I realized that I was growling like some kind of animal, and it was scary as fuck. I thought that this was going to be a great help in getting information out of him. Leaning forward, I said in his ear, "There's a monster inside of me that wants to rip your fucking throat out."

Yeah, now we were getting somewhere, I should have been mad as hell when I noticed that I was sitting on the lap of a man who was pissing his pants and on me. No; I was not upset. It only drove home my next point even more.

"Who is in charge of your operation?" I demanded.

"Captain Holmes," was his reply.

I didn't know who the fuck that was, and I needed a little more clarification, so I got a little more acquainted with his freshly broken knee cap. The scream was ear-piercing, and I only had so much time. Someone would be coming through that alley soon, and I didn't want to be seen getting out of a police vehicle that contained a cop who was going on disability for the rest of his life.

The wheels were spinning in his head, and I was taking no chances. My left hand was now around his throat, and I gave a gentle squeeze, which for him was a matter of life or death. He started talking real fast, but it was just gibberish until I backed off enough for him to talk.

"There is $20 grand in the trunk. Take it all."

That sounded good to me, but I needed to know if it was his money.

"No," he replied.

"Well, who does it belong to?"

Officer Ptacc hesitated for a fraction of a second, and the vise was back on his throat. There was drool coming from my mouth, and that growl was back. Ptacc was speaking clearly again after a couple of coughs.

"It belongs to the Company. It's the Company's money."

"What and who is 'the Company?'"

In less than three minutes, I had all the information I needed and some. I had to hit him in the mouth to get this coward to shut the fuck up. We went over his speech one more time about his excuse of what happened to him and that he would deliver that money to the Company as planned. I didn't need extra heat, and he would contact Officer Finney, and they would give me $20 grand in one week.

I ran back to where this clown picked me up, and still sitting there to my surprise was all my work equipment. Damn, I was lucky.

Slowly walking back home to clear my head, I did not know what to think. I just had the drug game broken down to me from a whole different angle. The police were selling drugs to the gangs and other distributors around the country. Yes, before you ask, around the country. Because it was Chicago, the second biggest drug market behind California. It was the hub of the Midwest. They brought it in by the truck load with police escort and protection. The gangs had to buy from them, or they were going to jail. The best place for this information was Lieutenant Sosa or

Agent James. Ptacc had given me some shit I didn't want, and its weight would smash an average person.

Walking into the door, I could hear laughter coming from the kitchen, and there was Poly, Ms. Tanggy, Ms. Diane, Mrs. Hubbard, and Lisa from across the street. They were having a great time with Walter. But as soon as I came around that corner, it was crickets. Not a sound, so I spoke to everybody and quickly excused myself. And the laughter started again. Whatever it was had to be about me.

Now I was laying against the wall holding my side laughing because in unison, they all started yelling: "ROACHMAN, ROACHMAN! GET YOUR HOUSE EXTERMINATED FOR $25! ROACHMAN, ROACHMAN!"

After I stopped laughing, I went back into the kitchen and told Walter that we needed some groceries in this house, and he needed to go shopping. And in true Walter fashion, he said, "I will if you give me some doggone money."

Now it was my turn to laugh as I reached into my pocket and grabbed the $200 from today's work and $75 from yesterday and threw it on the table. Now I had my hand up to my mouth, yelling, "ROACHMAN ROACHMAN!" I didn't have to say the rest as they filled in the rest of the words, and I swung my arms like a choir director. Lisa asked if could I do her house tomorrow, and again, I put my hands up to my mouth and yelled, "ROACHMAN, ROACHMAN!"

Knowing that I needed a shower, I headed to my room. Walter announced that he was about to go shopping and grabbed Dee and Lisa to take with him. Before I could come back, Mrs. Hubbard was going down the stairs. Ms. Tanggy had walked into the living room and picked up a pool stick and started to knock a few balls around on the pool table. Diane was sitting at the kitchen table with the last of the cocktail that she had from the hen session. We spoke again as if we had just seen each other for the day. I wanted to go over and hug her, but that was the thing that got me in trouble in the first place. Diane spoke first as she started to tell me that I was doing well with the business. I said thanks, adding, "I hope it carries me through the winter."

Diane stood and walked over to stand in front of me wearing a pair of jeans that had to be a size too small and an even smaller top. Extending both hands to stop her where she was before she got to close, I said, "Please go sit back down. We can talk from across the room." She walked back, reminding me of Winnie, my baby, when I told her no about something. It was no surprise that Diane turned around with her head down and her lips stuck out.

STAND YOUR GROUND. STAND YOUR GROUND. I had to win this battle. These two women would have me going into battle with a fucking toothpick. I needed a distraction.

"TANGGY, TANGGY!" I called from the kitchen, and right on cue, she replied, "Is this bitch about to burn down or something?"

"No," was my answer. Well that took away Diane's advantage. I asked them both to sit down, so we could talk about this meeting. Laying out my side was simple. The other side got a little complicated with who was related to who and who to trust. It came down to six women and the two officers.

I was not going to let the meeting end without knowing the truth about Mrs. Myra and how she ended up on my doorstep. They both sat there, looking at the floor. I thought that the awkward silence was good; now I got to see another side of Tanggy when her back was up against the wall and how she performed. I already knew how Myra ended up at my door. She was a second cousin to Tanggy. It was her mother's first cousin.

Diane started to speak, but Ms. Tanggy stood and cut her off.

"She is my cousin on my mother's side. When I took her to the police station, it was like they didn't give a shit, and we were desperate." She continued on to say, "It was the way that Diane talks about you, like you are some fucking Superman with all the kids... I figured that you must care, and I sent her over here just on a whim."

Looking straight at Diane, I wanted to know if she cosigned this shit. Still looking at the floor, Tanggy tried to lie for her, but I wasn't having it. I informed them both that I expected her to answer for herself, or they could get up and leave. I needed to know what they both looked like telling the truth and lying. I needed that on file for future reference.

These two were slick, and I tried to press the point that we could not have a partnership if they wanted to play games. Reminding them that I was tired and needed a shower, Tanggy had a relieved look on her face until I asked them to leave. Then Ms. Tanggy looked over at Diane as if to say "you didn't try the PUSSY play while I was up front?" It didn't matter. One way or the other to me, they both had to go. Yes, I already smelled their arousal a long time ago, but I needed to show some restraint of my own.

Gathering all their things, we walked down the front steps, which were sort of narrow. Diane was walking slowly in the front, and Tanggy was real close, pulling up the rear. We got to the bottom of the stairs and ran out of room. Diane turned to face me and gave another sad-eyed apology for lying to me. She hugged me and said again that she was sorry as she kissed me. I returned her kiss. Then I felt on my back those 38-double-Ds, and a soft voice whispered in my ear, "I'm sorry, too, James."

We stood there for what I hoped would be an eternity, just holding and kissing each other. Diane had turned me around, so I could kiss Tanggy. I was in heaven, especially after turning back around, and Diane seemed twice as enthused as before.

Twang time: "IT'S HOT AS HELL IN THIS HALLWAY ON THESE STEPS. ARE WE GOING BACK UP STAIRS OR WHAT?"

Back to life, back to reality.

"HELL NO! YOU ARE GOING OUT THAT DAMN DOOR." I slid to the side to let them out and said, "I will see you two at the meeting."

Diane asked if she could call me tonight. I didn't answer; I just closed the door.

What the fuck was I thinking? I needed to turn on the big head and let the little head shut the fuck up.

CHAPTER SIX

PUTTING A TEAM TOGETHER

Getting a grip was easy; it was just a matter of what you had a grip on. In my case, it was a lot. I just had to figure out what was first.

The kids were my first priority. This was not the kind of thing that you wanted to blow back into your household. These gangbangers didn't have a preference about who house they shoot up. They were in SUPER PREDATOR MODE. The park that was less than 200 yards from my house had had four shootings in the last month. I have seen crackheads get beat down for showing up to the dope spot with too much change; are they too good to count the change, or did some of them quit school too soon and never learn to count change? Change. That's what they were getting. The drug trade brought in a lot of money, and they only saw a fraction. Like I said: CHANGE.

There was also a meeting that I needed these women to sell what I was trying to do with the lieutenant and Agent James. I needed to see some Academy Award shit. I had instructed Ms. Diane to bring children and infants. I wanted them to see the carnage firsthand. I wanted them to see the hopelessness in their eyes. No one had to fake that; it was real and omnipresent.

Now to the largest problem of them all. Just today I learned of times, locations, and names of the second biggest drug trade in the United States of America. Ptacc really did have a bad knee. I saw that limp at the bar, and true enough, when I punched that knee and re-injured it, he couldn't stop talking. I had an FBI agent who was trying to work her way up the ranks and a lieutenant who just wanted to stick it to all those that laughed at him, which was every-damn-body. I knew that I would have plenty of time to think about it. I had an event for Ajaumu in about three hours.

Before I could sit down, the doorbell rang and kept ringing. I knew it was my brother and Sconey Dog. I took a deep breath and went to answer it. First off, they were loud as hell, and they both were trying to get a few dollars. I moved out of the way, and they flew right upstairs. Sconey wanted to know where Walter was because he said, "Dude be looking at him funny." He was just that type of dude. His hair was freshly braided and hanging down his back. And it was his style to be dressed even though he was not leaving the neighborhood. Today was no different; he sported a red and black two-piece walker with red and black cowboy boots. Red and black were the Nation colors.

Sconey Dog was up front about his initial purpose for his visit. He opened his coat and pulled out a 44. Magnum asked, "Do you want to buy it?"

By the time he had laid the gun on the pool table, my brother was in another room, the kitchen. I yelled back to the kitchen that it was cool; I didn't have bread for a gun, and I didn't know if it was clean. He assured me that it was clean and that's why it was still in the box. He kept talking and said that the brothers hit the trains and got an arsenal of shit.

Okay, okay, okay. Let's pause for the cause once more. I have been hearing this shit about people hitting the trains for guns since I was a kid. But now I'm an adult, and I think like one. We can't be fools here. Are you telling me that a bunch of gangbangers who can't find their own ass with the lights out, they can go find a train in a certain part of the city, and out of 60 rail cars they GUESS the one with the guns in it? Come on now. I can't be the only adult in the room…

Well, in this room I was in, I might've been. I made a mental note to ask him about that. But for now, I was trying to figure out how to get them out of my house. Telling Sconey that I had no money to buy a pistol, he said, "Don't worry about it. Hit me with four bills when you get it, but I need at least 25 as a down payment," and we shook on the deal. My scary-ass brother asked me how many guns I needed. I didn't even have an answer to that question. I just told him that THE REVOLUTION WILL NOT BE TELEVISED. They acted as though they understood, but I wasn't sure.

Keeping it moving, I explained to my brother that I needed him to pick up some food and deliver it to the church. HE LAUGHED AND SAID, "SO WHAT? ARE YOU A NOBLE MAN NOW?" I knew exactly what he was referring to. I drank and smoked as much as the next man. And I chased women just like the next man. Now that might be one of the bigger reasons that I was a single parent, but we were both guilty. I told you a little while ago some shit is harder to get a grip on.

Squaring shit away with those two, I went straight for a nap. When my alarm clock went off, I got straight up and wanted to go right back to bed. You can't tell an eight-year-old when to deliver the news. James walked up and hugged me and said, "My mama told me to tell you that the girls got to come home, or they are going to stop her check." An eight-year old-can only tell you what they know or heard. Man, where the fuck do I file this shit away at?

After taking a deep breath, I bent down to talk to James and give him a hug. Trying to assure him that everything would be alright, he said that he would go with them just in case. I didn't even have it in me to ask my eight-year-old son, "Just in case of what?" He was still a kid, but no longer a child. Our surroundings can rob us of our innocence way too soon.

After the long hug with James, I stood up and continued to go backwards into the wall. Walter and James rushed to my side to assist me. They were both holding onto me as I gained my balance and put one of my hands on the back of a chair. I stood there for maybe two minutes, which seemed like much longer, with Walter and James fussing over me. I knew right then and there that this had nothing to do with a physical element. This was mental; it was STRESS, plain and simple. There was a million pounds on my head, and the blow James just gave me was something that I didn't expect.

Yes, I knew what it was. STRESS. BUT BLACK MEN DON'T GO TO THERAPY.

I stood with the water running on me until the hot water ran out. That's what it took to help me out of this funk. Yes, it was bad, but now sitting in my room with this baby oil trying to get right for the evening...

Hold on—get your mind out of that gutter. No, that's not what I meant. I was putting on oil, so my skin was soft and not ashy. I was about to be a part of a live improv show, and I was just getting ready. I figured out the crowd that I was going to see; I thought a simple pair of Levis and a black half turtleneck would do nicely. Next was the jacket, which was black with a blue checkered pattern. It was swift, and I received lots of compliments on this jacket. I topped that off with a pair of loafers complete with quarters in them—not pennies. Well, you must understand that my attire was very appropriate for the yuppie crowd. Yeah, once again that dude from the Projects was hobnobbing with the Ivy League folks. Only this timem my trip was a lot shorter. University of Chicago. Well, this place didn't smell like money like North Western. This place smelled of prestige. I WISH I HAD A WAY TO SHOW THE WORLD THAT I WAS ON THE SAME STREET.

Yes, the same street. You see, I lived just a few miles away, just straight down 55th Street. You go from poverty to Nobel Peace Prize winners in everything from economics, medicine, and science, and more. To be honest, the University of Chicago was surrounded by poverty on all sides. Well, my question is, how does all of this knowledge and technology jump out to the rest of the world? Going forward out into the world, it never stops in the poor community, and we are right there next door. I guess we can't shut off the conscious mind. But I really wasn't there for that type of a social experiment. I was there for a different type of an experiment. Who knows? The participants in this study probably would have preferred that I came from below the poverty line. I don't know if it may be filled with some type of shit in the back of their heads. That's the reason that I put on my mask before I get in the door. If they are here for the games, don't let them draw you into their game.

I saw my old friend Ajaumu. He had a smile that was genuine and welcoming. This was his world, and he allowed me to come in and take a peek into it. He was a real psychologist. You know, the kind with the long white coats? And somehow he took to monitoring their behavior in studies to having them pay him to execute their fantasies. What part of the game was this?

Ajaumu introduced me to a few of the major players and a possible cash cow. Her name was Mrs. Bell, a radio and TV executive who he said could eat up a dozen men and spit them out before lunch. Ajaumu told me to get her number, and, "Be careful. She likes to humiliate men."

We walked into an auditorium that was really a glorified lecture hall that had lighting and sound as if it were a real auditorium. Lola greeted me and gave me another one of her famous hugs. I must have held on too long because I was told by Ajaumu that he would be checking her for fingerprints later. There were a few laughs. My mind was more on the stage and the view that the audience had since that's where I was standing, looking down at where I would be performing.

Lola pulled me to the side, and we did the necessary paperwork, then I was led to a dressing room. Men and women shared the same dressing room if you were a performer. The guests who paid big money to play had private dressing rooms. I walked in and saw five other people in the dressing room, and two of them I knew from other performances. We all spoke, and I was introduced, and we started to discuss the script. It was basic all they wanted to see was a live sex show and try to figure out why certain people get turned on in certain situations. Oh, these people put up a real front with legal pads to take notes and everything!

Lola stepped into the door and yelled, "Five minutes to show time!"

I was over in the corner trying to do a few pushups, trying to look fresh for the part. I was playing the role of Oedipus Rex. Well, if you know the story, then you know how freaky these WHITE PEOPLE are. But if you don't know, by fate and happenstance Oedipus met and married his mother and killed his father along the way. So please tell me again what type of research they were doing, other than getting off on some incest shit.

I couldn't complain too much when the mother appeared on stage. She was early forties but looked much younger. Her body was well preserved; what I call good maintenance and up-keep. The whole production ran maybe two hours. (You have to give perverts a chance to get off while they are taking notes.)

The final scene was a thing of beauty. There were four couples on the stage going at it to music and lighting that was amazing. I almost forgot what I was doing until the music changed, and that was our cue to switch partners. Three of us got curtain calls, and one lady got a standing ovation for her performance of Annie Oakley. She transformed herself into Annie Sprinkles and wetted a few people.

We all retreated to the dressing room. Lola was there and asked me to hold off on changing. I was dragged off to a small office space to meet a VIP. It was Ms. Bell. She thought it was entertaining that I was still in my Toga from my performance earlier.

Ms. Bell gave a nod, and Lola left the room. She gently slid an envelope in my hands and made it clear that it was payment for an evening of her choosing. I made it clear that I had a family and small children, so she would have to give me some notice time. She didn't skip a beat as she sat in a chair right in front of me and reached under my toga to inspect the package as if she was buying meat at a store. Hell, she was buying meat; she just wasn't at a store. She did this funny thing with her nose. Mrs. Bell started smelling my dick like it was an expensive bottle of wine. I think she was getting off on the fresh smell of sex from my recent performance.

Ms. Bell said, "There's more than enough to pay a babysitter."

Rising to leave, she did a sort of "throw the meat back on the counter" type of a thing, but it was attached to me, so she couldn't fling it anywhere. The message was given, but I wasn't humiliated at all. I just wanted to know what else she had in store for me. I could see something in her skin that I didn't see before. Her ears were a little bit darker than the rest of her skin. She wasn't completely Caucasian. Then came what she thought was the humiliation part. She requested that I not fuck anyone for four days before her event.

Back home getting undressed, I laid my thrift store jacket on the back of a chair. Yes, thrift store. I just put it in the cleaners along with the half turtle neck that came from the same shop. You don't have to spend a lot of money to look good. There was going to be no work on the schedule for tomorrow. I wanted to sleep in, plus I had two months of rent sitting on the dresser. No, I did not feel like a WHORE. Because the money was on the dresser. I actually felt proud, and I managed to get an advance gig that paid twice as much as I made last night. I lit me a joint because Walter and the three remaining kids were asleep. It was sad and heartbreaking to know that it would just be me soon. I put out the joint and put the bottle back up. I just laid across the bed and went to sleep.

The kids talked to me all the way to school. It was nice; we laughed and even got in a little prayer because James said that he was trying out for basketball today. That was a good thing. He needed something to help take his mind off of the adult situations that his mom put him in. I got hugs and kisses as they got out of the van.

Home, home, home, I was not clicking my heels together, but I was wishing for bed. My mind was pretty much clear. I left the money for Mrs. Hubbard for the rent when she came to Starbucks this morning. I was just hoping that everybody else was gone when I got back. I didn't need or want company. I just wanted my bed and a clear head for the meeting tonight.

All clear was my wish as I walked through the door. I went straight to my room and closed the door. I don't know how long it took to get to sleep, but I know that it was 4:17 p.m. when the small alarm clock on the nightstand went off. Getting ready for the meeting, This should have been easy, but life has a way of rearing its ugly head. Walter informed me that my ex wanted to come over to pick up the kids this evening. No, I wasn't going to cry, but Lord knows I could not stand anymore. This hit me right in the middle of my chest, and I felt a panic attack. I had no idea what to do, so I grabbed my running gear and started running. I don't know how fast I was going, but I ran straight to the school, and I was early for the meeting. Real early.

I had no keys, but Mr. Gant's car was parked on the side of the building. I walked over to the door where the maintenance office was located, and he was sitting there with the door propped open to get some air. He was sitting there looking at the racing form for tomorrow. He was a gambler like me. We would bet on damn near anything. He got out of his chair to give me a bear hug. We rocked back and forth like two old women. It was one thing to say we missed each other. He asked how the kids were, and I gave him all the bad news. Mr. Gant grabbed me and gave me another hug. He hugged me like Lola did, but without breasts and the perfume. We talked for about 20 minutes before Lieutenant Sosa pulled up in the lot.

I went inside and got the spare keys, letting Mr. Gant know that I would clean up and lock up later. I got a chance to talk with Sosa for about 10 minutes, and he really wanted to know who was giving me the inside info on the cops in his unit. I told him that I was the source. He didn't believe that shit because he pointed out that what I did was not random, and he knew that I didn't have a plug into a police station that I had never been inside of. I wanted to know what he knew about the Company. Just the mention of the Company almost gave this brave-ass man a heart attack, and he started to stutter. There was no reason for him to lie, and I was not going to accept one. Halting whatever explanation that he had, I didn't want an answer; I just wanted to confirm that it existed. His face and the stuttering confirmed that. Sosa told me that my life could be on the line for just knowing this shit. I didn't care. I just wanted to know which side he was on because I thought he was alright. Things had to be made clear that the Company was going to come down, so which side did he want to be on?

"WHAT THE FUCK? YOU DIDN'T TELL ME SOMEONE ELSE WAS INVOLVED!"

Like fucking clockwork, Agent Nora James pulled into the lot. Hell no, I didn't tell either one of them that the other would be there. Shit, I like surprises, too, and I wanted to know how well they knew each other.

"OH SHIT." There we go. Lieutenant Sosa had a twisted mouth and that little pencil thin mustache just would not stop wiggling. "You brought on another officer and didn't bother to tell me?" We were doing that whisper-shout thing, and he had no idea who was in the other vehicle. Now in a real loud shout whisper, he said, "THE FUCKING FBI?"

I had to take into consideration the fact that he didn't have a rosy past with the FBI. He still had no idea who was in the car as I tried to get him to calm down. It was going to be alright. I told Lieutenant Sosa that if I wanted to babysit, I would have stayed the fuck at home, so he needed to get his panties out of a bunch. I really didn't mean it that way, but the look on his face told me he made a mental note about the panties comment.

Agent James emerged from the vehicle, and a small amount of relief showed on the lieutenant's face. Agent James came over to shake our hands, and the two of them gave each other whatever look they needed to give each other. I was slightly distracted with my brother pulling up into the parking lot like he was in a race. The mofo came to a screeching halt when he saw the two police vehicles in the lot and me standing there next to them. Sosa and James both put their hands on their weapons. I raised both hands and got between them and the van. I told them it was my brother bringing food. I think we all calmed down as I directed my brother where to set up the food.

Slick got out of the vehicle and wanted to know what was going on; was I sponsoring the policeman's ball with all of this food? The next question was why I was hanging around with the Feds. I asked him to stay for the meeting; we might need him. Slick looked me in the face and told me to go catch something flying. He didn't specify what.

OH yeah, Slick was the nickname that I had for my brother, and he was that with extra oil on it if you are looking from a distance.

Head shaking and finger pointing is an argument. Well, that's what I saw from one of the classroom windows. James and Sosa were having a few words, and I was not going to interrupt, but I needed them to work together on this Nation Baby thing.

Here we go. Now a small car, something foreign, pulled into the lot, and the head shaking and fast talking stopped to take on a more professional look. But I bet they were over there doing that loud whisper thing. The car door opened up, and three women and four kids got out of the Toyota. The big one who was in the passenger seat had to unfold and stretch before she started walking. Sosa directed them to where the meeting was going to be, or at least he directed them to the door that I had entered. I held the door open for them to enter and asked them to help themselves to something to eat.

Within 10 minutes, all participants were there and ready for some answers. I jumped right in by introducing myself to everyone and told them we were all there for the same reason, adding this was too important to discuss with anyone outside of this room. I introduced our two officers and explained that they were there to gather information and pile up evidence for later arrest.

The twang started: "WE DON'T WANT NO ARREST LATER. WHAT ABOUT RIGHT NOW?"

I signaled for her to calm down and let us get our plan together. Each woman was given a chance to speak, and some even had additional information on names and whereabouts. We even had info on some of the Nation members who didn't live in the Town. It was all info that could be used. The meeting took almost an hour, and the eating took just as long. There were nine women there and 17 kids, all Nation Babies. It painted one hell of a picture for my two law Enforcement people. Sosa even got caught up playing on the floor with a couple of the boys. I asked those two to stay for what my final game plan was.

Ms. Diane and Ms. Tanggy were the last two to leave besides the law. I told them that I would be leaving after I finished my meeting. Diane's eyes were pleading, and Tanggy was very blunt.

"Well, we need to talk to you later if you have some time on your hands, Mr. ROACHMAN."

The ROACHMAN comment didn't get past anyone, but Sosa and Agent James didn't know what it meant, so they said nothing. The two ladies left the room shaking the shit out of their lady parts, and I noticed that Agent James was looking as hard as I was. Sosa had the "I don't eat fish look." Well hell, he wasn't going to be playing macho for Agent James, and I didn't care one way or the other. I thought about what Ms.

Dee told me about walls that leak. I chose my words carefully. Taking a deep breath and thinking about what I had to say, even if it came out slow, I said: "Do we all agree that there is a real problem in Englewood?"

Both nodded in agreement. I gave them the floor for a while.

I believe that I had heard all that I wanted to hear about evidence and witnesses and other procedures. I held up both hands because they were now discussing which department would be in charge.

"Please hold on. This will not belong to no one's department. This is going to be a blind mission, or those women who just left here will start to disappear one at a time. Either by murder, or they just won't help us anymore, and if we don't see their faces again it means that we FUCKED UP."

Lieutenant Sosa spoke first.

"Do you know what you are asking?"

Agent James seconded his question.

"Yes, I know what I am asking, and it is simple. DO YOUR FUCKING JOBS. PERIOD."

Both were older than me by between eight and 10 years. That didn't even bring into account the life experience that they had over me. I had to win this fight if it had to come down to a fight. Agent James realized that I was not going to give up, so she said, "Fuck it," and took a seat. Well, I sat down, and Sosa followed. Now that I had their attention, I brought up something that I knew that they both wanted a part of: the Company. Yes, this was only part of the bribe.

We sat and talked for the next 90 minutes, and a new partnership was born. We needed more officers, and we needed some media coverage. We needed a way to shine a spotlight on the problem but tell the truth. "No!" was the response from both officers on the media coverage. It was just like the gang thing but in reverse. If they got coverage for breaking the supply chain of the Company, they wouldn't last another week on the force, or living.

There was one more piece of business for the night. It was in my van. First thing's first, I had to clean the place up, and they both volunteered to help. It was the funniest shit ever. Sosa wanted shit nice and neat, and James just wanted to put the chairs back and get the fuck out of there. She even said so when Sosa was too particular about sweeping the floor. Looking at this new whatever you want to call it, all I knew was I was working with BITCH and BUTCH. Okay, okay, okay, I know that I wasn't supposed to say that. These were two people who had made a decision to put their life on the line because I asked them to. But hell, it's still funny.

That last piece of business now that we were in the parking lot. I waved the two of them over to my van. I opened the back door and reached underneath the couch to reveal the box that contained the 44, the Magnum that I got from Sconey Dog. I just wanted the guns off the street. There was no way in hell I was going to turn in Sconey Dog. Shit, that was family. But we needed to find out about the guns. The police both looked at me and shook their heads.

Lieutenant Sosa spoke first.

"What the hell is this, another surprise?"

There was no time for me to answer before Agent James chimed in, "Hey Sosa, I don't know about you, but I'm already putting my career on the line."

He jumped in: "And our lives."

When they gave me a chance to speak, I said, "These guns are coming off the freight trains into the hood, and the Nation just got a brand new shipment."

The filters were off, and I guess that we were now friends. Agent James went into a cussing fit about the fact that I kept coming up with all of these surprises. Sosa then told her about the possession charges he had to file against his officers. The two looked at each other, and I was on the ground stripped down to my drawers to prove I wasn't wearing a wire. I don't know, maybe that was because we don't trust people, but shit. From the police?

I thought they were going to let me up, but no; they had questions while they had guns on me. Not one word came out of my mouth. I didn't even ask to get off the ground. They had to pick me up and put away their guns before I moved a muscle. I wanted them to really know what it was to have a gun pulled on you by the police. They both knew the feeling was real because it was a few minutes before I said anything to these GODDAMN POLICE. I was pissed. I understand the no trust shit. With the info that I had, I get it. But I'm an ex-soldier, and I know that if you don't stand over people with your gun trained on them, it could go off. Pulling a gun is a nervous situation for anybody. There was no appreciation for that shit from me.

As I closed my van door, I made it clear if they ever drew down on me again, I was going to make an example out of one of them because I couldn't afford to lose two partners. Lieutenant Sosa asked about the gun in the back of my van like I was going to hand it over for evidence. It was plain to me I paid four bills for this; he needed to get his own.

The smell of the food in this city was driving me crazy. I was at A.P. Deli getting me a corn beef on rye bread with mustard and Swiss cheese. I knew that Walter was home, so I got him one to go and two for me. It's only hard to eat and drive when the food is good. All I needed to do was get home without tearing up some shit on the way. This sandwich was so damn good. The meat was falling off the sides and in my lap. I pulled over and demolished the sandwich. It was just my good fortune my brother didn't drink all of my beer. It went down so smoothly.

I drove the rest of the way home smiling. The meeting was the bomb, and we got a commitment for three arrests every other week on the Nation Baby thing, and we needed to take our time to make the charges stick. There were eight witness protection spots available. We never mentioned it in the meeting because we needed to know who was for real.

Back to life, back to reality. On the side of my house was Ms. Tanggy's car. She was sitting there with the window down, just waiting on me to get home.

"Well hello ROACHMAN." The twang was missing. I was well aware that she wanted something, and I was all out of favors and bubble gum, if you know what that means. I walked all the way up to the car and asked where the other half was. "She's around the corner at her cousin's house. She'll be back in a little while."

Tanggy told me that she was there to talk to me. I had no words. Silence. I needed her to speak first because I was not in for any more games. We sat on the back steps. Damn, it had been a while since my backyard was totally empty. No kids. I was hurt in a way that may be hard to understand. I had changed my whole life for those kids. They were left with me for a reason. They were all taken over some checks. Everybody got a check and some fucking food stamps. If you can't see how the system takes a part in breaking up families, then you are either blind or closed your eyes.

Out of nowhere Tanggy grabbed me and told me in my face, up close and personal, like nose to nose, "James, you handled that shit in that meeting today, and you got the FBI on our side! Man, we gonna fuck them bitches up! They all going to jail!"

I had to put my hand over her mouth and say, "You are telling the plan!" Ms. Tanggy put her hands over her mouth like she was stopping the words from coming out as I was reminding her that the first and the last thing we said before leaving the meeting was don't talk about this to anyone. Now I was worried how many others were so excited about the news, they just ran right home and told everyone. All I needed was for these people to help me help them.

Diane came from around the corner with that ass swaying from side to side. She sat right down on my lap. I leaned down to whisper into her ear, "Could you please get up?" It was a simple request. I got stared at with daggers, but it didn't matter to me. I needed to stay alive. Man, pussy will have you trying to cross an expressway with a blindfold on. I had to say my piece, so we all knew where we stood.

"Look, you two are very attractive ladies, but I can't be tricked into something that one of you wants done out of revenge. We have been lucky so far. We have not done anything dangerous yet. I know that I have been played by you two on more than one occasion. So please forgive me if I seem a little standoffish. I'm just playing the hand that I was dealt."

There were some tears and some apologies and hugs. I didn't stop them, but when they were done I asked them to leave no matter what my nose was telling me. I was a gentleman and walked them to the car and said my goodbyes. I had a long day and got a lot accomplished.

At the end of the night, I kicked those fine-ass women out of my place, and now I was here with this baby oil after my shower. What? I am home alone!

I hit the street at 9:00 a.m.

"ROACHMAN, ROACHMAN! GET YOUR HOUSE EXTERMINATED FOR $30! ROACHMAN, ROACHMAN."

I was totally numb. That's all I did every damn day. I tried to lose myself in my work. I took a few things off my list by giving Diane's phone number to the lieutenant. They made the list of which three Nation members would be arrested this week. There were a few people on the list that we had to wait to arrest. I had my plans for those individuals. Right now, information was king.

I had a separate meeting set up for Sosa and James. I had to produce big time for this to work. I asked them both to come up with three cops apiece who they trusted. We met at the lakefront with all six officers, and it wasn't a go from the beginning. I was not going to stand outside and talk to eight police officers in broad daylight. I asked them to get in the van. Now one of these big mother fuckers said that I didn't look trustworthy. Nothing from me; just silence. I figured that the lieutenant or Agent James would speak up, but no one said a word. So now I knew the deal. Each man had to prove his own metal. Again, I was the youngest in the circle but needed to prove the most. It was my belief that we could get shit done without VIOLENCE, which I was becoming better and better at.

"Excuse me, what is it that I have to do to get you to trust me?"

"You don't have to do anything," Sosa replied, "but I would like to know who you got on the inside telling you about crooked cops. I've been working with some of these guys for over 10 years and didn't know that they were crooked."

It was show time, and I didn't have long to do my thing. Mr. Big Mother Fucker was about 6-foot-4, and he looked like he could run through a wall. He was more of a dark caramel colored fella with wavy hair. He was very confident, and I thought that was a good sign. His name was Officer Daniels, a city boy who came up rough and wore it on his face like I did. I got as close to him as possible, knowing the size difference would make him laugh. I even bumped his body a little. Just as I predicted, that macho shit kicked in, and he started to push back. I turned on the power, and he couldn't move me, not an inch. I let the farce continue for about 10 seconds. One small push, and Officer Big Mother Fucker was on the ground about 15 feet away from the crowd. Before he could gather himself and stand, I was in front of him helping him up with force, not giving him a chance to refuse. In fact, by the time I got him to his feet, his legs were still wobbly. I was holding up a 280-pound man, and only he and I knew about it.

The next trick was almost spectacular. Still holding on to Officer Daniel's arm, I announced that no one could get in my van carrying drugs. I asked Officer Daniels to please remove the bag of dope from his back pocket before he got into my van. I did get a crazy stare from this behemoth of a man, but he got his ass in the van.

Officer Green was next. Giving her my best gapped-tooth smile, I asked her to please remove the dope from her bra because her breasts and perfume didn't hide the smell.

Now I think I had everyone's attention.

Mr. Acne and thick glasses was next. His name was Agent Oliver, an Ivy League man. He had no fucking idea how much I laughed inside, but he needed to get in the van.

"Yo Pimple Face. How much dope you got in that right boot?"

He didn't say a word. He just sat on the ground and removed the boot and put the drugs on the ground and climbed into the van. The show was over on that front.

We all piled in, and I turned the air conditioner on high and left a few doors open for a minute. Lieutenant Sosa had no shame. He wanted to know how I knew where the dope was. I wasn't telling and told him to stop asking. There were three more bags of dope in the van I was saving for later. Up front I made a bet with James and Sosa to have them hide one bag on their bodies, and I would find it. I just wanted them to think that they got away with it. Nora James spoke first. She told the squad, "This is James Madlock. He is a concerned citizen who wants to help us if we help him."

Officer Green wanted to know what I needed help with. There were strange looks when she said, "Nation Babies."

The only other officer who knew what that was was Lieutenant Sosa. He spoke up and explained the play to the team. You could hear a pin drop, and none of them had ever heard of such a baby.

I broke into the conversation. I was getting pissed at the fact that these officers kept frowning their noses at the fact that I smoked weed in my van. Raising both hands, I told all of them that I was not a cop, and I smoked weed, and lots of it.

"But if you don't want this chance to make a difference," I told them, "you can get the fuck out of my van."

Sosa turned bitch on me and said in a somewhat feminine voice, "HOW UNCOUTH."

I told Sosa that he could get his light skinned Cuban ass out, too. This brought some chatter from my guests. I decided to put an end to this charade that was going on. I had to say my piece.

Standing in the middle of the van, I made one thing clear. I had intel on the Company and other drug shipments. I wanted to stop the guns from coming in and stop this Nation Baby thing. Then I sat and told them to take the floor and say what they wanted out of this shit, and I even wanted to know why they were here. I told you that they were cops, not angels. I pulled out a quarter of a bottle of Martel, and Lieutenant Sosa stepped out of the van only to return with a bottle of scotch. There were no cups, and we just passed the bottles, plus I heard that alcohol killed all germs. One hour later, there would be some buzzed cops driving home.

As we exited the van, I had to do the last part of my job. I spoke to Officer Brown, who was the only white person on the crew. It was one of Agent James' picks to put him on the team even though he was not FBI.

"I need you to give me that bag of dope out of your hat."

Everybody stopped to look at him. He smiled and gave it up. There were three more bags of dope on the circle. It was getting late, and I was ready to go, so I asked if they would give them up, or did I have to point it out? No one moved, so I said, "Sosa, you are holding in your waist or belt area. James, yours is in the purse that you left in the car trying to trick me."

Agent Horde was my type of man. He said the least of anyone today yet he made the most valid points on how we would proceed. He didn't have dope on him. Officer Green carried her bag between the cracks of her ass. And a nice ass it was. Just as she was walking away, I grabbed her by the ass, and she turned to hit me. I grabbed her hand and lifted her by the back of her pants and spoke directly to Agent Horde: "If you carried your own shit, she wouldn't be in this situation."

There was some testosterone in the parking lot. A couple of the men bucked at me, and I let her down. I think I got my point across about each person doing their job. This was the time for me to properly introduce myself.

"I am Sergeant James David Madlock of the United States Army. I came home to find my family and neighborhood fucked up, and I want to do something about it. If you want to help, all you have to do is carry out your assignments for the week, and we meet up next week."

I needed to speak to Officer Green and apologize for grabbing her ass. She had no hard feelings about the whole damn thing. She knew that I was trying to prove a point. Now we had another problem. This little Philly was in heat, and the smell was loud, and I was what was turning her on. Straight after the apology, I asked, "Can we go to my place to get the frustration off?"

The look on her face told me that I had struck out on that deal and then she smiled and said, "I live a lot closer."

If you are writing, you should be some sort of a wordsmith. Well, that's not me. I'm just trying to find a way to tell you about this thing of beauty that I have laying on her own dining room table.

I sat thinking about the meeting while Officer Green went into the shower, but when she came out in that thin-ass, transparent robe, I picked her up and set her on the table. She was 38 years old with no children, and she worked out five days a week. She had no idea that she would be a meal. I had no idea that she would throw in the towel so soon. Only on the table for about 20 minutes, I was begged off to some hard breathing and a repeat of: "DON'T TOUCH IT, DON'T TOUCH ME."

Leaving my victim lying on the table, I frisked the fridge, looking for something that would produce some energy. I could hear a faint voice behind me saying something about chocolate on the nightstand. Shit, I had to find the nightstand because the dining room table was the furthest that we got. It looked to be a very nice house from what I could see. I figured that the bedrooms were upstairs, so I ventured off to find the chocolate.

The master bedroom was that of a single woman, a million pillows on the bed and nothing was out of place. No man around to make a mess. Triumphant in finding the chocolate I made my announcement coming down the stairs THAT I HAD FOUND IT. It fell on death ears. Officer Ramona Green was out like a light, still laying on the dining room table. The gentleman in me ran back upstairs and turned down the sheets to let her rest. That was not to be the case as I deposited the lady in her bed, and she held my hand and said, "Don't leave." Like LL said, pink cookies in a plastic bag. Well, the sunshine caught me leaving the next morning. It wasn't all about sex. We got a chance to talk, and I found out how she became a cop on a dare from one of her friends. She told me that she had run three half marathons, and her goal was to run the Chicago marathons. She looked fit enough to do it.

By 9:30 a.m., the ROACHMAN was on the job. I needed to make an appearance on the set of the Nation. I found out from one of my students where the new spot was, and that was my block for today. I walked over a couple of blocks to May Street. Just off of 51st Street, there was a large contingent of the Nation just milling around. It was showtime. I put both of my hands up to my mouth and yelled: "ROACHMAN, ROACHMAN! GET YOUR HOUSE EXTERMINATED FOR $30. ROACHMAN, ROACHMAN!"

I was set and ready to start my day. This recon mission was going to be easy. I did about four houses on the block before moving on to the next block. But while I was there, I talked to the customers. I knew that the extra traffic was new to them; it was a new set up. These old folks were ready to talk. I found out about all types of stash spots.

It is truly amazing what you can see looking out of a picture frame window. I was currently standing in the living room of Theodore and Margaret Turner. They had been in the neighborhood for 40 years. There was no love lost over what was happening on the block. I fed them information about coming home from the Army to see this mess. Mr. Turner was a feisty man, and he said back in his day, the fathers would have taken control of these kids. He sounded as if he wanted to get a belt and whip the shit out of them right now. Mrs. Turner was really heartbroken. They had lost a child to this struggle, a daughter who came around to beg for money or steal from their home.

I finished with my job 20 minutes ago. I just enjoyed talking to the old folks. They were who I wanted to see come back in the neighborhood. Leaving their home, I spotted Big Fred who was across the street, and it was showtime again.

"ROACHMAN, ROACHMAN! GET YOUR HOUSE EXTERMINATED FOR $30! ROACHMAN, ROACHMAN!"

There was some serious laughter coming from across the street. Fred's big ass was in stitches, and the rest of the crew were cracking up as well. This didn't bother me at all. Hell, I gave two more yells before I even acted like I saw Big Fred. Oh, the hook was in. Now he wanted to know, "What the fuck are you doing? What happened to that good-ass job you had with them white folks?"

I couldn't wait to respond.

"Man, you were right all along. Those people will use you up, man, and spit you back out." Fred just smiled like he was praying for another brother's downfall. "I'm doing this, so I can pay my rent this month," I explained, then I shut up to see what stupid shit would come out of his mouth.

"Look, bro, if you short, I may be able to help you with a few bucks to tithe a playa like you over." Again I said this was my new hustle. Big Fred simply threw out a number: "A grand for $1,500 in return. One week pay back." Those were fair prices for loan sharking in the hood. I wanted no part of it, but I needed to get close and asked if I could get $2,500. At first his eyes got big, and he was going all in. I had this big fish hooked on dry land. Fred said he would bring it to the apartment later at about 6:00. We both walked off claiming victory. I had made $180 for the day, and it was time to pack it in for the day. I didn't have a full evening on my hands, but with Fred coming over, I had to switch some shit around. Well, I thought better of it and left shit the way it was. A few calls, and everything would be alright. I had made plans for the evening as I was meeting Agent Oliver and Officer Daniels (AKA Big Mother Fucker) at my apartment. I called them to let them know what was up, and they had to come over as two of my Army buddies. No guns, and Big Fred would be there with whoever was running security on the money that he was bringing. Big MOFO wanted to know what was up with the meeting, and did they need back up? My voice was calm as I told him that he could not get into a dick measuring contest with Big Fred. I asked that he treat it like an undercover case, and Fred was the mark.

I got my shower and waited for the show to start. Big Fred was right on time. He had one of the Nation's boys with him, and I knew that he was strapped. I needed to pay attention. I didn't know him, but I knew his job was security on that money. Fred threw the money on the pool table, and his companion looked around like he was in a museum. I did have a nice crib. There was no furniture in the living room. I opted for a custom pool table instead, and the TVs were mounted on the walls. There was a small weight room off to the side. The dining room had a longer than usual table that I got from the church rectory when they redecorated. It was from old money. I had never seen one like it. and it came with a China cabinet and hutch. They even gave me the dishes inside.

The young man was snapped back to reality when there was a loud bang on the door. He looked shocked, and I knew that that Big Mother

Fucker was banging on my door like he owned the place. I holla'd down the stairs: "Come on up!"

As soon as the door opened, Agent Oliver went into a roll, coming up the steps.

"WHERE YOU AT? You good pool-shooting son of a bitch! I need to get at that ass right now!" he shouted as he came running up into my apartment. Agent Oliver stopped in his tracks, like he was shocked to see company. "OH, so you got some fucking backup today. Well, I ain't fucking scared. I got that Big Mother Fucker with me. He is parking the truck, and you know he walk slow as hell."

I yelled, "Hey man, you need to take them fucking boots off in my crib."

Agent Oliver went back over to the door to remove his cement-covered boots. I stuck my head out the door and said, "Take them boots off please," in a sarcastic tone to Officer Daniels.

I started making introductions right away, and I just wanted to try and take control of the room. I didn't know the name of the young man with Fred, so I let him take care of that.

After the first round of introductions. Daniels walked into the room and he and Fred just locked eyes like they had met their soulmate. Trust me, this wasn't about love; it was about "I am the biggest and baddest MOFO in the room." I made introductions and took over from there.

"Yo Fred, man, I need some weed before I shoot one game."

Big Fred looked at Daniels and threw the weed on the table, and it was hit with another bag of weed from Agent Oliver, telling them to put his shit up because he owed me and was paying up. I was right; I had to figure out Agent Oliver, because those are some thick-ass glasses and the acne. This dude was on 10, and Big Fred was eating it up. Big Fred excused the security; the money had been delivered, and two hours later, Fred was leaving. He was a little bit more than tipsy, but we were just as bad. Officer Daniels didn't smoke weed, but he could put away some liquor. Agent Oliver and I were a little worse for wear.

No sooner than the door closed, Daniels told me that he couldn't wait to take Big Fred down. There was lots of conversation about how we would proceed. One thing for sure was those two couldn't go on the Nation Baby raids. I didn't need them getting spotted.

Agent Oliver wanted to get our attention and stood up too fast, but Daniels caught him, and he turned to me and asked how I learned how to do the dope dog trick. I told him that it wasn't a trick. And for it to be a trick, they would have to be involved.

The last bit of business with them was Ptacc and Finney. I needed cover on them. My meeting was tomorrow, and I needed them to follow after. Agent Oliver brought his brain to the meeting. He informed us that the best way to tell what someone was up to was to follow them from early in the morning. What a criminal gets into before a crime is just as important as after.

It was set. They started their surveillance at 6:00 a.m. I just said okay because they were dedicated. I walked them to the door, and I almost lost it. Right there on my porch was my son James and his two sisters. My ex was standing there, trying to look innocent. She said that the kids wanted to spend the night. I let them upstairs and said goodbye to my company. This was simple to me; she had fulfilled her requirement to the state, and now the kids were back with me. Trust me, I wasn't a sucker or a sap, but this was better for the kids.

When we all got back upstairs, she was gone in less than three minutes, saying that her ride was downstairs. Walter came out of his room, and we had a ball. I ordered pizza, and we had ice cream. Shit was starting to look better already. We were full, and I watched my last kids' show of the night. They were all asleep, and so was Walter. I needed to do some thinking, so I called Officer Green, and she answered with a smile in her voice. I returned the smile through the phone. Officer Green asked how my day was and what made me call her. As if she didn't know. I didn't have to talk long before she said, "I want some Lawrence Fish, and I will open the door."

Shit, I knew the price of admission, so I was headed down to Canal Street. I must have lost my fucking mind. I took my dumb ass down there, and my nose and the promise of pussy made me spend $75 on some sea food. I was digging in the bag, eating shit on the way. That's the privilege of the runner, to dig in the bag. The fried oysters were amazing, but hot as hell coming straight out of the grease. Yes, I was doing that thing where you swirl the food around in your mouth when it's too hot. I did like last time. I parked about a block from her house and walked down.

Ramona came to the door with a smile and some Fredrick's of Hollywood on, and I went dumb again. I set the food on the floor and scooped her up, trying my best to have a great thinking session. We came up for air about 45 minutes later, and she ran to the bathroom to get a towel because she said my face was wet and I needed to clean it. I had to apologize for snatching the towel out of her hand, letting her know that she would be wiping away fond memories. She said that she would leave it there until we got ready to eat the fish. I agreed but warned her that I didn't think that she was ready for me to eat the fish again. I saw her face as Ramona closed her legs real tight and looked as if she was having a flashback of sitting on my face. I wiped my face with the towel as I went to get the food, and she said, "Thank you, sir."

We ate and talked about different aspects of our future work together. Of course she gave me the obligatory speech about no one finding out about us. I said what I was supposed to. I WON'T TO TELL A SOUL. Talking about her assignment for the week, Ramona got real emotional as she told me about getting all of the women and children photographed for their folders. I told her that we would hire a photographer who was mobile, and they could travel and get photos on site. We finished off our night with a challenge. Ramona was bragging about her head skills and said that if she couldn't do the whole thing, she was going to get further than anyone else ever did. Who was I to stop her? I wasn't really sure how to tell another human being that you can't swallow a small log, but her efforts were inspiring.

A pause for the cause: Fellas, if you are reading this, you should have noticed that I take pride in my oral skills. If done right, it shows a level of commitment to making sure both of you enjoy it. One last thing. It's not because I was asked; no, it's what I enjoy now. We enjoy. IF you don't enjoy what you are doing, don't waste her time. YOU ARE WELCOME, LADIES. You can't take your eyes off the prize.

Agent Oliver called me at 7:30 a.m. He was having coffee at a dinner in Bridge Port. He said that Ptacc met up with some other cops for breakfast. Agent Oliver said, "It looks as though they are distributors." He said that Ptacc was easy to follow on those crutches. That was my plan of action. Every time I asked him a question and he didn't answer, I was going to punch his knee again. I thought we were going to have a great line of communication. Oliver was getting pictures and wanted to get surveillance on all of them, and he was excited. My wake-up call to him was this was a secret mission, and this was not the FBI budget.

I was at the park in the uniform of the day. Oh yeah, I was not playing games with Finney and Ptacc. We were all to wear a tank top and a pair of shorts. No socks; they were too good with weapons, and my body was my weapon. Ptacc and I arrived at the same time, and we walked to the designated bench. I waited for him to sit down. He had a harder task than me with the crutches and all. I already knew that Finney would be late. I had Officer Daniels put a hole in his tire. I needed to speak to Ptacc alone, and I needed to scare the Bejesus out of him. I don't know if that's a real thing, but I heard my folks say it a few times.

Trying to not pay attention as he was sitting, I let him set his crutches to the side and get comfortable. I wasn't going to let him get too comfortable. Reaching between his legs, I grabbed a hold of the park bench that he was sitting on and ripped a large chunk of the wood that was attached to the bench. Pulling it out, a portion of the bench cut the back of his leg. Nothing life threatening, but it was enough to warrant medical attention. I almost said I was sorry, but I wasn't. I had his attention. It was like he couldn't take his eyes away from me. Ptacc had no idea what was next, and he wanted to get to a hospital. I didn't make things any better. I used the accident with the wood to my advantage. One end of the wood had a serious point to it.

I took that end and pointed it at his knee and asked how hard he thought that I could drive it into his knee. Better yet, how much damage I could do with it. The look on his face when I rattled off his home address and asked how it would go over if I came to his breakfast spot and drove it in there, that way all the mob boys and the cops could witness it…

Okay, okay, okay, just in case you missed my fuck up. I just threatened a mob connected cop and his family. I didn't say it, but it was implied. I didn't know if I needed to walk that shit back or act like my balls were made of brass and big. Fuck it, I went with the latter and balled up my fist, placing it on top of his knee and drawing it back. Ptacc lost all his pride as a man and caved. I really didn't believe that he could deal with another six-hour surgery with that knee.

I laid out my plan for our new relationship. He was going to tell the Brass because of his knee that he couldn't do the leg work. Yes, pun intended. This mother fucker tried to have me killed for the bag money. I still believe that my advantage in life was thinking. He had to get a job with the Company that would yield information, and I would not exact my revenge on him.

Ptacc tried to put on a tough look, but face it. When the man who's standing in front of you is the reason that you have these fucking crutches and now he is crushing the piece of wood from the bench with one hand and asking about your retirement plan, that's not really an option. I told him to steal as much as possible from the Company because they were going down and I would give him a 10-minute head start for his cooperation. I wanted two spots that could be hit in the next month and four officers who I didn't know about who were a part of the Company. He had a look on his face that said it all: "A month ago, I would beat your black ass." Maybe true in his eyes, but the powers or not, I ain't nothing to sneeze at.

Wait. I did get my ass whooped two times in the same month. And one time somebody almost killed my ass.

There had to be a final message and a nodding of the head that he understood. For us macho-ass men, a nodding of the head is like bending the knee in surrender.

"The money that you are giving me today is my protection. I have $30,000 of my own. But with the $20,000 that I get from you two today pays for the contract on your life and his. It's also my insurance. I will keep your family out of it, and you do the same for me. That's it. That's all."

With the nodding of the head, we now had an agreement. I don't know if I could sleep well, but at least he understood.

On my way walking off, I told him, "Finney didn't stand you up or run out on you. I just had someone put holes in his tires. I needed to speak to you alone."

Ptacc informed me that he had to leave, and he would get the money out of the trunk of his car. I knew that something wasn't right, so I told him to set it on the ground next to the vehicle and drive off. Ptacc had no idea that the truck parked 50 feet behind his vehicle with a guy standing outside smoking a joint was the FBI. I needed to speak to Oliver about his behavior.

The blood running down the back of Ptacc's leg had him trying to walk a little faster on his crutches. A taxi pulled up, and it was Finney getting out. They exchanged a few words. I yelled out to Finney to bring the bag. He walked over to Ptacc's car and got the money. He looked fucked up in those shorts and tank top. The leather jacket was better for his image. By the time he made it over to me, he was already sweating. DO THEY STILL GIVE ANNUAL PHYSICALS? I let him sit on the bench and stepped in front of him with the same shit, only this time, I reached to the side of him and started to slowly rip away at a piece of the bench. He could not only see it, he could hear the wood crunching.

While doing this, I asked what part of the South his family was from, and he said Memphis. Now was my chance to help save his life: "I need you to buy a piece of land down there as soon as your disability package is approved." I needed something in return for my generosity. He was commanded to talk about his involvement with the company and how the Nation and other gangs fit into this scheme with the Company. Finney talked for 10 straight minutes. I asked, and he answered. It was easy when fear was already in his heart. I even found out how those two got a chance to work together. The Company didn't mind selling dope to minorities, but they would not trust a black cop alone with the dope or the money, so a match was made in hell.

We were about to part when Finney looked at me straight in the eyes and asked, "How the fuck did you heal?" I had to reach up because of his height and placed my hand on his shoulder, driving him back down into the bench, breaking two of the back cross boards. It literally took his breath away. I got real close and sat on his lap, facing him. I was close enough to kiss him. I raised up Finney's head with my finger and started to growl like a fucking dog. I was foaming at the mouth, and some of it dripped on his chin. He was warned that if he ever spoke a word of this, I would come back to see him at his house, and I repeated his address to him twice. Once I explained to him about the hit money on his life, there it was; I got the nod. This fight was over, and I think I scared the Bejesus out of him, too, because his pants were wet in the back.

I had to get in touch with Lieutenant Sosa and Agent James. The only information that I didn't have about the Company was those cock suckers in a line up.

Once Finney pulled off in his waiting taxi, Agent Oliver and Daniels walked up to discuss what we learned from today and how to proceed forward. Giving props where they were do, I let Agent Oliver know that he was right about the early morning shit. He grinned, and I saw the set of gold fangs that he had. Top and bottom. I was still trying to figure him out, but I knew that I wanted to hang out with him.

Officer Daniels seemed to be distracted by something, and I needed his attention, so I asked, "Is there a problem, brother, that I can help you with, so we can move on?"

I followed his eyes to the bench and the pieces of wood on the ground crushed. Daniels stepped past me to pick up one of the pieces of wood and tried to crush it and didn't have much success. He handed it to me and stared at me as I dropped the chunk of wood to the ground. Officer Daniels scratched his head and thought about when he and I were chest to chest and the results. He wanted answers, but he was smart enough to not push too hard. I didn't ignore his actions and wanted to know if he wanted to be on my side or against me. Agent Oliver stepped in and asked what the fuck I was getting them into. This was the second time that they were around me and a large amount of money changed hands. Shit, I forgot about the money on the pool table the other day from Big Fred and the Nation. Turnabout is fair play, so I went through the whole spiel about getting in tight with the loan, explaining that the money today was a final goodbye payment from two very bad cops who were getting a pension instead of a prison sentence.

I was still not figuring out Oliver. He said, "We are dressed for the occasion, so let's play some ball!" He had a ball in his truck and on the way over politely explained that he and Daniels played against each other in the Illinois State High School Championship. I didn't have a story to compete with that, but someone was about to be surprised.

Wow, Oliver had one of the smoothest strokes on a jump shot you ever wanted to see. It was pretty. Officer Daniels was a typical power forward and had all the brutality of a fucking bull. He was a load down low.

We played two games against some other cats, and it was a wash. Those two alone would be enough. I turned on the speed and got five steals in the first game. Daniels got three dunks because his big ass hadn't even run back down the court yet. Oliver must have been some sort of an all-out dude. He asked me if we could play one on one. I quickly declined his request and started walking to my van. Yeah, this dude was straight up Ivy League. He went right to some psychology shit and called out my name loud as hell: "YO JAMES, you must be chicken!" and folded his arms and did a full chicken dance in the middle of the street.

I went straight to my van and got me a cold beer, and I drank half of it straight down. Daniels came over and asked what the hell I was waiting on because he got winners. I gave them some bullshit excuse about having to finish up some business. I really wanted to bust that ass on the court, but I needed to be patient. I wasn't going to let all the cats out of the bag too soon.

I set up a meeting with Agent James and filled her in on what was happening with the Company, and the photography was going well. Agent James didn't play any games. She asked me if Officer Green tasted as good as she looked. Now I got a shocked look on my face.

"WELL?" she screamed at me to get me out of my stupor. I snapped back as Nora grinned at me. "Was it that good that you couldn't respond?"

"Hell no! I was just shocked that you would ask me some shit like that," I replied, trying to reclaim a small amount of dignity. Agent James turned into an FBI investigator right in front of my eyes and read off my arrival and departure time and the fact that I parked a block away on another block. She told me that the leftover Lawrence fish was very good with some grits the next day. Just to stick the knife in a little more, she said the fried oysters were to die for, but she really preferred her fish from Goose Island.

I got out of the van and started walking fast. I didn't have a destination; I just needed to clear my head. I thought that I was calling the shots. Now I realized that my young ass was being played from all sides. I didn't know who to trust, and now I was thinking about Agent Oliver, the Chameleon. This man could fit in anywhere. If they were going to play me, I was going to need a soft place for me and the kids to land.

About five minutes later, I got back to the van, and Agent James was sitting there with a shit eating grin on her face. Well, if she knew this much, I needed to see how far she was willing to play. I told her that I was going to get this shit in one circle and not be stabbed in the back. She acted like she didn't know what I was talking about, but I made it clear we don't have to sneak around, and she left her work blouse from work the other day on the back of the chair.

"It was the perfume before you ask. And how did you like the cream pie that I left you?" She told me I needed to change my diet to more fruits and vegetables. TOUCHÉ. I needed to move this meeting forward because I was having a measuring contest with someone who didn't even have one to measure. But Agent James had plenty of BALLS.

We conducted our business, and I got the hell away from Butch. I was going home for a nap, and no one was going to stop me except Christina and Delilah. They were at the door waiting on me with a school project. We had to get poster boards and some art supplies. The projects were not due for another week, but they wanted to do it right now, and that's why we were at the store. I think we bought way more stuff than we needed. There was probably not a lot of adult supervision on this store run. All I knew was I was so happy to have them back, I might have bought an elephant. By 9:30 p.m., we were finished, and I was finished. They gave me extra hugs and told me that they knew they were coming back. James was on the phone, huddled up in the corner talking to someone. When I heard him laugh, I knew who he was talking to; it was Terrell, his brother who was in another state. They were both about to turn nine years old soon, and I wanted to do something special for them. I didn't know what it would be yet, but I wanted it to be something special. I don't want to sound like a sap of a man, but missing them was an understatement. I had had some really bad days and mood swings. I was worse when I was home alone. I knew that I needed to seek some help because I had another one of those dizzy spells. Just the truth of the matter was that black men didn't go to therapy.

I sat down next to James on the floor, and we talked to Terrell and the rest of the kids on speaker phone. We told jokes and talked about their new school. Corvell and his mom were not getting along, and he told me so even though he knew she was on the other end listening in her room. Happiness and depression at the same time, how could that happen? I don't know, but I believed those were my feelings at the time. I kind of chickened out by leaving them on the phone together, so I would not have to do the sad goodbye. Tonight, it was just better that way for me.

Walter had given me one of those yellow legal pads to write shit down on because he was tired of me forgetting to tell him things that needed to be done. There were a ton of things to be written down, but none of it had to do with me and Walter. It was all about the things that had transpired during the day. The recap was simple: Don't trust anyone, and break that little thing off with Officer Green as soon as possible. I really had to think about that one. It wasn't the sex; it was the exchange of words with Agent James.

I need to go back for a minute I have a problem. Yes, I am confessing I have a problem with sex, and the kinkier the situation the better. No, I wasn't an addict in that sense. It was that freaky shit. It started with my ex-wife. We were in high school…

No, that's not right. I was in high school. She had dropped out and was pretty much living on her own and doing grown folks' shit. I was way behind the curve. That was the problem. I was behind her girlfriend, fucking her while she munched on my ex. They had an apartment where they could relax and do whatever they wanted. The first time she said to me, "James, this is my girlfriend Clair," I thought she was saying that it was her friend. It wasn't until later that night when Clair got off work and climbed in the bed with us I realized otherwise. By the way, this was my first time spending a night out from home with a woman. I thought that I understood what she meant by GIRLFRIEND, and that was after some explanation, some action, and some more explanation, a little more action, and waking up with the two of them. That's when I knew what they were talking about.

Every book has to have a scene where someone wakes up with the sunlight in their eyes, waking them up to a new world. Well, this was mine. Clair was shaking my ex, Nat, and laughing. It was short for Natalie, but you knew that right? I was frantically getting dressed. I was late for school, and I needed to catch the bus. Clair thought that I was panicking because I woke up with two women and was running. Not the case, but I was still amazed that it happened. I didn't want to be late. I was already in an alternative high school, and I just couldn't flunk out of there. Nat jumped up and grabbed me and asked me to calm down. I told her that I needed to get to class, and I needed to get dressed. She held me tight with her naked body, and she calmed me down and riled me up at the same time. Clair got out of bed and came over. She said, "You can't go to class smelling like that."

My slow ass asked, "Smelling like what?"

"PUSSY!" they both yelled at the same time. I was so inexperienced that I really didn't know that it had a real smell like that. Clair told me to hold up my hands and smell them. It took two or three times for me to get it, but once I got that smell in my nose, my life was fucked up from then on. They took me into the bathroom and put me in the tub. I was so excited that I had an erection for the rest of the day. Two naked women walking around, and I was done.

Oh yeah, I never did make it back to school that week. I never did go back home. I went back to school the following week and got a job at Church's Chicken, where Clair worked. It was only three blocks from the apartment. This is where I started to get my stripes and bruises as a man. I was very undisciplined and one who would fight at the drop of a hat. Being introduced to weed and alcohol, I was learning on the fly. I didn't know that people were going to say things about Nat and Clair because of their lifestyle. They were openly affectionate with each other in public, so I came home with some bruised knuckles. I didn't know it was the false pride that was fueling that violent streak, plus the alcohol. Even when my decisions were bad, I was still looked at as the man of the house and their protector. I would come home from work, and there would be a party in progress. Up late, falling asleep in class, and no matter how late they stayed up one of them or one of their friends would want to fuck, and I turned down no one. I never knew that women used the word pussy so much. It seemed like just the mention of the word would get me fired up.

I ended up dropping out of school again. It took six more months to go back, and in the meantime, I was fucking and working. I worked double shifts or whenever they needed me. I didn't even try to keep much of my paycheck. I knew it was needed for bills. Nat didn't work, and Clair ran some weed for her brother for extra money. I didn't give a shit about being broke. I was doing the freakiest shit that anyone could imagine. I was really respected in this circle of young gay people, especially when we went out to party. Everyone knew to stay close to me, and I would fight for them. The gay guys in the group never hit on me, and if I walked into a room with one of them with their ass in the air, I would just close the door. We were something like a flop house for a little while. Young people our age didn't have apartments often, but we had friends who had to leave home for whatever reason. The leftovers from Church's Chicken fed us. Almost every day, there was either some rice or potatoes on the stove, because we always had chicken to go with it. Clair and I had gotten used to putting on extra chicken right before closing, so we had a large amount to take home. We were not the only ones who did it. Clair was the night manager four nights a week.

One last thing about how I became such a freak: I was curious. I would ask questions about everything. All I could think of about a pussy. I wanted to know why she trembled like that, or why this lady wasn't responding. I would lay down on the bed or the floor and watch up close. Pretty soon, I was having a pussy eating contest with other women. Sometimes I was declared the winner and sometimes not. But I had fun trying. The icing was put on the cake when I saw a woman SQUIRT FOR THE FIRST TIME. This was my goal no matter what woman I put my hands on. Nat had an amazing way of teaching me things. She would suck on my nipples to teach me how my tongue should move on a clit or how much suction to apply. This was also a time in my life that I found out about how many women eat pussy and why they hide it. We as men have some fucked up mentalities about the needs of a WOMAN, but she does not want to be poked every night. Sometimes, she just wants to be held by someone as soft as her without having to fuck them. You know, that cuddling shit that they crave. From what I learned if you don't do it, her girlfriend will.

The studs in the clique gave me extra props, and they all wanted a dick this big. I told you that some of the parties got wild, and Nat was in the middle of everything, and so my dick was in the middle of everything. One party got a little wild, and a fight broke out, and a young man was hurt badly. It was my fault. At least that's what the police report said. The arresting officer used to work at my old high school, and he did me a solid. He arranged for me to get back in school and take the test for the Army. SOUND FAMILIAR? We have to reach back to try and help, so WE can move forward.

Speaking of reaching back, I had promised Nat that I would come back and get her and marry her after basic training. I did just that, and well…you know how that turned out.

Now back to these damn cops and robbers that have hijacked my fucking life. Just a couple of months ago, me and my kids were doing fine, and playing in the backyard with a water hose was like the most satisfying thing we could think of. And then we went into the house and had some Mac and Cheese with some Scott Peterson Polishes cut up in them—or Parker House (those were my favorite). Now here I am trying to make a list of the shit that may or may not save my life. Yes, I had my own agenda, but I wasn't telling them.

Pros and cons that was the way that I made my list. Right now the cons were winning by a lot. I was going to have to make a lot of sacrifices for this shit to work. Before long, I had a list of cons that almost killed me somehow. I listed the kids one name at a time, and I knew that I had 14 other reasons that I couldn't fail this test. The very first test would come tomorrow, and it had to be theatrical. I did my ROACHMAN thing early in the morning and came back to the block. By 2:30 p.m., I had my grill going and the music playing in the backyard. This brought out the neighbors in droves. One hour later, Big Fred showed up to pick up the payment on the loan. He had one of the Nation boys with him. Shit was in full swing. We were getting it in, and I told Fred that as soon as I flipped the meat that we could go upstairs to get his money.

Showtime. Big Fred thought about running, but he was in the yard with me, and there were too many police around for his big ass to run. Three police cars descended on my house, and Agent Hoyde racked that shot gun in my face. I thought Fred was going to shit in his pants. Agent Terrence James held up a warrant for my arrest and threw me on the ground. They told everyone else to step out of the yard and let them do their job. Officer Brown just milled through the crowd and asked questions, as he was keeping everybody back. Before long, "ghettovision" was live and in color. All my neighbors watched me lay on the ground as the FBI and the Police went up to search my apartment. I could hear certain conversations coming from those who were spectating. It ranged from, "James don't bother nobody..." to, "He must have some serious shit. He got Chicago police and the FBI on his ass..."

It didn't take long for them to come down the stairs with a clear plastic evidence bag I insisted on. All the Nation's money plus another grand to make the paperwork look good. Criminals always want to see paperwork about a case. I had arranged the money in the bag so it looked like it was more than it was. Also, there were two pistols; one was still in the box, and I wanted Fred to see it. He knew right away that it came from the Nation.

There are a lot of ways to make a man sweat, and I was turning the heat up on Fred and the Nation. Looking at their money and one of their guns going with the Feds brought sheer panic. I don't think he stayed for the rest of the arrest. I was sitting in lock up, waiting to go to court. Trust me when I tell you that the Feds have a lot better lock up facility than the Cook County Jail. Yeah, that Cook County Jail thing… It was dehumanizing. They would take a hundred men, sometimes more. They all had to stand on a yellow line naked. The guards would beat the hell out of a couple of detainees to intimidate the rest of the prisoners.

I wasn't your ordinary prisoner. I had no fear of violence, and all I wanted to do was sleep. I must have laid there and slept for 15 hours. I didn't even ask for a phone call. Agent Nora James came to get me the next morning. She took me to court, and I was given a $100,000 bond. This meant that I needed $10 grand to walk. I asked for my phone call and called Ms. Tanggy. I needed her to get a word to someone that I had $5 grand cash and I needed five more.

I went back to lock up and straight back to sleep in the same corner. It was around 10:30 p.m. when I got bailed out. Walter was there waiting on me. He hugged me so hard, and I hugged him back. We walked to the van, and Dee sprung out and gave me a big hug and asked if I was alright. It was more of a motherly ask. I assured her that I was fine and everything would be alright. I didn't tell Walter about the arrest because I needed his natural reaction when the police showed up. Oh my God, Walter did not disappoint! He put on a fucking show. Agent Horde had to point his shotgun at him and tell him to shut the fuck up. This helped to sell the authenticity of the arrest.

I got home to Big Fred sitting in a really nice, brand-new custom van across the street from my apartment. I went straight upstairs to grab some cash I had set aside for him. When I got in the van, he pulled off before I could get the door closed. I handed him the stack of cash, and he pulled over two blocks away. He turned on the interior lights, and we both turned in our seats. Now I knew that we had some company. The Prince and a bodyguard were sitting in the back. I started to get up to give him a pound, and the Prince waved me off and said, "Sit down," kind of like a request and an order at the same time.

Let's see how smart he really is… I had been doing my homework, and by all accounts, he was pretty sharp; private school educated and spoke with a soft business voice.

Fred set the money on the table and got out of the van. Next, it was the bodyguard leaving. This had to be serious; he wanted no witnesses to what he was saying. I explained that it was $4 grand on the table, and I would get the rest in the next two weeks. I was told, "I don't want your money, I want your help."

Okay, James, shut the fuck up and listen…

The Prince started speaking. He let me know that he knew about the classes in my basement, and he wanted it to continue. The only catch was, he needed it to be 10 students at a time, and he would sponsor books and supplies. He continued speaking and let me know that he was at the funeral, and that's how he found out about the basement. I knew that this was just small talk. He wanted something, and it was big. I just had to listen.

The Prince started asking about my military experience. Before I could answer, he held up his hands and stopped me from speaking and asked where his manners were. I was given a shot glass and then passed an unopened bottle of Martel with a blunt. He was honest and told me that Big Fred bought the bottle. He waited until I was settled as we both watched each other, one trying to gain an advantage over the other. His calmness was his gift. He just came out and asked, "How far away can you hit a target?"

I told him maybe 500 to a thousand yards. He smiled, and I had a clue what he wanted. He was looking for a hitman with some experience, which his people didn't have.

Silence was my best option, and I listened carefully. The Prince asked if I needed to keep the money. I didn't answer; I just gave him a look that said "everybody needs money." He said that he might have some things on the horizon that were a fit for someone of my talents. I had to ask what talents he thought that I had.

"Well," he began, "I have a need for a man who can ensure that another man got lost and didn't come home for dinner."

Since we were playing cat and mouse and I wanted the game to go on longer, I said, "Young people find lots of reasons not to come home. Some just fall in love and don't come back home. Some people take extra-long walks. Some people meet with accidents."

A small smile came across his face. I think that we had a deal. Now he stood to shake my hand. I returned the gesture, and we both sat and had a drink to celebrate our new deal. We talked shit and kicked the BOBOs for a minute, then it was time for me to exit. The Prince picked up the money and said that it was a down payment. I was wondering when this part was coming. I was given two small envelopes that were sealed. There was no way I was going to open it in front of him and let the shocked face out. There was no telling whose information or profile was in the envelopes. I took one more poor man's look around this luxurious-ass van and made my way to the door. Before exiting, the Prince called my name and said, "The bottle goes with you."

Smiling, I thought, *THIS MOTHER FUCKER IS TRYING TO PULL ME OVER TO HIS SIDE, THE WAY I WAS GOING TO PLAY HIM.*

He held out the bottle, and when I reached for it, he held on even tighter. Looking each other in the face with the lighting being just enough to read a man's eyes, the Prince said to me, "YOU DIDN'T GET TURNED IN THERE?"

Still holding on to the bottle, I reminded him, "I had to borrow money from the Nation to get the fuck out, so that's the deal I made." We were still holding the bottle and looking into deadly eyes. I knew that Fred and the bodyguard were back and standing at the door.

I opened the door right as the Prince tried to alert me to what he thought was an insurance policy: "I HEAR YOU ARE PRETTY FOND OF WALTER."

Well, that was that, and the Prince was standing there holding the top half of a bottle of Martel. I crushed the lower half with my bare hand and didn't even flinch as I told him, "I am good at my job. Don't make me work overtime."

The bottle breaking got the attention of the two outside, and they were quickly waved off. I started walking home when the van pulled up beside me, and the Prince holla'd out the window, "We shooting pool or playing bones in the morning, mother fucker?"

I yelled out, "Bones, bitch!" and that's when I knew that we were alright. But I still needed to be careful. Man, it felt good to be able to breathe a sigh of relief. Please, no more cops and robbers for the night…

Walking into the apartment, Dee and Walter both hugged me again. Ms. Dee held no punches.

"James, sit your ass down in this chair".

I sat down but not in the chair that she specified, and Ms. Dee said it again. So I got up and moved, as it didn't really matter to me where I sat. Maybe it did, because as soon as I sat down there was a mirror in front of me. I don't know how I didn't see it at first. She went on to recap the last 48 hours, and it didn't sound good. Her closing statement was: "AND YOU BORROWED MONEY FROM THE NATION TO GET OUT?"

It was look in the mirror or hold my head down and just let it slump there. It was easier to do my acting job than looking into that mirror or at them.

"James, you must be crazy if you think that I don't know who was in the back of that van." Ms. Dee sat next to me and grabbed my hands. She sat silent for a second and said, "That soft-spoken little man is the devil." It wasn't that I didn't believe her, but I could not at any cost tell her what was happening.

After the long lecture by the two of them, I was ready for a nap. I KNOW, I KNOW. I just slept 25 hours or more in the lock up. Didn't my mama say that I needed more rest than the average man?

Back to the yellow note pad again, there was way too much for me to keep up with. I phoned Sosa first and told him about the offer from the Prince, adding that I might want to pursue that angle, just to see where it would lead. Tomorrow was our meeting, and we were having it at Lieutenant Sosa's house in the Chatham neighborhood. It was a small little subdivision called Mary Nook. It was Mayberry for black folks. I left out the part about receiving my first assignment.

Now for the grand reveal. I opened up the envelope, and there sitting on top was the photograph of one of the ladies in the Nation Baby operation. The second was a bit of a shock. It was Finney.

Agent James was my next call, and she pretty much got the same run down as Lieutenant Sosa. Well, I could hear it in her voice. She was fishing for info on something else. I didn't know what to tell her. I figured it might have something to do with Officer Green, but I was not going to bump heads with the bull again. I was tired of the games, and I said so. Agent James said that she had not heard from Officer Green, or Ramona as she called her, since the day before just before the raid on my place. I had no answers and no clue. I had no inkling about her life other than coming for the two visits. I had my head down most of the time, so I didn't observe much. Agent James got off the phone more stressed than when she got on it. I made my last few notes but withheld the info that only I knew of. All I wanted was some more sleep. It was like I was hooked on it.

One last thing before bed—well, two, because I was going to try and finish this fat ass blunt that the Prince had handed me. The other was to square some things away with Walter. I knocked on his bedroom door, and he came out. I didn't even let him open his mouth. I handed him $5,000 and told him thank you. That was all I got out of my mouth before he was all over me. He was beside himself, and I didn't want that little gown he was wearing to ride up no more. Once he stopped jumping all around the kitchen and calmed down, I got to properly thank him for his help. Now it was me, a fat ass blunt, and the Spinners—yes, the Spinners. It didn't last long. I was asleep in the attic in less than 20 minutes.

By the time I came downstairs the next morning, Starbucks was in full swing, and the usual crew was there. Waving as I walked past to my room, I just kept going. I saw the clock, and it was 9:15 a.m., which meant Walter had taken the kids to school over an hour ago. Someone was knocking on the back door, and Big Fred asked if it was cool to come up. I said yes and made my way to the bathroom to brush my teeth and wash my ass. Walter made them feel right at home with some of the Starbucks charm attached. I tried to be as quick as I could. This might have to be a great acting job for me. The Prince had a smile on his face when he threatened my family last night. He was expecting me to be like the rest of the people in Moe Town. No, this was not that movie. I told the Prince that we were playing Dominos on the back porch. And then all the sudden, the devil jumped up in me, and I asked if everybody was comfortable and did they need anything. Big Fred opted for more coffee, and the Prince didn't need anything, so I asked Walter to show the Prince what the "house special" was, and he said, "No, because he can't handle the house special."

The Prince was now curious about the house special. He tapped his watch, and that was some sort of signal to Fred that he had something to do. Fred walked out of the door. We continued to play the game. The young man could slam some bones. He won three games to my one. Shit, we had just forgotten about the time. Upon leaving, the Prince didn't forget about the house special, and he asked what it was. Walter handed him a plate with the food covered up, and the Prince removed the napkin. There before his face was a straight razor. He stayed cool and said that was not funny, and I responded, "Well, we can both tell jokes." I asked, "How fond of Walter do you think I am?"

There was no more calm on his face. I told him that if he threatened my family again, Walter would serve him a cup of coffee. I think we had an understanding. I think that it fucked with his pride that a gay man made his balls shrink up. We finished our game and discussed what was in the envelope that he gave me. After that, he was gone with the quickness.

Ms. Dee was at my apartment as soon as she saw him leave, and she let me have it with both barrels.

"How the hell you let them niggas walk up in your house like they own the place, and we got to leave because behind your back, Fred's big ass was shooing us off like it was time to go!"

I didn't have a leg to stand on, so I let her go for the next five minutes telling me that this was my kids' house, but it wouldn't be if I kept letting mother fuckers like that come up in here. I took my lumps and said that I would be careful and try to do better. Dee thought it was because I left my job and needed money that I was hanging out with them. Ms. Dee reached in her back pocket and pulled out an envelope and said, "If you need money this what I have, and you can pay me back later."

She threw the envelope on the table and left my house in tears. Man, I was fucking crushed, and I couldn't let her down. Other than my mother giving birth to me, this was the single greatest act of kindness ever shown to me. Walter asked me if I knew what I was doing. He looked concerned as hell.

I got in my van to run some errands, and this damn thing was sounding bad as hell. I didn't know what was wrong, but I couldn't get one block without that noise. I pulled over to see what was wrong. I wasn't a mechanic, but it didn't take one to see that there was a belt that was going around and around, and it was damaged. I drove straight to Al "the Alley Mechanic" Mack on the next block, and he was full; maybe five hours before he could get to it, and I had to go get the belt. Al made a recommendation to go see Fatima around the corner. There were a few whistles and catcalls about that. I knew her; never did business with her, but I stood in the alley and smoked outside her garage shop and even bought her a 40-ounce on a hot day.

I got to her shop, and she was under a car doing whatever mechanics do under there. I called out to her, and she said, "Pass me that 10mm socket, and we can talk." I didn't know exactly which one to get, so I picked up about five sockets and read the markings on the side until I found the right one. Before I could hand it to her, she wanted to know, "Are you slow or what?"

I passed her the socket. She was under there turning some shit and then slowly slid out from the vehicle on one of those creepers. It wasn't my first time seeing her, but it seemed like it took forever for her to slide her big, fine ass from under there. I reached down to help her up, and I had to pull hard and show off a little masculinity. Once she was up, Fatima looked down at me and said, "What's up, ROACHMAN?" I was a little shocked to hear that, but I just took it and smiled.

Let me do my best to describe Fatima. She had this long, wavy hair and skin that looked like she spread it on herself. I'm talking about smooth like the singer Sade. She had her hair hanging in two ponytails. She was maybe a size 14 in jeans with about 44-double-Ds. The only thing was, she was 6 feet, 2 inches tall, and I was 5 feet 8 inches tall. She did what she normally did when men came to her shop. Fatima got close up on me and asked what I wanted. I told her about the belt, and she said if I went to get the belt, she could have it ready in two hours. I needed to step back a little bit to look up at her to answer. I don't know where she got those teeth, but they were perfect. I stepped back a second time because she came forward again. I asked her to back up, and she asked, "Are you scared?"

Hell no, I wasn't scared. But I was in her shop. I slid to the side, and she said the quicker I got back with the belt, the quicker she could be finished with my car. I stepped out of the garage and asked what the best place would be to get one, and she told me to go to Murry's on 63rd Street. I think she wanted to assert her dominance and said, "Hurry up, sweet cheeks." It didn't even faze me. I just wanted my van fixed.

I broke out running down the alley to start my journey. I ran all the way and stayed in the alleys to keep anyone from seeing me move that fast. I was there in a matter of minutes, and my brain turned on while I was standing in line to order and pay for the belt. Damn Fatima was really aggressive. Now that I think about it, every woman who approached me for sex was aggressive. Maybe that's what it was; they saw me as a challenge, or maybe they were Alpha women from the start or something. I had time to figure that out; it wasn't like I was going to give up sex tomorrow.

On my way back, my nose was on fire. It was the onions on the corner at the doughnut shop. I bought six Polish sausages with fries and a couple of those big-ass, Texas-sized doughnuts. Shit, I was in Chicago, and the food is just amazing. I ran back a little slower; it only took about six minutes. I had some bags. I got back to the garage shop, and Fatima was explaining to a lady that she just needed to keep her oil changed, and she should not have any problem. This was totally different customer service than I got.

After Fatima finished with her customer, I gave her the belt and some of the food for her and her assistant. He was an oil-covered, small guy who was just working for his next crack rock. Fatima said it must be time for a break. Her voice was like that of a soul singer, but it had a raspy kind of a sound to it. It was just sexy. Fatima moved some stuff off a workbench and told me to sit. It didn't sound like a request, so I sat. I could see her out of the corner of my eye, and she was watching like I was going to steal something; or I was going to be her next meal. Fatima cleaned her hands as I unwrapped my food, and just being nice, I unwrapped hers, too. I got a big smile for that as she sat next to me.

Fatima thanked me for the food, and she handed her helper some bills, and he clicked his heels together and was at the crack house. Fatima wanted to know about the ROACHMAN thing, and I told her about me leaving my job and wanting to be my own MAN. I got another big smile, and I wondered, *How the fuck did she get those teeth?* Well, mine are all bucked with a gap. This woman was something totally different. It wasn't just her size, but she had an IT factor, and I couldn't figure it out.

Fatima started balling up the cardboard tray the food was in and said that it was good and she appreciated it. I decided to push the buttons a little bit and asked if she was ready for her second Polish sausage.

"Fatima, you know I'm looking out for you," I said and handed her another Polish sausage and one of the doughnuts. Man, ain't nothing like feeding a big woman. Before I knew what was happening, she picked me up out of the chair and hugged me real hard. I made it easy for her by standing as she did it. Now it was my turn to see if all those legs rubbing together while we ate was real, and she couldn't deny the smell that was in my nose.

Reaching up, I grabbed both of those pony tails and pulled her down to my eye level and looked in her eyes. I saw just what Natalie and Clair told me to look for. She was willing to be dominated; she only wanted to be in charge in public because of her size. It was her defense to keep weaker men at bay. Pulling her close to me, I simply told her that I was in charge of all her ORGASMS for the rest of the day.

Fatima tried to stand, but I was too strong and held her in place. She sucked in a big breath of air and closed her eyes with her head down. She didn't move, but her body trembled once or twice. Still holding her hair, I whispered in her ear a second time. The small orgasm that she just got was on the house, and she had to earn the rest. I released her and demanded that she close up the shop.

The doors were closed, and she came and stood next to me. There was not one word spoken as I undressed her, trying to pay homage to those 44s. I had a trick up my sleeve. Fatima's skin was tight, and it was almost the color of a very light caramel. There were a few stretch marks, but a man is supposed to kiss those to let her know that you appreciate her bringing our futures into the world. Fatima wore some green lace underwear. I thought that was pretty sexy for a mechanic and such a full-size woman. I nodded, and she pulled down her panties nice and slow. That was probably the last slow thing that we did.

Fatima wore a shocked face as she was being manhandled, and it was driving her wild. That chocolate frosting from the doughnut took me a while to lick off her, especially after that third orgasm. She couldn't keep still. She was at least considerate enough to ask if I could breathe while she was riding my head. A woman with this much junk in the trunk is not going to ride your face. She is going to ride your whole damn head.

I told her to sit on the couch in the garage. It had been maybe 45 minutes, and I still had my pants on. She must have been enjoying her role because Fatima wanted to know in a very soft voice, could she pull my pants down? I nodded yes, and we both got a surprise. Her eyes went wide, and she was surprised at my size. Less than five minutes later, I was surprised. Fatima really could swallow a small log. This was turning into a great session, and I wanted to end this with a bang. Fatima found herself in the air for the next 15 minutes with her legs wrapped around me as I talked to her in a very calm voice that she was going to be with this dick until she said, "I don't want to play anymore." But for now, we both still wanted to play.

The garage door was loud as fuck, and we knew this was over for now. Fatima yelled at whoever was banging to come back in 20 minutes because she was having lunch. She wasn't lying; Fatima had literally ate my ass up. I started getting dressed, and Fatima told me that she wanted to see me again. I was game, and this was the most satisfying encounter that I had had in a while.

I put money down on the workbench for the van while she was letting the garage door back up. It was one of those that you have to lift up manually, and it was nothing to this healthy girl. Before any company came, she told me that she liked the fact that I knew to get her two Polishes. I wasn't expecting that, but Fatima was down to earth. You will be surprised at what turns a woman on. Fatima asked if I could do her one more favor before I left. Her voice got soft like a little girl, and she said, "Daddy, can you pick me up just one more time before you go?" It was my pleasure. Fatima wrapped her legs around me again and kissed me the whole time her feet were off the ground.

I went home to get a shower; Lord knows I needed one. I smoked a joint after my shower and went straight to bed. Yes, I was getting my fix of sleep. Man, this was the best drug ever.

Ms. Dee was sitting at the kitchen table when I came out of my room. She just wanted to talk, and I listened. It was more of a concern for me and the kids, and she apologized for yelling at me earlier. We hugged it out, and Dee knew that we would be fine. I told her that I needed to get dressed and pick up my van before my meeting. Ms. Dee laughed and told me that Queen Kong brought my van back about two hours ago. Then there was that laugh again as she saw me smile at that. Dee didn't hold back any punches.

"So you are Sumo Wrestling now? Don't lie to me, boy, both of y'all had the same goofy ass grin on your faces."

I wasn't throwing any fuel on that fire. I went on in the bathroom. It was a lot easier than putting up with Dee and her laughing. I called Agent Hoyde to see if he could be there a few minutes early because I wanted to pick his brains about the photos in the envelope. He suggested that we meet up before the meeting somewhere else. I left immediately and wanted to be on time. Agent Hoyde was not one to fool around with, and I wanted to impress him.

When I pulled into the vacant lot, Agent Hoyde climbed into the van and spoke in his no-nonsense voice, "What's going on, young man?"

I handed him the envelope, and he looked inside. He recognized Officer Finney right away. I explained this as best I could. Hoyde didn't have much facial expression, but I could tell that he was thinking, and he informed me that these were capital murder charges for whoever gave me that envelope. I nodded my head, hoping he knew more about the law than I did considering his profession. He said that it would be best to speak with Lieutenant Sosa and Agent James on the matter without the rest of the team. I agreed, and we left for the meeting at Sosa's house.

Sosa's home was something like a small palace; it had good size, but it was the artwork showcasing his Filipino and Cuban heritage that was impressive. Sosa started off the meeting with a prayer and informed us that our task was about to get bigger dealing with the Company. The lieutenant had done some digging of his own and said that at least seven other precincts were involved, and the money kicked way up to the top. He didn't know how high, but City Hall was where he could track it so far.

Each team member reported on their assignment. I watched Agent James as Officer Green got up to report that she had 33 families photographed with blood tests on the order. James was smiling, which told me that they were alright. Agent Oliver had a list of VINs that I got from Ptacc, and they were all registered to the Chicago Police department but one, which was registered to the ATF. Oliver told us that these vehicles leave the motor pool only once a week, and all at the same time. Six vehicles at a time and heavily armed. Agent Terrence James provided us with a list of officers that signed them out on a rotating shift. He told us that it is about 260-mile round trip, according to the logbooks. We just had to figure out where they were going.

I raised my hand like I was in class. Lieutenant Sosa called on me like he was the teacher. Everybody laughed, and we got on with the meeting. I said I knew where they were going and what they were picking up. Sosa waved his arms to get on with it.

"The next pick up is going to be in three days, and the product is cocaine and weed. They are going to a small port that's closed to make the pickup."

We had three days to come up with a game plan. I suggested that we do nothing but just follow the first shipment and get a handle on how they did things. Sosa wanted to start arresting dirty cops right away, but Agent Hoyde spoke up, endorsing my plan and adding a few more pointers. This agent was smart; it was his idea, and he told me to bring it up, and he would second it, and everyone else would agree.

Officer Brown came through with all the surveillance equipment that was needed. Man, I was in with all the gadgets that he had. This was his specialty with the force, and he appeared to be good at it. We were all issued cameras and told don't be afraid to run out of film because every photo could contain some type of evidence. Lieutenant Sosa asked us all to join him upstairs, where he had a feast prepared for us. The food was amazing; there was a beans and pepper dish that was to die for. I made sure that everyone understood that I was going to try and take home any leftovers. That statement alone was enough to start a riot with this group; these were all good-sized people.

Somehow, I ended up sitting between Sosa and Nora James. We got a chance to cover a lot of things about the cases, and Agent Hoyde was signaling me to say something, and the only thing that I could think of was the hits that I had in the envelopes. Maybe he changed his mind about keeping a lid on this thing, so I produced the envelopes and placed them on the table. The eating slowed down to a creep, and Agent James asked me if she should open the envelopes. I took that to indicate that she didn't want any more surprises, or trouble out of me. I explained to everybody there that this was the request that came from the Nation for bailing me out the other night. I put all the cards on the table. It took Sosa about one second to put Agent Terrance James and Agent Oliver on that assignment of having an exit plan in two days. He wanted those capital murder charges to stick, and he said exactly that.

Officer Green wanted to know, "Why her?" She was talking about the lady in the photo from the Nation Baby case. I explained that she orchestrated a robbery of one of the safe houses for $200 grand. Green asked if there was any proof. I told her what I knew about her buying a new Suzuki Sidekick two weeks prior. She worked for the Nation, and her boyfriend was missing for the last few days. Officer Green informed us that her team had just photographed her and her children, and she was talking about leaving if the government would look out for her and her kids. It drew some sympathy from around the room but not from Sosa. He looked at it as she was about to use us as a getaway vehicle. He was right, but we had to do something or the Nation would take care of it. Again, Agent Hoyde was right about his opinion. He was gaining my respect. Plus he was like my Uncle Robert; not a lot of words, but the ones he said mattered.

Finney that was another matter. He was crooked, and the whole room knew it. There was still a hired hit on a police officer's life, and we got a surprise out of Agent Terrance James: "I will pull the trigger myself," he said, and the room fell silent. He spoke up to say, "I worked a case about four years back about his crooked-ass, but we had to let him go because the witness refused to testify because he threatened them with sending all three of her sons to jail, and then he dumped a bunch of small bags of dope on her dining room table."

I told them that I had an out on making Officer Finney disappear. My problem now was that I didn't know what type of proof the Nation wanted as proof of death. I told them about the going to Memphis thing with Finney, and Agent Nora James looked me in my face and put me out there in front of the whole damn crew.

"Who the fuck are you and how do you know so much about all of this?"

Agent James went on to explain that there was over a hundred years of law enforcement in the room, but they had nowhere near the intelligence reports that I had, and I kept coming up with these little surprises that kept getting all of us deeper and deeper in shit.

"Is there something that you want to tell us, Mr. Madlock?" she asked.

"No ma'a,m I have been straight up with all of you, but I can't reveal where my info comes from or I'm shut out on that end."

"Well, how do you know that he wants to go to Memphis?"

I was upfront and told her that he and I had a talk in the park a couple of weeks ago. Agent James wanted to know if I knew anything about his injuries. I told her no. Officer Daniels and Oliver both spoke up and said that they were already injured when we met in the park because they ran tails on them. Even though Daniels was giving me cover, he didn't forget what he saw in the park and gave me a look of remembrance. I knew that there would be a tail on me because Agent James wanted to know what the fuck I was doing, and with whom. I thought she was finished, but now she threw my rap sheet and a FBI folder on the table and looked at me and said, "You do have a propensity for violence, Mr. Madlock. I see that's how you got into the military, and that's how you got out. Violence, Mr. Madlock. So is there anything you want to tell your teammates, who are putting their lives on the line for this information that you somehow keep manufacturing?"

I stood and addressed the squad and made my shit plain and clear that I was on the up and up about the information.

"You guys are the pros, and every bit of information has checked out without a hitch."

Agent James realized Officer Daniels said the word "they," and asked, "Who the hell is they? I thought you all just followed Finney since he was the only one that came up."

Agent Oliver explained about Officer Ptacc and all the stops he made with other officers who are believed to be a part of the Company.

"Am I missing something?" Agent James asked, but we knew that she didn't want an answer because she kept right on talking. "So you are running side missions with our guys without us knowing," she said, nodding towards Lieutenant Sosa. Oliver explained that it was his idea, and he included the whole thing in his report that was still at his house.. Wow, this dude was good. She asked in a knowing voice, "What type of shape was Officer Ptacc in when he came to the park?"

Daniels jumped in to say that he was on crutches, and he had a cast on his arm. It didn't escape Sosa that both of his officers who came to see me were now filing for disability and that didn't seem odd to anyone else in the room. We were just letting that one sink in, and Hoyde tried to bail me out by asking what they put on their police report. Sosa screamed, "Fuck the police report. This is bullshit. We know that there is something else going on here."

I stood at this point and let everyone in the room know that what I brought to the table was real, and Finney and Ptacc were bad cops who were no longer on the force.

"I'm not sorry about that," I said. "I can prove that all the facts that I bring to you are real, and I'm not a fake." Lieutenant Sosa didn't know that I had figured out that he was playing a game with me. "I would like all of us to try the desert that was prepared for us today by our host. But the only way we can do that is if all of you fail your next drug test."

Sosa said, "That it isn't for you. A few of the ex-officers at a retirement home have cancer. I made them a little something to help with the nausea that comes from chemotherapy treatments."

We all understood that and moved on to the next subject.

Officer Brown was given a nod by Agent James, and he stood and walked over to me and asked me to put my hands on the table. I complied and was searched by Oliver and given a complete electronic sweep of my body. The waves from the device he was using were so strong that when it was up around my face, the fillings in my mouth started rattling or something. When that was over, most stood around looking at each other. I made one thing clear: If I was not trusted in this room, then we could just pass up on the whole thing and I would find another way to work out the Nation Baby thing, and they could go at the Company alone without my inside information, but this was not my number one gripe. I put both hands in the air to show that I was umarmed. This was my message:

"THE NEXT COP WHO PULLS A GUN ON ME OR TRIES TO SEARCH ME LIKE A CRIMINAL WILL APPLY FOR DISABILITY." I winked blatantly at Lieutenant Sosa and gave Agent James a nod, then asked, "Who the fuck wants to retire early. It's real fucking easy to do; just distrust me one more fucking time, and I promise you all that I will do what I do and let the chips fall where they may."

Officer Green, who I knew was on my side, spoke first.

"How do you expect all of us to trust you when you are being so vague about your information, and you want us to believe that you are a drug sniffing dog, and you took a park bench apart with your hands!"

Okay, she was with either Oliver or Daniels while she was on her hiatus from Agent James because they were the only ones there when I broke the park bench. This was bad, and I needed to run before pussy or ego fucked up this mission. Yeah, I needed to get out of there right now, and then the thought went through my head two more times before I even offered an answer.

"What the fuck do you want from me. I can't give up my sources." I continued, "There is not one officer in this room who will give up an informant. And if you would, I suggest you get the hell up and leave now because you won't be worth a shit to the rest of the room."

Agent James chimed in for me to, "Sit your speech giving ass down, because ain't nobody going nowhere."

That broke the ice as Sosa broke out a bottle of the good shit, and Oliver went to his vehicle and came back with a bottle of scotch that I never heard of, and they all cheered for the bottle. It must be some cop or Irish shit that I didn't know about. It was strong and smooth at the same time. We toasted a couple of times, and people sort of broke out into different circles to discuss whatever. Sosa produced a second bottle of the same scotch, and I started to beg off on that. They all laughed and told me that one bottle was for the start of a mission, and the second bottle was for when it was over. I knew that this was some cop shit.

I made my way over to Officer Brown and struck up a conversation that had nothing to do with work. I wanted to know how I could get a hook up on a video camera in my bedroom. He thought I meant a hidden camera. I said, "No, that's not it. I want them to know." I made it clear that I wanted something on a tripod right in front of the bed. I wanted them to want to be there and smile for the camera, like me. Brown just shook his head and said he could hook me up for a small fee. We shook on it, and we both kind of drifted to other parts of the room.

Five shots in and ready to talk shit, Agent Nora James slid up to me just as I was getting some more of those beans.

"So you think you got everybody fooled? Well not me. You are working for somebody that we don't know about, and they are feeding you intel. You don't have to tell me that I'm right, just remember I have seen this system eat up a lot of talent. Bright young stars out of the military. They put them in some tough situations, and they burn the candle from both ends."

"Agent James, I got kicked out so that disqualifies me from the start."

She said, "I can read. You didn't get a dishonorable discharge. You received a general."

"Well, that doesn't get me no benefits and shit either, so come again."

She stopped and turned to me and grabbed both of my hands. I didn't even move because here came the serious shit. Agent James started going straight to the fact that they had careers and lives depending on me. That didn't worry me. I didn't have any intention of firing a gun or doing any damn thing else that would endanger me. While she was still holding my hands, she asked if I was a noble man. I didn't give an answer because I wasn't sure what a noble man was and made a mental note to look it up when I got home. I think that I got her meaning. I had heard the term a lot lately, and I needed to be sure.

Agent Hoyde made his way around the room like a politician. He made his way to me and said it just felt right to put the information out at that moment, and he wasn't trying to cross me or anything like that. He really wanted to know about the picnic bench and how those officers got hurt. There was somewhat of a standoff; I wasn't telling, and he was just as stubborn. We made plans to meet up at a later time and place. It didn't matter where we met, it was going to be the same answer unless he saw something with his own eyes that he could verify.

It was getting time for me to leave, and I still needed to thank Oliver for the assist on the Ptacc thing. He was standing all tight with Officer Green, and I knew from the body language that there was something going on, but it wasn't romantic. I told Oliver to make sure he gets that report in, and they both laughed, knowing that it was bullshit. They both asked me to have another shot with them to celebrate the fall of the Company. I did, and it went down smooth, but I was not in charge of making sure that the bottle was empty. Home was on my mind, and these cops had drinking on their minds. I made small talk around the room, trying to head to the door. Sosa stopped me and waved over Agent Nora James for what I thought would be a slight side bar. No, they both took control of an arm apiece and dragged me off to a side room, and the door was closed. Lieutenant Sosa spoke first, "Who the fuck are you working with that can take this crew down?"

I asked for clarification because I didn't quite get his meaning of "taking down the crew."

"If they are giving you this much information on the Company and we decide not to play ball with them, what do they have on us to either keep us quiet or shut us down?"

In my most calm and convincing voice I did my best to explain that I was working almost solo on my end and just happened to stumble up on the Company and wanted to do something about it. I really wasn't expecting them to believe me completely, but I did expect some trust to at least start out with. This interrogation went on for a few more minutes, and I had to excuse myself. I had one last meeting set up for the night, and I was hoping that I was being tailed. I needed to use the Feds to scare the Bejesus out of Ptacc.

Why was I meeting with Ptacc again after he had already tried to kill me in Bridgeport before? I think it was my way of making him think that I wasn't too bright or that he had the upper hand. I ran around the meeting place three different times, and on my second trip around, I saw Ptacc talking to a group of guys in two different cars that were parked next to each other. On my third trip around, one of the vehicles had pulled around to the alley in the back of the building, and the second was now parked about 30 feet in front of Ptacc. Once he went into the building, I needed to be fast and efficient. The vehicle held three occupants. Now two after I snatched open the back door and removed the skinny blond guy with the shotgun. He laid on the sidewalk, trying to continue breathing. He was hit in the chest about five times before his body hit the pavement, and now we were all in the front seat of the big Lincoln Town Car that they drove. I wish I could tell you that I had some smooth-ass martial arts moves and took them out, but it was quite the opposite. I swung at them both with all I had. It was very cramped in that front seat. One of these fat-ass, linguini-eating mother fuckers weighed over 300 pounds and had a large knife. The second one had a damn cattle prod. He hit me with it one time, and I think it charged me up to hit him a couple more times. They were both out and didn't stand a chance. I was stronger than both of them put together, and I had a pool ball in each hand. Those dudes tried to kill me the last time we met, and they were rude. They didn't introduce themselves. Well, I told them who I was even though they couldn't hear me. I told them that I was, "James David Madlock. Don't be fucking with me," in my Uncle Chester's voice and his fury.

Officer Brown had those long-ass lenses pointed at me with either a camera or some binoculars. Well, he and Agent James were going to get an eye full tonight, and this was going to go a long way with the squad. Yes, I found out that he was the nephew of Agent Nora James on her husband's side of the family. He and all the rest of the agents were borrowed from Indiana, just across the border. They didn't know how far the Company ran, so no chances were taken. No shots fired so far, and I wanted to keep it that way. This had to be done with the least bit of a threat to my life, and I really needed to get home to my kids.

The second vehicle was sitting at the corner with four guys, and they were deep in conversation. The military teaches a lot about distractions, and I needed it to be believable and real. Walking up to the front of the Caddy they were in, I took one of the pool balls and threw it into the front windshield. It had the force of way over a hundred miles an hour. The glass shattered in the front, flying everywhere. The sound was loud enough to be a concussion grenade, which was the effect that I was going for. All the occupants were disoriented, and now it was nighty-night for everybody. I started swinging those other two pool balls as I pulled each one out of the Caddy. The first was bleeding from the face from all the glass that shattered in the front seat. After that, it was wash, rinse, and repeat. There was not one skull in the group that could withstand the pressure of pool balls banging off their heads. So like I said, nighty-night.

I also knew that Agent James and Officer Brown wished they had some popcorn for the show that was going on. I knew for a fact that Sosa and James would enjoy the show. With full knowledge that Ptacc could not run, I stepped out of sight of the officers and hustled around the block and jumped in the back of their surveillance vehicle, which was a carpet cleaning truck. I need to talk to them about that.

"Not one person is out cleaning carpet at 12:45 a.m. Get another vehicle," I said. "Hell, that's how I spotted you!"

Officer Brown thought he was fast with pulling out his weapon until I was sitting next to him, asking him to put it back or I was going to introduce him to a pool ball. Agent James started screaming loud as hell that he knew that I had something in my hand because no person could fight like that or hit that hard. I said, "Lower your damn voice! You act like you're at a fucking concert."

Officer Brown was looking at me with the two pool balls in my hand, and he still had to ask, "You beat them with those damn pool balls?" The look on his face seemed to indicate that somehow he didn't agree or wanted to say something. I knew 100 percent that this was the time for him to shut his damn mouth. I had a ball in each hand, and my arms were already loose from all the swinging, and my adrenalin was pumping. *Breathe, breathe…* is what I was telling myself; *Calm down and do not hit this scary-ass white man.* I also needed to calm him down. He probably thought I might hit him for real.

"Now that I have us all on the same page, we needed to get a plan together. Yes I'm going to scare the life out of Ptacc." I needed them to be the officers that they were and just follow my lead. We walked into the building where Ptacc was waiting, and sure enough, there was the obligatory guy behind the door with a shotgun. I threw one of the pool balls and put a shattering hole in the door. The force made him a little disoriented, and I threw the second one and hit him in the chest as he came from behind the door. This was right about the time that Officer Brown drew his weapon after the fact for the second time in about five minutes. I told him to put it up; Ptacc was not going anywhere.

It was time for the formal introductions. Ptacc didn't want to hold his head up as he was being placed under arrest by the Feds. I sat his dirty ass in a chair and explained everything that I needed as far as routes, times, personnel, and how far this shit went up. Ptacc said that he wanted a lawyer. I turned and walked away to retrieve my pool balls. At this point, Officer Brown pretty much begged him to talk to me. I was not in a hurry. I already knew that Ptacc knew what I was capable of, but the begging by Brown was making him think twice. By the time I got back to the chair, he finally saw what I had in my hands. I sat on the floor in front of Ptacc. Taking my time to slowly unlace his shoes and remove them from his feet, I was sure that Ptacc would try to play hard ball until the pain came. One thing the world needs to know about police officers is that they are so tough when getting caught because they want to be arrested for their crimes. If caught red handed, with the police unions, they are going to get off, so they don't fear arrest like they fear justice and retribution. Well, tonight was retribution and a little revenge.

I left the pool balls laying on the ground next to his feet. I went and picked up a 4x4 that was lying in the corner. I think they used it to prop the door open. When I got back, I propped Officer Ptacc's feet up on the block of wood. I could smell the fear from his body. Even Agent James, who was a fan of the pool balls 10 minutes ago, had a look of concern for this lowlife cop.

I sat back on the floor with my legs folded like a child playing an innocent game. Asking the rhetorical question of, "Can you hear me?" he nodded in an affirmative, and I ripped off a piece of fabric from his jacket and asked Brown to put it in his mouth to keep down the noise.

Telling Ptacc how the game was going to go was incredibly enjoyable: "I ask you a question, and every time you tell me the truth, I will hit this piece of wood with the pool balls." Well, since he could no longer talk, he had to communicate with his eyes and head movement, with a little bit of moaning in between. "Now, if you lie to me, I'm going to hit your feet with the pool balls. And yes, I am going to hit both feet at the same time."

I just didn't have a lot of time, even as Officer Brown gave me one last look of "don't do it."

"Are you Officer Ptacc?" was my first question, and he nodded yes. I simply said that he got one right. When I raised both of my arms to a stretched position and looked into the eyes of Officer Ptacc, he was dead set on being a cripple for life. His face begged for mercy, and I gave him a gapped-tooth grin that had evil written all over it. I hit the wood with the pool balls simultaneously, one ball struck between his feet and the other on the left side, where I knew that the knee was bad.

The wood shattered. I didn't know that someone who was gagged could scream that loud until I realized that it was Officer Brown and Agent James who thought that I had hit Ptacc's feet with the balls. Their screams damn near sent all the air out of their bodies. My next statement made them suck it all back in.

"We have no more wood, so it looks like all of the blows have to go to your feet now." I reached up and put my hand over his mouth and asked, "Do we have to do this?" The cloth was removed. When I told him that he was now the property of the FBI and all questions would be answered, he nodded, his long black hair bobbing up and down furiously. Officer Brown wanted to record the statement and said he was going to his vehicle for a tape recorder. Right after he left out of the door, I nodded for Agent James to step off. Leaning into Ptacc, we had a private conversation with me holding one of the pool balls in my hand, and he told me everything that I wanted to know and then some. Just for effect, I tapped the pool balls on the ground to keep him focused. I made sure that our part of the conversation was to stay private for the moment. I needed to have my own ace in the hole.

It was time for me to leave. They knew their job better than I did. Lieutenant Sosa and Agent James were thrilled with the news that they had someone on the inside who was going to cooperate. I don't know how pleased they were about some of my other methods. I stayed for about 10 minutes of the first questions and was confident that Ptacc would be truthful because I was giving him a free ride in a getaway vehicle driven by the Feds. On my way out of the door, I had to borrow a flashlight from Agent James, so I could find my other pool ball. I came here with four, and I couldn't find the one that I threw into the car window. Officer Brown came out as I was looking for the pool ball and wanted to know how serious I was, and did I know that I was holding up traffic in the street? Brown told me that if I quit holding up traffic, he would buy me a new set tomorrow. Shit, I stopped looking and walked straight to my van. Officer Brown walked with me as he explained that he had video footage of what happened here tonight and wanted to know what I thought he should do with it. I just smiled and asked, "Is it worth having a pool ball fight with me?"

Officer Brown did the zipped lip thing and walked away. On his way to his vehicle, I said that I shoot pool almost every day. Man, I needed my fix. I was headed straight home to get me taken care of. The door to my van was barely closed before I was reaching under my seat for my drink. I let the window down because Brown was still talking and said, "We have had a hell of a night!" and reached through the window and snatched my bottle and turned it up. Looking over at me, he handed the bottle back and said, "You need to get some help with that anger thing."

I needed a shower, but I wanted to sleep, and I gave Walter the keys as soon as I hit the door and said that I was tired and he knew that I would not be around in the morning. I wanted to clear my head of today and focus on tomorrow. Closing the door, I had a great, big-ASS smile on my face, and it matched my thought, FATIMA. SWIM, SWIM, KICK. The water was extremely cold, and I was standing straight up in the bed, and Sosa and James were standing laughing at my reaction. I missed the blanket, and now I was standing in the middle of the bed with nothing but morning wood. I was yelling, "What the fuck you doing at my house this fucking early in the morning!"

Before they could answer, I was stepping down from the bed and grabbing my blanket to cover myself. As I walked past the two of them, I asked how the hell they got in my house. Agent James knew that this was a vulnerable time for me with no clothes and that this was the best time to take advantage of me. She hit my available wrist with a pair of cuffs, and it instantly locked, and there was a gun at the back of my head. I kneeled down and let her put the other cuff on. I was not going to fight this yet, but this bitch was going to learn not to pull a gun on me again. I was helped up and led to the bed and held on to the blanket. Agent James put a folder on the bed and asked in a forceful manner if I wanted to come clean, or would I like to spend the rest of my life in jail for attempted murder of a federal agent. I didn't know what she was referring to, but I was silent. Just trying to soak this shit all in.

Sosa didn't have time for the bullshit and said, "One of the guys in the car was undercover. Now he is in the hospital trying to breathe because you hit him in the chest several times with a fucking pool ball. He was the one with the shotgun."

I apologized about the gentleman being in the hospital, but added, "I was in a situation where I had to defend myself. Now I have a question: Did you two know about the undercover agent before last night's incident?"

The look on their faces said no. I was a captive audience to hear about all the departments she had checked with, and none of them had ever heard of me.

"But after last night, you have proved to be quite dangerous," she said.

I wasn't proud of the increase in violence that was now in my life, but what was I to do? I tried my best to say that I was sorry again and asked if we could do this later because it was way too early for this shit. I thought to myself, *Where in the hell is Walter?* I reasoned that maybe he had taken the kids to school. Sosa calmly walked over to the folder and picked it up and violently slammed it back down on the bed, screaming in a high pitched voice: "It is 3:30 p.m., and we have been back and forth for you to get your sleepy ass up since 9:00 a.m."

Shit maybe he went to get the kids, and that only made things look worse. Thinking quickly, I told them that I had a sleep disorder that can put me in a stupor, and I couldn't do anything about it. They didn't believe that either. I wasn't going to go through this all day and demanded that the cuffs be removed or I would crush both of them in the next 10 seconds. Agent James took her time walking up to me and saying something about turn around, and I did, but the only reason I did was to put the blanket over her head and pull her over close to Sosa, and I dragged him to the ground by his belt. It was a hard slam to the ground; his knees hit hard, and he damn near fainted. Agent James tried to wiggle out of the blanket, and I helped her by tossing her in the air. She hit the ceiling and then the bed. Once out from under the cover, Agent James saw things differently. I was holding her gun and one of my own.

"LET'S PLAY COPS AND ROBBERS." This was my comment after I had their attention. Sosa didn't look amused at all. Nora was looking up at me from the bed with the same bewildered look as Sosa, and then I realized that I was naked again. I now had three guns pointed at them. They were all loaded. Bitch and Butch were the wrong crowed for that. I tossed the revolver on the bed and reached for the blanket again. This time, I wrapped it around me and put one of my guns back on the nightstand. I was not going to harm them, and they were not going to harm me.

Speaking first, I told agent James that we needed to find a common ground about this trust shit, or the next time I was going to be issuing disability slips along with some pain. I made it clear to Agent James that her next move was to get these broken ass handcuffs off me. They both looked at the cuffs and then me. I held out one arm and held the blanket with the other. Sosa was forceful about his views on a truce and urged Agent James to do the same. She reluctantly agreed, and we knew that this was the last time that I was to be harassed or else. No one knew what the "or else" meant, but I don't think that we had volunteers to find out.

We discussed what it meant to have a man on the inside of the Company. Agent James wanted to stretch out the surveillance to follow at least five people per day. We could map out buyers, dealers, and even trace the money. I didn't want to sound too frantic, but I wanted to track the money with Officer Hoyde. I got a couple of suspicious looks at that point. I didn't give a damn what they thought. There was an agenda for everyone on the team. Sosa said he would have to see about that because I was not an officer. I didn't care what he thought I wanted to follow the money. Agent James again with distrust, and Sosa stopped rubbing his knees to move over in front of me, blocking the path to her. At this point, I was really getting frustrated with her and her antics. Only this time, she was right, and I said so.

Sosa brought us up to speed on the Nation Baby arrest, and none were teenagers. All six so far would be held without bail to give us more time to build cases. The whole conversation changed to some crazy talk about morals and the code of the job. Lieutenant Sosa kept talking, and I sat on my bed and rolled myself a joint. James was furious about the fact that I was about to do something illegal in their faces. She knew what the options were and dismissed herself from the room and said her goodbyes. I don't believe that she was down the steps good before Sosa sang a whole new tune. He was on some straight up macho shit and wanted to know what made me use pool balls. I said that it was a last-minute thought as I was leaving out the door. Explaining that I didn't know what I would do with them, they came in handy. Sosa asked me if I knew about Chops and

Lunch Meat, and I drew a blank as I reached for my lighter and instructed him to meet me on the back porch. Walking out the door, he said that Chops and Lunch Meat were the two guys in the front seat of the Lincoln. He said that they had 13 felony warrants, and they had a reputation for working guys over. I got dressed and met Lieutenant Sosa on the back porch. I just wanted to know about these fucking nicknames. Maybe black folks ain't the only ones. Letting up the windows for some circulation, I smelled weed. It was coming from behind me, and Sosa was puffing away. Those pool ball stories really fascinated him, and he wanted to know more, but I made it clear that it would not be the topic of discussion. Sosa passed me the joint and informed me that he was about three months in on his chemo treatments. This really changed things. I thought out loud and tried to apologize for saying it that way, but he stood proud and said that his partner died a year ago of AIDS and now he was leaving soon, too. I must have hugged Sosa five or six more times before we parted company and even when I walked him to his vehicle. I wasn't worried about the gay thing because this was a human thing. He also told me that the only reason that I know about his cancer was because I acted like I gave a fuck. Wow, such an important man, and no one cared. This was a human thing. His last words to me that day were to tell me that Ms. Diane was a nice lady, and she was not trying to trick me. I guess they were working together on the Nation Baby thing, and they had been talking about other shit.

There was no reason for me to do anything else for the day. I had already made plans to go back to bed. It was now 7:30 p.m., and I had been talking to the lieutenant for several hours, and I didn't feel like any company. Walter told me that I needed to go to the doctor about my sleep problem. That was fair on his part even though he didn't know the truth.

The phone rang, and it was Agent Nora James. She wanted to talk, too, and not at my house. Asking, "Can this wait until tomorrow?" she said no. We needed to meet right now. I put on black sneakers and a black jogging suit and left out the door. I kept my movement low key and mostly in the alleys. I didn't want to get seen moving this fast, and I needed to travel eight miles to the meeting place, and I wanted to beat her there and not let her see me. My van would have been spotted right away.

Agent James was giving instructions or something to two other people when I got there, and I knew she couldn't be trusted. I walked up to her about four minutes later and made it clear that I didn't have time for her distrustful bullshit and got on with the conversation. Agent James was very clear that I was to keep my distance from her and that she had two snipers watching. They would take me out if I decided to throw her in the air again. I had no more intentions on touching her or getting any closer. The conversation was straight forward, and Agent James laid out her argument about her distrust for me and what was going on with me and the case: "You came back from the dead. You are stronger than any person I have ever seen. You know shit that no one else knows about the police, and there are 12 different government departments that don't know who you are, and you can smell drugs from a mile away. Tell me again that you are working alone."

There was a lot of things to address, so I tried to start from the beginning.

"I really don't know what happened at the hospital," I explained. "Everything after that just sort of fell into my lap. The Nation Baby problem came out of me while trying to find a missing girl in the neighborhood. That happened right before the hospital thing, and Ptacc was the one who put me in the hospital."

Agent James wanted to know if that was why he now had a set of crutches. I made it clear that he was not on my radar until he tried to kill me a second time, and that's when he acquired crutches. Finney was her next stop, and I explained that he hit me with those rings on, and I didn't appreciate it.

"Is that when Sosa first sent for you?" I nodded yes, and she continued, "What about the day I saw you lift Big Fred? There were bruises on your ribs."

I responded by telling her, "Yes, it was his work, and I was not going to let anyone else put their hands on me under the auspices of being a fucking cop."

Agent James waved her arms in the air, and I knew it was to wave her guys off after I explained that, "When I walked out of that hospital, this was the shape my body was in. I just sort of fell into this information about the Company and wanted to do something about it."

She knew that I was telling her the truth as much as I could tell her. Agent James stepped closer to me, and I stepped back. She asked what was wrong, and I told her that I didn't want her snipers to get the wrong idea. It didn't stop her advance towards me, and I just sort of froze. Agent James grabbed my hands again, holding on for dear life, and she said, "You really are real." I had no idea what that meant, but she started talking about being a noble man again and that her and her team would give me their loyal support.

Well, someone had to break up this sobbing shit, or I was going to throw the fuck up. It was time for me to go because I now had a police lieutenant pouring his heart out to me, and now this tough-ass FBI agent swearing loyalty to me. I still hadn't told her about the fact that she was going to have to uncuff her snipers; one from a tree, and the other from his steering wheel.

There was one last bit of information that we needed to discuss. Captain Mathew Holmes. He was Sosa's boss and currently running two precincts because of a freeze on promotions, and we knew that he was one of the cogs that ran to City Hall. She said that it was delicate, and we couldn't let on that Sosa was involved, or he would be transferred immediately. I saw it on her face; she was almost overwhelmed with problems. Agent James slumped her head and put her face in her hands and started to ask a question that I can't tell you what it was because once her hands went up, I was gone. She removed her hands and found out that there was no me to talk to.

Twelve minutes later, I was rounding the corner to my house, and again, I was going to sleep, and no one was going to stop me but Ms. Diane, sitting on my back porch with some flowers and a card. I didn't see the card at first. They were presented simultaneously with an apology. I wasn't going to be rude, but this was not on my radar at the time, and I invited her upstairs. She went in first, and I had to watch her temptation shake all the way up the stairs. I was going to be strong and not jump my dumb ass back into the fire.

We went into the dining room to talk where I knew the kids could be a distraction and Walter was floating around the apartment. The look of exhaustion on her face was enough for me. Diane started off with another apology, and I didn't have to worry about the tears because there were too many eyes watching. Trying a different approach, Diane said that the flowers were from Tanggy and the tickets in the envelope were from her. I didn't want to be too non-responsive, so I opened the card, and it had an apology written in crayon. It said, "Will you please go on a date with us? Please mark yes or no," with boxes for each and a box for "maybe." There was also a crayon to mark my answer with. I have no idea if I was being too harsh when I checked the box that said maybe.

Ms. Diane stood and said, "I guess we have to work a little bit harder for your attention." That was far from the truth. I just wanted to be in a situation where we could all trust each other.

She started to walk to the front door for her exit. I had every intention of letting her know that I was not being a hard ass. Do you know how many men the Nation has killed over the years? Stepping into the hall leading down the steps, Diane decided to sit where she was on the top step, and I joined her. We didn't have much room sitting side-by-side, but it was cool and cozy. Diane stopped me from talking, not with a kiss but with her voice and its seriousness. She told me that Ms. Tanggy had to break this all down for her that they had sent me to get a child back from the worst street gang in America, and I got that child back home without one problem. Now I was trying to help with the Nation Babies, and they did it all under the pretenses of really liking me and pussy. It was acknowledged at that point that she was not trying to trick me. She said that things got out of hand and started to move sort of fast, and they had no idea that I was going to bring all these police and the FBI. I should have been up front and let her know that I didn't know either. It just sort of happened. We hugged, and I told her that we just needed to work through the problems, but I needed to keep my distance. I could feel her body tense up when I said that I needed to keep my distance.

I was released about 10 seconds later, and we were looking into each other's eyes. Diane wanted to know why it was that a man could show up with flowers and an apology and all would be forgiven. Just for effect, she threw in the fact that she had concert tickets to see the Spinners and the O'Jays along with Franky Beverly and Maze. I had to make it clear that I was not turning down their peace offering; I was turning down the piece that they offered under false pretense.

Diane and I talked for about an hour. There were things explained and broken down to me about women, that when all else fails, they turn to the one thing that their grandmothers, mothers, aunts, and older cousins had explained to them for years. If all else fails, turn to the secret weapon. At this point we were still sitting, and she asked me to stand and she raised her right hand in the air and moved it slightly to keep my attention and repeated the statement.

"IF ALL ELSE FAILS, USE THE SECRET WEAPON."

I still heard the same statement and didn't have any more of an understanding. She repeated it for a third time, and I saw her left arm moving, but her right hand was still holding my attention. On the fourth time, she said it, "IF ALL ELSE FAILS, USE THE SECRET WEAPON," this time I followed her left hand, and it was circling over her crotch area like it was a magic orb or something. Wow, sometimes you have to break down the deception for us men like we are five-year-olds. I was allowed to ask questions along the way. The part that got me the most she called it "THE DO OVER."

I had a million questions about the do over. It was basically when a woman had taken the wrong path with a man and pretty much messed her life up, there was always the dude who liked her for years, and she would now conform to him to get her life back on track. It was usually some nice guy who was not so cool and worked hard and thought she was his reward for doing the right shit in life. She said that some of these women could keep up this act for years, and some couldn't pull it off for a week. I was told that some of these women grew to love them, and some grew to hate them. It was all about getting that roof over their heads and getting that loser's kids fed. It wasn't lost on me that I was still young as far as life's experiences go. I was willing to learn, but not at the expense of my life. I wanted to know if she and I were past that phase in our relationship.

Diane told me that she was never sleeping with me for favors. For her, it was the character that I had shown her, and that was seen by others, and it was obvious to her and them that they were not wrong. To me, it wasn't about right or wrong, it was about staying alive. All the facts in the world can't save me if I don't have my mind together, and one of these Nation members got some bonus points for putting a bullet in me.

On her way out of the door, Diane had one more message to deliver: "Tanggy said she can't wait to get her hands on you again."

I had one more question.

"So why didn't you explain to me about the two pussy tricks?"

Diane looked at the floor and then back up at me.

"It's not a trick. We both want you." That was her reply with a straight face. I didn't drink the whole cup of Kool-Aid. I just took a big sip. Diane told me that the concert was two weeks away, and I could think about it until then. The door was closed, and I could still hear her saying goodbye.

I must have slept great because I was up and around the house before Walter and the kids got up. He told me that he was taking the kids to school because he had some errands to run. I had no problems with it, and I was out on the hunt in the neighborhood, letting everyone within the sound of my voice know: "ROACHMAN, ROACHMAN! GET YOUR HOUSE EXTERMINATED FOR $30! ROACHMAN, ROACHMAN!"

I didn't know if I was going to get two customers or 20; I was going to do the whole day. It felt good to be back doing my own thing, and I got four customers and some enquiries on future work, so I left them with some of the altered flyers that Walter and the kids made up for me. I guess some jokes are just too funny to pass up, so I heard from the side of me "ROACHMAN" in a smooth voice, like they were almost trying to whisper or make a joke. I knew who it was in the back of the van and who was driving. I just didn't have time for the bullshit.

The Prince got out and walked with me for half of a block, and I was given instructions on a hit for three days. Getting this info, I had to cut my workday short and get this to the two heads of this squad. There was an emergency meeting called for 5:00 p.m., and we were all given the address. I had about three hours to kill and decided I would not torture myself any longer and went over to the garage where Fatima had her , and the first look that I got was not pleasant. I think the pizza box that contained the deep-dish pizza from Giordano's may have had something to do with her smile. I saw it coming before it happened. I had to brace for contact as the distance between us closed, and I had not moved. The softness of her body was something I had no problem feeling. I believe it to be true that a lesser man would have been smashed up against the wall. I don't think she cared that there was a customer in the shop along with her helper. The embrace was nice, but she had a look on her face as if something was missing, and I went right into action, lifting her off the ground. I heard a little girl laugh and realized it was Fatima just enjoying herself. I had to pick the pizza box up off the ground. I wasn't about to let her smash the pizza.

Fatima took a break, and we all ate some pizza. She and I sat in the same place as before at her work bench as her customer and the assistant sat on the old couch that I had a fond memory of. We whispered for a few minutes and swap a 40-ounce. I think it was the third time that Fatima warned me about the backwash as we shared the Colt 45 Malt Liquor. We made plans to go out to eat tomorrow evening after we both finished work. Nothing had changed; our legs were rubbing together under the bench. She gave me that smile, and those teeth were just as pretty as ever, and I told her so. This brought on another smile. From the look on her face, I knew what was going on. She was doing what most women do. She had started a relationship in her head and didn't tell me. This told me that we really needed to sit down and talk. I wasn't trying to be rude; It's just that I was damaged property. I was not ready for all of that, and she needed to know. There was also my side hustle. Which reminds me, I had a little rendezvous with Mrs. Bell, who paid up front and doubled it.

Needing to go get ready for my meeting, I said my goodbyes. The meeting was at a new spot, at some storefront that the FBI had to assemble for their raids and a surveillance hide out. Once everyone got settled, it was right down to business. The first hit was Officer Finney. The Prince wanted it public for proof of death, and he wanted it to send a message. Lieutenant Sosa and Agent James both gave their spiel about how important it was that we didn't fuck this up. Agent Hoyde was again right on the money with making it a family outing, and we needed some collateral damage to make it look real. It was decided that it would be him loading bags into the trunk of the car on a shopping venture with his family. "The Chameleon," Agent Oliver, was going to be the one who would be shot in the leg as he was walking past. The news coverage would be huge, and a closed casket funeral would be required because of the shotgun blast to the face. I told them that we needed to contact Officer Finney and finalize it. We knew that Agent James had this covered. It was her type of thing to just be in charge. To her, we were all her children. It just took me a little while to understand it. We had a couple of days to work out the small stuff.

I'm not sure who in the room was the most frantic to talk about the Company. There was so much information that it took almost two hours for each person to lay it all out. The increased surveillance had every officer in the room talking. I was most surprised that they were this naïve about the crooked shit that cops do and how careless they were. These were Chi-Towns finest. It was a feeling of not being able to be touched because you controlled the city. That was about to change.

The younger Agent James gave his report with a lump in his throat about what he had seen in just two days. This was now personal; he had watched police brutality and drug deliveries out the back of police vehicles. Agent James said that he saw two cops drop off drugs and then rob the courier 20 minutes later and drop off the drugs to another spot. Officer Green had a similar story, only the difference was it was one of her ex-partners who had hit a kid with a knight stick across his legs until he told where they were going to stash the drugs, so they could rob them later. Oliver brought another problem to the table. He followed some cops to what appeared to be a flop house for the Company. Wine, women, and song was the theme at this circus. It was part of the perks for being a part of the Company and being loyal. Officer Brown had tracking devices on the vehicles that would be used for the big trip out of town to retrieve the shipments.

Now for the icing on the cake. It was Agent Hoyde who figured out where the money was being stashed. I saw Agent James look over at me as I sat up in my chair, and she shook her head no. I didn't give a shit about her head shaking. They were all being paid by the government, and no one was handing me a dime. What the fuck was I going to do with a pat on the back and a few shots of some whiskey to celebrate? I needed a soft place for my kids and me to land, and a soft pile of CASH would do the trick. Agent James stopped Agent Hoyde from talking before he could divulge the information about the location.

This made me mad as hell, and I was not going to hold my tongue about it. I made it clear that, "I put my ass on the line to get this intel. Now you want to play games about info in front of me like I need a fucking security clearance to be in this bitch?" No one else in the room picked up on what she did until I said something. There was a slight rumble in the room, which told me that they didn't all agree.

"Before you give another speech, we don't need any unforeseen thing to happen."

Trying to calm down I said, "This whole operation is unforeseen, and how the hell am I going to rob a place with six armed cops there at all times and it's in the bottom of a police annex?" I'm sorry; I just had to get that out. She was being a real bitch, period.

The lieutenant jumped right in before anyone else, asking, "How the hell did you know where the money was when Agent Hoyde didn't say where it was?"

I gave him the finger, too. I couldn't wait to put the screws to the whole damn crew.

"I will be right here on Friday evening when all of you get paid. If no one stops by to split their paycheck with me, then shut the fuck up about crooked-ass money and crooked cops. Yes, my children have to eat, too. Plus I have tuition to pay."

Officer Daniels suggested that we go about this another way. I didn't respond with just a finger. Daniels was not backing down and let me know that they weren't those types of cops. He said that this was the reason that they were all here, to stop corruption. I said to Agent James that she needed to get on her job and stop all these damn speeches. I guess a little humor didn't hurt, and Daniels told me he understood my need, but he wasn't there for a robbery. Shit, it had to be clear that I didn't come to this table for a robbery. I was just going with the flow. And this shit presented itself to me.

Sosa said that he had a solution to the problem. The Whistleblower Program. It was a government program where a person turned in crooked cops or employees cheating the government, so that I could get 10 percent of whatever was recovered. That sounded good, and I was for it publicly.

Agent James asked me to raise my right hand, so she could do some slick-ass deputizing shit, and I wasn't raising my hand. She said she was not trying to deputize me; she just wanted me to promise that no one would show up with pool balls. I just told you that humor didn't hurt because the whole damn room thought this was funny. Officer Brown stood like he had a fucking speech to give. He even put his hand over his heart for effect.

"Well, I might be an accessory to robbery…" Then he reached down next to his seat and grabbed a bag with my new pool balls in it. Once he threw it on the table and the contents came out, there was more laughter.

Agent James screamed for everyone to shut the fuck up. I think Brown was going to explain why he bought them. She told him in particular to shut the fuck up. Agent James was holding her head as if she was having a migraine headache.

"He just beat the shit out of seven people with balls, one of which was an agent," she said. "And your dumb ass bought him a new set?"

The mood in the room was serious, so no one just laughed out loud, but it became hard to hold in. Brown looked at the floor while the snickers were going on, he said in a weak voice, "He lost one the other night..."

Agent James didn't quite hear what he said and asked him to repeat his statement.

Officer Brown held his head up and repeated the statement: "He lost one of his pool balls the other night."

"GET THE FUCK OUT, RIGHT NOW." Agent James was on fire, and the laughter was way out of control. Once the bullshit stopped, we got down to business about the Hit and the tails that would be put on the Company. No one was to make contact or an arrest. We could all follow from a distance and take plenty of photographs. Brown instructed us to get photos of diners that they stopped in to eat or gas stations. We could use their employees as witnesses. We needed to establish a frequency of travel and routes. There was more to these investigations than I knew, and they were serious about it. I got a firsthand look at why they were picked for the job.

No matter what, they were still cops, and the bottles came out. I found out that the store front had quite a few rooms in the back with a kitchen and two bedrooms for overnight shift work. Another 20 minutes, and I was ready to leave. I had my assignment for tomorrow. Agent James made it clear that she needed to speak with me after the meeting was over. I didn't have a problem with it, but I had another situation that was pressing at the moment. My nose was doing something that was driving me nuts. I needed to get away from Agent James, and the storefront was in a part of town called Hyde Park, and that Harold's Chicken was smelling awfully good to me, and there was a Ribs and Bibs on the corner. I was hungry. She was delaying something important. Sosa also wanted a word, and he told me that he would do whatever he could to get me some type of compensation for my work. I thanked him.

Now Agent James was leading me to the door. I was told to meet her at Officer Green's house in one hour. Looking over my shoulder. I was looking for Officer Green to get some type of confirmation on this from

Green, but she was nowhere to be found. Agent James said that she was in the back, and I could go back there and confirm if I needed to.

I walked out the door and went straight to Ribs and Bibs to get two large rib tips and sausage combos with mild sauce. It was sort of crowded, so I ran over to Harold's to order six wings and a half order of white meat with mild sauce. If you are not from Chicago, then you might not understand this mild sauce thing. Just so that we are clear, you might get your ass whooped for saying the wrong thing about it.

I gathered all the food and headed to my next destination with sticky fingers. I was digging in the bags as I drove. I was trying to think while I drove. Agent James had a smell of arousal to her, but that ain't what this shit was about. This woman couldn't stand me. We just had a working angle that somehow worked with a lot of bumps in the road. I got to the house, and the front door was open, and I didn't have a gun. I needed a plan and quick.

Pushing the door open slowly, it was sort of dark. There was one light on in the corner. It may have been a waste of good food. I was winding up to throw that food and attack after the food. At this point, I was too far into the house to retreat, and I had to move fast.

"SIT YOUR SCAREDY-ASS DOWN!" It was Agent James sitting over in the corner with a cigar in her mouth. I could see the red heat from the end as she took another puff. I wanted to know what she was doing sitting here in the dark. Agent James ordered me to put the bag on the table and have a seat. Surveying the room, I was just trying to find a safe seat. She was sitting there in what appeared to be a short men's bathrobe. I think I was being outclassed. I sat in the one single chair in the room.

My eyes were adjusting to the low light, and I realized she was wearing a smoking jacket with an ascott around her neck. The only reason I knew what it was because of those old Sanford and Sons shows. I didn't have money, and I didn't come from it. I think Nora was really enjoying seeing me on pins and needles. Well, that was not something that was happening; I was just playing my hand close to the vest.

No…that's not true. I was nervous as hell!

The music was nice and soothing; some dude named Kenny G. He was smooth, and Nora offered me a cigar. I declined it. Somehow I never got the hang of them. Pulling out my own joint got a frown, but she said, "Suit yourself." I didn't turn down the Johnny Walker Black that sat in the middle of the table. We toasted a shot together, and she said, "To good pussy."

I didn't want to be rude, so I said, "To good pussy," too.

She was ready to talk, and five or six shots in for the night. Nora told me that she wanted to see me use the dick that she saw this morning. It had been on her mind all day, and Ramona talked about it like it had a gold tip on it. She smiled at me and said that she might even come to one of my shows. Now I had that shocked look on my face. I was reminded that she was the FBI, and there was nothing she couldn't find out about me.

The talking stopped because the focus of the evening had just started walking down the stairs. Red heels were the first thing we saw. The legs went on forever. She kept coming down, and we were treated to sexiness; a red and black lace panty and bra set. That was amazing on a woman who came with her A-game tonight. The hair and makeup were flawless. She walked right past me to sit on Nora's lap, making a show out of crossing those long-ass runner's legs.

"So do we get a free show, or are you going to charge us, too?"

There wasn't even time to answer. Ramona reached in her bra and pulled out three $100 bills, threw them on the table, and said, "Do you mind singing for your supper?"

At that point, I should have run like the Gingerbread Man. I was about to stick my business in a situation where guns were involved. That ego shit kicked in, along with the Johnny Walker Black. I stood up and started to disrobe and make a show of it. Oh yeah, I flexed my muscles as I went. And right before I unveiled the package, I yelled, "Showtime!"

Nora didn't bat an eye. Patting Romona on the ass was her cue to get up. We started nice and slow to the music. It was a great slow dance, which brought Nora a little closer. Sitting on the edge of her seat. I was going for the kill right up front. Lifting Ramona up and turning her upside down, we became each other's meal. No one sits on their hands when I perform, and tonight, the FBI would not be an exception. Dipping Ramona's body over and bending down, I was able to make sure that Nora and I were eating from the same bowl. I used one hand to pull her face further into the bowl. A few minutes later, all I did was stand up and walk towards the steps with the bowl, and I had a faithful follower.

At 2:38 a.m., I got a chance to sit down and eat. Food, that is. Ramona was trying to feed me food and laughing her ass off about the treatment that Butch got. Yes, I beat that thang into a coma. At one point, I sat her in my lap to ride facing Ramona, and she sat on the floor and ate from the bowl. Actually, that was the first time Nora passed out. It was pillow talk time, and I wanted to know how they got together and who approached who first. They were taking a three-day law enforcement class to become instructors. She was away from home and was horny and targeted herself an agent. One hour after the first day was over, it was on. That was six years ago, and it had been good. They were free to date on the side since neither of them has a dick, but they have a collection of toys. I didn't think she was into men and said so. Ramona knocked on my head like it was a block of thick wood.

"Yo, is there anyone home? She has two daughters and was married for 11 years. Her husband passed away in the line of duty." We went one more round before I left, and Nora woke up just in time to find out that I did not change my diet.

Getting home was a thing of beauty. I was floating on cloud nine. My EGO was high, and I did'nt feel tired. In fact, I was feeling good as the sun came up. The shower before I left is the type of thing that makes a man want to come back to see a woman. Officer Green just let me stand there under the hot water and washed me with care and passion. OH, just for the record, when I say hot water running, I mean what a man can stand; not that scalding shit you women can stand.

I was in my running shoes by 5:45 a.m. and on my run. It was the recon for sure on the Nation and to get myself calmed down. I was pumped and ready for the day. I saw two spots that were getting that early morning crowd. I was on Cottage Grove down the street from Hales Franciscan High School, and I just stood as though I was waiting on the bus. The Projects across the street were buzzing. It pissed me off to see the local gangbangers shake down the Catholic school boys for their lunch money. I just had to mind my business and stay focused. The second spot was on Ashland and 63rd Street, under the train tracks. These young drug dealers had 40 adults standing in line. Teenagers were telling them what to do. This shit was unreal. I had no idea this type of thing was going on and how I did not see it before. Maybe I was like the rest of society, too busy trying to make a living to see the carnage that this CRACK MONSTER was doing to us. My eyes were now open, and I needed to leave because it was becoming emotional.

By the time I got home, the Feds were sitting about a block away on two different streets. This was going to be a busy day, and I was almost ready to get on my hustle. One joint, some breakfast, and a shower later, I was getting ready to leave when Walter said to me that they would be here in two hours. I told him that I knew, and everything was ready. The "they" Walter spoke of were the Madlock men. I needed help. There were a lot of those cops and one of me. I needed to be in a lot of places at one time. But for now, I still had to still earn a living.

"ROACHMAN, ROACHMAN! GET YOUR HOUSE EXTERMINATED FOR $30! ROACHMAN, ROACHMAN!"

I got my first one on Justine Street, and it was for roaches and mice. I made quick work of it and moved on. By noon, I had done three other places, and there was a small grocery store that wanted me to come back on Saturday after closing for a large rodent issue. I was happy, and it was time to head home and get ready for my date with Fatima. The Feds were still following me, and I was going to show them a good time.

Parked on the side of my house was JOY and PAIN. There was a long Cadillac Fleetwood and a Grand Prix, both with Missouri tags. This was family. I almost ran up the stairs. The first face that I saw was Uncle Shorty. He matched his name. Standing about 5 feet, 4 inches tall, he was a different type of man. He was built for the streets and the hustle. Rumor has it that he only had one job in his life. It was at the Fox Theater in St. Louis. It was said that he got his first paycheck and made a down payment on a Cadillac, and he had been pimping and running gambling houses ever since. We hugged and jumped up and down. He had two of his brothers with him, an ex-boxer named Molly, and Uncle Chester.

We were finished with all of the greetings, or so I thought, until I saw his young ass come out of my weight room. It was Poochie, my little cousin. This fat-ass kid was the busiest damn kid. I guess he wasn't a kid anymore; he was on a big boy mission. We exchanged hugs, and he whispered in my ear, "When are we going to get them Jew Town Polishes?" I had a meeting to conduct, and his fat ass was looking for food. I made it clear that we were going to get there. By the way, this was Shorty Long's son.

I got us all in the living room around the pool table to lay out the plan for later. We just needed to be on time and not sloppy. Uncle Chester was first to ask about the police and how many. I told him that it was six at the annex and the two that would be trailing me. He opened his jacket and removed twin .45 automatics and a sawed-off 12-guage that was strapped to his body with a leather strap. There was a grin on his face when I said this was going to happen without a shot fired. Shorty Long reached in his coat for the .357 with a 12-inch barrel on it. I tried not to laugh. The gun was more than a quarter of his height.

Poochie was next, and he showed his age by producing two 9mm and said, "My daddy said it might be trouble." Those toys were all the rage with the younger generation. Uncle Molly said not to worry; he had a handle on them, and no one was to have a drink until this shit was over.

I needed to get ready for my date. There was noise at the front door, and I almost lost my mind. It was more family, and where did they come from? It was Johnny Rhodes and his brother June. June didn't say much. He just backed his brother's play. They were like an old married couple. Somehow you knew that they would be together for life. They were cousins from the Cabrini Greens Projects, and this was a problem. Johnny was the other bookend to my Uncle Chester. He was not alone. Uncle Roosevelt from Georgia was there, and he carried a bag. A big bag, and I didn't want to know what was in the bag. Last but not least was Willie and Mack. They were brothers. When my family left the Lee Plantation down in the Mississippi Delta, they came with my family. Shooters, flat out shooters.

After about five minutes of hugs and handshakes, I got everybody settled. It became a fucking joke about how many guns were on the table. Willie and Mack preferred their work close up, so they both had a set of .44s, and Uncle Roosevelt was not carrying; his was in the bag. Johnny Rhodes had two pistol grip sawed-off shotguns. I wanted to call this shit off. I didn't call them, and I wanted to know who the fuck did. No one spoke up at first. Uncle Chester said he worked better knowing that Willie and Mack had his back. Lil Poochie spoke up and said, "I was rolling with my daddy, and he said you had some trouble with somebody named the Prince. And we are going to see if this mother fucker can sing or play guitar?"

The whole room started laughing as I looked over at Walter. He looked at the ground. I knew who sent out the red alert. Once the room got quiet again, I did my best to explain the situation. This job was set up to need only four people. Any more than that would be overkill, and we ran the risk of being caught. The snicker and laughing coming from behind me was getting on my nerves. It was coming from Willie Riggins. I turned around to see his signature hat cocked to the side. He wore one of those big-ass Godfather hats. He and Shorty Long were deep into something. I stopped talking to let them have the floor, or at least tell us what was so damn funny. They were laughing at me, "Little James." I didn't know that I was about to lose control of my meeting.

They started telling jokes about me and my first hustle with them. I was the runner at my Uncle Shorty's Crap house. They would shoot dice on the first floor. It was Uncle Molly's apartment, and I had to take the cut money upstairs to my Uncle Zo's apartment. I was scared as shit when Willie handed me the Saturday Night Special. He said where the bag goes, the pistol goes. I put the gun in the bag, and laughter was all in my face. Willie wanted to know why I put the gun in the bag. I responded that the gun went with the bag. He said, "Yes, but not in the bag! If you get robbed, they are going to get the bag and your gun." I was 13 years old, and they started laughing, just like they were doing now.

I got them to settle down after a few more jokes, and Mack said, "Little James, you running your own hustle." Didn't they know that I was going to grow up at some point? Explaining that the thing with the Prince and his boys didn't have anything to do with this, we were not at war, I let them know this was about the police and the police only. It was a separate matter that we could discuss later. Right now, it was time to get ready for my date and for those on this mission to get to work.

Right after, the next fucking interruption of my screen door being banged on occurred, and it was Tommy Rivers from Napp Town and Uncle Tommy Lee from Mississippi. They came on up the stairs, and the whole apartment was a buzz again. There was cursing and loud talking for quite some time. I noticed in the corner, sort of quiet, was a young kid I didn't know. He was dark skinned with these thick glasses. I asked who he was and was introduced to him as Junior. He was from Lima, Ohio, and was a Madlock. Tommy Rivers said that he was a future and upcoming hustler. I gave him a hug and a pound. His face lit up when he saw all the guns on the table. He said, "What's up fam? We bussin who tonight?" And then he removed two of those new 9mm and turned them sideways like he was ready to shoot something. I didn't care about embarrassment at the moment, I put both of my hands over my face and screamed, "LORD JESUS, I NEED UNCLE ROBERT RIGHT NOW."

The room laughed and then went silent as Uncle Roosevelt put his hands in the air. His country twang came out.

"If we are all here, it has to be about family or money. Let's get our shit together and get this money and protect our family."

For the next 15 minutes, we went over what was to happen. I informed everyone that I was hot. There were two Fed cars outside watching my house, and they were probably trying to figure out why so many people were at my house. There were a few strange looks, but I let them know that they were a part of the plan, and they would be leaving with me, and if they left a car behind to send two cars to the store at different intervals. They would have to follow. I gave out the uniforms that were needed. Everybody knew their jobs, and they just had to wait until I left for my date with Fatima.

I went to my room and grabbed Walter on my way there.

"Please tell me how they all got to my house at the same time."

He told me that he and Ms. Dee were talking, and they were worried about the Prince and his people.

I hugged Walter and said thanks for his concern, but I had the Prince and his people covered, and I had no intention of getting into a gunfight with anyone. I had to close my bedroom door to make a phone call. It was Fatima, and I asked how long before she would be ready, and she said about half an hour. I asked for her to come to my house when she was ready. This was all a part of the plan.

My next call was to Eli Banks, the city garbage worker. I needed him to be on time like his life depended on it. With the crowd at my house, his life did depend on it. I took my shower and got dressed. This gave me more time to think. I had decided that we were going to change up a few things. We had the personnel; why not use them? The job went from four people to 10. Extra security never hurt anyone.

It was my time to show off. The doorbell rang, and a female voice called out, "James, are you upstairs?"

There was a lot of chatter, and when she asked the second time, she was a little louder. The whole house got quiet, and I told her to come on up. She just had that "IT" factor. I was standing there with my mouth open just, like all the rest of the men. Tommy Lee was the only man in that room six feet tall, and she dwarfed him, too, with her heels on. There was a gold ribbon around her hair that was loose and wavy, hanging on her shoulders. Our mouths opened made hers open hers. They saw her and that smile. I felt 10 feet tall. I had no idea that my feet were on the ground. I was walking on air. The gold low cut blouse and black mini skirt, and the heels were an amazing touch. This woman had just knocked out a room full of men and never threw a punch. I got a big-ass hug and kiss.

Because of her height, she could see right past me and all my short relatives. I was trying to make introductions, and she was trying to see all the hardware on the table. Fatima almost pushed past me to get to the pool table. The first thing she picked up was one of the pistol grip shotguns. Fatima racked that mother fucker, and the whole room started ducking, and Uncle Chester stepped straight up to her and removed his shotgun from her hands. We all stood back up. Fatima laughed and asked, "What are you getting ready for, war?" Standing in the middle of the room, Fatima pulled out her .380 Mangum and said, "Let's go, dammit."

I had to ask her to wait in my room for a minute. I went over the new security plan, about security. It was like getting ready to go to war with real soldiers, only this time the Madlock name was the uniform. Fatima and I joked around with my family for a few minutes and took some pictures before our date. Most of them took pictures with her and some even sat on her lap. The two teenagers in the room were bonding with each other while at the same time keeping an eye on Fatima. They got photos, too. Fatima was the center of attention and had a question for Poochie.

"Do you know what the back of the milk carton is for?" He said no, and we were all curious. Fatima told him it was for his picture if he didn't quit rubbing her legs. The whole room went up laughing because he had taken his picture five minutes ago and he was still standing next to her copping feels.

After the jokes, Uncle Shorty Long took off his Godfather hat, put it over his heart, and apologized for his son, saying that he was just trying to be like his daddy.

"My old lady at home is about your size, and I think he wants one."

Again the room was loud, and it was time for us to go. They all got more hugs, but Poochie and Junior got their hug together, one on both sides. We left the house trying to make a show of leaving. I needed the Feds to get on their job and follow me. As expected, one car stayed there. My brother, who did not come up to the house, was on his job. The second Fed car was still there. He went into the house to get Poochie and Junior and take them to Jew Town to get some Polishes. The Feds came out smoking. Junior was told to wait until he got downstairs before he tucked his gun into his waistband. This got the Feds attention. The very first alley they pulled into, the gun was tossed. Uncle Molly walked into the alley to search for the tossed gun. It took about 10 minutes, but he found it.

The whole squad was at work. The lieutenant was in Hyde Park at the surveillance headquarters, and everyone else had to tail one of the vehicles in rotation. The way it was set up was so that I would be watched at all times. This was to be over by 9:30, and we were to meet at the surveillance headquarters to discuss the findings. Follow the dope was the mission, and then following it to the distribution spots.

My date with Fatima was going great. It was my first time ever going to this type of steak house. I was really impressed; it was first class. It was called Lawry's Prime Rib House. I didn't know the difference between a steak and prime rib. It came with a meat carver at your table. He brought the food in a big silver cart. We both got the biggest cut of meat they served. It melted in your mouth. I was trying to be romantic and do a little hand holding and have some conversation. Fatima was not having it; she was getting down with no shame. When she looked up with that smile, I was at a loss for words. We literally ate in silence. We had some desert. It was the fanciest looking thing that I ever had in my life. I had made up my mind that we were going to get the entire downtown date package.

We talked a little bit after eating, but what we needed was a long-ass walk before we fell over in these seats. I paid the bill, and we headed for the door. Walking straight past the valet parking, we walked east to the lakefront. Half an hour later, we were getting into a horse drawn carriage. We made out a little, but it was sightseeing time for us. We lived in this city, but we didn't get to enjoy it all the time. We were what you would call the working poor. I wanted to go to Ronnie's Steakhouse to get a step in, but we were on a tight schedule, and I needed the Feds to be able to keep up. I had already informed Fatima that I was on another mission while our date was going on. She said, "Good because all this romance shit is amazing, but I need to go home alone," so there was not going to be any action tonight. This wasn't my first date. But I got a raincheck for some action for next week.

We went back to the restaurant to get Uncle Shorty's Cadillac. I was on a date, and I wanted to look good, too, so I borrowed his pimp-mobile. We cruised down Lake Shore Drive. The music was nice, and we held hands all the way home. I was happy. I think loud music and a lot of people might be enough reason to have your house raided. We had the music up loud, and the fourth phone call to the police should do it.

Oh shit, the FBI and the police at the same time. It was sort of a race to get upstairs. The cops were there because of the loud music. The FBI was there because someone robbed the police annex and took a police captain and a cop hostage. The music was turned off, and we were all on the floor. The apartment was searched, and I was brought to my feet and taken into another room. Sosa and Agent James were furious with me. I didn't care one way or the other. I recognized the squad even though they were wearing masks. I had one request.

"Let my minor relatives out of the house and leave them the hell alone."

Sosa told me that if they were involved, he would send my whole family to jail.

I told him, "If that's what you have to do, do your fucking job." He knew that I was right, and he sent word out of the room to let the two minors go. There was nothing found in my apartment. Not one gun or even a joint. I told Sosa and James that I was still a part of this squad, no matter what they suspected me of doing. I would be at the briefing in an hour like the rest of the crew. Agent James asked, "Is that where you want to be?"

"Can you and your Storm Troopers get the fuck out of my house?" Yeah, I'm in a lot of deep shit, and they were looking for two officers and a shit load of money.

Pulling around back at the surveillance spot, I made a lot of noise kicking in the back door. My hands were full, and I didn't have time to knock. The back room was quickly filled with cops who had guns drawn . I really didn't give a shit. I was carrying two duffel bags full of money and a rotten-ass police captain who I was willing to put a bullet in his head personally. I dumped it all on the floor in front of the squad. Guns were still pointed at me, but some were lowered.

Daniels ran over first to check on his captain. He was unconscious but breathing. At the end, Agent James didn't put her gun up; she was on that bullshit again. It didn't matter to me. I was feeling good; my stomach was full, and I had a good joint to get to in my van. I walked past them all and straight to the liquor cabinet and found that bottle of scotch that they cherished so much. I took a big swig out of the bottle and offered it around the room.

Agent James spoke first.

"How the fuck did you pull this shit off?" she demanded, gun still in hand.

I asked in my nicest voice for her to please rest her side arm. She didn't, and I said it a lot louder, "PLEASE PUT YOUR GUN AWAY, OR START FUCKING SHOOTING."

Big Mother Fucker knew where this was heading and put his big body between us. Not lowering my voice I didn't ask her to put her gun away. I told her to go sit the fuck down somewhere. Agent Hoyde was who I needed at that moment. Just plain and simple English; let's find out what's going on first.

The lieutenant led us all to the meeting room, and I got a lot of stares when I grabbed Captain Holmes and drug his trashy ass with us. I told them if he woke up, he could join the meeting, but in the meantime, I wanted to keep an eye on him. Agent James asked if I wanted to start off the briefing with some answers. Shit, that part was easy.

"That's around $2 million in those bags, and I want my fucking 10 percent off the recovery. That piece of shit right there has been beating the shit out of us black folks to get some bad confessions. I don't have my pool balls with me, but I can still make him talk."

The room was quiet, and I knew what they were waiting on. How did I come into possession of the money and the captain? There was not going to be an answer from me. They knew to take their evidence and move on. They had photos of me 30 miles away from the scene of the crime, and they were getting almost $2 million back because I didn't run off with it. I let them all know that it would have been easy for me to run with the money, or even put a bullet in the captain's head as payback for all of the brothers he had wrongly convicted. They had done TV specials on his rotten ass.

I didn't have anything else to say. I got about 10 different questions at the same time from around the room. It looked like I was at a news conference after a big game. Lieutenant Sosa gave me a folder with photos of my relatives and their rap sheets, if they had one. Willie and Mack were on parole, and Uncle Chester had a warrant. He had all their plate numbers, which told me they would all be stopped and searched on the way out of town. I said to Sosa, "If you need to arrest them, be my guest."

He now understood that I would do something to offset whatever he did. I wasn't going to get away Scott-free. Even I knew that. It was the moment of proof as to why this team was put together: "Are we going to turn him in along with the $2 million?"

No one spoke at first. I wanted to take a crack at why there was so much silence in the room.

"Am I the only one thinking that all of that money does not have to be turned in?"

There were a few grumbles, and we started the briefing. It lasted about one hour. The truth of the matter on Captain Holmes was Agent James was taking him to a black site, so they could flip him. After the meeting, I got some sidebars about the money or where it came from. I had no answers for anyone. I just wanted justice to be done. In the case of the Captain, we were talking about a man who needed the book thrown at him. I wanted justice for all the black men he had harmed over the years. For all the families who had suffered because of him—almost 300 confessions on his watch. The torture needed to stop. Plus he was the link to City Hall for the Company.

Agent Hoyde got up and left the room with no words spoken. I had no worries about him. From there, we went on to figure out how the raids could be conducted without anyone knowing who was behind it all.

These people played for keeps, and that was almost too high of stakes for me. Agent Hoyde came back into the room carrying a tray with scotch glasses and a big-ass smile. We all looked his way, and he spoke. The real black man in him came out.

"We need to salute this young soldier." He didn't give anyone in the room a chance to speak. "Captain Holmes has been a thorn in my side for years. He has gotten past four or five investigations that I was involved in. This son of a bitch is trash. If we can't convict him, I will give up my career to put a bullet in his head." He went on to say, "There will be no deals made for him. Prison or death. Those are his only two choices."

The room was silent. I didn't know what to say, and neither did anyone else. I didn't know if this was good or not, but Hoyde volunteered himself and Officer Daniels to escort Captain Holmes to the black site. We all sat silent as he went around the room pouring us all double shots. I stole a peek at Officer Green and Agent James. They were on two different ends of the rainbow. Green was proud of me while James wanted to wring my neck. Less than 24 hours ago, we were in a different position. I needed to figure out how to have a one-on-one conversation with her to see if I could get her off my back.

Once all the glasses were filled, we stood still and held them high in the air. Sosa did a one, two, three thing. I thought this was some more police shit that I didn't know about. On three, they all yelled out: "ROACHMAN, ROACHMAN! GET YOUR HOUSE EXTERMINATED FOR $30! ROACHMAN, ROACHMAN!" I was red in the face. I had no idea this shit would cross over here. I couldn't stop them from laughing. Finally, we had a real toast and to my surprise it came from Agent James.

"TO THE MOST MYSTERIOUS AND TOUGHEST MOTHER FUCKER I KNOW. GOOD JOB, ROACHMAN!"

We turned them up and turned them down when they were empty. A few side conversations were had, and Oliver confessed that he was one of the people trailing me today, and he let the squad know about the ROACHMAN thing. He said that he didn't know how I really made a living until today. We briefly talked about my military and foundry time, and I wanted to be my own man. We all have to start at zero unless you had rich parents like him. Again it came up, "How could you turn all that money in?"

"Maybe I'm foolish," was my answer. I said it to seven more people before I left that night.

On my way to the van, Sosa walked me out. He said that he saw life differently now. Not as a cop, but as a human being. He would have kept the money. I asked Sosa if he could look back at the building and imagine who was inside and have them dogs chasing me and my kids. He looked at me and just nodded. I felt like I was a part of something when he said to me, "SQUAD MEETING SUNDAY NIGHT."

How big can a man smile? I was driving down Garfield Boulevard (to us Chicagoans, it's 55th Street) straight to the crib. But I just had to make one stop. Leon's BBQ. Yeah, I was going to treat my family to the best 'que on the south side. My order was large. I had a while to wait, so let me feel you in on what really happened today.

First off, that damn Eli Banks was late, and they got to the annex late. By this time, the shift change had occurred. And so this put Captain Holmes in the parking lot getting head when the city garbage truck arrived. He had a straight view of the back of the annex. Ptacc couldn't carry the bags, so he had to let Uncle Molly and Uncle Chester in the basement to carry the bags. Yes, I was robbing the police of some money that they cannot report missing. Being in a hurry, my uncles had no chance of seeing Captain Holmes standing in the doorway with his service revolver pointed at them. The five bags were dropped on the ground, along with Captain Holmes. Shorty Long hit him with that big-ass pistol. Man, that had to be one hell of a sight! Them two country boys stomping the shit out of the most prejudiced cop in Chicago. Willie and Mack dropped those Stacy Adams on him a few times. Thank God for extra security.

The bags were loaded into the garbage truck with Ptacc and the captain. Eli closed up the back, and they drove off. We had a total of three cars running security on the way home. Some people would have just split with the money. That's how you go to JAIL. Remember, if all else fails, use the secret weapon. In my case, it was the brain. I never worried about what the hand was covering. I was more attracted to the distraction. I knew I would be followed from my house this morning. I knew that their plates on their vehicle would be photographed. I didn't know that there would be so many. Officer Ptacc provided the schedule and the inside interference. Eli Banks got about two ounces of dope to borrow the garbage truck and drive. I can't tell you where Officer Ptacc is. He took one of the bags, and he got his 10-minute head start. As for me and my family, we are okay. I needed the police to come and search my house. They needed to know that it was clean. Ms. Dee made the calls about all the noise with one from Mrs. Hubbard. As far as the FBI being there, where else was Agent James going to go looking for the money? She brought the whole squad, all masked up. I even saw her count the balls on the pool table. Agent James was looking for anything. They all missed the PLAY. I made it my business to argue with Sosa and James about the minors, who I didn't want caught up in this shit. Well, Poochie and Junior were on a bus back to St. Louis. Yes, they were both carrying $750,000 apiece. A total of $1.5 million. Ms Diane and Ms. Tanggy were waiting for them in the park.

On the way to the bus station, things were quiet until Poochie wanted to know if they could stop and get him a couple of those Jew Town Polishes. It brought out laughs in a very intense situation. The ladies took care of them and put them on the bus. I wasn't worried about the money; these two had four guns and eight clips.

When I got home the party was in full swing. Lisa from across the street and Dee rounded up some ladies in the neighborhood. My uncles and cousins were being entertained by the ladies, and they cheered when I walked into the room. We literally shouted for joy. The food was passed out, plus I splurged a little on my family. I threw $2 grand on the table.

"Ladies, can y'all please take good care of my family?"

I saw Uncle Roosevelt sitting off to the side. Making a quick enquiry about why he was not participating, he said that Ellanor, his wife, was the only woman for him. I got the hell out of there. All I wanted to do was get some peace and quiet. Two blocks later, I was knocking on Fatima's door. She came to the door with her flannel gown on and damn-near snatched me in. She had to pump her brakes. I had an arm full of food and drink. Fatima was happy to see me, but said I thought, "I told you there was no sex tonight." I told her I just needed a soft place to land for tonight.

I don't know when I went to sleep. I was comfortable, and she was soft. All women don't know how to leave a man alone and let him sleep. Fatima wasn't bad at it. I rolled over about 4:00 a.m., and she was still asleep. Once movement was detected, she came right to life and smothered me with a big hug. I was cool with that, and I knew it was time for some pillow talk. This is one of the most precious things about a relationship. That's when you find out whether you want to be with a person or not. It's the soft conversation and the rubbing of skin. It lures you in unsuspectedly.

We were having a great conversation until she started to lay down the law. It was cool with me. I needed to know how she viewed men and what she thought their purpose was in a relationship with her. My questions were answered before I could even ask. There was no dependence on a man, no matter what. She made it clear that she was not ready for a commitment and was hoping that I was freelancing a bit with Ms. Diane. No, I didn't see that coming. Fatima told me that it was neighborhood gossip for quite some time, and they actually knew each other from another circle. There was one more cat to let out of the bag, and that was Ms. Tanggy. Fatima confided in me that they were a package deal, and I needed to be careful with her. Okay… I needed to know what there was to be so careful about.

Just sitting back and listening, I was told about how she shot one of the Nation members in the park in broad daylight. He grabbed her ass, and she slapped him. Because of the size difference, she was on the ground being stomped before anyone could get over to stop what was going on. Tanggy went to her house, came back, and put three bullets in him, then walked off asking if anyone else wanted to get a handful of ass. Ms. Tanggy was also the bag lady for the Nation at one point, and some rogue members thought it would be a good idea to rob her. She shot two of them in her apartment, and the third was shot in the alley while she was still wearing her panties and bra. It was January with snow on the ground. Shit, I ain't that damn tough…

Fatima was trying to read my face to see if this was affecting me. She was looking in the wrong place. For some strange reason, this story was turning me the fuck on. Shit, I needed to put Ms. Tanggy's ass on the Squad. My next question was, "So if you knew about Ms. Diane, why did you have sex with me?"

Fatima rolled over on top of me, which felt amazing, and I was told that I had a lot to learn about women. I was all ears.

"James, you run around that park all the time half naked. Sometimes you don't have on a shirt, and sometimes you have a bunch of kids with you. Well, we women look, just like men do. We discuss who we want to knock off and who we don't. Your ass was at the top of the list. Me and my girlfriends have sat in the park getting our bubble on. And here you come running by, chest all out and that thang swangin. Shit I had plans when you bought me a cold beer last summer, but you never came back around."

I can't lie; I was flattered. This pillow talk was very informative, and Fatima was so soft. Again, like any other time there is pillow talk, I had some questions.

"So what about all these codes of honor that you women have?"

Fatima told me that it still existed, and it was the men who did not understand it. Until he puts a ring on her finger, he is still fair game, but it had to be kept quiet.

"Once he produces that ring, we will back off," she said. "There are still about 25 percent who don't care because that's just their nature." Then I was told about how most of them compared notes about us. Fatima said, "A man in the area who had more than seven inches and had a thirst for eating out, he would be passed around the neighborhood and would never know." She laughed and said, "He probably thinks he's a player."

At this point, I wanted to know where I stood. Fatima said, "Your black ass ain't standing nowhere, because you are laying in my bed."

I got the joke and gave it a HAHA. Again I asked the same question: "Where do I stand with you and Ms. Diane?"

I got a low grade, and we were cool. Depending on where you are from, that could mean several things. And the first thing that came to my mind was that I saw Fatima with a gun this afternoon. Plus, you just told me a horror story about Ms. Tanggy shooting multiple people. I wanted a full explanation. *JAMES, GET YOUR DUMB ASS UP AND RUN NOW.*

Fatima didn't answer right away. She appeared to be thinking. At the same time, she dropped her right hand down and started playing with my package. Plus I got the pretty smile, not as wide as when I show up with food, but it was big enough to be a warning that a curve ball was coming. Fatima lowered her voice as she said that she and Tanggy were cool, but they had history from another era.

"You are talking in riddles," I said.

At this point she had the package out and was having fun, or so she wanted me to think. Diane came to mind: IF ALL ELSE FAILS, USE THE SECRET WEAPON. Taking control of her hand, I made it clear, "It's not going to sound better with this in your hand."

"We were in juvie together." Okay, that's a start. "We all came from the same hood, and we fought together; we ate together. We had to bond together or be taken over by the BDs, GDs, Latin Queens, and whoever else that was reppin in juvie." I was trying to be patient, but she was taking too long.

"So have you and her ever fucked around?"

"What do you mean?" was her answer.

"Stop playing. You know what I mean."

She was still vague about her answer. I needed to get her back into submission mode. This was the easy part. I reached up and grabbed a nipple and squeezed. For most submissives, a little pain lets them know that the game is back on, and the master wants to be served. I didn't want sexual favors; I wanted answers. No man in the world wants to be caught in the middle of two women with guns and estrogen issues. Fatima fell right in line and asked, "What do you want to know, Daddy?"

"Tell me about you and Tanggy."

That explanation took a little while to bubble up to the surface, but when it came, Fatima was all guddy and smiled a lot. She made it clear that she was not gay, but they fooled around as 17-year-olds in juvie hall. It was made clear that she didn't eat pussy, but she did enjoy all the things Tanggy did to her. I wanted to know if it was a one way street. I was told no, but eating out was not her thing. She enjoyed the softness and comfort of a woman. All this damn talk, and she still never answered my question. I needed to be a little more direct.

"Will there be violence if you two are in the same room?"

I got an eye roll and a small sigh.

"She was my first love," she replied. Fatima tried to turn her head and talk to me. I still had a nipple, but decided to let it go. I made it clear that she didn't have to say anything else. The emotion on her face told only part of the story. I was a little bit surprised at the second part of the story. Fatima said, "Too many people worry about young men when they go to jail. But what about the young ladies? Especially the ones who have never been loved properly. Very little education, and no promise of a future, so we just held on to whatever or whoever was in our circle. This sometimes led to love, no matter how misguided."

Oh shit, here came the tears, and I didn't know why she was crying. Well, what was I supposed to do? After calming her down, I had to get up because I was not sure where this was going. There were some men at my house who needed to get on the road. We hugged and smooched for a while, but I needed to get rolling. Her children would be up in about 45 minutes for school.

On the way out, I saw a picture on the wall and asked if it was her parents. She said yes and proceeded to tell me that her mother was a Samoan and her father was from Trinidad. Judging from the picture, I now knew why she was so damn big.

When I got home, there were people everywhere. Some had clothes, and some had none. I slammed the front door, and this started a slow train of people getting up and moving. It took about 10 minutes for the five women to get themselves together. And then the door to my bedroom opened and out came Uncle Shorty and Willie Riggins with Lisa from across the street, taking that walk of shame. The only difference was she had a smile on her face and walked a little funny. Lisa rolled her eyes at me and kept on walking.

Once the house was clear, we had to get down to business. I made it clear that all guns would be left at my house. Each of their vehicles would be stopped and searched. No one should have over $300 in their pockets. Uncle Chester wanted to know about the money. I told him that Uncle Roy and James Cage would run security and pick the boys up from the bus station. Uncle Molly pulled me to the side and asked what the hell was wrong with me. I didn't get what he was talking about. Uncle Molly said that James was a loose cannon, and he might shoot somebody. James Cage was another one of my cousins; he was just a little older than me, but he was handy with the steel. I laughed hard because that's who Uncle Robert told me to call. With that much money on the line, I wanted someone who would kill all that was in sight. Plus Uncle Roy was borrowing one of the school busses from his job, and that's how they would ride to Uncle Roy's house from the bus station.

We had one last piece of business to handle before they left. I wanted us all to get together and thank Walter for treating them so well. I was informed that Walter had a date, and he was still out. I was not going to touch that subject. Not with these damn fools in the room. They all have felt the wrath of Walter before. But they told jokes while he was not around. And even when he was.

All five vehicles pulled out together. Uncle Roosevelt prayed for their safe travel, knowing that they would all be pulled over once they were on the Dan Ryan Expressway. I wasn't worried that everybody was clean. I put on my running shoes and hit the park. This was going to be a great day. All I had to do now was kill a man in cold blood in public.

CHAPTER SEVEN
HOW FAST ARE YOU?

After my run was over, I came home and went straight to my weight room. I needed to get a little more stress off my chest. The workout was going fine until Walter came in fussing about the fact that my ex-wife didn't have the kids ready for school. I did my best to calm him down. It was almost useless. I just let him rant about it for a while.

I got a call from Lieutenant Sosa to tell me the hit was set for two hours and my ride would be there to pick me up in 20 minutes. I went straight for the shower. I was in there for about two minutes when the door opened. To my surprise, it was Officer Green. She was early and said she needed to talk to me about Agent James. I didn't have a problem about her being there, or even talking about Agent James. I wanted to know what happened to Agent Oliver and was there a change in plans? She said that they were all at the mall trying to get things set up. I made my shower quicker than normal.

Officer Green was standing there with a towel as I stepped out of the shower. She started to dry me off and went straight for the package. I took the towel and asked what was so important about Agent James that she had to talk about. There was a slight hesitation on her part.

"James, this back and forth between the two of you has to stop." She continued on to tell me, "You don't understand the life of a cop. They are sworn to certain things, and you are breaking the law right in front of us. This doesn't sit well with some of the squad, and Agent James is at the top of that list."

Officer Green reminded me of the fact that I showed up with almost $2 million and a police captain who was kidnapped. There was a second officer missing from the robbery, and an agent who just got out of ICU this morning. I said that I was glad that the Agent was going to recover. She went on to say that some of the information I brought to the table was a little out of the reach of a civilian like me.

I wrapped a towel around myself and went to my room. Officer Green followed like a small puppy. Her banter about my actions did not stop. She said that no one on the Squad wanted to see me go to jail.

"James, you are pushing the envelope, and we can't ignore everything that you do. There must be a better line of communication between you and the squad." I had no disagreement with that. There was another warning: "Whoever you are working with will be arrested when found out." I made it clear that she would have to arrest some crooked ass cops first, and that I had nothing personal against Agent James. Green interrupted me by saying that she was also a cop, and some of my tactics bothered her. I asked what I could do to satisfy her and the squad that would make this easier for everyone. She said, "Be more open about what you are doing. And stop putting people in the hospital and on disability."

I informed her that I don't carry a gun, and my risk was much greater because of my lack of protection. Officer Green jumped to her feet and said, "That's my fucking point. If you are up front with us, we can help protect you, and shit will work out better." I had no disagreement with her statement. I just had no way of explaining some of the shit that they would see, and the questions would not stop, like the fact that I couldn't explain how I knew that she was more aroused than she had ever been around me. I could smell it, but I couldn't say how I knew. There was only one thing to do in this situation, and that was to bend her over the bed and be 15 minutes late for the meeting for today. We enjoyed each other's company. But I will never understand the FREAKINESS of a woman. Right in the middle of me giving one of my best performances, Officer Green looks over her shoulder in the middle of some great sex, if I should say so myself, and said she wanted to know when she could meet Fatima. Yes, she said Fatima. I was shocked for about five seconds. And five seconds after that, I was as hard as Chinese arithmetic. I could not stop the speed or the force of each thrust. Officer Green was loud as hell, and I grabbed her panties off the bed and put them in her mouth. This only muffled the sound and turned me on even more.

On the ride to the mall, we talked, and I asked about the work for today, and she asked about Fatima. Green gave a confession about her being the tail on my date with Fatima. I wanted to know about Agent James' feelings about this little twist. She said it wasn't her business, and she was a grown-ass woman. I could not disagree.

It was not a long ride to Ford City Mall. We pulled into one of the outer lots. Four members of the squad were there, and the plan was laid. I was given a 12-gauge shotgun with a pistol grip. Officer Finney wanted to check the shotgun to make sure that it was filled with blanks. Considering our past, I did not blame him at all. I sat with Officer Green as the rest of the squad got things in place. My heart was beating so fast. I got out to get some air and to try and breathe. Officer Green got out with me. She knew right away that something was wrong. I think I was having another one of those panic attacks from the stress.

BREATHE, BREATHE, BREATHE... I WAS TALKING MYSELF DOWN OFF THE LEDGE. I needed to talk to someone. But black men didn't go to therapy. Remember your training.

The radio call came in from Agent Hoyde, and Green asked him to hold on. She leaned over me and asked, "Are you alright? Do we have to abort this hit?"

I told her that I was fine; "We were still a go."

We climbed back into her car, and we rode around to the parking lot. There was one pass made to see where Officer Finney was parked and where the rest of the squad were posted.

Going back to the drop spot, I told Officer Green that what she was about to see could not be told to anyone.

"This is a part of the reason that I can't be upfront with Agent James," I said as I took the long jacket from the back of the vehicle. Officer Green kissed me hard and wished me luck. I did not put the jacket on, I just put the shotgun under it. We were parked about a quarter of a mile from the lot, and I was off. Stopping just short of my target, I signaled Agents Hoyde and Oliver that I was ready. Officer Finney was told to go.

Officer Finney went to the trunk of his car. Four shots were fired from the shotgun, and I was gone. I had turned on the power and moved through the parking lot at well over 30 miles per hour. Agent Hoyde never saw me. Agent Oliver fell down when he heard the shotgun. Officer Brown was somewhere in the parking lot, doing his tech thing. The shotgun was placed in its pickup spot. Now as for me, I was on 67th and Western at Petey Boys getting me an Italian beef sandwich with mild peppers and cheese, dry not dipped. Shit, I smelled it as I was running, and it was across the street from my pickup point.

I was almost finished with my sandwich when Officer Green got there. Signaling for her to come across the street, I handed her the three extra sandwiches that I ordered. She took the food and gave me a look like she had a question for me. I told her to ask away. Several really deep breaths were taken and then she came out with it: "WHO THE FUCK ARE YOU?"

I tried to answer her as honestly as possible.

"James David Madlock," was my answer. I got up to leave, and Officer Green sat down. I informed her that we needed to get going. She would not move, so I sat with her.

Her next question was, "You do know that I am a runner, right?" I nodded my head yes and she continued. "I have been a runner since high school and for two years in college." Her voice went up, and she forgot that we were in public. "THERE AIN'T A MOTHER FUCKER ON THIS PLANET WHO RUNS THAT FAST."

I put my hands up to get her to lower her voice. She went to a shouting whisper and reminded me that she was in a car and I still beat her there, adding, "Not to mention you ordered food and ate a fucking sandwich before I got here."

My humor did not help when I told her that I had to stop for a couple of red lights. Officer Green lent in close to me and said, "Do you really think that the whole squad is going to trust you doing this type of shit?"

Again, I had nothing to say, so I remained silent and started to walk towards the vehicle. With almost reluctance, Officer Green followed me to the vehicle. Once inside, I reminded her that she had made a promise to not speak of what she saw. She was driving and talking a mile a minute. Brown lied for you when he said he didn't have footage of the pool ball shit, and Daniels and Oliver did not exaggerate about the bench. Daniels brought a part of the bench as proof of what happened. I let her talk. This was some news I didn't know. She told me that Agent James had orders to arrest me if I got out of line. I now wanted to know why she was telling me this, and she said that she thought that I was a noble man. She also said that she thought I was trying to do right. I needed to look up this noble shit. Plus I was on some bullshit of the first order.

I had a picture of Officer Green and Fatima in my head. I couldn't wait to make the introduction. I asked Officer Green to pull over before we got to my house. She followed my directions. We got out of the vehicle, and I told her to get the food. She pulled her jacket over her gun to conceal it. We walked three garages down, and there she was. Fatima was bending over under the hood of a car. I walked over and tickled her in the side. Fatima yelled out that she had a wrench in her hand, and she was not for any games as she came out from under the hood. I got a big hug and a frown. Fatima looked over my head and saw a cop in her shop.

"Yo, James, do I have to clear out my fucking shop?"

I replied with a quick no. Officer Green picked up on the animosity. She wasn't smiling either. I looked around the shop to see a few neighborhood people and her assistant. I had to take control of this right away. This was not a butch situation like Agent James. We were looking at some feminine shit like scratching your eyes out, and "who is this bitch?" Plus they both had guns.

I made a quick introduction, then I informed them that I had bought them lunch. Officer Green held up the bag that she was holding, and Fatima smiled at me. She gave me a big hug, and I was on my way out the door. Officer Green gave me a funny look. I simply said, "You wanted to meet her." I told her I was tired because I was out running and needed a rest. She gave me a fucked up look because she still had that running shit on her mind. I left the two of them talking and jogged off.

The park was my next stop. I had to find Big Fred or the Prince. It was a little windy, so they were sitting in the Prince's van. I walked up to the security, and he asked if I was packing, and I said no. He moved aside and let me in. There were about six of them there. Big Fred cleared them out with a nod. He was about to exit also. The Prince told Fred to have a seat.

This van was top of the line. The fridge had a glass front door. I could see cold beer and reached out to get one. Nobody said a word. I drank the whole beer and reached for another one before a word was spoken. I told the Prince to go home and watch the news. No one was even given a chance to ask a question. I was gone. I gave the others a good look as I passed by them. I needed to remember some of their faces.

I got home and called Sosa to see what the report was that he had gotten. There was no answer. I called Agent James to get a report from her. She answered the phone almost in a rushed manner. I informed her that it was me calling. Agent James burst out in tears and said that Lieutenant Sosa had been shot. She was on her way to the hospital from her downtown office.

I headed straight for the hospital. I got there before any of the squad. Agent Hoyde was next. We had a chance to talk about what happened, and we came up with a quick plan. Only officers from his precinct should go up to visit. The rest of the squad had no reason to even know him. That meant telling Agent James that she could not see him or she'd risk exposing the rest of us. The agreement was made, and we needed to find out what happened to Lieutenant Sosa. Most of the squad showed up at different times. We all had our thoughts or suspicions. I gave Officer Brown the names of four other officers who were a part of the Company. I got that info from Ptacc at the warehouse. I knew that Agent James was about to dig into every part of their lives. I almost felt sorry for them.

I made it home at about 10:30 p.m. I was tired and needed some sleep. The Prince was parked on the side of my house. It didn't even matter to me. I just walked from my van straight to his. The door was opening as I approached. One of the bodyguards got out and started to frisk me. This was the wrong day. I was holding on to his hand like we were dating, only he found out that love hurts. Especially after the knee to the back of the leg. He was released and I entered the van. The Prince didn't even flinch. Big Fred got out to help the security guy up. Before I could sit down, A brown paper bag was tossed to me. Twenty grand has some weight to it.

I saw the box with the bones in it. He followed my eyes. I got up to exit almost two hours later. I'm not sure how to describe what was going on, but the two of us couldn't stop talking as we played. He had a decent game. The Prince asked when he could send his first 10 students. I just told him soon. On the way out, I apologized to the young man. I also explained, "If you don't touch me, I won't touch you."

Big Fred said something under his breath. I was not shocked. He had to make it look like some sort of an attempt in front of the Prince. It had no bearing on me at all. I just wanted to go to sleep.

I went up stairs and got my fix. At this point in my life, there can't be anything better than sleep.

I was out the door by 8:30 a.m. The ROACHMAN was on the job. My first two jobs were perfect. The third was not so great. I was standing in Mrs. Myra's living room being introduced to Nikki for the first time. I didn't want to see it, but I did. Her eyes told a sad story. A story of innocence snatched from a child. She, too, might be carrying a Nation Baby. I bent down to shake her hand. Nikki did not understand the look on her Grandmother's face as she made the introduction. I told Mrs. Myra that I needed to get to work. She had a lot of roaches. She read between the lines, and I knew that we would talk later. Whether I wanted to or not.

This was some emotional shit. I kept my head down and did my job. It was the thoughts of my nieces and my Winnie that brought a certain tightness to my chest and the loss of breath. This was going to be my last job of the day. My head was fucked for the day, and I had to work later.

I went straight home. Ms. Dee was there having a coffee or a cocktail. I was not sure which one. My face must have shown some stress. Dee walked up and hugged me just like my mother would have. She just told me not to say anything. Just breathe. I didn't know that Mrs. Myra had called her about my visit. Mrs. Dee was about to get another shock. I asked Walter to give Dee that brown bag of meat in the freezer. That envelope she gave me that day when she thought I needed her money had $1,400 in it. I had to peel her little ass off me when she saw the five stacks in the bag. I told her it was interest on the money she gave me.

Agent James came up the back stairs about 10 minutes later. She looked about as subdued as me. Only I knew what was eating her. Lieutenant Sosa. We just embraced and got a little bit of relief from each other. He was going to live because he was wearing a bulletproof vest. One slug got in near the collarbone. Agent James had found out about the cancer. This was some emotional shit for me, and I needed a way to calm down. We talked about the possibilities of what may have happened to Sosa. Her contacts gave her a few more names of Company members we had no clue about. On that list were maybe 20 names. We both looked it over, trying to make a connection somewhere. And there he was—number 11 on the list. Officer Canen was the very first cop that I told Lieutenant Sosa to check for dope. How could we talk to him without outing the squad?

This was going to take some work. I needed to speak with Agent Hoyde. I needed answers and help. I explained why I needed to talk to Hoyde. Agent James understood. On her way out the door, she gave me another big hug and reminded me that I was not a cop. In my mind, this meant letting the police handle it. She said, "I hope you have a couple of those damn pool balls when you talk to Canen." She informed me that he had been a bad man for a long time. With that, she was gone.

I had about four hours before work later today. I grabbed my running shoes and hit the park. On my run, I saw one of my students, and we talked for a bit. I wanted to know who in particular put their hands on Nikki. He looked almost afraid. I made it clear he didn't have a choice or I would put Sosa on him. He said she was G Black's property the whole time she was in the building. He has a thing for young girls, and when he got one, he never shared with anyone. G Black was going to be the next one on the arrest list.

My running route changed in an instant. He needed to understand that little girls were off limits. I got to the spot where they all sat and talked shit. And there was G Black. I had no game plan. I just walked up and kicked him in the nuts. As he fell, his jaw was dislocated and his orbital bone in his face was crushed. I wanted to hit him a few more times, but I needed that time to deal with the other three Nation members who made the mistake of coming to his defense. There wasn't even a second thought. I just started swinging. It didn't matter what part of the body I hit. My job was simple: Stop the assault and cause some pain. I put my foot on G Black's chest and told him what this was about.

"Little Nikki sends her regards. Do I have to come back here?"

I didn't wait for an answer. I was gone. My run wasn't finished, and I still had to work in a few hours. I went straight for the block that I knew the van was parked on. The Prince stepped out before I got close. We shook hands, and I told him why I was there.

"You have a few soldiers on their way to the hospital. If you want to discuss, it we can." I saw him stick his hand in his pocket. I wanted to know if there was another member of the Nation that needed hospitalization. He said no and pulled out a lighter and lit a blunt.

"Yeah, we will discuss this as soon as I go check on my people."

I wasn't worried at all, but you still have to watch out for those who would shoot you in the back. I wished that I could go tell Nikki what I had done. For my own selfish reasons, I wanted to see her smile.

It was 6:30 p.m.; time to go to work. I had the information and was a little excited. Winnetka II, a stretch of land on the shores of Lake Michigan, about an hour's ride from my place. I had time to think. Sosa was somewhat skeptical about searching for Officer Canen. Maybe there was something there. I just had a feeling that somehow the Company might know about our squad. Either way, we needed to make this right.

I couldn't believe that Agent James wanted me to use violence against those responsible. It was hard to believe. Finding the address was somewhat simple. It was the "close your mouth before you catch flies" mode that I was in. This place smelled of money, and I was hoping that the owner would be present.

Seven acres of land perfectly manicured. Two acres faced Lake Michigan. I was escorted to the rear of the estate. There was an elaborate coach house set up for a party. A young lady took my jacket and my Kango. I was wearing a form fitting, black button up shirt with some Black and burgundy checkered slacks and color coordinated Fotti shoes, two-toned.

Mrs. Bell came to me with a nice hug as she escorted me to the living room. There were a lot more people than I expected. It was not intentional, but I was the last to arrive. I found out later that there were a total of 16 women there and nine men including myself. Mrs. Bell gathered everyone in a circle. The rules were explained. Each woman got her pick of men, and he was obligated as an employee to cooperate. In other words, do as you are told. She stated, "You have all been paid in advance."

Mrs. Bell raised her arms, and two of the women brought forth a box with some fancy decoration on it. The box was sitting in the middle of the room on a glass table. The room was abuzz after we all saw the contents of the box: $5,000 cash. The women would vote at the end of the night, and the best performer would get the cash. WINNER TAKES ALL. I needed to do this right.

Let me describe Mrs. Bell. She was about my height, and the heels made her a little taller. It was her hair and body that made her stand out. She had a 36C breast on a frame that held hips that looked like she had never given birth. But that ass came from the Spanish side of the family. She stayed manicured from head to toe. Her attitude was her sexiest feature. She took what she wanted.

Okay, I understood the contest, and the money as motivation. Maybe my mind was preoccupied with other things. I walked over to the refreshment table. I made myself a stiff drink and took a joint out of my pocket. Stepping through a set of sliding doors, I wanted to be alone for a minute. I could still see inside; people were pairing off for the start of the evening. I would love to win the money and bragging rights.

Just as I was getting ready to put out the rest of my joint. My motivation walked up and hugged me from behind. She reached around and grabbed my joint to take a puff. I thought I told you before, no one in the world gives a hug like Lola. I stood there and started a slow rock to her rhythm. Exhaling the smoke in my direction, Lola asked if I was bored or had a plan to come in with some heroic plan at the end to capture the prize money. It sounded good, but I had no such plan. When she turned my body to face her head on, she rubbed the sides of my face with her soft hands.

"James, I have assembled an amazing cast of the horniest CEOs in the city, and some of the most gorgeous women anyone has seen anywhere." She let the cat out of the bag that the money on the table was just peanuts. There is a side bet with the ladies. "We are betting on a winner, $5 grand per woman."

"I want to know who you betted on."

She gave a sly smile and said, "I'm betting on my man to win." Lola applied another hug. I had never touched Lola sexually even when we did three shows together. For that amount of money, I wonder if that would change tonight. Lola was what we in the hood call FINE.

People can tell if you are fantasizing about them if they have to call your name three times to snap you out of it.

"James, don't think that some of the CEOs won't tell their guy that they are being betted on."

"Is that what you are doing?"

She gave a resounding yes and, "Dammit, you better come through."

Now I wanted to know, was she just hosting or are you a participant?

"I'm the one that's going to close the show, just follow my lead," she said. Lola told me to stay away from Mrs. Bell. She said Mrs. Bell could wear out three men. "If you run into her early, you may not last the rest of the night. There is also an Asian lady out there who has incredible stamina. Stay away from her."

Shit, it wasn't just those two I needed to stay away from. This place was crawling with naked women. The smells of the perfumes. The smell of arousal.

Lola said the rest were easy pickings and told me that she would bring Mrs. Bell to me towards the end of the night.

I had never seen such a more beautiful group of women in my life. It was like a naked beauty pageant for middle-aged women. I was still the only man left with clothes. I had done between 15 and 20 of these shows, and this one was filled with the most amazing bodies. Male and female. There was one guy who was literally carved out of stone. There were two guys who were twins and could have been on a magazine cover. I knew two of the other guys. They mostly made their money as male strippers. Talk about bringing out the big guns. Nine inches and extra thick was the smallest dick in the house. There was pure muscle in that room, and I was still dressed. Mrs. Bell came over to me and asked if I was Chi or maybe I had something special for later. Telling her the truth—that my mind was not in it—that was not going to work. So following the excuse that she gave me, I made it clear that I was saving the bomb for her and Lola. I think that I read somewhere that people remember the last thing they saw. Not the action scene at the beginning of the movie. Thinking outside the box, I found Lola and asked if the staff could run and get a dozen long stem roses. Lola thought that I was tripping. I explained that it was about me winning the $5 grand and her winning the big pot. The flowers were for Mrs. Bell. I wanted to present them to her as we double-teamed her for the last act of the night. Lola smiled and said, "Her birthday is tomorrow. That's why she is hosting this shindig." We gave each other that look, and a new partnership had been formed.

I just milled around the room just kind of flirting or helping out one or two of the guys. This group had to be some of the most well-kept women in the world. I was approached by a woman who wanted to know why I was still dressed. I told her that I was waiting on her to undress me. Mrs. Bell said that we were to perform no matter who asked. If I was having a dream on my own, there was no way a prettier woman would show up. I walked right past her to the oversized cocktail table. It was solid wood. I climbed on top of the table and yelled, "SHOWTIME!" This got a lot of attention. Even though I didn't know it at the time, the room needed a time out. Those twins were eating and beating their way to a victory. A couple of the other men were on a mission. This was a day that I almost felt sorry for pussy. These boys were putting in work. Now that I had their attention, I needed to keep it until Lola got back. That part was simple. I turned the coffee table into a small stage. This curious lady followed me. I picked her up and turned her upside down. Holding her by her ankles, I spread her legs apart in the air. I spread her legs and pulled her to my face. Not even the strongest men in the room believed what they were seeing. To hold someone in the air was one thing; I was now going on five minutes. This was the most innovative 69 that I ever had. I saw Lola's face, and it was riddled with mystery. Mrs. Bell had not closed her mouth in the last three minutes. I decided to get fancy. I stood on one foot for 60 seconds. I had won this shit, and I was still dressed, except for my package hanging out. No one knew about the power.

When I stepped down from the table, I walked straight over to Mrs. Bell and turned this beautiful woman in the air so that she was facing her. I asked Mrs. Bell if she would like to share a birthday meal with me, as this was her first present of the night. I presented the Scandinavian Beauty for the offering. Because her hair fell forward, no one saw us slightly clash heads getting to the meal. Maybe 60 seconds went by. She wanted to know how I knew about her birthday. I just winked at her as we shared a clitoris.

Man, I love my city. I was heading back to the Southside $10 grand richer. Lola gave me $5 grand from the $80 grand that she won. I'm on North Ashland at Pero Brothers getting me a couple of calzones.

Yeah, back to the money. I carried Mrs. Bell around the room singing *Happy Birthday*. Mrs. Bell had an even harder time closing her mouth. She was being royally fucked as the rest of the guests joined in on the *Happy Birthday* song. Right after I gave her the flowers that Lola had brought into the room, shit, I was on a roll, asking for her forgiveness for being late.

"I just didn't want to ignore your birthday," I said. Even though I had her engine revved up, I invited the rest of the guests to give her some birthday LICKS. You know they all LICKED, some more than once. Lola and I put the work on her for the next 40 minutes. A person fading in and out of consciousness can't really vote for a winner, but the people who witnessed it can vote for the last thing they saw.

The next morning, I finished my coffee and headed for the door. Agent James was coming up the stairs. She had a coffee mug in her hand. She told me that we needed to talk. Walter cleared the kitchen. He took Lisa's smiling ass with him on his way to taking the kids to school. Agent James told me that I was right. Officer Canens shot Lieutenant Sosa. He saw Sosa coming out of the men's room at a restaurant. He was pissed about the firing.

"We can't prove it in court because the source was anonymous," she explained, "and they said that they were undercover." I wanted to know what she wanted me to do. She said nothing but, "There is a squad meeting tonight at a different location."

I was out the door, and a half of a mile later, I was yelling, "ROACHMAN, ROACHMAN! GET YOUR HOUSE EXTERMINATED FOR $30! ROACHMAN, ROACHMAN!" It was all about the hustle, not how much money you made right then and there. It was about building something to last a lifetime. I needed this business to work. My kids needed to be able to look at me and see something PRIDEFUL. It's a different world to know your family is proud of you. I have seen all of the welcome home from jail parties in my family, but I haven't seen a lot of graduations in my family. This is what I wanted to change.

My mind was on the task at hand. That's how the van got up on me before I knew it. Big Fred was driving, and the two security boys were in the van. As the door opened, I climbed in the back. The Prince sat in the back on the couch. I think it was more for safety reasons. I decided to test my theory. I made a move to sit back there with him, but my way was blocked. I had my answer. Now what?

Big Fred drove straight out of the neighborhood. One of the security guys gave me an envelope. I put it in my pocket. I was more worried about what was happening right now. Fred stopped the van, and the Prince and I got out, just the two of us. I was more surprised about where we got out at. We were on 65th and Loomis. This park was rival gang territory. He saw the concern on my face and explained that he did not live his life by territory. The Prince told me that he understood the whole thing about G Black and the child molestation thing. He also made it clear that there were Nation members who wanted some get back at me. I asked what he wanted. He said that he wanted some peace and quiet in the town. I went back to G Black and these girls who were being molested. The Prince swore to me that it was an isolated incident. I had no reason to believe him. Then was the point and time that shit changed. We got a chance to talk for real. He didn't ask for this life. It was an inheritance like a building or money. The Prince said that he had been trying to stop all of the "free sex shit" as he called it. I had nothing to say. I wanted to see how much information he was willing to give up. I was informed that this shit ran like a corporation. His father was the CEO; there was a board, and he was the face of the company. I instantly concluded that his father did not know that private schools would change his viewpoint on life. This young man was more trapped than I was. He said that he was trying to change the Nation from the inside. We stopped our walk. He was now relying on his instincts and education for this conversation.

"James, I wish you could get a thousand of our kids at a time and put them back in school. The old way of thinking like my father and his generations is over. They believed in numbers. If you had the most members, you had the strongest gang. It ain't that way anymore. \ I could take 10 smart guys and wipe out and replace a hundred dumb guys."

I wanted to know why we were having this conversation. The Prince said that he wanted a New Nation, something that did good in the community. He wanted to open up social centers. I could hear Mrs. Dee in my head saying to me, "That little quiet spoken man is the Devil." I wanted to believe that we were having a breakthrough.

"So why are you in this shit if you don't want to be?"

That statement was met with a very stern correction.

"I am where the fuck I want to be. You may not agree with it, but I am who I am."

I got off that subject quickly. I had something else in mind. I wanted to know about guns. I never got a straight answer. He said something about someone else who had that connection, and he didn't know who. We talked for maybe an hour. He really thought that he could change shit from the inside. I hoped that he had more faith inside of him. That drug money was corrupting a lot of people, including him. All that fancy shit he had and wore was not cheap. Not to mention the Fleetwood Caddy in his grandfather's name. He had the meanest old school Impala with all the switches. The cost was ONE SOUL. It sounded like the Prince might want his back.

I had one more thing on my agenda. I needed to meet with my guy Oliver Stone. Not the movie maker. This was an ambitious young Thunder Cat that I met out west. He had a nose for hustle. Plus he knew how to mind his business and keep his mouth closed. I gave him five bills to follow Agent Oliver. I needed to know how far I could trust the squad. They took charge of Captain Holmes and Officer Ptacc. I wanted Officer Canens. This was not something for the justice system. There is no justice if the police went to jail and they were kept separate from the other prisoners. I wanted suffrage for this man.

Stone met me not far from my house. We exchanged a pound and a hug. He was cool with being in the town. He was a Nation member from out West. I think in K-Town, but I'm not sure. I knew not to enlist him in work against the Nation. SHIT, he was solid as a man, but he still might shoot my ass if I didn't come correct. I was told about a big farm that Agent Oliver owned in Indiana. He raised dogs. I asked Stone what kind of dogs, and he said big ones. He went on to tell me that this dude must be crazy or something. I let him continue. He said that he had all types of medieval shit around his house and a bunch of guns. It dawned on me that Stone said that he was in the house. I asked him what about the dogs. That's when he nonchalantly said, "You owe me $81 for them steaks. And $150 for the sleeping pills. Stone laughed and said, "Man that dude got a lot of dogs." I did not argue. I added an extra three bills to the five I was about to hand him. Good help doesn't come cheap. He filled me in on a few other things that I needed to know. He went to the Internal Affairs office three times in one week. This man was a real chameleon. I needed Stone to give me three more days of work.

The meeting started on time with some emotions. We had to settle our nerves. Agent James started the meeting off with a prayer. Officer Brown was an atheist but he remained silent. Once the meeting started, we all wanted to know the best way to proceed. Agent Hoyde spoke for everyone in the room.

"We have to proceed with caution, and we cannot let any of your coworkers know that we are working on this case. We need to find an extraction point where Canens can come up missing."

I was asked for my opinion. I didn't address the squad. My question was to Agent Oliver.

"Can I use your farm to question Canens?" Before he could answer, I asked, "What type of dogs you raise?

The room was silent. Agent Oliver said that he raised Cane Corsos. I did not know much about them, except for the fact that these were big dogs. He finally said, "Yes, if it would benefit the squad." He still wanted to know how I knew about his private life. Agent Hoyde spoke up to break the tension. He wanted 24-hour surveillance on Canens.

"If we learn his schedule, we can pick him up. He's not an officer anymore, but he is still carrying. We might be able to get some extra info from him."

Officer Brown was on his job. He said, "We do not have to get close to track him." He had put tracking devices in both of his vehicles. We were ahead of the game. Officer Daniels was not there. He was babysitting Captain Holmes, but the rest of the squad all got a chance to add their say. The meeting was breaking up, and Officer Green said she needed to speak to me. I made time for her, but the room never emptied out. I thought this was private, but it turned out to be public. Officer Green wanted to know if I could smell anything other than drugs. I was not about divulging any information that was not needed. She told me that she had a case that they were working on and the department was in a funk on evidence. The lab would take almost three months to come back with something.

"Okay, what are we talking about?"

She threw two pairs of men's boxers on the table. She said that they were evidence in a rape case that she was working. She wanted to know if there was anything on them that I could smell. I looked around the room. It was time to read faces. Was this some type of police initiation joke or what? I wasn't into that so called funny frat shit.

Agent James said, "This is legit." I picked up the first pair and immediately threw them in the direction of Officer Brown and started walking for the door. Agent James tried to block my path along with Green. I didn't have time for their fucking frat games. The exit was blocked by the two of them. They were both talking at the same time. I wanted to push them out the door and keep going. Agent James told Green to be quiet, so she could explain.

"There have been eight women raped in the last three months, and we needed to know if you knew the difference in the evidence."

"Why the hell am I smelling Brown's funky-ass boxers?"

"We needed something to compare the evidence to, so we borrowed his for the comparison. The other pair is from the crime scene."

Officer Green gave me that relationship look. I didn't even know that we had a relationship. I walked back to the table and picked up the second pair.

"Men's cologne," was my answer. "That's what I smell on the boxers. It's old. An older brand, something like an older gentleman would wear."

"So we are looking for an older man," Officer Green said with confidence.

"Stop, you're going in the wrong direction. I never said it was a man, I just said that it was a man's cologne. A lady wore those shorts." The entire room froze. And that was the moment I fucked up. In my eagerness to help I just said something that was too much information.

"How the hell do you know that?" I was looking at the younger Agent James in the face. He said that he had picked up and examined this evidence 20 times. He had been over it with different types of lighting. I told you I just went too far. Now I was trying to backtrack a little.

"Look man, I'm not trying to knock what you do, but there is a female secretion on the inside."

He looked at the boxers again and changed his tune.

"We need your help on this one. Eight women have been raped. And we don't have a clue."

Trying to break the ice in the room, I said, "Well you have one now." It was not funny, and the tough crowd let me know it. I wanted to know what else they had as evidence.

"Just a few items at the station."

Once I looked at Agent James, he said that he would bring it to my apartment. I had to put a hold on that. This man looked and smelled like a cop. The kids in my neighborhood could spot him. We set up a meeting for a different location. I wasn't sure if he was married, so I was going to meet him at a bar.

Growing tired of the police shit, I was ready to roll. Agent Oliver wanted to talk. He knew that someone was following him but never got to see a face. There had to be a way to get him to relax and know that he was no longer being tailed. That was not his concern. Agent Oliver was looking for a different type of hook up. Because of the glasses and the acne, he was incredibly shy. He wanted a date. I wanted to know what he was looking for. Agent Oliver shocked me with his wish list. He wanted ghetto and a big ass. He didn't mind a smart mouth. His last request was the kicker. He was a rich man, and he wanted to be dominated. I told him to be patient and be ready for an interview. My buddy Ajaumu was going to get a kick out of this one. I received a lot of information in one day. But it shouldn't make your forehead cold.

Agent James was in mother mode. She held me in her arms next to her bosom like I was her child. The rest of the squad were standing around, looking with concern. I was lying on the couch. This time no one was there to catch me. I don't know at what point that I went out. The squad now knew that I was not invincible. They hovered over me like I was some sort of a lab specimen. My head was not hurting, but it was spinning. I knew as soon as I regained consciousness, it was another anxiety attack. Only this time, people were around. I need to fix this before it consumes me. BUT BLACK MEN DON'T GO TO COUNSELING.

A PAUSE FOR THE CAUSE: BEING A BLACK MAN IN AMERIKKKA. That was stressful enough. There is PTSD associated with it. We as black men have been conditioned to be strong and tough in public even though the odds are stacked against us. Get help if you need it.

There was nothing that I could come up with to say that I was good. Officer Green gave me the look along with Agent James. It was settled before I even said a word. Officer Green was going to either drive me home or to the hospital. I settled for home. I didn't even have health care anymore. Shit, I was no longer at the foundry, where it came straight out of my check. I needed to get my shit together.

The ride to my house was good. Officer Green drove and rubbed the back of my head the whole way. She got me excited and burst my bubble at the same time. Fatima would be picking her up for a date next weekend, and I was not invited. Damn that hurt. We talked about the rape case. She told me that each woman was drugged after having drinks. I told her again that a woman had been wearing those boxers. I was also told about the second pair of boxers found at another rape scene. I asked if she had ever seen a case where the rapist leaves their underwear. She said, "No."

"Well, someone is trying to frame a man."

That was the last we spoke of the case that night. Green had a second motive for wanting to come back to my house. She wanted to do what everyone else did at my house: hang the fuck out with Walter. I don't know how long they talked; I went straight to bed. Man, sometimes you have to share the wealth.

I was back on the grind bright and early. My nose told me that I was going to eat first. Cottage Grove and 63rd Street. The breakfast was amazing. I was at Dailys. Parker house sausage (we call them hot links), three eggs over easy over hashbrowns with a side of strawberry covered waffles. Man, I love my city. The coffee always came quickly. I was in heaven, or so I thought. An older gentleman slid in my booth, opposite me. It was Mr. Millner, who lived downstairs from Mr. Gant, my old supervisor. I knew that he wanted something; I just didn't know what. He was direct and asked me if I had any money. I thought nothing of it. It took nothing for me to peel him off a sawbuck and offer to pay for his breakfast. Mr. Millner said he didn't want or need my money. It was Mr. Gant, who was in the hole with a local bookie, about $3 grand down. Mr. Milner said that they came by the building where they lived. He didn't say anything else. He just slid out of the booth and left.

I didn't need any more stress. I made a mental note to stop by and see Mike about the debt. He was the local bookie that held the debt. For my own sanity, I needed to get started with my day. I was on 64th and Ellis, yelling, "ROACHMAN, ROACHMAN!" GET YOUR HOUSE EXTERMINATED FOR $25! ROACHMAN, ROACHMAN!" Going back to $25 was my way of giving back.

The rest of my workday went smooth enough. It even put me in a great mood. But my day was just getting started. I still had to see Mike the Bookie. He normally had a crowd around him. I didn't want to put things in a bad mood with him. There was always some young punk trying to make a name for himself. Mike's office was in the back of his beeper shop on 66th and Cottage Grove. He ran construction and a garage out of the same building, just in the back. I really didn't know him.

Once I got to the shop, there was a collection of motorcycles. They lined the back wall. I was distracted. Someone was saying, "Hey you"; this brought me back. Even as I turned to answer, the chrome was amazing to me. I never had this type of stuff in my life. I was like a kid in a candy store. To me, they were life-size toys.

Once I got to the office on the second floor, I wanted to know if we could have some privacy. One of the four goons who lined the walls like furniture made it clear that this was as private as it gets. I enquired about Mr. Gant's debt. Mike said that another man's debt is private. I made it clear that I understood the rules, adding, "But there is going to be money in your pocket if it's taken care of."

Some people are just snakes. Mike let me know that debt is sold all the time for the right amount. I was not going to negotiate with him for too long. I wanted it understood that I would pay the debt plus the purchase points, and that was all the money I had. He laughed and said that he could not forgive the interest on the money. I asked the final price, and he said $4 grand could clear the debt. All I wanted to know was where to bring the money. One of the goons said that I was saving the old man from an ass whooping. Turning to him, I asked, could he not be so disrespectful? I had no beef with them. I just wanted to pay the bill and be done with it. I told Mike that I would drop a bill if the money could be picked up at my place. I had no beef with these people, and I needed to get moving. I gave them an address about two blocks from my house.

There were other things on the agenda. I was driving straight out to Indiana. On the outskirts of Gary, that's where Agent Oliver lived. He met me at a gas station off the expressway. I followed his old pickup to a big-ass farm. He said that it was almost 300 acres. His parents left it to him. He was a prideful man. He wanted the world to know that despite the silver spoon, he worked hard. I felt that when he told me.

We had a couple of beers and discussed my plans for Canens. I got a chance to see those dogs. There were 14 of them. They were big, some weighing as much as 160 pounds. Agent Oliver screamed when I jumped over the fence to rub and pet his dogs. What the hell was I doing? These were not my dogs, and I had no idea why I jumped in here. Oliver was running to the gate to save me as the dogs jumped all over me. He stopped right in his tracks to see them playing and not trying to bite me.

After about five minutes, I got out to a cold beer and some choice weed that Oliver grows on his farm. I thought he was full of mysteries until we started talking.

"HOW FAST ARE YOU?" Again, we were back to the questions. This was about the hit. "James, you were running faster than I have seen anyone move."

I stood my ground to the fact that I was scared and just started running. My explanation got some eye rolls. We had to get back to planning. I wanted to bring Officer Canens and Captain Holmes to his place and question them. It had been almost a week. And his ass was still missing in action. He was on the news every day. Oliver wanted to know why his place and how the fuck did I know where he lived. I needed to clear the air on that.

"I do my homework," I told him, "and I am serious about making the squad work. I picked out four dogs and requested that he separate them and not feed them for at least 24 hours. Agent Oliver smiled and said I wish I had thought of that. Not sure exactly what he thought I was going to do. I was just glad he was game. Seeing how this man thinks, now I wanted to see the collection of medieval shit he had in the house.

As we walked towards his house, he asked me again, "How fast are you?" Before I could answer, he said that Agent Hoyde and Officer Brown both said it looked to them like I was definitely moving well over 30 miles per hour. My answer was that a scared man can run faster.

WOW, this had to be the real shit. The trophy cases that held over 50 different weapons from a time long gone by us.

"What can I borrow for my interrogation tomorrow?" It was a rhetorical question. Any piece of this shit would scare anyone. Agent Oliver was fishing again about the speed thing. I was more interested in the artifacts of a young, rich kid. We had sort of a bonding session. I was almost too high to drive home. Oliver said that I couldn't be who I said I was. He had researched me from birth. There were no clues. We were both pretty high. He wanted to know why his dogs did not tear my ass up like they were raised to do. I stuck out my chest and told him that a BIGGER dog came into the yard. Shit, since we are asking questions, I asked, "What the fuck are you doing making all of those trips to Internal Affairs?"

He didn't even try to lie.

"I work there."

"What does that mean?" I asked him. Agent Oliver told me that he was an Internal Affairs officer, and he moved from one station to another every 18 months to be able to see how the departments are run. I wanted to know what kind of a chance I had if the police don't trust each other. I also wanted to know if I had made it into any of his reports. He said, "No, not yet." At this point, I made it clear that I had to remain anonymous. If I was outed, I would walk away.

Man, that drive home was brutal. I had to stop and eat again. Morrisons Soul Food was my stop. I think I got a double of everything, even the peach cobbler. There was going to be a long run and workout in the morning.

I didn't have time for bullshit, but it was at my door whether I wanted it or not. Agent Hoyde was parked across the street from my house. I acknowledged his presence and drove off the block. After about a mile, I pulled over so we could talk. I can't say that I was worried. It was Agent Hoyde, the person I thought was the most solid person on the squad. Well, not today. He got into my van and straight lit into my ass.

"You can play games with other people if you want. The superhero shit that you do. It's cool to help us, but if another person follows me, we are going to see what you are made of."

I had no clue of what he was talking about. I did not have him followed.

He said, "One of your goons from the Nation was following me for two days."

Again I made it clear that it was not me. Agent Hoyde wanted to know if I would follow Oliver, what the fuck made him any different. At a loss for words, I sat silent and let him talk. Once he described the vehicle, I knew who was following him, and it wasn't Oliver Stone. I made it clear that I would take care of it. The younger Agent James must have a new hobby. It was his second vehicle that was described to me. I don't know why I didn't tell Hoyde who it was. Maybe I had other plans for Hoyde. I needed him to get me a prisoner by tomorrow night. I wanted G Black to be at the farm for the interrogation. Agent Hoyde wanted to know what I had in mind for the interrogation. I was honest and said I didn't know; that it could be played by ear.

Then the subject changed to the hit and how the fuck did I move that fast. I gave the same answer again: A scared man runs faster. We both laughed. He asked me if I wanted to see the video tape that I was not on.

He said that Officer Brown was set up to record, but there was only one problem. When he heard the first shot, he looked up to aim the camera, and I was already gone.

"I never saw you fire one shot. I just heard them."

I needed to know, "What was Officer Brown's reaction?"

"He said that you are the fastest person that he never did see!"

We both got a laugh out of that one. I decided to come clean at that point about a little knowledge that I had. I asked Agent Hoyde, "What'd you do to have the Feds following you?"

There was no blank stare or an excuse. He said, "Two months ago, I stole $300,000." My info was correct. I made it clear that Agent Terrence James was a member of the squad that was following him around town. Now the truth came out. Agent Hoyde told me that he took the money from a raid he was doing as an advance party check for a later sting. He was sent to stake it out alone and figured out the best way to do the sting. He found eight bags of money in the warehouse. He took one. He had no clue how they knew, and he didn't give a shit if the Feds found out. His daughter was going through her last round of breast cancer treatment. She was 28 years old. Agent Hoyde said his only regret was that he didn't take more. Before I knew what was happening, he flipped the script.

"So why did you turn in all that damn money?" Agent Hoyde asked the question loud and angry. I had no chance to say a word. He unleashed on me about how the system is fucked up, and I had a chance to get money that me and my kids will need in the future. I was six weeks shy of my thirtieth birthday, and this black man was 58 years old. Somehow we felt the same about the system. This was a common thing for us. We just had to talk a little bit more. We had more in common than we had apart.

I told him, "It would be too hard to hide with so many kids." But there was an unwritten agreement in both of our eyes: GET THAT MONEY. In this case, what was understood had no business being said. I told him about my plans for Oliver's farm. Agent Hoyde was pleased. He wanted in. I had no problem with it. I just wanted him to bring G Black. He was next on the arrest list with a slight detour.

Fatima was the thought going through my mind. I called her as soon as I got in the house. One of her daughters answered the phone. I could hear her teasing her mother about a man on the phone. We spoke briefly because of her daughter, but the plan was set. I got a quick shower and waited for her to pull up. We went straight to the lakefront. Our evening went well. We ended up at the Ramada Inn in Hyde Park with a nice lakefront view. We asked for a late night check out. We still were not ready to leave. It was a mutual thing. We found each other easy to talk to. After a shower and some more messing around, she wanted to know why I didn't ask her about Officer Ramona Green. I told her that I was curious, but it wasn't my business. For some reason, she just wanted to talk about it.

"James, you seem to be a decent man, but you still don't know much about women. You have to learn how to read between the lines. Sometimes we don't want a man in our business. There are times when we want you to be more forceful and guide us." I didn't want Fatima to think that she was talking over my head, but since we were standing next to each other, she was literally talking over my head. Fatima told me that it would be easier for me to ask more questions instead of acting like shit don't bother me.

I guess it was my turn to respond. Without hesitation, I made it clear that I was already damaged goods from other women. I let people do what they want to do. My next statement must have been too much: "Chasing PUSSY has fucked up my life enough, and I don't have the capacity to mentally handle all of the emotions that come with playing games."

Fatima's face and voice changed.

"WHO THE FUCK DO YOU THINK IS PLAYING GAMES WITH YOU?"

I drew my whole entire body back from her. At this point, we were going to need a stiff drink on the way home. Once I got her to calm down, I started my explanation.

"Fatima, you just gave me three different emotions about me not asking about the two of you. You're hollering at me for answering your question when I told you up front that it was none of my business."

Fatima came close and wrapped her arms around me. She gave me one of her big smiles and said, "If we are both going to be your women, you can ask all of the questions you want." I never tried to escape her grasp. I wanted to be close to her ear as I spoke.

"You just told me a couple days ago that there is no room for a relationship. Fatima, you even said that women were not really your thing." She tried to let go and back up. I was not allowing it. I was the one doing the grabbing for her not to escape.

She simply said, "James, you need to read between the lines."

I noticed she was trying to move. I wasn't allowing it. This was my chance to get my point across.

"The reason you can't move is because I am strong. Not just physically strong, but I love this strong. If you were my woman, you would feel my love, but at the same time my pain and lifestyle would crush all emotions."

Fatima wanted to know what I meant.

"Ms. Diane is somewhat a part of my life. So do I kick her to the curb?"

Fatima's emotions changed some, but she really didn't give a fuck about that. She just wanted what she wanted. I was somewhat having fun with this conversation.

"Hey Fatima, what am I supposed to do when the gun fight starts?"

She said that there would be no such thing, so I let her go to do the math on my fingers as if she was slow.

"There is one dick, five pussies, and four guns." It was as if she saw a ghost and told me that I might die soon, and I would not be the first man that PUSSY killed. I didn't think that shit was funny. For some reason, she never stopped laughing, but after words, she wanted to know how I counted five women. My answer was Diane and Agent James, who also carried a gun. She was quick to tell me that I had a problem on my hands. Just as quickly I told her that this shit was none of my business. Nothing shy about me informing her that I was willing to go on about my business. That would be a lot better than DEAD. Fatima wanted to know why I would jump out just as the fun was about to start. Yes, this whole situation was scaring me to death. But I was more turned on at that than I had been all night. Oh hell yeah, I rode her BIG ASS into the sunset, which cost another night's fee at the hotel.

The next time I woke up, it was already 7:30 p.m. Fatima was in the shower, and I needed to get moving. I had a meeting to get to at Agent Oliver's place. She wanted to know what my hurry was. I told her about my meeting and that I needed a ride since I rode with her. She said she needed to call her kids' aunt to come over for a while. Arrangements were made, and we were on our way. Stoney Island to the expressway. Fatima was not happy to hear that she could not stay and that I would get a ride home. Women are really emotional.

Once we got there, Fatima gave me a sideways look. I had no real way of explaining all the police vehicles. Her first question was, "Are you a snitch for the Feds?"

I understood her concern. I told her flat-out: "No." She asked again about all the police cars, then all the sudden, she stopped talking to me. Her mouth was open. I followed her eyes straight to Officer Green, who was escorting G Black to the back of the barn, where the dog pens are. Fatima was out of the car before I could stop her. She got out of the car and stopped short of G Black. She knew who he was. They made eye contact with his one good eye. The other one was still fucked up from our park encounter.

Officer Green passed G Black off to Agent Hoyde. She made a beeline right to us. There were no hellos. Just venom. I explained that Fatima was just giving me a ride. Office Green said that it was too late because she had already seen the prisoner and she knew the location. I sort of got her meaning, but I was not a cop and didn't really give a fuck about all this protocol shit. I was about the results.

Fatima walked to the back with us as if she was invited. We got to the back, and the dogs went wild. They were barking at a loud and attention-getting pace. There were three prisoners sitting on the ground. They were each hand cuffed. G Black, Captain Holmes, and Officer Canens our shooter. Half the squad was there. I wanted to know from Agent Hoyde how much latitude I had in the interrogation. He said that they were prisoners, and they were not going to let me break any laws.

Something happened; I have no idea what it was. but I turned and walked straight over to the prisoners. They sat on the ground at the back of the barn in what looked to be some sort of an old tool shed at one point. On my way to them, I saw the toys on the table. Oliver had brought out about seven or eight of his medieval weapons. The path to the prisoners took me right past that table. My speech was simple: "If you lie, the dogs will get you. On your second lie, I will pick a weapon from the table." I asked them to nod their heads if they understood. I saw three bobbleheads. They could see the dog pen about 40 feet away. They could also hear them. On my way back to the dog pen, I yelled, "SHOWTIME!" It may sound corny, but that was my thing, and nobody will sit on their hands when I perform.

Officer Daniels asked me what the hell was I doing when he saw me climb up on the gate to the dog pen. I gave him a wink and jumped in. Officer Brown screamed stop twice before my feet hit the ground. I was mobbed by the dogs. We wrestled and played for about five minutes. I was covered in dirt and dog shit from the ground in the pen. I was rolling around with the dogs. I was having a ball. This was something different, and I was getting a better understanding of the power. It was raw and animalistic. It was something PRIMAL about it. Nothing and no one existed outside of that pen.

When I emerged from the dog pen, I was a fucking mess, but I was feeling like something out of the woods. I got down on all fours and crawled over to the prisoners. By the time I got to them, I was foaming at the mouth and growling again. I still don't know where that comes from. It was something inside of me that was now part animal. Once I reached the three detainees, there was foam and shit coming out of my mouth. I told them to remain still or they would be eaten alive. Their five eyes stayed on me. Fear was thick in that barn. Not even the police knew what was next.

Standing to go back to the dog pen, I made a left turn to the pen on the side. It contained the four dogs that had not been fed. I opened the pen and had no leash. I petted and played with them for about two minutes. Leaving that pen must have been one hell of a site. I was on all fours again. The dogs followed. Even Agent Oliver was shocked. But he had done what I asked for.

A box of steaks. One steak was placed on the lap of each man right over their packages. I asked if they could all hear me. Each responded with vigorous head shaking. I let them know that we had not fed these dogs in three days, even though it was only one. My words stopped as I started to growl at the prisoners. Now the dogs were growling. Officer Brown wanted to know if it was okay for him to approach the first question. I said yes and grabbed one of the steaks from Captain Holmes' lap and threw it to the dogs. Not one of them moved. The growling was at a fevered pitch. I pointed, and they all came at the steak. It was devoured. The barn was silent. I wish that I could tell you that the others didn't have fear on their faces.

When the steak was gone, Officer Brown started his recorded questioning. I never got a chance to use any of the medieval weapons. Each one gave up enough information to do several life sentences. I could smell the piss and shit that was in the back of the barn. It all came from the prisoners. Their fear level was off the charts. That smell of fear would be with me for the rest of my life. It gripped my soul to see these once powerful men, lying there begging and telling everything that they knew. Canens offered to sign a confession if we took the dogs away. I even got a lead on who handled the gun shipments.

Information about the Company was plentiful, from beginning to the end. We had enough info to get them all right now. The problem was evidence is what we needed. We had info on more Nation members than we knew what to do with. I didn't move the dogs from in front of them until each confession was given verbally and in writing.

I was coming out of my trance-like state. That's when I noticed that everyone in the room was looking at me. I did not know what to say exactly. I had forgotten all about Fatima being there. Her mouth was open, and she was holding on to Officer Green. Now I saw that they were holding on to each other. She even turned her nose up at my smell. No one even mumbled anything. I was looking for the other steaks to give to the dogs. I ended up giving them the extras that Oliver bought out of the box. Once the dogs were put up, Agent Hoyde was the first to speak. He asked if I was alright. I gave him a weak nod, trying to get my head on fucking straight. It was like trying to get my balance. I kneeled, and Hoyde was right there. He helped me to a sitting position. I sat on the slab of concrete. It felt cold. I was glad I was sitting because it was not a soft place to land.

Man, I had to piss bad. I got up and followed the light to the bathroom. I knew that I wasn't home. The floor had carpet, and it smelled good as hell. I just didn't know where I was. I finished my business and flushed the toilet. The sound of the toilet brought on a herd of footsteps. I was still at Agent Oliver's house, and so was everyone else. Not one person left. In fact, Agent James was there as well. Maybe she really was the mother. I don't know if I was proud or embarrassed, walking back to the bed with all of them looking.

The small digital clock on the nightstand told me that it was 4:37 a.m. Oh shit, I must have passed out again. Fatima rushed past everyone to get to the bed. I thought she was going to get under the covers with me. After her show of affection, Agent James said that we needed to get down to business because the confessions would probably not hold up in court without the evidence. She also said that as soon as Officer Canens got in front of Union lawyers, he might change his story. I made it clear that he should not get to see a lawyer. I had to remember that I was in a room full of cops. I think that's why they were not smiling. I knew that Daniels and Hoyde understood. Our justice didn't have to match their justice. Maybe sometimes professionalism jumps out the window.

Agent James put both hands on her hips and asked, "WHAT THE FUCK IS THIS I HEAR THAT YOU TURNED INTO A FUCKING DOG?"

The truth is always best. I explained to her that I blacked out and did not have a clue what she was talking about. I just woke up in time not to use the bathroom on myself. It's clear to me that someone would have to tell me what happened. There were a couple of snickers in the back of the room. Fatima looked at whoever it was from her perch. The snickering stopped. Daniels was the only person in the room bigger than Fatima.

I was trying to piece some things together in my head. I remembered the dog pen and the dirt. Agent James asked if this was some more of my bullshit. An emphatic yes was my answer, because I was definitely not about to give her some bullshit. My answers were going to be based on whatever they told me they saw. The younger Agent James wanted to know why I didn't respond some of the time. I asked what he was talking about. He was a psychology major.

Fuck it, this was my out. I made a point of getting everyone's attention, saying, "It's a mental concentration thing. You all need to understand that I have learned how to hypnotize myself for short periods of time. It allows me to do things that others may not be able to do. It drains me, and that's what produces the black outs. When I am done, it takes a while to recuperate." I put on the most apologetic face I could muster and apologized for not being up front. I was trying to read faces to determine who was buying it. Shit, I was fishing and caught them all. Hook, line, and sinker on dry land.

Except Agent James. He wanted to study me in a fucking lab. I made it clear to him that if this got out, I don't play fair with others. I saw him visibly swallow like something was caught up in his throat. Mind reading did not come with the powers, but to me it was clear, he didn't want to face me and those dogs or the pool balls. I needed to make this clear to the squad: "We can't speak of this with others." All agreed.

Agent James went back to running the squad. We had urgent business with the Company. They had a shipment moving out to New York in three hours. It was transported in trucks with cattle. Bulls to be exact. We needed to ground this shipment. Hoyde wanted to make sure that it never got on the road. We had an address to a warehouse in Homewood, Illinois. It was not far from our current location. Hoyde laid out a makeshift plan to hit the warehouse. Officer Brown wanted to know if I was well enough to participate. I told him yes even though I wasn't sure myself. Agent James said no. She wanted me to rest and get myself together. There were a few mumbles from the squad. Fatima volunteered to stay with me. At this point, a light went off in Officer Green's head. She said, "We are all going." There was a new plan made on the spot. IF ALL ELSE FAILS, USE THE SECRET WEAPON.

Thirty minutes later, we were sitting in a field watching the warehouse. Fatima and Officer Green approached with a flat tire. No warehouse employees, just cops—three of them to be exact. Officer Green banged on the door. It really was showtime. The officer came to the door with a shotgun in hand. Green spoke with him for a few seconds. The door was closed. We made our advance to the rear of the building. No visibility, but I could smell a large concentration of drugs in a small trailer. It was fenced in. I didn't think that was a problem until Brown showed me a wire running to the fence. Shit, I was about to get fried.

Agent James fed us info from a safe distance. There were two cops out front helping the ladies. Through the window we could see the third officer. He was maybe 20 feet away. He was distracted with some sort of electronic device. Agent Terrance James was right on time. He had one of those new Taser gun things. One shot, and the officer was on the ground. I want one of those. Maybe two.

The ladies performed great. Both officers were in handcuffs, and Fatima hit one of them with a brick. Ten minutes later, we were gone like we were never there. But we now had three more officers to flip or interrogate, it did not matter to me; 3,010 pounds of dope—pure, uncut COCAINE. This was going to cause a big wrinkle with the Company, all the way to CITY HALL and straight to the Mayor's Office.

This cops and robbers shit got me hungry and horny. I didn't know which one was going to be done first. I still had the keys to a hotel room in Hyde park. I was formulating my plan before the squad parted company. Agent James pulled me to the side and instructed me about Fatima. She said that she was not authorized to be there, and she needed to go through a debriefing. I did my best to vouch for her, but Agent James was not budging. She pulled out Fatima's rap sheet. It was long, and she had a past affiliation with the Nation. I asked for time to speak to her. I was told to get it straight in 24 hours.

Oliver and Hoyde both wanted to speak to me about the last 12 hours. Oliver was more on the street of congrats on the work. Not Hoyde; he said to me that I just did hero shit and didn't do it for free. That's millions of dollars' worth of drugs. That 10 percent shit. You need to get that money for your family. He assured me that I would get my share.

What the hell was wrong with these people? I was trying to get out of here. Now Agent James was holding up a plastic bag in my face. I had to step back. He was so close. He said, "That these are the other pair of boxers I wanted you to smell." We all knew what he was talking about except Fatima. She asked if I was sniffing drawers now and fell out laughing. She wasn't the only one laughing. The whole room was.

After checking them, I told him that a woman had worn them, but it was not the same woman. We made plans to meet up later because I had some ideas about the case. I gave him Mr. Gant's address for a meeting later in the evening. I needed to make my last statement before I left. I made it clear to Officer Green, if she didn't meet me at the Hotel it would be the last time that she would see Fatima. Green turned to face me with her hands on her hips to let me know that was not my decision to make. It even had some neck roll to it. I gave her my famous gapped-tooth smile, then I explained that I was going to FUCK Fatima to death if she didn't come and help her. I had never seen her laugh so hard. Everyone else stopped what they were doing. I didn't say another word. I just grabbed Fatima and walked out the door.

I drove, as Fatima had a million questions. She wanted to know about everything. She asked about the guns, Nation Babies; she asked what they were going to do with all of that dope. She had questions about the dogs. The shit was coming like rapid fire. I had to slow her down. It was too much to answer at one time. I pulled the car over on South Chicago at Mrs. Biscuits. It was like a great hood secret. The breakfast was off the chain. We put in our orders to go. Yeah, we ordered too much food. We waited in her car because she had more questions. In public was not the place for the answers. I was trying to give her info as the questions kept coming.

Fatima was full of energy and questions. She didn't realize that she was filling me in on parts of what happened as she talked. Putting my head down to keep her from reading the shock on my face, Fatima described the eating of the steaks. She said that the dogs and I ate the steaks off the laps of the prisoners. I was wondering what happened to those steaks. Fatima said that this produced the most fear from the prisoners. That's what made them all decide to confess to anything I wanted. This brought on another problem in my head; I needed Fatima to swear that she would not tell anyone about what she saw.

"James, you don't have anything to worry about from me. I don't ever want to see you and those damn dogs again." I was a little confused by her statement. I asked for clarification. I thought she was saying that she never wanted to see me again. Fatima made it clear that she didn't want to be an enemy of me and those dogs. She leaned in and kissed me, telling me something that I already knew. She was turned on by the animalistic shit. She said that she and Officer Green gave me a bath at Oliver's place. She said that the two of them couldn't wait to get me alone. I was ready.

We got our food and made a beeline straight for the hotel. Officer Green was sitting in the parking lot. We all went up to the room. I was in heaven. Two beautiful women, plenty of food. What else could a man ask for? They started to get undressed as soon as the door to the room was closed. I saw that first kiss…

And for the life of me, I couldn't figure out why the fuck I was so damn wet and trying to swim again. Agent James and Lieutenant Sosa were pouring water on me to wake me up. Both were laughing. Once I was sitting up in the bed, the water stopped. I didn't know that Sosa was out of the hospital. He gave me a one-armed hug. His other arm was in a sling. Lieutenant Sosa had a big smile on his face as he explained that it was the only way for them to wake me up. It was the next day. I slept for 21 straight hours.

My head was slowly clearing up. I came into this room with two beautiful women, and now I was with Butch and Bitch. Something must have gone wrong. I didn't even know where to start. These two went straight to work. It was about all the cops we had in custody. Lieutenant Sosa said that we could not turn them in no matter how much evidence we had. I drew a blank. I had no idea what he was talking about. Agent James said that they would try to hide behind the Police Union. She said that the first thing that they would do would be to out everyone on the squad. The Company was too well connected to let that happen. I needed to know what our next move was. Sosa said that we would be meeting with Agent Hoyde to plot our next move. Even I knew that having five officers missing without a trace was not good. It wasn't all over the news, because the Company couldn't stand any bad news coverage.

I listened to him and Agent James for the next 10 minutes. I only heard about 50 percent of the conversation. I was trying to figure out what the hell happened. I saw two naked women kissing, and that was the last thing that I remember. These two who were now in the room were not helping my mental picture. I formulated my first real question after the water.

"Can we use Agent Oliver's place to store them until we figure out a plan?"

"That's kidnapping." Agent James was as serious as I'd ever seen her. I shut the hell up and listened. Now that I was quiet, the whole damn room was quiet. We were thinking like mad scientists. I asked if we could put this on the back burner until I had time to get my head on straight. I wasn't sure what straight meant, but I was hoping for a better outcome and some clarity. Agent James said that she would wait downstairs until I came down. Once the door was closed, Lieutenant Sosa hugged me so hard, I started to feel uncomfortable, especially with the fact that I was in my drawers. Sosa expressed how proud he was of what has been accomplished. He said that the squad could do so much more if we could remain a secret. There was no way that it could stay a secret if five cops knew our identity, plus a well-connected gang member. We had to come up with another way. I was fresh out of ideas.

Sosa wanted to know about the thing with the dogs. I told him the same story that I told everyone else. I learned how to hypnotize myself, and that it took a lot out of me. That was the reason that it took me and my body so long to recover. I made it clear that the other night with the dogs was the longest that I had been under. This was Sosa's moment of truth. He said that he had extra information on the Company. There was another person he wanted to bring in on the squad. I made it clear that it was not my call.

Getting dressed and down to the lobby, Agent James had taken care of my bill with the FBI's budget. We did our best to brainstorm as we rode to my neighborhood. I was not about to get out of this car in front of my house. I had them drop me off two alleys over at Fatima's shop.

As soon as we pulled up, Agent James saw Fatima. She got out of the car to have a word with her. I was saying my goodbye to Sosa when the volume got really loud. We both rushed over to see what the problem was. Fatma didn't take too kindly to Agent James' approach to "keep your mouth shut." Fatima told her to get the fuck out of her shop. I found out she also threw in a warning about Officer Green. We got them separated. Fatima was right. All this ESTROGEN AND GUNS, I was going to die.

A PAUSE FOR THE CAUSE: PUSSY AND GUNS DON'T MIX, as I was about to find out. Fatima used her long reach to swing at Agent James. She got in a solid punch that spun her around, or so I thought. It was just a move to come around the other way with her gun drawn and placed under Fatima's neck. Fatima yelled for her to put the fucking gun up. Agent James said no with force. Sosa was the only one that saw Fatima's move. She wanted to know how we liked our pigs—with two or three holes? She had her gun out, too. I wanted to run, but this shit was turning me on. It was like a cat fight on steroids.

I realized that they were not going to shoot each other. Shit, I got brave and said with authority, "Put the fucking toys away. We can play with this shit later."

Agent James told me, "Fuck you."

And Fatima licked her gun and said, "I will if she will," in a sexy voice. Sosa and I had to grab Agent James. Fatima was pushing her buttons about Officer Green.

I don't think Sosa knew exactly what the licking of the gun was about, or what else was going on. He was just doing his best to help keep the piece at the moment. It took a few minutes to get Agent James to the car. She drove off mad as hell. Two minutes later, the shop was closed, and Fatima was open, spread out on that old couch with me trying fuck her to death. No Officer Green to save her. I know that I should have run, but this was excitement on a whole different level.

Now that we'd gotten our rocks off, we had a little time for conversation about Agent James and Officer Green. I didn't think it was a good idea for the relationship to continue. Fatima gave a big laugh at my suggestion and said that she was definitely going on her date with Ramona Green. It was now tattooed in my brain that I was going to get shot. I knew that I had a choice as to which direction to go. It should have been simple—run the fuck on like a good little boy. In my mind, I wasn't a boy. I was a MAN. That's what I kept telling myself all the way home.

Back to life, back to reality. I was hoping that Mrs. Dee won the verbal assault battle. I was getting it from both sides. Walter was bitching about me not coming home for three days. Dee was talking about the raids that had been going on all over the city on Nation members. It wasn't just them; G Black had given us info he had on rival gangs, too. No, I didn't think that it was fair. These young gangbangers were going to jail, but we can't figure out a way to lock up the Police. The system is fucked up. People like me used to think that I was a little smarter than most. Well, that's not true. Most people go straight through school and don't end up with a police record at a young age. You see, the way the whole country is set up, I'm supposed to fail. I don't know why this was on my mind. I think it was my way of drowning out Walter and Dee.

I was closing the door to my room by the time they realized I didn't care. Shit, I was back home and staring at my bed. Just as my head hit the pillow, Walter was at the door, yelling, "The phone is for you."

It was Mrs. Bell. I said hello with a smile on my face. She was just as pleasant. She congratulated me on my performance and win. Mrs. Bell wanted to know if I was available for Saturday night about 2:00 a.m. I didn't give it much thought.

"Yes ma'am, I can clear my schedule for that." She told me that I would receive the location on Saturday morning. Shit, that was another pay day for me. Who the hell was I kidding? I would do this freaky shit with these people for free. This is the part that needs to be understood: The freaks come out at night. I have never had a daytime performance. The people who show up for this shit never look like the type that stays up later than the nightly news. I got off the phone and called Diane to give her a big congrats on all the Nation Baby arrests. She greeted me with a nice hello and a laugh. She was teasing Ms. Tanggy about a bet they had made. She won five bucks because I called. Diane said that she knew I would call about going to the concert with them. *Think fast, David, think fast.*

"Oh yeah, I thought the two of you were going to pick me up. Like clockwork."

"Well, have yo ass ready at 5:00 p.m. on Saturday." Tanggy was not on the phone, but she was close by. I got off the phone only to realize that I just made an appointment with Mrs. Bell and a date with Diane and Tanggy. I needed to figure out a way to fix this shit.

Somehow, I came to my senses and decided to go for a run. It was just the natural thing to do. Without a doubt, the baddest Mofo in the city of Chicago was the wind. Some people just called it the Hawk; either way, it was getting to be that time of year. It was somewhat nippy on my run. I had a planned route in mind. I wanted to see for myself if these places were raided and closed down. Right around the time I got to the first raided crackhouse, I felt good. It was almost a reason to shout. I was hoping that the ladies of the neighborhood would be happy and proud. I even felt as though I could hold my head up.

This whole fight was a long way from over. There were just too many things going against our people, and I'm only one man. I promise that I will try. IF I DON'T GET SHOT FIRST.

I ran over to Mr. Gant's house where I was meeting young Agent James. I had a few ideas about this rape case. The cologne on the boxers was old, something that I had smelled before. We got there around the same time. I explained who Mr. Gant was to me, and we would be only a little while. Mr. Gant came to the door with his pistol behind his back. He wanted to know if I was speaking or creeping. I let my old friend know that I was speaking. If my answer was creeping, he would have shot Agent James. We were allowed to enter, and I made my introduction. I told Mr. Gant that we needed to check out his cologne and aftershave collection. He led us to his bedroom. There had to be 50 bottles, dating back 40 years. All we had to do now was find the right one. With a bright and helpful smile, he said, "I have some more in the bathroom." Agent James had a hard time holding in his laughter.

We spent over an hour sniffing and smelling all kinds of scents. It took a while, but we found it. You would not believe there were two colognes: one was called Hi-Karate, for which I had seen their commercials as a child; the second pair of boxers had Avon cologne called Wild Country.

Agent James was already putting that big brain of his to work. He had started making a list of all the places that these ladies had in common. Six of the eight rape victims had a couple of places in common. The CheckerBoard, a blues club on 43rd Street. The other one was a steppers joint called the 50 Yard Line. It was on 75th Street. One thing I knew for sure was we were looking for an older person. Also, there was the fact that something was put in their drinks. I had been sniffing this cologne for almost two hours. It did not escape me that Mr. Gant had a pot of pinto beans and some hot water cornbread going. He even had some smothered pork chops in the oven. I immediately call a halt to this work shit. I think I scored enough points with Agent James. I had some questions that had to be answered. I needed to know what his report on Officer Hoyde was going to be. Agent James said that it came down to how he was going to explain the money. Hoyde was a proud man, and he was not going to lie. I wanted to know why he was not brought in for questioning. He said that the information about the missing money came from a not-so-trustworthy snitch, who just happened to be a dope fiend.

My next question was, "Why don't they drop this shit?" I was told that it was the large medical bill payment he made for his daughter, which came only a couple of weeks after the money went missing.

"If he can't vouch for the money, what am I supposed to do?"

A proud man really doesn't have to say much in life. His body of work speaks for itself. I didn't need a thank you from Mr. Gant about the gambling debt. He just gave me a nod at the table. Man, this country boy from Arkansas could flat out cook. The three of us were full as a tick. Agent James almost ate his body weight. Mr. Gant made it clear that he didn't have lunch for next week and started to prepare another pot of beans before we left. I did not know one person who could have a mean bone in their body after that meal. We even killed a good amount of beer with that meal. That's why I was in a vehicle with Agent James. I was too full to run around the corner.

I went back to the subject of Officer Hoyde.

"Hey man, you need to write this shit up in his favor." I got one of those "I'll think about it" looks. I guess emotions are emotions. That's one thing our faces can't lie about. So I proceeded to make a deal with him on the spot: "If you can find it in your heart to help Hoyde, I will try to find it in my heart to not mention your girlfriend and child on the side to your wife."

The vehicle was pulled over, even the engine was turned off. I knew the play before it even came. He wanted to threaten me about my knowledge. Not a good idea. I started screaming in the car. I did not want him to say one word. I needed him to listen before this got out of hand.

"I have no intentions of telling your wife anything. I just need you to put on Hoyde's shoes for five minutes. Which one of those women and children that you love, which one would you steal for to save their lives?" I made it clear that I did not need an answer. I asked that he start the vehicle. I still had to meet with the brain of the squad. I needed to see where his head was. I drug him into the meeting with me. Shit, he was a member of the squad, too.

We sat in the back storage room of a local business. It amazed me how many places the police could hide and observe people that they wanted to keep an eye on. Agent Nora James was glad to see her nephew, but we had no time for a family reunion. Sosa jumped right in with a chart and graphs that he had made. It showed the connections between the Company, City Hall, police precincts, and all of the gang drop off and pick up points. We had something new on the table. Mob boys who got looped in from the surveillance that were being run. I was not surprised about Bridgeport. I just didn't know anything about those boys in Melrose Park and Tinley Park. These were different suburbs around Chicago. One was to the west of the city and the other to the southwest of the city. Sosa made it clear that we couldn't collect anymore prisoners.

"We are stretched thin now trying to watch them all," he said.

Hoyde was all about getting these crooked mother fuckers broken down to their knees. He wanted to hit all the holding spots. If their bread was short, they would have to go to work and make mistakes. He wanted to make it hard for the cops to pay up the chain. Hoyde made it clear that we could hit five of the places in one day, three belonging to the mob boys and two that belong to the cops. All these places had minimal or no security. Officer Brown was using some type of new recording device that came on only when there was motion. He had made a schedule and given it to Hoyde.

Agent James wanted to know how much time we had and when we'd start. She was shocked to learn that the first hit was in less than two hours. He said, "60 pounds of dope and maybe some cash." At this point, he gave me a knowing look: "GET THAT MONEY FOR YOUR FAMILY." We were all briefed on what was to go down. This was something run by professional police officers. They got suited up and ready to go to work. In my ghetto language, they were "hoodied and masked up." I wanted to know if we had enough people for this shit to run all night. They said that the rest of the squad was on the way to the city.

I asked, "Why we don't split up to get more places hit in less time?"

The breakdown had already been done. I was working with Officer Daniels, Oliver, and Hoyde. The rest of the squad made up the second team. All the spots were residential homes except one. It was a warehouse not far from our current location. The only problem was covering the distance from the gate to the building. Maybe 80 yards of open space, and the one guard was facing the gate. He had a small monitor to help him. Hoyde volunteered our team for that job. I knew that there had to be money at that location.

We got there, and sure enough, we needed to get close to that guard shack. I asked Oliver if he had one of the new electronic gun things. He had one and Daniels had one. I collected both. The fence was held up at the bottom, and I was gone. I turned on the power and ran straight through the door of the guard shack. There was no time for the guard to act. It only took one shot from that Taser thing, and this guard was out.

We went into the warehouse and retrieved the money and the dope. Hoyde said that each one of the spots were scheduled for a pickup in the morning, which meant that they all held a large amount of money or dope. On the way out, Officer Daniels stopped by the guard shack to destroy the camera system and get the security tape. It had footage of me running very fast.

Our night went smoothly after that. I waited in the vehicle while they did raids on two of the private residences. We had four garbage bags filled with money from the warehouse. I wasn't going to let Hoyde down. He still had close to $300,000 worth of medical bills for his daughter.

I guess the rest of the night went smoothly for the whole squad. We had more shit in that storage room than we knew what to do with. This wasn't just evidence; this was break your back type of shit. There was dope, weed, and money piled up everywhere. We literally had nowhere to sit.

It was 6:45 a.m. As a group, we were tired and hungry. I needed a shot of something to pep my ass back up or put me to sleep. Sosa and Daniels both had bottles in their vehicles. We got some glasses and made a toast. It started out simple: "TO SUCCESS." Young Agent James was somewhat emotional as he said this squad was the most successful thing that he had ever done. That brought on a second toast, and we were on our way to getting drunk on empty stomachs.

I got a few strange looks when I picked up a two-pound block of weed and put it in a bag. There was silence in the room. I wanted to know what the fuck were they starring at. Daniels said that I could not just take evidence like that. I told him that I was not a cop and all he had to do was come and take it from me. He took two large steps forward, and I quickly gave him the weed and told him that it was not enough for me to kick his ass over. The room was shocked. They were even more shocked when I picked up a bigger bundle, maybe five pounds. That's when I said to Officer Daniels, "Now this bundle is worth kissing your ass for."

The whole room started laughing. We needed to break the tension.

I wanted to know who was giving me a ride home because we were going to have some weed in the car on the ride to my house. Officer Green volunteered to give me a ride if I bought her breakfast. I said it was cool with me, and Agent James damn near swallowed her tongue trying not to say shit. I knew that this was not a real job for me, but I also knew that pussy and work don't mix. I got out of there with the biggest bag of weed I had ever seen. The car door closed, and I was glad. I did not want the others to hear Officer Green screaming. Part of it was directed at me and the other part was on her. She wanted to know why I would take Nora James to Fatima's shop. I didn't have a good answer. But I didn't have a bad one. I sat and listened. I learned from my eldest sister, if you have nothing good to say, then don't say anything at all. The anger only lasted for about two blocks. Then Officer Green couldn't hide the excitement on her face. She wanted to know about the gun play. I didn't really have a chance to tell her what happened, because she went on to explain to me how excited Agent James was when she got home. The gun play and the physicality of Fatima put Agent James in a whole different mood. Green said that she came home to a dark house. She was sitting there with her robe open wearing the largest strap on that they had ever used. She figured it was brand new. They played a few rough games until it was time for sex. She said she had to soak in the tub for two hours. Officer Green said that she was fucked for a little over an hour in every position imaginable.

Yes, Fatima was all she talked about. Fatima had pushed some buttons. Now I needed to get the fuck out of the way. PUSSY AND GUNS DON'T MIX. Green saw the look on my face and told me straight forward, "We cannot FUCK," with lots of emphasis on the word. A confession was made. Agent James beat that thang up. She said it needed kissing not sticking.

I said, "Okay, what do you want me to do? I can take care of that." She declined, only to tell me that this was a job for a woman not a man. My mind went right back to the lessons of Nat and Clair. Sometimes men are not needed. The dumb man in me spoke anyway. "Well, can I watch?"

The vehicle was pulled over at that moment.

"James, please get the fuck out of my car."

I did, with about a mile and a half to get home. I knew not to ask about breakfast.

"Run your fast ass home," was her reply. I did exactly that. It was still early. We had been up all night. I still had work to do. There was money in a dumpster that needed to be retrieved. Yeah, while they were in the second house, I got out of the vehicle and stashed some cash for Hoyde. Those medical bills were not going to pay themselves.

I got home around 7:30 a.m. My first call was to Oliver Stone. I needed to pay him and get the rest of the information about the squad. Shit, they were following me. I put on my work clothes and headed out. I got the money from the dumpster. I was headed to an area called Roseland. Don't let the name fool you. We called it the "WILD WILD HUNDREDS." It was mostly gang territory. The whole area was composed of middle-class black people who were now feeling the crunch of the crack epidemic and being left behind by the politicians. It was the perfect place for me to be. I got on with my job. I was on 105th and Wentworth, yelling my new theme song: "ROACHMAN, ROACHMAN! GET YOUR HOUSE EXTERMINATED FOR $25! ROACHMAN, ROACHMAN!"

It was a good day. I made a couple hundred bucks and got some promises from others that they would give me a call later. I felt good riding home. I needed some food, plus I couldn't wait to see Fatima. I went to the hoagie shop on 111th Street. I got myself a steak supreme and Fatima a couple of hoagies. I had a few stops to make. The first was to meet up with Oliver Stone. He was worth his weight in money, and then some. We met at the designated spot. I gave him a big bonus. I didn't count the money; I just reached in the bag and grabbed a handful of bills. This move was going to buy mee some loyalty and some continued great work.

Stone wanted to talk to me about a party that was going on at the Brothers Palace. It was a steppers' joint on the Westside of Chicago. He told me that he would book us a table. I had no problem with it. Even though I preferred to step at The Rose if I was out west. It was a place on Madison Avenue; a bigger dance floor and less gun play. The last one is the most important.

Back to business. I was only told about the girlfriend and child of Agent James. Now I was looking at photos. This had to be enough to get him off Hoyde's back. I gave Stone an address to drop off the money in the garbage can. Hoyde just had to take it out. He told me that it was a little hard for him to follow Officer Brown because of where he lived and the surrounding area. There weren't a lot of black folks in Skokie, Illinois, so there were less chances for him to blend in. I understood that. Man, I was glad for the information that he had given me. It let me know what I was dealing with. Please don't forget, I was the only one who did not have a badge. If shit went south, I needed to have a soft place for me and the kids to land. As we parted company, I hit the brother off with a half-pound of that shit I got today.

I was starting to feel like fucking Secret Squirrel. All these fucking meetings. I was sitting at a table with the Prince and one of the prettiest women I had ever seen before in my life. She was his wife and the mother of his children. He made the introduction, and I had to come back to reality. That was when I was able to speak. We were sitting at a back table at Salom's. It was amazing. I had the curry chicken with all the sides I could get. He talked more than I did. It was partially the food and partially her. I didn't want to appear disrespectful. They invited me here to talk about my next class of students. The Prince wanted me to do 20.

She wanted it to be 60. I had no idea how they were so far apart. Plus that wasn't the number that I had told him. I saw several things sitting at that table. One was young love. The other was an enthusiasm for bringing a change to the Nation and Moe Town.

First off, I was holding these classes in my basement. I wasn't a real teacher. I barely got out of high school myself. I let them know up front that it was too much for me. They laughed at me like I was telling jokes. Once the laughter stopped, they told me that the Nation was going to sponsor everything. My next thought was I needed a space large enough to hold everyone.

Damn James, hold up. For starters, this man paid you to kill a man, and now I am waiting on the next instructions. Something about this just doesn't feel right… Then, *On the other hand, if they are paying, I can get more students. Shit, this is what the hood needs.*

Who was I to turn this down? In the back of my head was Dee saying, "That quiet, soft-spoken little man is the Devil." I slow played it and said, "Let's take the time to set up a plan and find a facility." We agreed and made plans to keep an open dialog. We had some desert. Small talk was being made for the next half hour. She told me that I must be a special person for him to invite me to dinner. She also said that he talked about me a lot. That's what the dinner was about. She said that he wanted to nail me down on a commitment because he really wanted the school to work.

Now was my chance to test his commitment. I had an idea that I wanted to put on the table. I didn't know how much latitude I had, but fuck it; I went for it.

"If you want these kids educated, then you have to show some initiative first." They both sat up and let me know that they were listening. I took a deep breath and then I said it: "WHY DON'T YOU GIVE THESE KIDS THEIR LIVES BACK AND KICK OUT EVERY KID 16 AND UNDER? MAKE A LAW THAT THEY CAN ONLY RE-ENTER AT 18 IF THEY WANT TO."

The table was silent. He knew what just happened, but he couldn't say it in front of his wife. I wasn't testing his manhood. Far from it. I was not that stupid. I was testing his HUMANITY. How can you be a MAN sitting at a table with not only your wife but the mother of your children, but you won't let these kids free? It was an unasked question: "Sir, where is your humanity?"

He was definitely up for the conversation. He made it clear that it was an interesting point of view. He even gave supporting arguments on why it was a great idea. He also played politics, saying that it was not his decision to make. His wife wanted to know how often we hang out. He answered for us by saying, "Not often enough."

I think my gapped teeth were showing when she complimented me on my manners compared to some of his other friends. And she shocked us both when she said, "You are not afraid of him."

OH shit. It was time to go. I thanked the two of them for a lovely meal. Making my exit, I shook both of their hands. We said that we would continue to have a running dialog about how many students. Like someone was chasing me, I was gone. I was gone. I made a mental note to only meet with the Prince, not her.

I got home at about 9:15 p.m. I was full, plus I got some extras for Walter. The kids were already asleep. I had phone calls to make. Hoyde was the first one on the list. He confirmed the delivery, and his voice was smiling through the phone. We kept it short. I needed to talk with Mrs. Bell. I wasn't trying to cancel work with her; I just needed her help. We spoke briefly, and she was interested in my idea. She just thought it sounded a little farfetched. I was headed for the shower. When the phone rang again, it was the Prince. He said that he and his wife would do about $200,000 for the GED program. Shit, maybe he did have some HUMANITY. He said that I had an interesting way of presenting things. It came with a stern warning: "DON'T MAKE IT A HABIT." I made it clear that we were on the same page.

My last call before washing my ass was to Diane. She answered with a smile. I wanted to know if she could stop by the house for a few minutes. She wanted to know if everything was okay. I said yes; everything was fine. I just had something for her and Tanggy. Diane didn't answer, but I did hear, "We will be over there in 15 minutes." That's when I realized something I already knew: They really are a couple.

I was shit, showered, and shaved by the time they got there 45 minutes later. Shit, I was even dozing off when they came into my bedroom. I was a little shocked, so I pulled the covers over me. Before I could focus my eyes, the twang rang out: "I KNOW THE FUCK YOU AIN'T BASHFUL. WHO ARE YOU HIDING FROM?" I did my best to compose myself. It was hard. I didn't even invite her.

I got up and hugged them both briefly. I was heading to a pair of basketball shorts. I just needed to get a few things out of the way. The first was giving them a half a pound of weed. They both smoked, so I thought it was a good thing to do. There was a loud scream from Tanggy. Diane just stood there with her mouth open. She gave me a big hug with a, "Thank you, baby," which I knew she meant.

After the hug, it was Tanggy rubbing all over me and jumping up and down. I put these shorts on for a reason. I needed to get them calmed down enough for the second surprise. It came with a little speech.

"Thanks for inviting me to the concert."

"See I told you he got some excuse. That's why he gave us this weed."

I sat on the bed with my palms on my forehead. I wasn't going to say a word until she finished. Diane got up and grabbed her and kissed Tanggy. That was their first show of affection around me. She told her to sit the fuck down. I thanked her. Nodding over to Tanggy, I was checking to see if it was okay to finish. She nodded back. I didn't even stand; I just said my piece.

"I have another job that I would like to invite you to after the concert." Tanggy knew not to say anything. Diane wanted to know where I worked. I told her that I was doing a little acting on the side. She had the biggest smile that had a small laugh attached. I answered her question with a question: "Do you want to see me perform or not?"

With the same smile she said yes. I looked over to Tanggy to let her know that it was alright for her to speak. She simply said she was going to be there early to get a good seat. They wanted to know where. I didn't have an answer. I explained that it was an underground thing, and the locations changed. Tanggy said like the house music thing used to do. We all cheered for that. If you are from the Chi, you know what it is. It makes you jump without trying. We own that. I made it clear that I would give them a location by noon on Saturday. There was also a little warning: "This may determine if you two want to keep seeing me."

Diane leaned in with her forehead on mine. She wanted to know if it was that serious. I said yes with a truthful yes. I think my mood was a little too serious for her. She quickly gathered up Ms. Tanggy and hit the door. I wasn't trying to be rude, but I was putting my cards on the table. I wasn't going to hide what I did. If they wanted to be with me. They needed to get the news firsthand. I had spoken to Fatima earlier today. She was happy about the hoagie sandwiches. I must have a thing for big hugs. Fatima showed her appreciation with a big hug. It almost rivaled Mrs. Lola. I wanted to get me a couple hours of sleep before she came by. We made plans to hook up at about 1:00 a.m.

I just laid there thinking about all of the shit I had gotten into over the last three months. I wasn't a poor man anymore; I didn't have to be here. I could just pack the fuck up and leave. There were no strings attached. Out of this neighborhood, I could fight for my kids. There was a world of opportunity out there. All I had to do was reach out and grab it. I was getting spooked about some of the decisions that were coming. The Prince, I was literally close enough to lock his ass up for the rest of his life. That's not what I wanted. I had a need to see him change the Nation. I did not know if it was possible; we just had to be patient to find out. He and his wife had pledged a large sum of money, but I wasn't fooled about who he was. What other voices in Moe Town could make dozens of gangbangers go back to school? I was going to do all I could to help him and his wife.

Two officers were now retired, one way or another. I didn't feel sorry for them. They got away with a large sum of money. Officer Ptacc was instructed to give 40 percent of his take to Finny. I wasn't sure how I felt about that. I knew that they were crooked when I met them. They also provided a lot of information. Some of it, I still haven't shared with the squad. It was my way out if it all went sideways on me.

We had a better-than-expected arrest record on the Nation Baby thing. We had people ready to testify and be moved under witness protection. Diane was keeping the list together as other information came in. I was just amazed at how fast these so-called tough guys start to tell on each other. That shit was comical. Because of all the snitching, the squad could hardly keep up with all the raids.

Man, it was a tough job playing cops and robbers in real life. I didn't want to play in the first place. I can't lie; this shit was kind of fun, but I couldn't let them know it. Just think, at 3:42 a.m., I was hauling ass down an alley carrying almost $500,000. I hid it over a mile away and was back before they even knew I was gone. That macho shit in me was on a high. I needed to keep my eyes on the prize. A soft spot for me and the kids to land. Right now, a move to the country was looking pretty good, but I wanted to see this shit through. I also had no intentions of getting shot. The danger and the women involved were really driving me. I also needed to stand up and be a man about not leading anyone on. What the hell was I saying? I sounded like a fucking choir boy. These were adults; let them make up their own minds. Yeah, that was the excuse I was using to get all the sex I could out of my situations. I am a man, that's my excuse. Besides, I'm single.

I needed to get the hell out of town. My son Terrell's birthday was coming up. I must be there. His mom was planning a skating party. I spent extra money to try and make it a blast. My only question to myself was, what constituted seeing this thing through? I had to pull out at some point. I came into this damn room to get some sleep, but I was still looking up at the ceiling. I didn't want to take a shot just yet. I wanted to wait for Fatima.

The telephone ringing scared the shit out of me. It was Officer Daniels. He said that we needed to talk right away. There was an urgency in his voice. I told him that I was on my way. We met up at an empty lot. His face looked worried. He said that one of the prisoners got out for a brief moment and made a call from the phone in the barn office. He said he got to him as quickly as possible. Agent Hoyde's name was yelled out along with his own name. We had no idea who he was talking to. I thought it was best that we contact Sosa and Agent James. He also agreed. I made a mental note to introduce our new prisoners to the dogs.

Officer Daniels wanted to talk. We were alone, so all I could do was listen. He said that he wasn't trying to be a hard ass about the rules, but I needed to learn a little more about tact. He let me know that not one cop in that room had an objection to me taking that weed. He told me that it was the way that I did it, out in the open. I was told that it was as if I was challenging their authority to say anything. Yeah, I understood where he was coming from. I let him know that I would work on it. His last statement was I HAD TO GIVE SOME RESPECT TO GET SOME RESPECT. I KNEW THAT I WAS TALKING TO A MAN.

A small box was passed to me that he had retrieved from the passenger seat of his vehicle. He said that it was from Agent Oliver. Officer Daniels made it clear that the message was not from him. "THESE ARE FOR YOUR BALLS." It appeared to me that it was two leather socks. I just took the box and placed it on the seat as I drove off. Now I had more shit on my mind. How would we keep these officers safe? Not really sure why it bothered me so much. This was the job of the police, but I was taking a crash course in humanity. Once you get to know someone, they just become a part of you. It really has nothing to do with the person; it has to do with what is inside of you. You either care or you don't. Not only did I look it up, but now I was starting to understand this noble man shit. It had more to do with putting others ahead of yourself. That's just my interpretation of its meaning in my life.

Walter came to my door with a message.

"You have a box in the weight room. It came earlier today. Your cute ass mailman sat on the steps with this box until I came from shopping." I had good reason to hide my excitement from Walter. The mailman waited because I gave him $200 to make sure it got to my house. It was hard to contain myself. I closed the door to my room after bringing the box in. It was well over $300,000. This was some of the money from the heist. I still had well over a million stashed somewhere in Mississippi. Each family member received 25 grand for their efforts, no matter how big or small their role was. I got squeezed for an extra 30 Grand by Uncle Shorty and Uncle Chester. It wasn't something to worry about; I was just surprised that it wasn't more money or more relatives. Once that box was opened, it seemed as though a weight had been lifted off my shoulders. My kids were going to have a good time next week. We were going to order room service. Winnie could have her own box of cereal.

I had to find a hiding place for the money. Dee was my first thought. I went straight over to her apartment. Her brother Cordell owned the two-family flat. He was a veteran like me. He was a railroad worker. Good man, but currently in love with an undercover crackhead. The cover was coming off faster than she knew. Her secret was out.

When I rang the doorbell, Cordell answered with a big smile. It was just a façade for the moment. His girl was in the apartment. I could hear her arguing about money.

A PAUSE FOR THE CAUSE, this is a perfect time to explain that whole comeback thang. His girlfriend was a very dark-skinned lady. I would say that she got teased a lot in school about her appearance. She had four daughters, all very light skinned with long hair. It was not lost on me what I learned from Diane about those women who go out and have children by a loser or some Pretty Ricky. Now her life was fucked up. She was using a hardworking man in the neighborhood to get her life back on track. In this case, she was dragging him down also to help take care of some losers kids. He loved those little girls as if they were his own. You see it every day. No one says anything because one of your relatives or friends is the one pulling the shit. All we say in response is, "So and so found herself a good man." IF ALL ELSE FAILS, USE THE SECRET WEAPON.

Back to the story. The box was locked up in the attic. Dee was given more than a little something for her troubles. I got home just in time to see Fatima take off all her clothes. She broke the bands on 40 grand that was laying on my bed and laid down on the money. She had her eyes closed. I guess there was some fantasy going around in her head. I just stood there and watched her roll around in the money. We were both heavy people, so I couldn't just dive on top of her and break my bed down. Once she opened her eyes, we knew what was about to go down. And "go down" it did. This passion went on for almost an hour. We were both excited about the money.

Reality is a mother fucker. All those fantasies about making love on a pile of money is bullshit. We both had at least four or five paper cuts, and they hurt like hell. I had my head down between Fatima's thighs. I was trying to apply some alcohol on two of her paper cuts. This shit turned into a laughathon once we figured out our mistake.

Fatima was a true player of the game. Not once did she ask about the money or where it came from, not even in pillow talk. I was the one with the questions. I wanted to know about Ramona and Nora, AKA Officer Green and Agent James. Yes, I was like a woman. I wanted all the gossip. She told me that it was too bad I missed a great session in the room with her and Ramona when I fell asleep. She said that her size was a big turn on for Ramona, and she was so turned on that she almost kissed that thang. Then came the conversation about Agent James. Fatima was frantic to talk about that shit. I was told that it might have been one of the biggest turn-ons in her life. Fatima said that this was going to be an ongoing thing in my life, whether I like it or not. Fatima said that it was a hard thing to find a gay-friendly man who knew his place. I didn't take it as an insult; I was just trying to follow the lessons that I had been taught by Natalie and Clair. Don't push, but most importantly, let it come to you. Don't be so nonchalant about it; pussy needs to know that you are interested and chasing. It needs to feel wanted. It does not like to be pressured.

Fatima told me that me being a man was one of the reasons I would always have this problem. I sort of laughed about her saying that. It was obvious that I was a man. We just finished fucking, and we were out of breath. She told me to shut up, because I didn't have a clue what I was talking about. Now I was stuck. It was relayed to me that, "Yes, you know that you are a man. That part is simple." She said that the one blaring thing I didn't understand was I never had to tell anyone that I was a man. It was an aura about me. She put on a fake male voice as she beat on her chest, saying, "I'M A GROWN-ASS MAN! YOU WILL NEVER IN LIFE HAVE TO SAY THAT." Fatima said that I smelled and looked like masculinity. "James, that's your hold card over women. It's a curiosity thing." It was hard for her to hold back her laughter. As she said, "You are a big-ass man, you are just short," I didn't take it as an insult. My ego was too big for that. Plus she was about to get the shock of her life.

"Fatima, I have a second job." She just sort of gave me a dead stare.

"I don't think anybody really knows what you do for a living," she replied, pointing to the pile of money on the floor. We threw that cutting ass money on the floor. "You didn't make that killing roaches." Again she never asked where or how I got it. She went right on with the conversation. "So what's this secret job?"

I made it clear that she could make up her mind at any point to leave as I explained, "I have a side job as an actor."

Fatima's enthusiasm was crazy. She jumped out of the bed and grabbed my gun off the dresser. She did an action movie spin and posed in a shooting stance with the gun. She said, "We are going to Hollywood. I can be your costar! They won't know what hit 'em!"

Again, I loved her enthusiasm, but I had to break the news that we were not going to Hollywood.

"Well, what kind of acting do you do?" Before I could respond, she said, "I know you don't do them boy movies…"

Waving both hands, I made it clear that, "I don't do noooooo boy movies."

She said, "Good," like it was a relief. We discussed the fact that I would be performing in two days, and I wanted her to see what I do. She told me thanks for the invite, but she had a date with a pretty police officer. I made it clear that I was not trying to cut in. I was already told that I wasn't invited. Ramona made that clear from the start. I told her that the performance was at 2:00 a.m., and they were both invited. She was still standing there naked with a gun in her hand. She also realized that I was no longer talking. Fatima knew what time it was.

I got out of bed and rolled us another joint. I poured us both a drink. Fatima said that this is what she was trying to explain to me earlier. She said that the look on my face as a man told her that as soon as I finished with my drink, I was going to FUCK her until the sun came up. I didn't say a word. I just nodded my head. Fatima decided to give me some motivation. I got an incredible masturbation show while I finished my joint and drank. Her smile was amazing. I didn't feel too manly as she laughed when I had alcohol coming out of my nose, but I was trying to down my drink so I could get with the program. Fatima said, "Calm down, I'm not going anywhere." I hope that Fatima understood that her big pretty ass did something for me.

Somehow, we got on the subject of what I was doing with the police. She thought it was a good thing and a help to the community. I didn't need the pleasantries. I wanted to know what she thought as someone who had been on the hustle.

"Street people won't like what you do, James. It's going to knock a lot of hustles." I was about to get another part of the dope game. Fatima brought up the dope that she saw the squad get. She said, "When the dope is in short supply, it's cut too many times. The youngsters on the street catch hell because this weak shit is harder to move. You are solving one problem on one end and causing chaos on the other. That's not counting the wars that come over customers when shit is short and the dope is bad. The money has to flow up the chain, no matter what."

The next question shocked me. She wanted to know how she could get involved to help. I wasn't sure what she wanted to do. This woman was a mystery wrapped in a problem. She was right to the point: "All their arrests have been men?" I said yes. Fatima said, "Don't you get it? Y'all need some women on the team." She went on to say that nothing distracts a man more than pussy. I knew she was right because the whole time she had been talking to me, I had been watching her rub that thang. I was stuck. That was one way to get her point across.

I must be honest. I didn't ride that thang until the sun came up. I stopped about 20 minutes before it came up. No one in that room was complaining. In fact, we both fell right the fuck to sleep.

Walter was banging on my bedroom door, and I rolled over to find Fatima gone. He was yelling, "Get the fuck up!"

The police were at the door. I threw on some basketball shorts and ran to the door. It was Agent James and Oliver. I let them in. We got to the top of the stairs, and there was a traffic jam. I don't know which one of them saw Walter first. No one was moving. I was in the back. I could hear Walter saying to them, "Don't block the door and close your mouths. Flies don't really want to go in there." They proceeded into the apartment. Walter invited them in for a cup of his famous coffee. We all walked to the kitchen. I didn't realize that we had company, plus a newcomer to Walter's Café. I turned into a fucking retard. I was standing there with my mouth open. Lisa spoke first.

"Well, ain't you going to introduce us to your friends?" When she said it the second time, my brain had kicked in. I started to make introductions around the room. Dee was laughing again, not because I was half naked in front of Walter, I went retarded again. The young lady in the corner stood to introduce herself and shook their hands with grace and elegance. After that was done, Lisa was talking.

"She wanted to come over to talk to you about some school."

Let's just call her "the Princess." I still couldn't get a word out before Dee said, "How are they going to have a conversation? He can't talk!"

At this point, I needed to breathe. I needed to calm down and get this lady out of my apartment. I decided to distract myself by telling the room those two cops were old army buddies of mineand I was shocked to see them. Walter jumped in by offering cups of coffee. Just as I was shocked about the Princess being at my house, Agent James and Oliver were glued to Walter. He had on a colorful gown with matching fingernails. We made the best of a crowded kitchen. In fact, it was quite cozy. This went on for the next 20 minutes.

Young Agent James was getting a little nervous, so I pulled him and Oliver into my room. No sooner than the door closed. I saw Agent James take a deep breath. He wanted to know who that lady was. I tried to slow play it because of who her husband was. I said that she was just a neighbor. Oliver told us to get our heads together. Another deep breath was taken. They both started talking. They knew who the call was made to. It was to Canen's wife. She was a desk sergeant at one of the precincts. Daniels was arrested but not booked on any log sheets. Oliver said that he thinks that he is being held for a trade. Sosa was trying to pull some strings to see if he could find out where Daniels was. He was using the excuse that Mrs. Daniels was in his office trying to find her husband.

Just as we were talking, the phone rang. It was Officer Daniels. He was given a phone call to set up a trade. I think he called me because he didn't want to lead the Company to the cops in the squad. He said that they wanted all the dope back plus Officer Canens. 6:45pm was the time that they gave me. We had several hours to plan the game plan.

I grabbed a shirt and my toiletries. I was headed for the shower. All I had to do was keep my head down and make it to the shower. I was almost there, but my path was cut off. She wanted to know when we would be able to discuss the students and find a facility. The Princess said that she had put in an order for 40 GED books that also came with work books. As calmly as I could make myself, I replied that she was getting us on our way. I even got it out that I thought that my kids school might have two or three classrooms for rent, I just needed to finalize the pricing. This was met with a cheer and a big spontaneous hug. I didn't move, my hands stayed to my sides, and I repeat, I didn't move. No one said a word except Dee. She said, "Talk shit to me again. I know what to do for you now."

I needed to get a run in. I needed to think. Officer Daniels said that I had to make the drop. They wanted no cops and no guns. That wasn't very fair. They were cops, and they all had guns. "Don't get shot." I think that is my new motto.

On our way out the door, Oliver wanted to know if I got his gift. I was not clear at first, then I remembered the small box with the leather socks. Oliver thought that was funny as hell. He said that they were not socks. Now I was confused. Oliver walked over to the pool table and said that they were for the pool balls. Still not comprehending, he told me that they were from his collection. The light went on right away. A new weapon. Then he told me that it was one of the weapons used by the ancient Romans. They would put rocks in them and swing them to knock out an enemy.

I broke free for my run. My head was jammed to the max. I might have to run all the way to Mississippi before I could get myself together. I was now on 79th and Western at Mrs. Muffins getting me some breakfast. On my way home, I stopped to scope out the exchange location for the night. It was a warehouse on 59th Street off Loomis Street. I had no intention of going into that building without knowing how to get out. There were no cameras. I saw lighting on the outside of the building. I was not sure if they worked; it was still light out. I needed to see inside of that building. I wished that Agent Hoyde was here to help me figure this out.

Once I climbed up on the shipping dock, I could see that there were three entry and exit points. I made a mental note to lock one of those to limit access. I needed to see where they would possibly put a shooter. I walked to the end of the dock to see what was on both ends. There was a large shipping container on one end; I could hide behind it, but it wouldn't stop a bullet. The other end only had weeds and an eight-foot-tall fence, so I made a mental note: *Don't run that way.* I would be trapped if I couldn't get over the fence in time.

I landed a heavy shoulder on the old wooden door. The third floor is where they would put a shooter. There were three different tables or work benches near the windows. Two of them would give a clear shot of the lot. One was kind of off to the side. I broke the legs off the first two and left the third in just the right spot for someone to be able to creep up on them. I wasn't worried about them moving the workbench. It was old factory shit; it was not going to move. The second floor was also a large open space. Nothing that caught my attention. The first floor was different. It had little cubby holes and different office spaces. There were two hallways leading different directions. I took some time to move some office furniture. One hallway was blocked. The two boxes at the top were empty. This would be the direction I would run. These were smart people.

I knew that they would take the path of least resistance down the open hallway. I don't know anyone in the world with built in night vision.

I started looking for the janitor's closet. I put a half of a bottle of liquid soap in a gallon of water. The mops and brooms were broken, so they had a point on them. I used the power to jam the back ends into the wall from knee high to chest high in eight different places down that hallway. I didn't think you could come down this hallway in the daytime without hitting one of them. Nighttime was going to be a bitch. I poured the soap solution on the floor. Even five hours from now, it would still be slippery. I needed to get the fuck out of the building. I had been in there too damn long. The Company was going to scout this bitch, too. Last thing on the list, I knocked out all the lights in that hallway.

I made it home to a slew of messages. Sosa was the first call that I made. He was sounding frantic. I told the lieutenant about a plan that I had, and he said that we needed to be real careful. Sosa told me that I needed to meet up with the squad in one hour, and everyone would be there. I washed my ass and got in my van and hit the road. I was nervous as hell. I just hoped that Oliver brought everything I needed. I had two leather socks with pool balls inside. Each one had about an 18-inch reach. I needed to be as safe as possible. I pulled into the lot where I saw the enclosed trailer from the very first warehouse raid. If all the dope and money was in it, there would have to be about 5,000 pounds of dope. I didn't have any idea about the amount of money. It was a lot.

Oliver had not arrived yet, but Officer Brown was in the lot having a cigarette. We spoke for a brief minute, and he let me know that I didn't have to do this. Brown said that this was a police matter. He knew that the Company was coming with force. Officer Brown was not the only one concerned for me. Hell, I was scared, too, but I was excited. Trying to get in the door, Officer Brown told me that he had that video equipment that I asked for. Sosa met me at the door. We went right to work on a game plan. Hoyde didn't disappoint. He gave me two hand grenades. He said to me, "If you don't come out, no one comes out." We were both soldiers. Nothing else had to be said.

There was about three hours left. Oliver finally showed up. I had a big list, starting with five of his dogs. He had something like a luxury kennel for the dogs to travel in. Agent James watched with fascination. She had never seen me with these dogs before. We played for maybe 20 minutes. At this point, I wanted to take a nap. I used one of the rooms in the back. It didn't take me long to doze off. It seemed like it didn't take long for them to wake me up. I had a charge on my battery. Reality struck when I saw them all in tactical gear. I was getting briefed on all the things that they went over while I was asleep. I told them about the adjustments I had made in the factory. We all seem to be on the same page.

As we got closer, I had my eyes peeled. I was looking for some flashing lights and a broken-down vehicle. It was Oliver Stone doing some advanced recon work. I pulled over. The three vehicles that followed pulled over, too. Agent James got out of her vehicle to see what was going on. I waved her over. Stone had a look of distrust on his face. First, I had him spying on the police, and now I pulled up with a caravan of them. This was not his shit. It took a couple of seconds. I got him calm, and he told us about who was in the building. Eleven officers in all, six inside the building, and one had a long gun case. That meant one sniper on the third floor. Stone described exactly where he saw light on the third floor. Two cops were under the dock one on each end. I figured the rest were on the first floor. Oliver Stone asked if I needed any help. I told him thanks for the info. Even though I didn't say it out loud, only in my head, I declared: *IT'S SHOWTIME.*

I got back in the truck that I was driving. It was just Agent Oliver's old cement truck with the enclosed trailer attached. I drove to the entrance, which was locked. I waited maybe two minutes before the gate was opened. Two police in riot gear walked next to the truck to let me know where to park. I got out of the truck with a mask on and three dogs. The police were on alert after seeing the dogs. One of them told me that the dogs had to go back in the truck.

"No sir, that's not going to happen," I told him. We continued to walk towards the warehouse. A man and a woman stepped out into the light. She asked about the dogs. I made it clear that I did not carry a gun, and my pets were my protection. Just for humor, I asked her how fast she could run. No one thought that was funny but me. She seemed to be in charge. She wanted to know where Officer Canens was. I nodded over to the truck. She asked, "Did you come alone?" I said yes, and that I was unarmed.

One of the officers decided to do his job and frisk me. BAD IDEA. All three dogs gave him a full-tooth smile that came with a lot of growling. He made a hasty retreat. I made it clear that no one was to touch me. I needed to know where Daniels was. She said to give them what they wanted, and I could have Daniels' worthless ass back. It was something about the way she said it that made alarm bells go off in my head. I knew that Daniels was hurt. He may not be able to stand or something. She didn't sound like a fair trade was going to be made. They asked me to pull up my hoodie and t-shirt to prove that I was not wearing a wire. There was a reason that she was slow dragging this. There was no urgency in her voice, as if she was stalling for something or someone.

It hit me that this was a matter of the heart. She was Mrs. Canens. She had to know that her husband was safe. I gave a warning with the keys to the truck and the trailer: "Walk slow. The officer will have an escort when he leaves the trailer. Plus, there are two other officers in there with him."

I stood still trying to get a gauge on the shooter or see if I could get control of this shit. I made a loud protest about Officer Daniels. The lady spoke again, only to give the order to roll him out. One of the bay doors came up, and he was pushed out in an office chair. I couldn't see him clearly in the dark. This was a big proud man who didn't sit slumped in a chair. His body was almost folded over. I could hear him moaning in pain. Him being tied to the chair was the only reason that Daniels didn't fall over. They had worked him over pretty good. I called out to Officer Daniels to ask if he was alright. I heard him say, "ROACHMAN, KILL ALL THESE MOTHER FUCKERS!" The distress in his voice alone got the dogs all fired up. I had to start petting them to keep them calm.

The two officers were coming back with Canens and the other two prisoners. I said that they had to live up to their end of the bargain. I needed to see Officer Daniels off that dock and walk away with me. She told me that I would have to untie him, which would mean that they would be gone. That's why she said that he was tied up. They needed a cushion to be able to leave. Canans got close enough to see the dogs, and he went straight shell-shocked. His wife hugged him to calm him down. This was also her excuse to get out of there. No one was going anywhere. My dumb-ass EGO kicked in. No one was going to leave early when I was performing.

The happy couple took about three steps. I left the back door open to the truck. The other two dogs had come up behind them. The growling of the other two dogs not only made her turn back around, the dogs turned Officer Canens into a basket case. He started to moan and cry. While I was petting the dogs, I retrieved one of the hand grenades from his collar. The other cops were waiting on some type of signal. It was too late. I made it clear that we were all going inside. I wanted to see Daniels in the light.

With the dogs walking so close to me and the grenade, no one was going to run or attack me. It was dark out, so we all stayed close together. I didn't want to give their shooter a clear shot. I was right in the middle plus we were moving. I stopped everyone at the steps of the docks. I patted two of the dogs on the back, and they were off. They found the openings under the docks before I spotted them. A 120-pound dog and a cop in a small crawl space. It happened twice at one time. We were close enough to hear the carnage. They all cringed at the screaming, except for one officer. He put his gun in my face and ordered me to call them off. I showed him the grenade, and he said, "We will all die." That wasn't going to happen. I waited another 15 seconds and gave a whistle. My babies came running back with haste, looking up at me for some hugs and rubs. I didn't disappoint them. I petted the dogs as I observed Mr. and Mrs. Canens on the ground. She was trying to calm him down. Just hearing the dogs' attack sent him over the edge. She could not get him to stand. When Canens got loose at the farm, he was placed in the back of one of the dog pens. Three dogs were chained in front of him. He had 14 inches of space between him and the dogs, and if he didn't keep his back to the wall, the dogs could reach him.

I nodded for us all to keep walking. I was no longer worried about her or him. She was trying to collect the shell of a man that she married. While petting my babies this time, I retrieved my pool balls with the leather sock from around their necks. I now had both hands in my hoodie pocket. I asked as nicely as the situation would allow, "Could one of you please roll him into the light?" I was now looking at the other four cops from the Company. They saw the look on my face as I saw Daniels. I told you a while back that our face would tell on us. I was mad as a MOTHER FUCKER. Someone was about to pay.

The cop who put the gun in my face was an experienced soldier. He tried to make sure that he was within striking distance of me at all times. My steps were careful as he and I did our dance. I wanted Daniels untied, so we could leave. The other two officers who were in the trailer wanted a gun, and they wanted one right away. I said no. It was easier for me if they didn't have a gun.

That dance was still going on, only I was where I needed to be—less than ten feet away from the furniture that I stacked earlier. I knew if one of those officers got a gun, the shooting would start. I produced the grenade from my pocket and made it clear again: no guns for them. We heard a jingling sound. It was the shooter from the third floor. He had come down because we were now inside. That's what I was waiting on.

Mr. Gun in my face was first. He got a pool ball to his temple and two more blows before his body hit the ground. You know, nighty night. I had a clear shot with the balls in the leather socks. I had a clear shot at everyone in the room. The dogs were creating chaos. And I was moving around faster than they could imagine. The good part was that I could wind up and swing without getting too close. Hitting a knee with a pool ball had a different feel to it. I wasn't worried where I was hitting. I just needed to make contact. One of the cops had his weapon drawn. He was trying to shoot one of the dogs. I hit him across the hand. He shot one of his guys in the hip. The sniper was trying to run with two dogs on his ass. At some point, he dropped his rifle. It didn't increase his speed. Me or the dogs made a mistake, one of the cops from the crawl space had recovered and started firing shots. I wish I could tell you that I was out of there. That wasn't the case. I needed to get Daniels, who was still tied to a chair. I turned on the power.

Moving as fast as my legs could carry us, I was pushing the office chair out of the door and then along the side of the docks. At this point, the squad was there to clean up the mess. Agent Nora James was leading the charge. Her first two shots took out our gunman from under the dock. They came in guns blazing. Me and the dogs were on the dock waiting to see what happened. I was untying Daniels from the chair. Two of them snake-ass cops tried to exit a side door. These babies rocked them to sleep. By the time I called off the dogs, these boys were not going anywhere. I was missing something. There was something that just didn't feel right. I was missing something.

The reunited couple was gone. I looked up to see them pulling out of the parking lot with the money and the dope. I was gone; the power put me almost next to their vehicle. As luck would have it, they got caught by a light on 59th and Ashland. They would have run the light, but the two vehicles in front of them stopped. I never slowed down. All they heard was a thumping sound as I went by. The back window was down. The grenade rolled under Canen's seat. I was over a hundred yards away as I watched the grenade do its job. They got blown the fuck up.

A news crew was there before the police. Another news crew was at the warehouse to film the carnage. The Company had just taken a major loss. The squad was gone without a trace. Even three of the dogs were gone. The other two followed me as I chased the truck. It was incredibly important to show the truck leaving the parking lot of the warehouse, which meant that Canen and his wife were somehow implicated in the warehouse scene. I couldn't wait to see the news. This was my request from Mrs. Bell, who was a TV and radio executive. I gave her an exclusive as long as I or the squad was not on the tape. They had close ups of the happy couple who pulled off with maybe 40 pounds of dope. The rest was at Oliver's place. All the money was not there either. Hoyde made sure of that. They got a chance to get photos and video of the dope and money burning. My favorite shot was of the two partial bodies in the front seat. They still had on their seat belts. I guess seat belts do work.

The shit at the warehouse was something to see. In that hallway were three officers who ran that direction, all impaled on those broom and mop handles. None of them died; it made for some awesome pictures. Well, it depends on which end you are looking at it from. If you get my point. I wasn't sorry for their pain. We had our own worries.

Officer Daniels was in bad shape. He had lost a lot of blood. There were three teeth missing. His teeth were not knocked out; they were pulled out. Four or five of his fingernails were missing. In different lengths. He was tortured for information. I was deep in thought when a horn blew. I look up to see my dude Oliver Stone. He let down the window to see if the dogs were okay and told me to get in the vehicle. I said yes, and we were off. Stone wanted to know if I was the police. I knew that he had a gun within reach, and he was not a fan of the police. I gave him my best gapped-tooth smile and said no. I could not erase his memory of him seeing me with them, and it was three cars and a truck. I had no idea how much he saw at the warehouse. I explained that it was a con that I was running. Stone was no fool. He saw and delivered a large bag of money, plus he got paid extra from that same bag. Before he even moved the car, he said, "I want in." Shit, I needed to know what the hell he was getting in on. Stone didn't know what it was, but he wanted in on the money. I told him that I would give him a call if something came up. I had him drop me off over two blocks from the meetup spot. I knew that he would follow me. That's what he does. Not tonight though. Me and the dogs hit the alley, and it was history.

I walked into the back door. Officer Green was crying. She grabbed me right away. Her body was shaking really hard. I just held her. There was nothing for me to really say. After she calmed down, Lieutenant Sosa gave us the best run down on Daniels. His condition wasn't great, but he was going to be okay. Sosa wanted to talk to me privately for a moment. First, he congratulated and thanked me for the work for today. He said that I was free to leave. I didn't know what he was talking about. Sosa reminded me of the fact that I had kids. He said that shit was about to hit the fan. He let me know that the Company did not play fair. I asked him if he thought that I played well with others. Lieutenant Sosa said he had no idea if I even knew how to play any games. Agent Oliver was glad to see his dogs back. He gave me the grenade that was still attached to one of the dogs. Hoyde didn't say anything; he knew that I was keeping the grenade. When Agent Hoyde looked at me, all I could do was think, *Cha-ching*. He had something else that he wanted to discuss with me. He had a way to shut down the Company, or so he thought. I was willing to listen. He said tomorrow at lunch we could talk more. On my way out both Agent James and Officer Green wanted to talk to me. First they said that it was good work out there. Nora said that I had a fucked-up mind to put those spikes in the wall. She was at a loss for words when I told her that it was three broomsticks and two mop handles. She told me that I was going to have to be patient. I was only in a hurry to get out of there. She nodded towards Hoyde. I followed her eyes.

"He wants to kidnap the head of the Company. If you do that, we all die."

I was somewhat following her. She said they both just found out who runs the Company. Hell, I want to know that. Agent James shut down on that front. I didn't see Hoyde walk up. My little pokey sticks became the topic of conversation. Even Green jumped in, talking about how devious of a plan it was. They all cringed when I told them about the soap on the floor. The trick was to start the soap about 10 feet from the door. You want them to get a good running start.

I needed a ride home. I didn't feel like running. Green volunteered. OH SHIT, PIMP ON THE SET. Agent James spun around and admonished her right on the spot. She said, "You better mind your DAMN manners and know your DAMN place." Shit changed quickly. Green's voice changed to a softer, "I'm sorry, can I drop him off?" Agent James rubbed her hand across her face as if she was stroking her mustache and beard. The whole move had a slight pause for effect. Then she gave the nod. The little filly went to get her jacket and keys. I gave her some dap for the player move. I confessed a long time ago that I was a MAN with an EGO. I asked James who she thought was the biggest pimp. She did that face stroke again and started smiling with her head cocked to the side. I knew that look. Somehow, I was having another measuring contest with someone who does not have one. It was made clear that Green wouldn't be needing any dick tonight. It was my pleasure to tell her that she lost the pimp contest. Before she could respond, I whispered in her ear, "YOU LIKE THIS DICK, TOO."

Officer Green grabbed my arm, and we were off. I fell asleep on the short ride home. When we got in front of the house, I was told that my ride was over, and she could not come up stairs. I just laughed and thanked her for the ride. I opened the door to leave, she grabbed my arm and said, "She didn't say we couldn't fool around for a few minutes."

I really wasn't in the mood, but I did ask if she would be joining Fatima at my show. This got a good laugh, and she replied, "I wouldn't miss it for the world."

I was in my room getting my shit together for tomorrow night. I was going to the Westside. The Brothers Palace. Your shit had to be together. I pulled out the navy-blue two piece with the silver pin stripes. The navy Stacy Adams boots were in order. I wasn't old enough for the big hat game. I made a mental note to buy a couple down the road. The kango was still fresh. You can't get this sharp without something special on the arm.

I went straight to the phone. I had a friend from the Projects in Altgeld Gardens. She was a bonafide stepper and easy on the eyes. Even though we were just friends, whenever she was around, my friends would say that I was bringing out the fine China. The thing was, it was all about the stepping. She was the best I knew. Not only that, I knew that she had my back. She carried the Baretta strapped to her thigh. Our call was brief. All she could talk about was burning up some Westside ass. She asked what color I was wearing. I gave her the colors and told her to swing by my apartment in the morning. I had some shopping money for her. A little screaming on the phone, and we said goodbye. Hell, what woman don't love to shop?

I didn't have a lot left in the tank. I needed to talk to Walter before I turned in. I needed him to deliver a couple of messages. I gave him a thousand dollars. He asked me three different times if I was sure. My answer never changed. A bed is an amazing thing.

If you sic your brain on a man, you may never have to ball up your fist. I was out working. The fall air was a little nippy. It was not a problem at first. After about two hours, I was cold as hell. I didn't feel bad about calling it a day. I had to get ready for Hoyde and pick up my suit from the cleaners. It was Friday, and I was going stepping tonight. I got home, and my boy Stone was sitting on my porch. We spoke and went straight to the apartment. I was heading up the stairs, and he stopped me. He said that we had to cancel the stepping thing. It was due to the fact that the raids were taking a serious effect on the Nation. The leadership was down to a skeleton crew. I had to play dumb. To me, that meant everything was going well. The con that I was running was the next subject. I put some of my cards on the table.

"This is not a regular hustle for me. This type of money comes around sparingly."

Stone said that he wasn't greedy; he just wanted to do something that mattered. I asked for some sort of an explanation. He said that it was cool to see those cops go down today. Plus, he made some money in the process. I asked that he be patient. Stone had one last question. He wanted to know if me and the Prince were friends for real. I told him that we were associates. That was good enough for him. He had seen the Prince a few times out west but never got a chance to talk to him. Just two hand shakes in passing.

We need to get something straight. There are millions of our young people out here gangbanging and never met who they are banging for. For most, it's just an idea; for some, they just want to be loved and to belong. I don't know who I blame this on.

Once I gave Stone the rest of his bread, he was gone. I had some other shit to get done. We had two higher ups in the Company who were extremely vulnerable. I needed to put them in some sort of a vice. I needed them to flip on the Company. This wasn't about pain. It was about honor. One was a City Hall executive who thought no one knew who he was. That bastard was already in the trunk of the police vehicle. The second one, I had to go collect. It was lunchtime for him. I knew that he would be eating at his favorite restaurant. It was called Dorothy Browns. It was in Hyde Park on the third floor of a court way building. I ran through the door with speed and force. It shattered into small pieces. I had one of those new stun guns in one hand. There was a leather sock in the other. It was going to be bad either way.

Officer Daniel Roscoe came running from the bedroom, pulling his gun out of the holster as he ran. He was butt-ass naked. I think he had the wrong gun out. It didn't really matter. A pool ball to the chin, a stun gun to the ass cheeks just as he was hitting the ground, and I had no sympathy for this piece of shit. He was the money man for the Company. He took care of the books. We needed him to talk.

You can't pay too much attention to your handy work. Dorothy Brown came up and hit me with a baseball bat. I was shocked more than hurt. It must have been reflexes. She was now laying on her back, just as naked as the bookkeeper only now she had a big-ass knot in the middle of her forehead. It got big real fast. I think that I am in love with these leather socks.

She never saw my face. Me and old Roscoe were heading down the back steps. He was wrapped and tied up in a couple of blankets. I threw his ass in the trunk with the other loser that Hoyde had collected. He was Tony Quarters. His last name was Tucci. That didn't sound good. Plus, he had several occasions that he paid up to the boss with change. Someone said that he had keys to the city parking meters. We needed to get this shit done, and fast. We had a house that the FBI used to stash people before court trials. It helped that there was an attached garage. Yeah, this shit was about to push all of our luck or fortunes.

Two minutes later, the doorbell rang. It was another camera crew. Only this time, Mrs. Bell was there too. I asked her to leave. She needed to have no connection with this. Mrs. Bell whispered in my ear that she was not going to miss this shit for the world. I brought in both prisoners one at a time. They were chained to a wall. We all wore masks. Each man had been given something by Agent Hoyde. I didn't know what it was, but they both looked dazed to me. I was in the back, but I heard the voice. It was Walter and two of my neighbors. Yeah, those two big ass gay boys. I came out to speak to them about what I needed. Walter had given them money to just show up. I was giving them money to do a specific job. Agent Hoyde gave them masks to hide their identity. I didn't want to see this carnage. Mrs. Bell's freaky ass couldn't wait for the action to start.

I left to get something to eat. It was my lucky day. I was not that far away from a place called three corners. Right outside of Altgeld Gardens Sols BBQ. This shit was heavenly. One of my old neighbors from the Gardens was the owner. There was a bar next door. I ordered my food and went next door for a double Martel. I ordered enough for everyone. I don't know if I could have held down a meal and watch what was going on at that stash house. Roscoe and Tony were thoroughly being fucked on film by those two big boys I brought over. They wore their masks, but both of the Italian boys had close ups of them being penetrated. They were also filmed with their mouths and throats filled.

I got back just as they were finishing up. I sat the food on the table. I walked back to the bathroom, got a bucket of water, and threw it on them. They came to with a start. I could see them looking around trying to figure out where they were. The bright lights for the cameras kept us from a clear view. I smacked both of them extremely hard. I needed their undivided attention. They were shown some photos on a screen, and some film footage was rewound for them. At this point, the film crew was paid six months salary each for less than an hour's worth of work. The twins were grinning when they got the $5 grand each. Mrs. Bell just wanted to get her rocks off. I didn't have time, but we made a date for something later. Now it was just Hoyde, the two mob boys and me. It was made clear if we got the answers that we want, the photos and the film footage went to them. If not, it goes on the news and to the *Chicago Defender* and the *Chicago Suntimes*. Hell, I threw in WGN because it sounded good. They looked at each other. I think a deal was made between the two of them. Hoyde took about 30 minutes with each one of them in different rooms, so he said that each would have plausible deniability if they ever got found out. The information from those two literally shut down the Company. It was Tony Quarters' property that was used to store the dope for the mob and the Company. We also found out that he had a key to the change room for the Chicago Transit Authority change room. One of his relatives had an outside contract to clean the place. Each was given the option to leave town. We needed to check out their information. The squad was busy for the next few days. If you don't have money or dope, you might be out of the Dope game. The bookkeeper Daniel Roscoe was so afraid of the photos getting out, he gave up his own personal money he was stealing from the Company. We didn't take his personal money. They were released and disappeared into the long goodnight. We never told Agent James about the kidnapping. We said that those dogs could make a man talk.

I needed to get to the cleaners to get my suit. I was headed over to Hood Cleaners. No, that's not why it had that name. The man who owned it, his last name was Hood. He had been on 59th Street for years. When I got home and got my shower, shit slowed down. I rolled me a fat-ass joint, poured myself a drink, and fell slap the fuck out.

It was 11:15 a.m. when I woke up. That was because Walter was beating on the door with a package for me. It was the location of tonight's performance. It had the location and a few cheesy lines. It wasn't about the acting. They wanted to see the carnage of the flesh. We are all weak to the flesh. That's all I'm going to say about that.

I got on the phone and called Diane to give her the location for tonight's performance. I knew that I was going to see her later. I just wanted to speak to her to see where her head was. She wasn't in a good mood the last time she left my house. Tanggy answered the phone and took down the information. She also spoke to me in a different manner. It was pleasant. I was not going to mess this up. I stood up a good woman last night. There was nothing romantic between us, but I still owed her an apology. I grabbed James Jr., and we were off to Cain's Barber College on 51st and King Drive. I needed to get the fade tight. I had a date with some women I needed to do some making up with. James wanted to know about the new business. He said that I had been working a lot lately. I knew that this was in reference to the fact that I have not had a lot of time with them. Walter had told them that I had gotten a lot of work from the city. I did not want to lie to my son, but I also could not tell him that I had been running around playing cops and robbers. I just went with the city contract thing.

After the haircuts, I could tell that he was really my son. Not just the lips and the gap in his teeth; he had style. James pulled out his little roll of money, tipped the barber two dollars, and thanked her for cutting his hair. She thanked him and gave him a hug and a kiss, which he wiped off with his hand. I also saw him smirking a little. We spent the next couple of hours getting some food and buying me some new cufflinks and a tie and handkerchief set. Of course he picked the shiniest cuffs that he could find with a tie clip that was the same. I had a great time with James.

CHAPTER EIGHT
THE DATE

BACK TO LIFE BACK TO REALITY, I got home to see a Fed car down the street from my house. I thought that this surveillance shit with the squad was over. I sent my son upstairs. I was up close on their vehicle before they had a chance to react. It wasn't the squad. One of them gave me a sealed envelope with Agent Nora James' signature across the back. They drove off immediately. It was simply a message telling me that I might have to lay low for a little while. It seemed that one of the officers from the warehouse remembered hearing the name "Roachman" from Daniels. Not only that, one of those twins called me "Roachman" and the mob boys remembered that. Now they were looking for a fictitious character named ROACHMAN. This cops and robbers shit just kept getting better.

I went upstairs and told Walter that we needed to move soon. The first thing out of his mouth was, "I TOLD YOU TO LET THE FAMILY TAKE CARE OF THAT PRINCE BITCH." He walked off switching and still talking. By the time, I got to him to explain that it was not the Prince, Walter was washing dishes at a fast pace, trying to ignore me. I told him that it was about Sosa and Nora. His tone changed, and we had a civil conversation. It was getting time for my date, and I had not looked at any of my lines for tonight. A lot of it was adlibbed for the most part. I sat in my room for the next hour looking over this corny script. I was playing two parts tonight. Not only that, I was a part of the very first scene.

It was cliché as hell. The hot and sexy aunt and her nephew, who just happens to need a place to stay while in town going to school. I was also in the last scene. It was called "THE SCARLET SISTERS." I was a little twisted about this scene. It was about two rich sisters during slavery. They bought male slaves for their personal enjoyment. I was to be the prize on the auction block. I was just starting to learn what it was to be a black man in Amerikkka. I had spent time in other countries. There are a lot of places that my black skin is hated. There are also places that my black skin is loved. I am back in Amerikkka now.

I got a call from Ms. Diane. She let me know that they would be ready in one hour. My next call was about our transportation. Black Mike the Bookie also ran a limo business. Yes, I was going all out. He was now in debt to me. Some of the information I had gotten had his name on it. I paid him a visit and saved him some jail time. The Company was about to sacrifice him and his crew, so their arrest numbers stayed high. He shut down and moved his operation.

I got straight in the shower and got ready. I even shaved off the peach fuzz on my chin. When I came out of the room dressed, I only had time for a few pictures with the girls and Walter. James Jr. was next door at Ms. Dee's house. When I came down the stairs, there was no one at Dee's house; they were all on the porch. Even nosy-ass Lisa came from across the street. Yes, I was sharp as hell. "Casket ready" as my older relatives would say.

The ride over to pick up my dates was short. The limo driver got his first tip early. He had stopped and picked up the flowers that I ordered. The front door was open; the glass storm door was closed. I could hear Ms. Tanggy telling Diane that I was in a limousine. Okay, she was a little louder than usual. Tanggy opened the door to let me in. I was trying to compliment her on her hair and her dress, but I could hardly get it out. She was on 10. The twang was there, but it was a happy twang, if you could call it that. Diane came out of the room no different than Tanggy. They both wore form fitting dresses of the same autumn orange. Tanggy had on a shorter version of Diana's dress. It was just below the thighs and nowhere near her knees. Diane's dress was just below the knees. It clung to her all the way down with a little flair at the bottom. Both women had a flawless make-up job.

Tanggy ran over to me to give me a hug. I had to move the flowers, so that she would not smash them. She was jumping up and down. She even managed to get a large smear of lipstick on my collar. I didn't mind at all. When she stepped back, I handed her one of the dozen roses. It was almost comical. She did one of those curtsy things that little girls do after a play or recital. She even said, "tThank you, sir."

Tanggy stepped over to the side. It was almost as if she was revealing something. There was even an arm wave to present Diane to me. She was beautiful. There was no running up like Ms. Tanggy. She was walking towards me, but it looked as if she was floating. Nothing but elegance as she walked her arms rose to embrace me with love. Her hug was different. It was slow, a full body thing with a soft whisper, "BABY, I MISS YOU."

We messed up some lipstick. It was a very passionate kiss. *WHY ME, LORD? WHY ME?*

Tanggy grabbed my hand, saying something like, "No, you can't mess up her hair like that!" I didn't even know that I had my hand on the back of her head. The kiss was so good. I think I understood how much I missed this woman. I handed her the flowers. I got an amazing smile. This woman was a class act. Following Tanggy's lead, there was one more curtsy done, only this time, it was flawless. Maybe it was her who was flawless. There was something else going on here. They had a surprise for me. Diane reached over to the table and handed me a box. I was surprised. It was a tie and hanky set complete with cufflinks, all in that same color of orange as their dresses. We as men don't think on that level.

We got into the limo. It almost seemed too perfect. I was sitting in the back with two women. WE had all that we needed. Tanggy had brought along a bottle that she got from work. It was some type of bourbon, and the label was fancy as hell. I couldn't wait to light up a joint. We all made a toast to a good fucking night.

The Regal Theater on 79th and Stony Island was popping. We pulled up to the door. The chauffeur opened the door. I stepped out first, so I could give the ladies a hand. Let me tell the truth here, the weed smoke got out first. There were people standing outside who said so. People will not keep quiet for shit. As I reached for their hands, I was trying not to smile too hard, but it was hard. I had just taken the ride of my life. I was trying to block the view of the ladies just a little, preserving their dignity as they got out. Neither of them was wearing underwear. I had a matching pair of orange lace panties in my jacket pocket.

We'd taken an hour for a 20-minute trip. Tanggy started out by saying that she always wanted to get it on in a limo. I wanted to know what was stopping her. She said nothing and jumped right on me. There was a lot of kissing. I told the driver to "take the scenic route"…whatever that means. I was in between them for a few minutes. Somehow, it became them two as I reached to refill drinks. I never slid back over between them. I sat back and watched the show.

Tanggy was a very aggressive lady. You would have thought that she was the dominant one in the relationship. I was turned on as I watched her remove the first pair of orange panties. Tanggy wasn't a bad carpet muncher, and then something happened. Diane got up and told her to give up her panties. I thought she was going to take them off. No, she raised both legs, and Diane took five minutes pulling them off. It was slow and sensual. Diane kissed thighs, kneecaps, feet and toes. She was slow and deliberate. After she pulled the panties over her feet, again she slowly kissed her way back down her leg. When she got to that bowl, it was slow. It was intense.

I finally slid out of my seat to get a better look. I didn't want to disturb what I was looking at. This wasn't that porno junk or even what I do on stage. This was love and passion. So much so that somehow that "don't mess up her hair" thing, it went out the window. Tanggy had a handful of hair. That twang turned into a moan from the gut. I was watching two lovers. A couple of times, Diane reached over to kiss me, just sharing the fruits of her love but never neglecting to go back to her work. We drove around for another 20 minutes or so. Just for them to get themselves together. Diane made it clear to me that it was difficult to share that part of her life with me. We looked each other in the eyes. I told her that it was hard for me to open up about my acting, so we both understood.

Now, I was presenting them to a Chicago Night scene. They stepped out of the limo looking amazing. Tanggy had a little bit of a glow. They both held onto an arm apiece. We looked good, but we were not special. We had to get our ass in that line like everybody else. It was a little nippy out, and we were close to the lakefront. This gave the ladies a chance to show off their matching wraps. I saw Tangy shake and offered her my coat. She said it wasn't a chill. Diane leaned over to whisper in my ear, "That was an aftershock." Damn, 20 minutes later. Hell, I was shocked. They just laughed at me and said, "He's just a man," and started laughing again.

We talked to other people in line. I was impressed with all the older cats with the hats and shoes to match. Let's be clear about this: BLACK FOLKS IN CHICAGO CAN DRESS. The fur coats were out. The ladies had the heels working. By the time we got to our seats, I was feeling no pain. I was in a grove. That EGO shit kicked in when I heard some of the old cats talking about me with two women on my arms. They clung tight to me. The "what's up, dog?" was not lost on me. It was Big Fred. He was sitting a couple rows over.

We both got up to shake hands in the middle of the aisle. Part of it was to shake hands, the other part was to show off these suits and shoes. While we were standing, there Minnie came over to give the ladies a hug. The matching outfits were not lost on Big Fred. He just had to say something. He was not quiet either. He asked, "How the fuck did you get a two for one sale?

I gave him that old player hunch of the shoulders and said, "I shop differently from you, dog." That got some of the ear hustlers nearby laughing, plus a round of five slapping from some of the old players nearby.

The concert was amazing. The Spinners stole the show. Even the gentleman who replaced Philippe Wynne was great. Okay, I brought that up to let you know that PHILIPPE WYNNE is the greatest lead singer of a group in history. END OF STORY. Franky Beverly was just smooth; no other way to describe him.

We danced our way to the limo. This was another surprise that I had for the ladies. There was Harold chicken and Italian beef sandwiches. Those sandwiches were Diana's favorite food. I have watched her tear one of them to pieces after a long day at work. She was crazy about that damn mild sauce on her chicken. I saw Big Fred and Minnie walking to their car. I had the driver pick them up. They got in, and the volume went up way past 10. There was yelling before they got in. They were not alone. There was another couple with them. The gentleman, I had seen before. He was from the Town.

They all got in and the party was in full swing. Introductions were made as we partied. I needed to get their attention for one minute. I turned down the music and saw Diane put her hand over Tanggy's mouth before she could say anything. I told them that the limo was rented for the night, and there would be a ride back to their vehicle, but for now, we were headed to the East of the Ryan to get some stepping in. I'm glad I didn't have anything else to say, because no one would have heard me. The noise was loud as hell. I passed around a couple of joints. The gentleman with Fred was Greg. He was a baller from the park and let me know that he was waiting for his turn. In fact, he worked for the Park District. I knew what he meant. It's just something that ball players do. I made a mental note of that statement.

Before I could get back to the party, Minnie was moving me out of the way. She was trying to make herself a plate. With great logic, she said, "There's too much alcohol in here to have a damn empty stomach."

We all snacked on different things. I saw Diane enjoying herself with an Italian beef. She had her eyes closed. You guessed it, my freaky-ass mind went to her earlier meal. In the back of the limo, no one can tell what you are thinking when you are in a cloud. There was smoke everywhere, so I got away with that one.

It only took a few minutes to get to East of the Ryan. Just straight down 79th Street. Even when we got there, we stayed put for another 20 minutes. We were high as a kite. Tanggy, of course, was outside the limo, screaming, "Party over here!" No not on the ground, she was hanging out of the sunroof. Thirty seconds later, all four women were screaming, "Party!" Minnie's big-ass made it tight in that sunroof. I got out and started heading for the door, hoping that everyone else would follow. I don't know how hard it is to herd cats, but I know herding drunk people was not an easy job.

Once inside, it was on. The music was great. There was no time for bullshit. There were two dance floors, so we decided to opt for the one in the basement. A lot less people. The stepping could have been called amazing. I must have danced about 10 songs in a row. The icing on the cake were the songs that I got to step with Minnie and Diane at the same time. They were great spinners. Minnie had really good footwork. Her stepping helped to keep us in a better rhythm. It was really like showing off for the crowd. I need you to understand, there were a lot of people out there putting in work on the dance floor. It's a Chicago thang. We all think that we are the best.

I was about halfway finished with one of those sweet daiquiri drinks. I had long abandoned the suit Jacket. I was hot and about to overheat. This drink was cold and good. Diane snuggled up next to me to let me know the time. I had 45 minutes to get to my next job. She looked a little shaken when she said it. I think she was still nervous about what she might see. I made the announcement, "The train is about to leave the station!"

Once in the lot, it took a little extra to get Minnie and Tanggy back in the limousine. We dropped off our guests at their vehicle. I got to the University in only a few minutes, straight down Stony Island. I think Mrs. Bell really likes this venue.

I didn't have a lot of time. Tanggy was still fired up. She saw Fatima and lost all control. They were loud. I needed to get going, so I ushered everyone to the door. Diane was staring daggers at me. She didn't just come out with it, but she wanted to know: "Why are they here?" I told her that I invited some friends to watch the performance. Once we were admitted, I did my best to get everyone settled. Even on my way to the back of the theater, I could still hear Fatima and Tanggy.

The first person I saw in the Back was Mrs. Bell. She gave me a big hug as she reminded me that I owed her a favor. I explained that I needed to get to the shower to get ready. Also I was asking for a favor from the host. I needed my guests to have some drinks and food. She just nodded yes.

I was off and running. My shower was so fast it was like what my mother and other relatives called a "hoe bath." On my way out, I had a towel around me when Lola met me with the paperwork. After I signed it, she gave me one of those hugs. I even remember closing my eyes, anticipating the feel of her. It was a brief hug. Watching her walk off, that's when I found out that I was not alone. Ajaumu was standing there. We were watching the same hips sway, only they belonged to him. I was caught with my eyes on someone else's paper in class. He didn't look upset. It was as if it was some sort of a setup. He told me that I could relax and slow down. The show would be delayed for about 30 minutes. Three of the performers had a fender bender. Mrs. Bell had sent her car to pick them up.

I was a little bit relieved about the time issue. Ajaumu wanted to talk. He was more serious than I had known him to be. He asked me if I knew how he tapped into these fantasies of so many people. I immediately told him no and shut up for an answer. In my mind, the GURU of sex was about to speak. He looked me in the eyes and said, "I am one of them." No words came from me. I was waiting on the other shoe to drop. I thought he was changing the subject. When he said, "Lola is not a leper, and she won't break." Looking at my blank stare, Ajaumu knocked on my head like it was a block of wood. Then he put up his hand with his thumb and pointer finger only about an inch apart. It came to my slow ass when he started to point his thumb at himself. Ajaumu was a hot wifer. At that moment, Lola came into the room and asked her husband, "Is he ready?" like I wasn't standing there.

The other three performers were arriving. In my mind, she was doing her normal backstage management. Before I walked off, I was told that Lola would be playing the hot aunt. There was a twist to the plot. Her husband would be in the closet watching. There was no way that I can be convinced that this was for research. I don't care how many of those yellow note pads they had. They were just flat out freaky.

I figured I had time to take one more look at the cheesy script. It was all leading up to some serious voyeurism. Hearing people walk around in high heels was nothing new around here, only this pair stopped right in front of me. Legs forever. A soft voice said, "Hello Ace." Walter said that flies really don't want to be in our mouths, so I better close mine. It was Mrs. America from a few shows back. She could see the blank look on my face. She provided a hint: "North Western."

Yes, now I remembered. A light went off in my head. Her husband said that she had one of those black buck fantasies. I stood, and we embraced. She smelled amazing. Shit, she smelled expensive. With an angelic politeness, she informed me that we would be working together. She asked if it was alright with me. *BREATHE, JAMES. BREATHE.*

I managed to eke out a soft, "My pleasure." We shook hands as we parted, and she said her name was Jessica. She left, heading to her private dressing room. I don't know how he knew that something was wrong, but Ajaumu was there with a glass of water and two pills. He said, "You are having a panic attack." He told me to just sit still and don't move. He raised both of my hands above my head. Ajaumu started counting to four. He had me breathe to his count, long deep breaths in and blow it out slowly. I came back slowly. I sat there not moving, just breathing. It didn't stop my mind from working. I was about to perform in a few minutes. The man helping me get myself together just told me that he wanted me to perform with his wife. Mrs. America just walked in, and the script calls for a passionless rough scene with her. This shit only gets worse. I had four people sitting in the audience who would be deciding if they wanted to see me again. This game of cops and robbers, I didn't want to play. To top it all off, the police were looking for ROACHMAN. The most important part was, I had not seen my other children in two months. I had a psychologist in front of me. All I needed was a couch and a big-ass oxygen tank, so I could breathe again.

Aujauma was talking to me in a very calm manner. It was like his voice was guiding me back to some sort of normalcy. He stood as the door to the dressing room was opened. I heard Ramon before I saw him. He was with Sylvia, one of the regulars. There was a rather thin looking guy with them. I got up and shook his hand for the introductions. My mind was so full at the moment, I didn't remember the name for 20 seconds. Ramon was there to do a gay part. It was of a father who found his son and one of his friends masturbating in the garage and joined them. I said it before, freaky people.

"Two minutes to curtain," was the call. I got a glimpse of Lola as she made the call. She had changed into an alluring nightgown.

The house lights went down. Mrs. Bell whispered to me that I would love the new sound system. She said that there were speakers closer to the audience. I could hear high heels walking across the stage. It was Lola getting into position. These new mics were loud. The curtain went up on the opening scene. Lola was up in her room. Her name was Aunt Kimberly. I was in my room, studying for a test or whatever. There was a loud crash of boxes and a startled scream coming from Aunt Kimberly's room. I jumped up to see what was wrong. The audience was already laughing. Of course, they had seen her fake the calamity. And watched the old, perverted husband go into the closet. I came in to check on her, and the boxes were on top of her and on the floor. Rushing to her side to offer my assistance, Aunt Kimberly said, "Oh Bryant! Oh Bryant, I don't know what happened! The boxes all just came tumbling down."

I helped her to her feet as she gave an over-exaggerated need for help, getting in a few extra rubs and telling me I was so strong and not a little boy any more. I was trying to pick up the boxes as she clung to me, the whole time telling me how much she needed my help around the house. It was my turn to get a little laugh. My outfit was a tight white shirt with a pocket protector. It came complete with the nerdy glasses. I was doing my part to act shy each time she touched me. At one point, I was putting up one of the boxes with those tight ass pants on, and Aunt Kimberly came up behind me with a hug, and I almost jumped across the room. I could actually hear Tanggy and Fatima laughing from their seats. I put on somewhat of a bashful teenager's voice and asked Aunt Kimberly what she was doing. She said that she was just thanking me for coming to her rescue. She sat down and patted the spot on the bed for me to come sit next to her. I gave a nervous, slow walk while biting my fingernails to show my fear.

I was told that I had been a great nephew. She complimented me on my grades and helping around the house. All the sudden, she threw both hands in the air and screamed that her back was hurting from the fall. For some reason, her nephew needed to rub it.

Aunt Kimberly laid out on the bed with her back to me. She couldn't see me stand and face the audience. I did an evil scientist hand rub and rolled my hips around in a circle real fast. The audience laughed, and she turned around to see me standing there again in my nerd pose.

"Are you-you sure about this, Auntee?" I stuttered out the words. Aunt Kimberly said yes and sat up on the bed. We made eye contact, and the rest of the script went out of the window. In my mind, this was Lola with the great hugs who always smelled amazing. We crawled towards each other. The first kiss may have lasted the entire scene. Somehow, we got undressed, and our bodies never separated. It was the sound that drew the audience in. They could hear the rustling of clothes and were moaning as if they were lying next to us.

The dialog was almost perfect. They could hear us saying to each other how long we had been waiting to be together. They were hearing the truth, just not as aunt and nephew. The sounds of flesh and wetness, the passionate kissing. The scene called for several switching of positions to give the audience a better view. This only happened once; it was only for Lola to roll over on top of me. Our bodies never even separated. The view didn't change that much.

The end of the scene was to have her beautiful breast covered. That didn't happen. The climax was inside. We didn't have to tell the crowd what was going on. We could actually hear them holding their collective breaths. We were covered in sweat from head to toe. The small group of spectators were clapping. Mrs. Bell had to tell us more than once to get up. We were in an afterglow that took us some time to move. I could even hear us breathing hard through the sound system. Once we were on our feet and walked to the front of the stage. We got another round of applause. Ajaumu came from the closet, grabbed her hand on the other side, and we all took a bow. This was the first time Ajaumu had ever participated in a show.

We walked off stage, smiling. A young lady came running up to us saying that we blew the entire scene. She wanted to know what happened to the oral sex and the position changes. We didn't have a chance to answer. Mrs. Bell was there to tell the intern to shut the hell up.

"DON'T YOU KNOW PASSION WHEN YOU SEE IT?" she scolded. Mrs. Bell came over to us to tell us that she appreciated the fact that we still had passion for the work. I didn't say a word. It was something about the way those two women hugged each other that said it all. I heard Lola say to her, "Thank you."

I needed to get to a shower and one of the cots that were in the back. Sometimes I watch some of the other performers, but not tonight. I saw the intern after my shower and said that I was going to lay down. I knew that it was at least 90 minutes before my next performance. I had a lot on my plate. I needed a nap like a kid in preschool.

The rest of the night was a blur. The four of us were in the limo headed home. Diane split somewhere just before the last performance of the night. It was weighing on my mind. The sun was coming up, and Ramona said that she lived close by. We were off to her place. She read the concerned look on my face.

"Don't worry, James. The big bad wolf is at her own house tonight."

I tried to turn on some music, but that shit was turned off. The questions came fast.

"How did you get into this business?"

"What the hell did they give us those notepads for? Was I supposed to take notes?"

"Who was that first lady?"

"How many times have you done this?"

"I hope you don't do what those men were doing!"

I wanted to answer that one right away.

"No, I don't do no men when I am acting."

Fatima and Tanggy wanted to know if I called that acting. I don't think I got many words in before we were at our destination. I felt great getting out of a limo at daybreak with three women. Now that we were inside, Tanggy said to me, "James, I'm not sure about what I saw tonight. Was that all acting?" She said that they all sat at the table together holding hands, praying for that pretty white woman and her sister who bought me at the slave auction. I tried to explain that the extra body moving and kicking was for effect. It was just acting.

Ramona spoke up, "Not those sounds."

I tried to explain that away with the new sound system; "It puts you in the middle of everything."

"We have all been with you. That was different. It was like you were trying to get some get back from SLAVERY," she said it with emphasis, and they all high-fived each other. The cheering was still going on when I left the room to get my script from my jacket pocket. I brought it back just to prove to them that I was doing what the scene called for. This time, Fatima had something to say.

"Well, if you ever try to treat this pussy that way, you better bring a second one with you." The room went silent and reality hit. Tanggy and Ramona both said at the same time, "Don't worry, baby, I got you." Fatima looked at me as if to say "help."

I walked out of the kitchen, saying over my shoulder, "YOU ARE THE ONE PIMPIN' WITH TWO WOMEN." There were some minimal giggles. I don't know what they discussed from there. I was in Ramona's spare bedroom, trying to get some sleep.

I came to at about 5:30 p.m. The house was quiet. Agent James was there. She was waiting for me to get up. There was no mention of the night before. She told me to get dressed; there was work on the schedule. She told me that we needed to pick up someone. It was an ATF agent. I asked if he was a new member of the team, and she said no. Agent James pulled the vehicle over and told me that he was the supplier for the Company. There was not a chance for me to speak. She said that he was the last one we needed to collect. He did not supply the drugs. They came in from other countries, but he was the guy who coordinated everything for all of the companies around the country. Half of the shit he distributed was confiscated by his team, the other half were from deals he had with cartels. It was a tool for letting them bring their drugs in.

I wanted to know where the squad was. Agent James said that this was a one-man job, and she wanted him to feel some pain.

We drove to a house in Tinley Park. It was a really nice house. Agent James said that this was our only chance to get him. He had a flight at O'hare Airport in three hours. His ride would be there in 10 minutes. We peeked into a back window. There was a gun on the nightstand about 10 feet away from him. There was one problem. He was a large man. I told her to go start the car and open the trunk. She said no. I didn't understand what was in her eyes. It was personal. She let me know that she thinks he is responsible for her husband's death. It was his ex-partner.

I picked up a brick from outside the window. I told Agent James to throw it through the window on my signal. I went to the opposite side and waved. The brick was a great distraction. I was dragging his ass to the car by his feet. He moaned once, and she hit him with her gun and told him to shut the fuck up. Agent James was curious about the way I subdued our new prisoner. She asked if I was an ex-boxer or something. I said no in between laughs. I told her that my technique was called "SWING, NIGGA, SWING." She thought that shit was really funny.

I knew that our ride would turn serious at some point. This was that point. To my surprise, it didn't start out like I thought. I was speaking to a real parent. She asked me if I remembered her daughters. I said yes, and they were some cool, attractive young ladies. This did not sit well with her. I was confused as hell. She made it short and simple.

"My oldest daughter just turned 22 years old. She graduates in the spring, and she wants to come over and ask you out on a date." I kept my eyes straight ahead, and my mouth shut. Her voice never changed. I was scared.

Agent Nora James asked if I ever noticed her daughter. I lied, "NOOOOOO." Trying to play stupid, I asked which one she was talking about. Agent James made it clear that she could drive just as well with two bodies in the trunk. My chest was getting tight. I let down the window to get some air. I started searching my pockets for the other pills that Ajaumu gave me. Putting two pills in my mouth without water was not lost on her. She tried to add a little humor by telling me that I didn't have to kill myself. Hell, I was trying to stay alive.

We got to the exit for Oliver's farm. Agent James made it clear we had only a short time for this interrogation. That was the least of my concerns. I wanted to know how much latitude would be given. She said to me that each one of the prisoners would be going to a tribunal. It was quiet time for me. I needed to learn as much as possible about what was going on. I found out that a tribunal was for people who were an exceptional danger to the Nation. Not that Nation. I mean to the country. These people were never allowed contact with the outside world. One phone call or a Christmas card could cause an Embassy to blow up or some of their enemies to be killed. As far as the world was concerned, they were either dead or missing. I didn't miss the point. It was a place for people like me who could not be controlled by simple means of imprisonment. I knew the rules.

We pulled into the back of the barn. Our prisoner was awake. We could hear him kicking the trunk of the vehicle. The dogs were excited. I took two of them out of the pen. The trunk was opened. The first thing he saw was Agent James. Our faces will tell on us. He was guilty as shit about killing her husband. He was even hesitant about getting out of the trunk. I don't know which one scared him the most. The dogs or Agent James. She was growing impatient with not moving.

"HIGGENBOTTOM, get your ass out of the trunk!"

Oh shit, we had kidnapped my ace in the whole. This was the name I had been given on two different occasions as a get out of jail free card.

Higgnbotom raised up a little too fast. Those dogs were on high alert. I needed to work fast. He was put in the back with the rest of the prisoners. Seven cops and G Black, all chained to a wall. They saw me walk into the storage shed with the new guy and the dogs. I could hear the groans and moans. They knew that something was about to go down. I figured, why wait? I spoke to the prisoners as calmly as I could. I explained that I didn't want to get the dogs excited. I wanted to put the dogs on their minds, so that when I walked in with them later, it would strike fear. I didn't have the two dogs with me on a leash. Each one weighed at least 120 pounds. I paced back and forth as I spoke.

Right in front of the prisoners, I put a stick on the ground. I told them that I was assuming that it was 18 inches away from the wall, give or take an inch. This is going to be the dog line. I pointed to their side of the line and said, "The dogs will not reach this side of the line. Your back must remain up against the wall. If you fall forward or down, however you end up on this side of the line, The dogs will get you. Nod your head if you understand."

Each man nodded. It was showtime. Sosa and James had not seen this before. Hell, the rest of the squad were looking as if it was something new. Oliver and young Agent James went to work on removing all their pants and underwear. Each man had a steak placed over their package. While this was going on, our two leaders were glued to the dog pen. I was rolling around with the dogs. I took off my shirt. I was covered from head to toe when I exited the pen. I took out eight dogs. I got down on all fours, and me and the dogs walked over to the prisoners. I stopped at the stick. My growling excited the dogs. A couple of the dogs walked up and smelled the steaks. I made them retreat. There was not one leash. I had to be careful, I had to pay attention.

Officer Brown approached us. He was walking slow and with his back to the wall. He sat down on a small stool. He had a notepad plus a small recorder. Officer Brown went over the ground rules: "If you lie to me or don't answer my questions, your dog in front of you will eat the steak. Nod if you understand." Each man again nodded with enthusiasm.

Every question was answered without hesitation. We found out about shit that we could handle. We found out about shit that was above our paygrade. These men would be damaged for the rest of their lives. Two of them were as bad off as Officer Canens, and some were not as bad. After the last question was answered, I fed the dogs a full three boxes of steaks. It was 21 of them in all. There was a meeting going on while I was in the shower. I knew that they were planning raids. Only this time, they had to coordinate with other federal forces. At this point, I was more worried about getting home. Agent Hoyde volunteered to take me home. I think that Officer Green thought about it, but, well, she might still be on punishment.

On my way out, the younger Agent James said that he was waiting on a search warrant for two lounge workers. Both had worked part time for both of the bars in question. He was hoping to find that old as cologne at one of their houses. I said that it might help if he searched their vehicles also.

On the way to my apartment, Agent Hoyde was like a kid in a candy store. We talked about the money that would be available. There had to be over $5 Million sitting in different locations. He said that it was money he had found out about. It was mostly to get out of town money. You know, just in case shit got hot. Hoyde said that these criminals were prepared to run at a moment's notice. After the first one offered up his stash to let him escape, Hoyde just worked the rest of them one at a time. He made it clear that he would need Roachman's help to get the money. I was not clear on that one. It dawned on him that I was not at the meeting. Hoyde said that it would be too dangerous to say my name around other people. Sosa thought it would just be better if they all used the code name of "Roachman" when referring to me. That was not a good idea to me. I still had a business to run. Hoyde started laughing at me. He said that I didn't have to work another day in my life. I don't know where he got that shit from.

Hoyde was right; we made three stops before we got to my house. I started out with four different bags. Each had money from one of our stops. We were sitting in a garage of a friend of his. We didn't have time to count the money; we were trying to consolidate the money from so many bags. He said for me to be careful with what I took. The money in the rolls was usually the money that was collected and not clean yet. Hoyde said that these rolls sometimes have $5-$10 grand per roll. I told him that I could smell the dope on the money. That's not what he was talking about. I learned that the money with bands around it came from a bank. It was clean to take some of it now. Lesson learned. I trusted him to hold on to the majority of the money. I had maybe a quarter of a million dollars in a bag.

It was 11:15 p.m., and my heart was racing like hell. I was standing at Diane's door. My chest was feeling tight. It was different from the panic attacks. This was a real matter of the heart. When the door opened, it was a lukewarm welcome. She asked me to come in. I sat the bag by the door. To my surprise, Diane hugged me and even kissed me briefly. I asked if she had a cold beer. She said yes, and I followed her to the kitchen. Diane told me to sit down. It wasn't a request; it was a command. I sat like a good little boy.

She passed me the beer and took a deep breath. I knew that she wasn't going to yell at me. Her daughter Kasey was at home. She had school tomorrow. Diane took a second deep breath. Still there were no words. I had to know, so I started the conversation.

"Did I hurt you that badly?"

Still no words, just a soft nod of the head. I knew where this was going. Diane was about to leave town. I stood in front of her and held out my arms. We stood there, two hearts beating for each other but headed in different directions. I wasn't trying to hurt anyone. The tears came and went; it was brief. Diane wanted to talk to me. She wasn't on one of those kicks with all the screaming and hollering. She just wanted to get her point across and go off into the good night. Her eyes and her gentle soul were her rage. It was a shock when she asked me, "How dumb are you?" I didn't think that I was dumb at all. I knew it was a rhetorical question, so I didn't answer. She had both hands on the collar of my shirt. She said, "What the fuck did you think was going to happen? Did you think that we would all just jump into your fancy sleigh and ride off into the sunset?" Not letting me go, she added, "That is shit that happens in a ghetto-ass fairytales. It was a great date, James, and you pull this shit at the end?"

I was looking at her. She was beautiful. This is what will make a man stop all that he was doing to marry her. I'm not that man. I wasn't there yet. I wish I was. Again I knew that I was damaged goods. Diane started talking again. I had to resist the urge to reach up and kiss her. She started telling me about all the changes that were coming in her life. Diane was leaving in the morning to go to Birmingham, Alabama. One of her stepsisters lived there. She said that she was going to look at an apartment. I didn't know when it would be appropriate for me to speak my piece. Diane had a lot more to say.

"James, you are the first person to see me do what I did in the limo." That was understandable to me, or so I thought. There was more to it. She said that she was leaving Tanggy, too. Damn, this woman was hurt. It wasn't just the emotional shit; it was the city, the neighborhood. She wanted to save her son before these streets killed him or he was sharing a cell with his father.

We had the same problems. I took my shot at helping out, but Diane shot that down right away. She said, "Your persona and your dick will keep you in trouble. James, you don't know how to turn off the neon sign on your forehead. You are too young for the type of life that I am looking for." She tried to tell me that it didn't have anything to do with me. She was tired of the cold, the police sirens, the ambulances, the shootings, and the drugs. It was all getting to be too much. Diane said that her mother was going, too. She finally let go of my shirt. I saw her face with her teeth gritted.

"You made love to that woman in front of me. She told me that she knew what sex was, and she knew what fucking is." Her hands rained down on my chest as she repeated that I was making love to that woman. I had to let her get it out. She said, "What I saw wasn't about acting. I felt that shit all the way over where I was sitting. James, I can't unsee that."

I just had to say something. I didn't like the entire picture that was being painted. I asked if I could speak. She nodded yes. I made it clear that it was her decision as to what she does. There needed to be some clarity. I let her know that I needed to be upfront about my life. She was right. I wasn't ready for the Shady Hills rest home, but I was looking to make some changes. I had a few more loose ends to tie up, and I was leaving the neighborhood.

She said, "Good for you."

Diane wanted to know about the "haram," as she called them. I made it clear that this was an all-volunteer army. She could still come and go as she pleased.

"NO THANKS," was her answer. All this time, we were still standing in the same spot.

This was a little intense for me. I don't think that I am good at this relationship thing. I don't know how to make myself sad if someone else is feeling sad. Diane was right. I didn't know how to turn off the neon sign. I never thought that I would be glad to see Mrs. Tanggy. She came rushing through the door with my bag in her hand.

"Whose fucking bag is this? I almost tripped over it at the door!" She saw me and ran over to give me a big hug. It was vintage Tanggy. "I GUESS YOU HEARD WE ALL GETTIN FIRED."

Diane quickly got on the defense told her not to come up in here with that bullshit. I grabbed my bag and said that I didn't want to interrupt. Tanggy said, "Sit your scaredy-ass down. You don't want her to go, just like I don't."

I sat right on down, but made it clear that if she spoke to me that way again, she better have a gun in her hand. I just needed to draw that boundary with her. Tanggy kept right on talking, but she gave a nod to my statement. I realized that she was fighting for something. The passion that I saw between them was not a one-way street. She was just as hurt as Diane. She had a 14-year relationship on the line. I wanted to know what her intentions were before she saw the show. Tanggy said, "Tell him right now."

Diane was sitting there with her head down. I thought she was going to take the normal route of shy, discrete Diane. She said to me that she told Tanggy that they were going to get me to leave with them, even if they had to kidnap me. Shit, that's kind of forceful. It also told me that she was serious. I asked if we could do some sort of a reset. I was grasping for straws.

"Can we just go upstairs, take a deep breath, and smoke a joint?" Two thirds of us were willing.

Tanggy said, "Fuck a joint I want her to know that I love her, and she can't leave me." She grabbed Diane and held on. I was just looking at the ball of human emotions. You can only separate from something by not being there. I picked up the bag of money and headed for the exit. Diane somehow got a grip on the back of my shirt. She put on a fake man voice and asked, "WHERE IS YOUR SCAREDY-ASS GOING?" I dropped the bag and followed them up the back steps. They got a kick out of the scaredy-ass joke. Shit, they got me curious now. Diane said it was because I asked to do everything. She said at her mothers house, I didn't sit down until after I asked if it was okay. They said that I spoke slowly and too softly. Tanggy said that I was killing her with the "Ms. Tanggy" shit. Diane said that she and I had been sleeping together almost a year, and I was still calling her "Ms. Diane."

"You look like a man who could take any-damn-thing you want. So why are you so soft?"

Well, they got me there. How was I going to argue with two women who were hot as a tea kettle? Why rush? I knew that this would be the first and the last time the three of us would share a night together. I wasn't soft; I was hard all damn night.

I got home and put the bag with the $150,000 under my bed. Yeah, it was a hundred grand short. I really loved Diane, and I just didn't want to see her struggle. She was going to be shocked when she found it in her underwear drawer. Maybe she could catch back up to society. She once told me that she wanted to go to nursing school.

It was 6:15, and I was on track. I was getting ready for my run. Officer Green was standing outside with her running gear on. I didn't have a clue as to why she was there. She said that she wanted to test the speed for herself. I knew that this was a front for something else; I just didn't know what. It doesn't take long to find out shit. Not even two miles into the run, Ramona told me that she wanted out. I let it be known that we did not have a commitment in our relationship. That was not what she was talking about. She wanted out of the police force. Sixteen years was enough for her. I made it clear that she had a choice to make that had nothing to do with me. When she said that she wanted in, the picture was getting a little clearer to me. She needed or wanted money. There was too much of it floating around.

I stopped at the next corner to see if she was serious about this. Ramona said that she could run and talk at the same time, but I needed to see her face as we talked.

"What do you really want?" She got quiet for a few seconds and came to the realization that I wanted to hear it from her mouth. Looking right in my eyes, Ramona said, "I need some of that money." She turned and started running again. Nothing was said for the next eight miles.

"How much do you need?"

She was breathing hard now. Through a ragged breath, she replied, "Is it possible to get a half of a million dollars?" She stopped running. We were about a half mile from my place. We started walking to cool down. She told me that she wanted to invest in some new fitness chain in L.A. The money would get her in on the ground floor. Her excitement level changed. There would be people from all over coming to these places to work out. For the first time since I had known her, she was really excited about something.

Ramona told me about a shipment that was going to be a money transfer. It was going to be done in public. The two sides don't trust each other. She couldn't attest to that, but she knew that after the transfer, the money would have to be alone for about one hour. She said that she needed Roachman to get the money. I asked why. She said that the house had four dogs in the yard. I didn't give her an answer. I wanted to consort with Hoyde on this first. She said that she had been doing the recon on this for months.

By the time that we got to my house, I had all the information on the job. Not very risky if we could keep the dogs quiet. I needed to get Oliver Stone over to look at the property. It was secluded; only one road in or out. We would have to travel through the woods at night for maybe a mile. PUSSY IS AMAZING. She was sleeping with a white bank executive who cleaned money for the Company and the mob. This explained the disappearances that kept Agent James up at night. She was meeting him there after one of his transactions.

"How do you know this man?"

Ramona said that he was her college boyfriend. They ran into each other about a year ago. Then his bank came up as a possible money laundering location. The connection to the Company came up with one of your sessions with the dogs. A prisoner mentioned him personally. I asked how sure she was that the money and him would be there at that time. Women have a bigger ego than men. She looked at me with her hands on her hips as she replied, "Because the pussy is good, and I saw it in his appointment book after I knocked his ass out."

I could not argue with that. I needed to know if I could bring Hoyde in on the deal. Again with her hands on her hips, she said, "He's in already. I followed you two last night. On his way home, I hit the lights and pulled him over. We had a chance to talk. He said that I could only get what I was in on."

"How much money are we talking about?"

"Somewhere around $2 million was her answer." She also said, "I'm in on the Daniels thing. We were going to give him 20 percent of whatever we got." My back gate was locked, so I walked to the front where she was parked. I was reminded that we only had one day to pull this off. Mannnnnn, I was confused as hell. I got sucked into this from the start by Diane on some sex shit, now here was a woman asking me to commit a robbery while she gave me the most passionate kiss goodbye that I ever had. I stole money with Hoyde last night. I kidnapped a man with Agent James yesterday. The list was too long to recap in my own damn head. If I had a mirror in front of me right now, I wouldn't be looking at a NOBLE MAN. I needed to get off this roller coaster. The violence was getting to be too much. I didn't have any pool balls with me when we picked up Higgenbottom. Agent James threw the brick through the window. When he turned to the dresser for his gun, it was already too late. I scooped him up by the legs and kept running into the bathroom. Higgenbottom didn't make it into the bathroom. The top half of his body hit the door frame and the wall. At first, I just thought it would be easier to get him in the trunk that way.

The running gave me some time to think, and I needed an exit fast. My first call was to Oliver Stone. He sounded excited to hear from me. We exchanged pleasantries for a short time. I was trying to build a relationship for the future, and I needed his help again. I needed him to sit on that location for the next 14 hours. My next call was to one of the realtors who I exterminated houses for. I literally begged her to make my house her first stop. We agreed on 9:00 a.m. plus 500 for a consulting fee.

Agent James was already on the premises. Walter's Café was just opening up. She got her coffee and knocked on my bedroom door. I opened the door. She walked right in, talking about the long day ahead. Daniels would be released from the hospital today. Agent James said that I had to go see Lieutenant Sosa today. I asked if I could call him. She said that it had to be in person, and by noon. I got back from dropping the kids at school. I had ten minutes before my meeting with the realtor. One call was made to Brown. I needed to know if he had something that would give me a clear vision at night. He said, "Yes, if you have something going on that will contribute to my pension fund."

WHAT THE FUCK IS IT WITH THESE CROOKED-ASS COPS?

I said that I would have to check with the other person involved. Brown said that there was no need. He was sitting with Officer Green now having coffee. Who's zoomin who? I let him know that it was her call. I was glad that the door to my room was closed. I didn't want Walter to hear me scream that loud. Not only that, I was cursing at a rapid pace. I was feeling frustrated. How the fuck did Officer Brown get involved? If too many people know something, it is not a secret!

I gave the wooden dresser one last bang and a straight loud "f&%#" three times in a row. Then I took a deep breath and walked out into my dining room. The realtor was sitting there with her hands folded like she was in class. I'm sure they were over her mouth a minute ago. She had to hear me. I rushed over to shake her hand. Somehow, I was trying to get out an apology and a good morning at the same time. I must have sounded like an idiot. It was Walter to the rescue. He handed her a cup of coffee and a pastry, telling her to sit down and don't pay me no attention. He said that I was having a rough morning. I went with his excuse and started rubbing my hands over my face and head, giving another apology.

She stood and shook my hand again as if we were starting over. This time, I got a chance to get a good assessment of her. The mustard yellow leather suit was killing it. Not a hair out of place, she shook my hand as if she had already won the negotiation. I asked if she would excuse me for one minute. I went into my room and retrieved the bag from under my bed. I walked in and set the bag on her lap. There was a slight pause. I wanted to see if I could make her flip over her words a little. She gave me a questioning look. I nodded for her to open the bag. She took her time opening the bag as if a snake was going to jump out and bite her. The zipper got stuck and she pulled it open with her hands. It wasn't unzipped all the way, and she could see that it was money. I just realized that I handed a bag of money to a lady, and I didn't even know her name. I just called her Miss GG because that was on the personal plates on her Jaguar. She threw the bag on the table and said her fee was only $500. I said that there was $150 in the bag. She knew that I meant thousand.

"Well, Mr. Madlock. What can G.G. Realty do for you?"

I started to explain what I needed from her. I had to excuse myself for a minute. I went into the kitchen and asked Walter for some privacy. My nose had not lied to me yet. I picked up the bag of money from the table and grabbed Miss GG by the hand. We negotiated what I needed for the next hour. I wanted something in the suburbs; a good school district for the kids; a big yard. She asked if the yard had to be big enough for horses. I think she got confused, because she was riding one. I wanted a pool and room for a basketball court. Her mouth kind of opened in shock as I tried to put it into her that I needed a few other properties in the city with storefronts for other business. I made it clear that the money in the bag was just a down payment. She looked fabulous in that mustard leather suit again after getting dressed. I handed her the $500 for the consultation. We shook on it to consummate the deal.

I made an impulse stop on Western Aveunue at one of the car dealerships. They sold new and used vehicles. I was there less than 20 minutes. I gave a salesman $5 grand and asked him to take care of the paperwork. I made a promise to be back with another $2 grand. I left my driver's license, so he could run my credit. I was buying a 1990 GMC van. A 2500 Series. This was the one with the extra set of captain's chairs. It was three years old, but it had all the bells and whistles. I was smiling from ear to ear. Only 41,000 miles. Me and the kids were going to ride.

Next stop was Lieutenant Sosa. I wasn't sure how to tell him this had to come to an end for me. We sat in his office for what I knew to be the last time. He had a need to skip the pleasantries. He gave me a list of names with a folder. I was told that these were some arrests that his officers had made recently.

"Do you have any more room in class for a few extra students?" I didn't know what to say.

"Yes," came out before the brain turned on. There were 13 names on that list. Thirteen new second chances at life. I needed to go nail down those classrooms with Mr. Gant and Father Fitzgerald. I stood to leave, and Sosa handed me another envelope. It had my name on the front and the US Treasury. He was not smiling. I took it and started to walk off. Sosa called me loudly and said, "Open it." I took a deep breath, and I was nervous. It was a letter promising to pay me $213,000. It was 10 percent of the money turned in from the heist. I was really shocked to find out that there would be a much larger check coming from all the dope that was turned in. He said, "The squad decided you deserved it."

You have to know how to negotiate with a man, even if you know that they are on your side. Mr. Gant was in the maintenance office. We hugged each other hard. Not macho, just love. He wanted to know if I needed some part time work. I laughed and said, "Hell no! But I will help you mop the cafeteria if you need me." I handed Mr. Gant the bottle of scotch that was meant for negotiating. At that point, Big Redd was coming through the door asking what the hell was I doing in the office and saying a kid had thrown up on the third floor. We all laughed. I did not miss those days. By the way, I can strip and wax the hell out of some floors. I told them about needing three classrooms for one year. Cash up front on the rental. Mr. Gant said that I might be able to keep my money. He would talk to Father Fitz for me. He said, "Just pay the janitor for cleaning after they leave."

Red yelled out, "Cha-ching!" with a big smile on his face.

Mr. Gant told me he had been laying off the horses lately. He was walking me to the car. He told me that I needed to stop whatever I was doing. The streets were talking about me being seen with some Feds. He told me that he didn't know the source of the chatter. He just told me to see the door man at the Taste Lounge on 64th and Lowe. I was filing that away for later. I needed to get home and pack. I was going to see my kids tomorrow. I said the hell with packing, and I walked into Marshall Fields in Evergreen Plaza. I bought everything new, even the suitcases.

I am lazy as hell. I put everything into the two suit casas and rolled them right to my van. Shit, having a few extra dollars was nice. Officer Brown was bringing me some night vision equipment. The drop-off was quick. We only had a short time to talk. I know that he was with Officer Green today. He should have more info than me. Somehow, he just asked one damn question too many. It was already 2:30 p.m. I needed to pick up my new van. Fatima was my first thought. She could give it the once over before I signed the paperwork. By the time, we walked out of the dealership it was much later than I needed it to be.

I was now pushing the time. I needed to meet up with Hoyde and get to the location early. We were headed southwest of the city to a small Suburb called Matteson Il. Mostly farmland just off I-57. It was hard to find Stone in the dark. He hit a flashlight a couple of times. Even in the dark, you could see and hear the stress. Stone wanted to know what we were scoping the place out for. Hoyde and I looked at each other, wondering if we could tell Stone the truth. He cleared that up for us. "I hope this ain't for no robbery. And if it's for a meeting, y'alls boy is already in there."

"What boy of ours are you talking about?"

He said, "The white boy that meet up in Hyde Park at the meetings."

Hoyde said, "Brown?"

Stone nodded yeah. I made a mental note to ask about the Hyde Park thing. Stone broke down the layout. There were two guys in the small storage building. Officer Brown was in the house with another guy and the Banker. He said that the two guys in the storage shed had two dirt bikes in the bushes. They don't work anymore. Oliver Stone held up a handful of wires. Hoyde smiled and said, "I like this lil mother fucker." I saw the wheels turning in his head. He said that we had to run in the direction of the dirt bikes. "That's where we take out those two."

All talk stopped. We just got our signal from Ramona. She was in the back bedroom window, opening of the curtains with all the lights on. She wasn't alone; there was a male figure standing next to her with a gun to her head. She was stripped naked.

Hoyde said that we had to go to the front door. I still had the one grenade from the warehouse and my leather socks. I told Hoyde that I would meet him at the front door and watch out for the dogs. Stone said, "Don't worry. His dogs like steaks and long naps." This young man was on top of his game. I asked if he had a Gun. Stone also likes those new 9mm.

"Stone, just keep the car running," we instructed.

Hoyde went towards the front door. I turned on the power and ran right past the small storage shed. The grenade at the door after I banged on it should be a big surprise. I was coming around to the front of the house when the grenade went off. The Banker and Brown were at the front door. They were both ducking from the blast. Their guns stayed on Officer Green. Brown asked me to drop the pool balls on the floor. I had to give them up. Hoyde started to negotiate. He said that we could all walk out of here alive. No one else had to die. I knew that I wasn't fast enough to get there before one of them pulled the trigger. The Banker spoke up. He wanted us to put our guns on the ground. Agent Hoyde assured him that. He was not putting down his gun. The Banker asked about me, and Brown told him that I didn't carry a gun. I was still trying to figure out where the last guy was.

I was sniffing the air, trying to find that other shooter. A curtain on the second floor moved. I had his ass. Hoyde was in the process of at least getting them to lower their guns from her head. That part went okay. My feet were not comfortable on those big-ass rocks on his landscaping. I laid on the ground in a surrendering position. I said that they could trade me for her. I was the one they were looking for. I told the Banker that I was the Roachman. I was the one responsible for the Company's money and dope being taken.

Brown nodded over to the Banker. He had a big grin on his face. The Banker stepped forward and Kicked me in the ribs. I couldn't make a move. Brown had his gun back at her head again. After the third kick, Hoyde created a standoff. He was right up on the Banker with his gun in his face. The kicking stopped. The edges on these sharp ass rocks were digging into my skin. For the briefest moment, Brown got caught up in telling the Banker to pick up the pool balls. He didn't see any pool balls. They were inside of the socks. He didn't know what to look for. Brown waved that gun just a little too far away from Green. She gave his slow-ass a palm of the hand to the nose. The Banker was never going to kick anyone else the rest of his life. He got two of those jagged-ass rocks. I jammed them into the top of his foot. Before I could stand, Hoyde was letting loose at that second floor window. He was firing two guns at a time. The Banker did finally find out where the pool balls were. Several swings of those long ass socks. I never even got close to him before he crumbled to the ground.

Brown was fucked up. Officer Green had him up against the wall, delivering another blow to his face. On my way passed them to the second floor to make sure that our shooter was taken care of, I ran straight into Brown and knocked him into one of the back walls. The shooter was hit in the shoulder. He never saw me coming. A half dozen strikes with those pool balls, and that was over. When I came downstairs, Hoyde and Green were searching for the money. The front door was still open. Stone walked in and said that he already got the money out of the garage. Green grabbed whatever clothes she could find. Hoyde said that this was too sloppy. He walked me to the kitchen and ordered me to pull the gas line out of the wall. He took a cigarette lighter out of his pocket and asked, "How fast are you?"

Hoyde walked out and got into the vehicle with Green and Stone. I wasn't about to take a chance. I set the furniture on fire in the living room.

The Banker had been propped up on the couch next to Brown. I turned on the power. I cut through the woods and was sitting on top of Hoyde's police cruiser by the time they were coming down that long, winding road.

I never did make it to see my kids that week. I was in the hospital. On our way back to the city, I passed out. I never saw it coming. I had no idea if it was a panic attack or the power needed to be recharged. When I woke up, it was two days later. A few of the squad were there at the hospital, plus Diane and Fatima. I knew that I had pushed it too far with the power. Now I knew what my Uncle Horse meant when he said that the POWER could kill a man.

It was a new couch, much more comfortable than the old one. I knew that anything that I said was privileged information. Plus, I trusted my old friend Ajaumu. This was my fifth session in the last six months. I haven't had a panic attack in a long time. He gave me the same advice every time I left his office: "Remember to breathe. No more dangerous work." The last part of his advice was the best part. "Hug and love them kids every day."

Ajaumu told me one day that the human heart needs to feel another human heart beat up against it. He said, "It keeps us calm and makes us happy." His assistant always asked the same questions after I left.

"Dr. Yofi, do you really believe all that stuff he said?"

Dr. Ajaumu Yofi looked her right in her eyes and said, "EVERY DAMN WORD."

THIS BLACK MAN DID GO TO THERAPY.

While I was at the doctor's office, we had a visitor. A well-dressed lady in a fur coat and hat with a chauffeur outside. She came into the pest control shop. OH yeah, I have my own business now. I'm on a busy street in Chicago. There are a couple of storefronts that I rent out. I have three apartments upstairs that I rent out. When the bell rang on the door, the twang wasn't as bad. Yes, Ms. Tanggy was the lady behind the counter. The middle aged woman asked if she could speak to someone because her husband was missing. Tanggy referred her next door to the detective agency. The lady repeated the fact that she was not looking for a detective. She left her card on the counter and said, "My husband is missing." On her way out of the door, she said she needed a ROACHMAN. I don't think she paid much attention to the young man in the corner who was now following her. No one in the shop had ever met Mrs. Bell before.

I was going home to do my new favorite thing. I have taken up cooking. I loved putting meals together for the kids. I now had nine kids in the house again. My kitchen at the new house was a dream. The timer rang, and I turned off the oven to go pick up the kids from school. They all piled in. I don't know how, but I could hear about all their days and respond at the same time. Maybe it was just our way of communicating. We pulled into the driveway. The older kids went straight to the basketball court. It had an Air Jordan logo in the middle. The inground pool was nice, but it was too cold for that.

Winnie and Nelson grabbed my hands. We walked into the living room. The three of us sat down on the oversized couch. I thought to myself, *WHAT A SOFT PLACE TO LAND.*

Agent Terrence James now runs an FBI lab.

Officer Brown, he cooked in the fire.

Officer Daniels, AKA Big MOFO, is coaching basketball at his old high school. He has the freshman.

Officer Ramona Green invested in some fitness club in L.A. She got in on the ground floorand is now RICH.

Agent Oliver now gets mistreated in front of an audience. He pays Ajaumu well for the torture.

Agent Hoyde owns the detective agency next door. We're partners. He has six units upstairs that he rents out.

Lieutenant Sosa lost his battle with cancer.

Agent Nora James is one of the many FBI directors.

Oliver Stone is still around in Chicago. He might be following you.

Big Fred got 30 years for sexual molestation of minors.

Diane moved to Alabama; she just started nursing school. Her son just got 20 years in an Alabama prison.

The Prince, well…that's not so simple. I never turned in the money for the hit. That took the Capital Murder charges off the table. I did my best to run interference for him. In the meantime, he and the beautiful Princess got GEDs for 142 gang members. I had a real love for this kid. He was eventually arrested on some other charges. He has not seen freedom again.

Fatima rents out three of the six garage spaces in the back and an apartment. Okay, she don't pay rent.

Walter Jackson died some years later of AIDS. WE LOVE YOU AND MISS YOU, WALTER JACKSON.

CPSIA information can be obtained
at www.ICGtesting.com
Printed in the USA
LVHW032037160223
739687LV00009B/313